Praise for Sharon Lathan

"The everlasting love between Darcy and Lizzy will leave more than on reader swooning." ~ *A Bibliophile's Bookshelf*

"If you love Pride and Prejudice sequels then this series should be on the top of your list!" ~ *Royal Reviews*

"Exquisitely told with a brilliant flourish of language and so rich in detail." ~ *Rundpinne*

"I defy anyone not to fall further in love with Darcy after reading this book." ~ *Once Upon a Romance*

"It's a book that I found almost impossible to put down until I finished it and then immediately read it again. I laughed. I cried. And when I closed the covers after the first reading - I felt drained and satisfied that things were now as they should be."
~ *A Curious Statistical Anomaly*

"Lathan's writing is lyrical and perfect for this genre... Jane Austen would be proud to read how her characters have flourished, lived, and loved in this continuation of her beloved story. "
~ *The Good, the Bad and the Unread*

"In true Jane Austen style, this story is filled with period details and witty dialogue... a very pleasant read!" ~ *Romance Reader at Heart*

"Sharon really knows how to make Regency come alive. Her descriptions of people, places, and things suck you in and refuse to let you go. " ~ *Love Romance Passion*

Darcy & Elizabeth

&

A Season of Courtship

A Darcy Saga Prequel

by

Sharon Lathan

Books by Sharon Lathan

ఴ

The Darcy Saga
"Pride & Prejudice" Sequel Series

Mr. & Mrs. Fitzwilliam Darcy: Two Shall Become One

Loving Mr. Darcy: Journeys Beyond Pemberley

My Dearest Mr. Darcy: An Amazing Journey into Love Everlasting

In the Arms of Mr. Darcy

A Darcy Christmas

The Trouble with Mr. Darcy

Miss Darcy Falls in Love

The Passions of Dr. Darcy

The Darcy Saga Prequel Duo

Darcy & Elizabeth: A Season of Courtship

Darcy & Elizabeth: Hope of the Future

Dedication

છ

To my wonderful husband Steve.
2013 was a wild year!
With love and the grace of God we saw many of
our dreams come true. Thank you for our new life in
Kentucky, and for ensuring I fulfill my dream of
writing full-time.
I love you ~ yesterday, today, and for eternity.

Table of Contents

ℰℭ

PROLOGUE

Hope Enters on a Whirlwind

*T*he chalked end of the stick hit the white ball precisely as aimed. The sharp *thwack* of impact was rapidly followed by sharper cracks as the cue ball bashed into the triangle of red balls.

Fitzwilliam Darcy watched the balls scatter across the green felt surface. His keen gaze evaluated his potential next shots as one red ball dropped into a corner pocket and three others slowly rolled into favorable positions. Now came the option of choosing an easy point over a maneuver that required extreme deliberation and application of his skills. Considering the purpose in his solo game of billiards, the latter was the sensible choice.

A week ago, he had departed Netherfield in Hertfordshire and returned to London and his house on Grosvenor Square. His preference would normally be Pemberley, especially this time of the year, when hunting was exceptional and the fall foliage burst forth in vivid colors. The thought of his beautiful Derbyshire home, sitting on a pastoral rise on the edge of the River Derwent, brought an ache to his heart. But the pain of homesickness was a mild sting compared to the agony eating at his soul. Mounting his horse and riding away from

Hertfordshire—*from her*—had proven far more difficult than leaving Pemberley ever had.

A week of busy days with his solicitor, working at his desk, fencing at Angelo's, riding at the track, and a dozen alternative activities depleted his energy and prevented his musings from incessantly drifting to contemplations of what Elizabeth Bennet was doing, who she was talking with, what she was wearing, or—most dangerous of all—whether she was thinking about him even a tiny bit. Unfortunately, his cousin Colonel Fitzwilliam was not in Town, although Richard would probably bluntly call him a coward and a fool for being here in the first place. Since Darcy fought daily against accusing himself of that very thing, it was probably for the best that the colonel was away on some sort of military mission.

It was late in the afternoon and the windows of the Darcy House billiard room were open to encourage the entrance of cooling breezes. Even in crowded London, where breezes of any sort were scarce, one could reasonably expect to obtain some relief by opening windows during the first days of October. But not today. Unseasonably warm weather gripped the city. Those citizens who could not escape to country estates added the heat to their list of daily complaints. Not that Darcy was remotely aware of what anyone in London was grumbling about. He was too preoccupied with his own miseries, none of which had to do with the weather.

For the present, he welcomed the heat because it contributed to the mild sweat he had worked up after three previous, intense games of billiards. Never mind that he was playing alone and not keeping score; the activity of hitting balls accurately necessitated discipline and concentration. Both were excellent for distracting his mind from dwelling upon his love life.

Or lack thereof.

Billiards proved a better choice than reading, so he bent over the table to line up what would be a jaw-dropping shot if successful. But the test of his expertise would remain eternally unknown in this particular instance. A sudden tumult from the corridor caused him to straighten from the table, and a half second later, the door burst open and smashed into the wall.

Lady Catherine de Bourgh charged through, not unlike a raging bull toward a fluttering red cape.

Shocked speechless, Darcy stared at her advancing body and forgot to bow or relinquish the cue. A white-faced Mr. Travers, the butler, trailed behind her, his pleas falling unheard, and after a stunned nod from Mr. Darcy, he practically bolted from the room.

Darcy did not have time to envy the butler's escape. His aunt was already talking—or yelling, to be precise.

"Darcy, I have passed the most unpleasant morning as a result of alarming reports, scandalous falsehoods that I intended to deal decisively with at the root, in the same manner as one employs to destroy a poisonous weed. My intentions were honorable and wholly of sound reason, I can assure you! One anticipates that a person will be reasonable, especially when confronted with logic and facts by a woman of my breeding and station. To say that I have never been thus treated in all my days is a vast understatement. I had no wish to burden you with this vicious scheming, Nephew. I hoped to ease your load and spare your sensibilities by talking to the chit myself. Never did I expect a girl of uncommon pigheadedness! Such hideous lack of propriety and decency! Rude as I have never before encountered! How could I have been so blind as to not see her for the creature she is? No wonder she could presume, as unworthy as she is in every facet, that she could use her wiles to reach above where she rightfully belongs. I shudder to imagine what our well-ordered world is degrading to if this brand of selfishness and, yes, evil abounds! Of course, considering her upbringing and low connections..."

After no less than five attempts to interject into Lady Catherine's tirade, Darcy surrendered the effort. He stood at the edge of the billiard table, the cue finally laid onto the felt surface, and focused on his obviously furious aunt. The worst of his surprise passed, to be replaced by concern and confusion. Her disjointed harangue made no sense to him whatsoever, and with the dearth of concrete facts as to what the "scandalous falsehoods" were, Darcy failed to muster a personal concern.

Lady Catherine, on the other hand, was red-faced and sweating! Rather than losing steam, each sentence appeared to rile her more. Darcy began to fear she might faint or collapse from an apoplectic fit. As he stepped forward to commandeer the unstable situation, Lady Catherine's most recent remark finally penetrated and instantly doused his concern.

"What did you just say? You were at Longbourn? Are you speaking of Miss Elizabeth Bennet?"

His cold inflection and abrupt stride toward her accomplished what his previous, soft interjections had not. Lady Catherine's voice stuttered to a halt. She misinterpreted the icy anger visible in his eyes and the hard set of his jaw, made evident by her next words.

"Indeed I am speaking of that horrible girl! Nephew, you have no idea the degree of scheming amongst that family. Tragically the eldest has sunk her claws into poor Mr. Bingley, although perhaps there is hope for him yet. The scandal of a broken betrothal is minimal compared to the devastation of marrying into *that* family—"

"Enough!" he barked. "I refuse to listen to slurs against the Bennet ladies or Mr. Bingley. Are we clear?"

Lady Catherine merely stared, neither agreeing nor disagreeing with his command. Then her eyes narrowed. "I was certain it must be impossible. Please tell me there is no truth to the claims, Darcy. Surely the Master of Pemberley is too wise to be drawn in by a pretty face and seductive advances. You would not forget your promises to Anne and stoop so low as to actually offer marriage to that girl, would you?"

"Lady Catherine, my personal affairs are absolutely none of your business. Not now, not ever. And I will not listen to another word, from this day on, regarding Anne and me. That topic has been closed for a decade or more." He stepped closer, fury warring with panic and causing his insides to churn. "As unfathomable as it is, evidently you accepted rumors from God knows where and then traveled from

Rosings to Longbourn for the express purpose of confronting Miss Elizabeth Bennet. What, exactly, did you say to her, Aunt Catherine?"

"Only the truth. That it had been reported to me by a reliable source, by my rector, Mr. Collins, that not only had the eldest Bennet contrived to receive an advantageous offer of marriage, but that *you* were to soon be united with Elizabeth Bennet! Impertinent girl that she is, a straight answer to my request for clarification was not rendered. By her evasion and shameful arguing, *with me* no less, I knew it to be a vile lie. Nevertheless, she persisted in countering every logical reason I gave for why a match with you is unacceptable."

During her reply, Darcy turned and lurched to the window. Blindly, he stared outside. Darkness, borne of murderous rage and plunging despair, engulfed him. Coherent thought was nearly impossible, and his aunt's words sliced as painful as a dagger thrust into his gut.

Yet he had to know the whole sordid tale—not out of any possible hope in salvaging the damage she had done, but because his honor required he attempt to apologize to Miss Elizabeth at the least.

"What reasons did you lay at her feet? Tell me precisely what you said made… us… unacceptable."

"Well, there is Anne, of course! Whether you acknowledge it or not, Darcy, it was the wish of your mother, and Anne is your destiny."

He spun about, clutching on to the curtain sash for stability. Lady Catherine clamped her lips on "destiny" and involuntarily stepped backward, his expression clearly alarming her.

"Not. Another. Word. And never mention my mother again. Ever. Consider that a warning, Aunt Catherine. Now, tell me what else you said."

Straightening her spine, she complied, in fine detail, unquestionably relishing the words. Numb, Darcy was unable to wince at the familiar reasons she recounted. Had they not once crossed his lips? Undeniably in a nicer tone, and after expressing his love, but equally as harmful. This debacle coming on the heels of the

Wickham disaster was a sure death knell to any chance he might have had with Elizabeth. He struggled not to strangle the woman standing before him—or fall to his knees weeping.

"I am deeply disappointed in you, Darcy. I fail to comprehend how you can toss aside your honor, family interests, and position in society to entertain an alliance with Elizabeth Bennet. As unfathomable as the prospect is to me, imagine how Lord Matlock would receive such an abhorrent woman. Promise me that you will not make such a disgraceful connection!"

"I repeat, Aunt, my personal affairs are outside the realm of your authority. I judge for myself and reach decisions based on *my* wishes and desires in *all* matters. I am not beholden to you and will certainly never extend to *you* a promise to do, or not do, anything. Just as I never promised to marry Anne, so will I never promise *not* to marry Elizabeth Bennet!"

As if that is an option, his soul sobbed, *but it is worth the shock on her face to pretend otherwise.*

"Have my points of fact fallen onto deaf ears, Darcy? Are you to be as unreasonable as she? Refusing to promise entering into an engagement, you must know in your heart is utterly wrong, just as she did. Are you resolved to have her despite the consequences? Like her, you would face contempt and ruin? For what? I know why she is determined to ensnare you. But what is your motivation? Is it love," she sneered, "or is it simply lust?"

Darcy frowned, creases marring his brow as he ruminated on her references to Elizabeth being as unreasonable as he, refusing to promise as he did, and being determined to ensnare him. The curiosity of those oblique statements overrode the offense at the last slurs. As if he would discuss love or lust with his aunt!

Suddenly a number of the comments during her tirade were seen in a different light.

"Elizabeth argued with you. Is that what you said?" He spoke slowly, examining her face and holding up his hand when she opened her mouth to speak. "A nod will suffice. Thank you. She did not back down or agree with your bleak assessments of a union between us, is that what you are saying? Ah…interesting. She has always been a woman who speaks forthrightly and with courage."

He smiled, and in spite of the tense aura in the room, his heart lifted in fresh admiration. *God, she is amazing! Facing down Lady Catherine de Bourgh, no less! What an incredible Mistress of Pemberley she would be!*

"Darcy, listen—"

"One more question," he interrupted, his voice calm but as stern as his granite gaze. "I presume, by what you said, that you attempted to extract a promise from Miss Elizabeth not to accept me? And she refused to make that promise?"

Lady Catherine flinched and glanced away, the reaction quickly covered by her hastening to grab the cloak she had tossed onto a sofa back. "I can see that you are overwrought, Nephew, so will leave you. Please dwell upon my—"

"Answer the question, Aunt. Did she refuse to promise?"

"Yes," she snapped, "and that alone should reveal the depth of her recalcitrant… ambitious… horrid nature!"

"Oh, it reveals a great many aspects of her nature indeed, just none of them as you have listed. I wish for you to leave Darcy House this instant, Lady Catherine. I have had enough of your interference."

He crossed the remaining space until he was only a foot away, never diverting his hard gaze from her eyes. She was angry still, that was obvious, but also worried and, perhaps, a bit frightened. Good.

"Listen to me closely, and have no doubt that I mean this as a threat. If you *ever* go near Miss Elizabeth, or any of the Bennets, I cannot say precisely what my response will be but can assure you will not like it."

"Threats do not become a gentleman, Darcy."

"Irrelevant. Of course, if you prefer, consider it a *promise* rather than a threat. You know the way to the front door. Good day, Lady Catherine."

Without a bow or backward glance, Darcy exited the room.

Mr. Travers, once again his calm self, stood at the end of the corridor and watched his master approach. "Mr. Travers, please ensure that Lady Catherine is safely escorted to her carriage. Immediately. Then have the groomsmen prepare my horse and carriage. I will be departing within the hour."

"As you command, sir. Should I be informed as to your destination?"

"Of course. I will be joining Mr. Bingley at Netherfield in Hertfordshire."

CHAPTER ONE

Declarations at Sunrise

D uring the course of a person's life, there will be days or hours, even brief minutes, that become etched upon one's memory vividly. Decades later those unique, pivotal times will be recalled with clarity of vision and emotion.

The day when Fitzwilliam Darcy proposed marriage to Elizabeth Bennet for the second time would not merely inhabit the list of special days in their lives. Rather, it would hold a position within the topmost tier, remaining there on into eternity.

For Elizabeth, the element of surprise enhanced the memorable event.

Surprise in the realization that Mr. Darcy still loved her. Surprise in discovering the depth of desire and love she felt for him. Surprise that quick-witted and saucy-tongued Lizzy Bennet was unable to articulate the emotions pounding in her heart.

How do you tell the man previously rejected that your feelings have profoundly changed? Can it be expressed in words when you barely comprehended the yearning within your soul?

"My affections and wishes are unchanged, but one word from you will silence me on this subject forever."

Mr. Darcy vowed that *one word* would silence him on the subject of his affection and wishes, and in no way did Lizzy want him to be silent on that subject. Considering it fortuitous that her mind reeled, she clamped her lips and waited, eyes luminous and fixed upon his face.

Then, as he hesitantly stepped closer, she detected a tentative light warming his eyes and a faint relaxing of his facial muscles. Never removing his gaze from her face, he inhaled shakily, his voice husky and tremulous as he continued with his declaration. Shivers raced up her spine as he revealed his love for her, claimed with conviction that his body and soul were bewitched by her, and divulged his wish to never be apart from her.

Some might argue that a proper marriage proposal it was not. To Lizzy his words were the sweetest music.

Perfection.

So perfect that she was overcome with the desire to freeze the moment, ensuring she would never forget the tiniest detail or nuance. It was the nakedly pleading expression on his face that made her gasp through the paralysis affecting her lungs and feet. Suddenly she *needed* to be near him. Three short steps brought her so close that the impact of his presence—impossibly handsome and utterly male— combined with the welter of emotions flooding his face once again overwhelmed her senses.

Abruptly dry of throat and devoid of words, Lizzy glanced downward to restore a semblance of control. Accidentally, perhaps, her gaze fell on his hand where it hung limp at his side. Inexplicably, a mingled surge of sadness and protectiveness pierced her heart. In that moment, she saw his empty hand as symbolic of his loneliness. It was a loneliness she understood, even if the emotion was not one she would have admitted feeling hours before. Instinctively she pressed his cold hand between hers and lifted it to her lips for a gentle kiss.

There was a minuscule pause before he gently squeezed her fingers. His understanding of her acceptance was conveyed in that simple gesture. No more than three heartbeats had passed, yet the strength flooding her body from the simple connection of their hands was enough to dispel her nervousness. The pages of words etched within her heart tickled her tongue with a yearning to be spoken aloud. All of them were lost the moment she lifted her face and met his eyes.

He looked honestly stunned! His parted lips and wide eyes comical if in a different situation. Lizzy's smile was a bare upturn of the corners of her mouth, yet enough to flood his face with relief and light his blue eyes with joy. So enraptured was she by the transformation in his countenance that the tentative touch of his fingertips to her cheek and the exhilarating cascade of sensations ignited by his feathery touch astounded her.

Instinctively, Lizzy leaned into the warmth of his palm and closed her eyes to better *feel* the wonder. When he bent and tenderly rested his forehead against hers, his sigh of contentment wafting over her sensitized skin, Lizzy could almost hear the walls of past misunderstanding and distance disintegrating.

Magical.

The connection between them was instantaneous, even though no words had been uttered. There was a dreamlike quality to the event augmented by the sunlight shining upon them as a benediction. Entranced as she was, a flash of clarity shone through, and of all the words she knew must be said eventually, the three vital ones rose to the top.

"I love you."

Darcy inhaled sharply and jerked as if stuck by a pin. His eyes flew open; they were so close she could note the individual flecks of colors in them.

"Say it again."

"I love you...Fitzwilliam."

He shut his eyes again and released a sibilant moan. Then the brilliant smile she had so rarely seen burst forth, and he opened his sparkling eyes.

"Elizabeth. Lovely, precious Elizabeth," he breathed as delicate fingertips traced a line of fire across her jaw and chin, finally lingering on her lips.

Lizzy's breath caught in her throat, and her muscles trembled from the raw emotion written on his face.

Kiss me!

Her silent plea echoed within his crystal-blue eyes, and she honestly did not know if living through the disappointment of him *not* kissing her would be worse than the drowning bliss if he did! She could see the harsh struggle he waged, his desire as strong, if not stronger, than her own. Somehow he conquered his urges and, with a visible shudder, withdrew a pace. He clasped her small hands between his broad ones and gazed at her with such intensity of love and thankfulness that any shreds of disappointment Lizzy felt at evading a kiss were dissolved.

"Elizabeth, there is much to say, much for me to apologize for, although I do not deserve your forgiveness. I did not plan this...rendezvous, and it is not how I intended to proceed in winning your affection. I wanted to court you properly, allot you time to improve your opinion of me, and maybe, if I was so blessed, have you love me. I never entertained the notion, even after my aunt restored my hope, that you felt a fraction of what I do."

"I do," she murmured with a nod and smile.

Darcy exhaled a happy sigh and shook his head in amazement. "Elizabeth, clever phrases and spontaneous conversation are not my forte, as you can attest. Luckily, fate has gifted me with this opportunity, and considering how atrociously I botched my well-rehearsed proposal, fate has also proven to be wiser. Simplicity appears to be its recommendation. Therefore, on that note—"

Without releasing her hands or diverting his gaze for a second, Darcy bent onto one knee. "Miss Elizabeth Bennet, I love you fervently and with all that I am. Will you honor me by becoming my wife?"

"Yes! Oh, yes, you know I will!" A wavering sob accompanied her shout. Lizzy was powerless to stop the tears or the launch into his body. He nearly fell, but rallied and stood while encircling her with his strong arms. His rumbling laugh vibrated the broad chest she was instantly pressed against.

Never had she experienced this level of intimacy with a man. Never had she felt such protectiveness, belonging, and unity. Never had anything, or anyone, felt so *right*. Remaining thus entwined longer than propriety would dictate, the sensations educed by the embrace were indescribable. He radiated heat, his heart beating powerfully under her ear, and his arms firmly but tenderly encompassed her body. Combined, it created a haven she never wanted to leave.

"Elizabeth," he whispered hoarsely, as his lips brushed the top of her head and warm breath tingled across her scalp. She recognized reluctance as he clasped her elbows and gently pushed her away from his body. Looking up, she noted his joyous smile and gleaming eyes. He wiped a lone tear off her cheek, eliciting a fresh wave of heat that made her gasp. The smile did not lessen, but a hint of sober intent muted the brightness within his eyes.

"Miss Elizabeth, is your father currently at home? With your permission, I would like to speak with him as soon as possible."

"He is at home, yes. And you have my permission, Mr. Darcy— wholehearted and unwavering."

He was taken aback at the vehemence in her voice, she could tell, and before he glanced away, she detected a flash of—Doubt? Disbelief? Fear? Instantly she understood his conflicting emotions. Goodness knows she had given scant reason to anticipate her exuberant response. Perhaps patience and time were required to wholly convince him of her love, but there never had been a challenge Elizabeth Bennet did not rise to.

A good place to start was eagerly taking the arm he offered and steering determinedly toward Longbourn and Mr. Bennet. It was difficult to collect her thoughts, however, due to the closeness of his body as they walked. She did not feel shy or uncomfortable. Rather, her senses were acutely aware of his presence—the musky cologne and faint smell of horse emanating from his jacket, his exposed neck

13

and glimpse of chest, how the damp linen shirt clung to his muscles, and the sheer height and breadth of his figure were more than enough to hamper logical thinking. Add to that his constant sidelong glances that clearly had him as captivated and addled, and it was easy to fathom why her head spun.

"Do you prefer to be called Fitzwilliam, or do you have another name?" she inquired abruptly, as startled as he by the unexpected question and interruption to the silence.

"My full name is Fitzwilliam Alexander James Darcy," he replied calmly. "James was my father's name, and Alexander was his brother. Fitzwilliam was my mother's maiden name. It is the surname of my uncle, the Earl of Matlock. Consequently there are quite a few Fitzwilliams about at family gatherings." He laughed, the sound beautiful to her ears, and she mentally noted to tell him so. "My cousins are often addressed as Fitzwilliam. Colonel Fitzwilliam is my cousin. Did you know this?"

"You mentioned it once. In your letter." She murmured the last, gazing momentarily at the ground before shaking off the unpleasant remembrances.

"Richard, that is Colonel Fitzwilliam, is two years my senior, but we grew up together and have always been friends as well as relatives. To answer your question, my family all call me William. It is what I prefer, although I think you, dearest Elizabeth, could call me by any name and I would find it delightful."

"Your family is so illustrious. Mama will be pleased," she teased, ducking her head to hide the rosiness that had risen in her cheeks at his last statement. "Lords and ladies abounding!"

His smile faltered and tone grew somber. "Yes, although, I fear my Aunt Catherine has proven how a title does not indicate worth— or an assurance of proper manners. What she did was unpardonable, Elizabeth, and I apologize for any pain she caused."

"An apology is not necessary, especially when the event led to this positive conclusion. Besides, it livened up the dreariness of a normal day at Longbourn. Nothing quite as effective as an argumentative confrontation to upset the boredom!"

"Indeed," he chuckled, his expression both amused and proud. "Fortunately, you will discover my uncle and his wife quite different. They will adore you, I am certain."

The radiant smile breaking over his face rendered her breathless, her rapt attention to his countenance distracting from careful attention to her steps over the uneven terrain. She faltered, Darcy immediately steadying her, with one hand gripping her elbow while the other slipped around her waist. The rescue brought her even closer to his body.

"Are you well, Elizabeth? Steady now."

Neither moved. His eyes were inches from hers, Lizzy unable to do more than nod. She had always been captivated, even in her annoyance and pretended indifference to him, by how penetrating his gaze was. His vividly blue eyes, fierce as a raptor's and burning with intelligence, never failed to intrigue her, especially in how they would darken when fixed on her—exactly as they did now. Previously she had erroneously decided it was disapproval and disdain. Now she understood the staring and the reaction were about his enthrallment, love, and…passion? Desire for her?

Blushing from the heat surging through her body, Lizzy tore her gaze away and resumed walking. Injecting a normal, jesting tone, she said, "Proper manners or otherwise, having peers of the realm as relatives will win you points with my family! Mama, especially, will likely faint dead away, so be sure you lead with that fact." Her laugh faded when she glanced to see him trailing a step behind, his expression grave. "Mr. Dar…William? Whatever is the matter?"

"I love hearing you speak my name, Elizabeth," he whispered.

"How providential that you do, since you will be hearing it so uttered for the rest of my life!" She unthinkingly lifted a finger to the tiny furrows between his brows, rubbing lightly. "What troubles you, William?"

Catching her hand and kissing her fingers, he held on and resumed walking. After some minutes of silent contemplation, he spoke slow and deliberate. "I am well aware of the fact that I made a poor impression on the citizens of Hertfordshire, aided partially by Mr. Wickham but primarily due to my own surliness. Frankly, I remain dumbfounded that you have not only managed to see past my errors and attitude, but have also grown to...care for me."

Lizzy frowned at his pause, sensing he started to say *love* but caught himself.

"Mr. Bennet has no reason to approve of me as a suitor—wealth or family connections notwithstanding—nor do I wish him to render his approval based on those inconsequential facts. It is imperative, Elizabeth, that he knows I love you and deem your happiness of the utmost importance."

She touched his chin with her fingertips and forced his gaze to hers. "Mr. Darcy, my father is a reasonable man. Be honest, as I know you only can be, and say to him what you have said to me. He will not refuse you, especially after hearing my feelings on the subject."

He searched her eyes, still frowning. "Does he know what happened...with us...at Rosings?"

"No one knows about that but me and you."

His brows arched. "Not even Miss Bennet?"

"No, I never told anyone. Did you?"

"My cousin suspected and knows pieces. Only Georgiana knows fully. She extracted the information as only she can. In truth, I was a bit of a wreck after Rosings, and she was worried." He shook his head, but before Lizzy could ask what he meant by being a wreck, he laughed.

"What do you find amusing, sir?"

He caressed one fingertip over her cheek, eyes sparkling with mirth. "It is humbling. I manage a vast estate and intricate affairs of business, domestic and abroad, without flinching. Yet, here I stand, daunted by the prospect of a confrontation with a country gentleman.

Of course, not one of those ventures has ever been as critical to my existence as this one."

"I suspect you are brave enough to handle my frightening father, Mr. Darcy."

"We shall see. It will be a test of my worth as a husband to someone as brave, forthright, and independent as you, Miss Elizabeth." He lifted her hand for a firm kiss, his eyes amused and serious at the same time. "Elizabeth, I love and respect you more than I can express. It is vitally important that you understand how valuable your opinion is to me. I want to talk to you, at length and honestly, about Rosings, my letter, Lady Catherine, Bingley and Miss Bennet, my abominable behavior, and the rest, so there will be no further miscommunications or…discord between us. Presently we do not have the time, as I dare not keep you alone for much longer. If you have any doubts or wish to wait until we can discuss—"

"No," she interrupted emphatically. "I have no doubts. Nor do I need to consider further or discuss unpleasantness from the past. I know my heart, and I *do* love *you,* Mr. Darcy. The rest can be dealt with, if it must, later. For now, the only important task is to face my father. I shan't let you back out simply because he is a terrifying individual!"

Darcy chuckled at her jest, his relief evident even if he still looked mildly amazed. Then he squared his shoulders purposefully, squeezed her hand, and turned toward the house visible through the trees. "Come then, Miss Elizabeth, my love. Our destiny awaits!"

❧

Lizzy waited in the empty corridor while Mr. Darcy remained closeted with her father in his library. *They have been talking for nearly an hour!* She bit her lip nervously, paced several steps down the hall before turning to pace back, glared sternly at Kitty and Mary—who were peeking through the parlor doorway—and attempted to ignore her mother's incessant declarations of shock.

By a miracle, she and Mr. Darcy had entered the house without encountering a single Bennet. They made it to Mr. Bennet's library door undisturbed, and it was as Lizzy knocked on the door, after squeezing the hand of the nervous man she hoped to soon be officially betrothed to, that Mrs. Bennet rounded the corner. Her gasp jolted both of them, but before either could respond or release the hand they clutched, the door was pulled open to reveal an equally astonished Mr. Bennet.

His gaze lowered to their hands—Darcy dropping Elizabeth's as if it were a hot brand—and the stunned expression rapidly evolved into a stern glare.

"I see you have matters of importance to discuss, Mr. Darcy." Mr. Bennet flicked his gaze to Lizzy's flushed face and then back to Mr. Darcy's composed one.

"I do, sir. If it is not an inconvenience, I beg your indulgence in granting me an audience without delay."

"Without delay, is it? Hmm. Very well. Elizabeth, stay close. I will be talking to you next." And after only the barest of glances from Mr. Darcy, she was left standing in the corridor.

The silence lasted half a second before her mother shrilly asked what was going on. Only the fear of Mr. Darcy overhearing Mrs. Bennet's confusion over Lizzy choosing *that man,* with his arrogant attitude and unpleasant personality, prompted Lizzy to leave the area. Jane was the only one who made any attempt to listen and support, but even she was clearly flabbergasted at the idea of Lizzy and Mr. Darcy. Finally, after some fifteen or twenty minutes of questions and berating from her mother and sisters, Lizzy threw up her hands in defeat and ordered them to stay in the parlor.

Nervousness at what was transpiring behind the closed door mixed with dismay over her family's reaction to the news. Furthering her anxiety were bleak thoughts as to what it portended.

Lizzy had all but forgotten the general opinion of Mr. Darcy in Hertfordshire. Even when he alluded to it while walking back to Longbourn, her happiness overrode the concerns. The majority of local citizens she had known since birth, some especially dear friends. Thus it was a worthy goal to convince them of Mr. Darcy's excellent character and the truthful reasons for marrying him. Hopefully she would succeed, but if she failed, so be it.

When it came to her parents and sisters, indifference was not an option. Based on the immediate reaction to her news, gaining their acceptance and understanding might prove tougher than she'd imagined! As for her father, Lizzy knew of his preference for her and anguished over causing him distress. Would he believe she was unwise in choosing Mr. Darcy? Would he easily grant approval, as she had assured Mr. Darcy?

Abruptly, the door burst open. Mr. Darcy breezed out, and Lizzy was so tightly wound that she sped right past him. Halfway through the door, she turned. He smiled wanly, his expression indecipherable. He did not appear distraught—nor overjoyed. His general demeanor was one of exhaustion. She smiled encouragingly, mouthed *I love you,* and shut the door.

Mr. Bennet was agitated as she had rarely seen him. The first words out of his mouth made her wince. "Lizzy, are you out of your senses? Mr. Darcy? Have you truly accepted his proposal? Have you not professed your hatred of him time and again?"

She lost track of the minutes passing after that opening. Her need to thoroughly explain all that had transpired between them was of the utmost importance. Tearfully, she assured him of the intense love she felt for Mr. Darcy, enumerated with vigor his numerous excellent qualities, related what he had done to prove his devotion to her, and spoke of his constancy and patience. She did not give the finer details of his first proposal at Rosings, saying only that she refused because she had not loved him at the time. Lizzy feared Mr. Darcy's poorly chosen words would incite Mr. Bennet's anger as fiercely as it had hers, and when he interrupted to ask how Mr. Darcy had proposed, the dark gleam in his eyes confirmed her fears.

"What did Mr. Darcy tell you?" she asked, rather than answering.

"Only that he spoke in a manner unbefitting a gentleman and with words he was too ashamed to repeat. He refused to divulge further. Despite his persuasive articulation of remorse and assurances that his attitude is altogether changed, I am not happy at the idea of my daughter marrying a man who once insulted her character."

"What Mr. Darcy left out, I am guessing, is that I insulted his character equally as much if not worse."

She went on to tell him of her misunderstanding and Mr. Darcy's regret over his influence with Mr. Bingley. Then she spoke of Wickham's unsavory relationship with the family. In that, she said only that Mr. Wickham had attempted to "seduce a member of Mr. Darcy's family as retaliation," the timely rescue saving the young woman from the fate Lydia nearly fell victim to—if it had not been for Mr. Darcy's intervention—and contributing to why Wickham spread lies of Mr. Darcy's character across Hertfordshire.

"We all fell prey to deception in regards to Mr. Darcy, Papa, but none as severely as me. He is too kind and too generous to lay conviction at my feet, yet there it should be laid as harshly as any directed toward him. You must understand that we are not purposely keeping secrets from you. Rather it is that these are private matters between us." Mr. Bennet's lips crunched together until not the thinnest line of pink flesh was visible, the tension lessening when she pressed a warm palm over his hand and continued in a teasing tone, "If we can forgive each other for painful words, mature in our understanding as a result, and fall in love, is this not a positive sign for the rigors of marriage?"

The conclusion was Mr. Bennet granting his permission to the match, albeit reluctantly and with professed reservations of their compatibility. Lizzy squealed with glee as she rushed to embrace her father.

"Erase your fears, Papa. We are perfectly matched, I assure you, and you will soon see how wonderful Mr. Darcy is and his abiding affection for me."

"I will be watching, my Lizzy. I could not bear to lose you to anyone less worthy."

She kissed his forehead. "In that, I do believe Mr. Darcy would agree!"

Sprinting from the room with her father's chuckle following behind, she dashed into the empty corridor and then into the parlor. Suddenly frantic over the barrage the poor man had probably been subjected to, she stopped short when her rapid scan of the room revealed only her mother and three sisters.

"What have you done to him?" she blurted.

"Oh, Lizzy! Mr. Darcy? Are you certain of what you are choosing? What pin money and fine carriages you will have—and a house in Town too! Quite wonderful, and a saving boon for us all, but he is so disagreeable and…"

Mrs. Bennet was atwitter, clutching at Lizzy's hand and gasping as she went on about Mr. Darcy's wealth and negative qualities in running sentences. Not wasting time to reply to any of her mother's ramblings, Lizzy glanced to Jane, who inclined her head toward the garden. Mrs. Bennet's voice followed behind as Lizzy flew down the steps and the well-trod path to the garden. She slowed when she saw him, her heart skipping several beats and butterflies dancing in her stomach.

He sat on a stone bench, hunched over with his elbows on his knees, and nervously twisted a mutilated flower between his fingers. He looked up and then lurched rapidly to his feet. For a moment she thought he was going to leap toward her, but instead he stood frozen, staring at her with a panicked question.

"It is official. I am yours."

The expressions that crossed his countenance would have been vastly humorous if she did not feel his turmoil. She laughed gaily, and swiftly reduced the gap between them until they were standing less than a foot apart. He enveloped her petite hands with a steadfast grip, face jubilant and awash with liberation, and placed their entwined hands against his throbbing heart. At the same time, he bent and settled his forehead on hers, releasing a mighty sigh.

As delightful as the sensations were, a giggle escaped her smiling lips.

"Are you laughing at me?"

"Only a little. Did my frightening father scare you after all, Mr. Darcy?"

"He can be rather intimidating when he wishes it, Miss Elizabeth. I relinquished my pride and bared my soul. I confess that I never recognized how deep his love for you. Of course, this emotion, while of a different nature, placed us on equal footing to a degree. Nevertheless, he put me on the defensive and refused to completely grant permission for our engagement until he spoke with you. Under the circumstances, I could not fault him that, but as he held my entire future happiness in his hands, I am not ashamed to confess being overcome with tremendous fear."

"I shall have to tell him. I doubt Papa has frightened anyone in his entire life! He will be amused."

"How pleased I am to be a fount of amusement for the Bennet household. I believe I have also adequately supplied the daily portion of entertainment for your mother and sisters."

She burst out laughing. "Poor William! Mr. Darcy, who hates to be teased, has received his allotment today."

Releasing one hand to smooth the loose strands of hair away from her eyes, he smiled unabashedly and replied, "I suppose I should be chagrined, but I find that teasing does not annoy me as much as it once did. Levity appears to have entered my existence along with you, dear Elizabeth, and it heals me."

"So, are you better now? Your heart continues to pound."

"I judge my heart shall forever pound when near you." His voice deepened, and tender fingers traced over her features, darkened eyes following. "Elizabeth, you are incredibly beautiful. I so love and adore you. I am the happiest of men."

Once again Lizzy was breathless and mesmerized, captured by his eyes and the renewed thrills racing through her body at his touch. His eyes and fingertips reached her parted lips, feathering them lightly.

"Elizabeth, please, may I kiss you?"

Unable to speak, she nodded faintly. As if in a dream of exquisite beauty, he lowered his head slowly while cupping her face with his strong yet tender hands. Instinctively, her eyes slid shut with the first gentle pressure of his mouth brushing against hers.

His kisses were restrained, pure, and delicate; yet the sensations flowing through her body were torrential, dynamic, and astonishing. Simultaneously they shivered, matching sighs of pleasure escaping their lips.

"Is it supposed to feel so…incredible?"

He laughed softly and shook his head. "I would not know, but I believe it should."

Without another word, he claimed her mouth again. His kisses were temperate, and his hands traveled to her neck for soothing strokes. Of their own volition, her hands tentatively explored the muscular contours of his chest and shoulders, and then moved up to encircle his bare neck, her fingers entwining in his hair.

Reflexively, Lizzy parted her lips. The delicious pressure of his mouth was glorious yet inexplicably increased her yearning for more. Precisely what the *more* was that she craved Lizzy did not consciously imagine—until he skimmed the tip of his tongue over her bottom lip. Not sparing a particle of a second to analyze why this simple act felt unfathomably fantastic and spiraled her senses, she gave in to impulse. A faint sigh escaped when she opened her mouth farther and hesitantly touched her tongue to his.

Fire ignited! Sheer ecstasy!

Darcy groaned. The sound and vibration woke something buried inside Lizzy's body that had lain dormant. When he followed with a penetrating invasion of his tongue, that unnamed something roared to crazed life. This manner of kissing's warmth and intimacy was

23

beyond her wildest imaginings. Oddly, rather than being overwhelmed or fearful, she yearned for even *more*.

Abruptly he left her mouth and planted kisses all about her face. He pressed his face into her hair and inhaled deeply, and then proceeded to rain soft nibbles down to the sensitive flesh behind her ear. He moaned her name before gently drawing her earlobe between his lips. Ceaselessly he caressed her arms and back, pulling her closer to his chest. Ardently, as if starved, he returned to her receptive mouth, giving her a taste of the *more* she craved.

Lizzy was dizzy from the sensations yet wholly aware of the bliss coursing through her veins. She matched each of his motions and responded with greater boldness. She was intoxicated, and wildly abandoned to the sensations he roused within. With a husky groan, she clutched his back and head, and fused herself to the entire surface of his body. She reveled in how the unyielding muscles of his chest crushed her breasts and, innocent though she was in many respects, thrilled at the rigid length jammed into her belly.

Despite that obvious indication of Mr. Darcy's enjoyment of their interlude, or most likely because of it, he harshly clasped on to her shoulders and frantically shoved her away. Staring at the ground, he hoarsely stammered between ragged pants, "Elizabeth...Miss Elizabeth, I beg your forgiveness! My behavior is... ungentlemanly and unforgivable! Please...accept my heartfelt apology."

Lost in a daze, her heart fluttered so alarmingly she thought she might well faint! Feeling bereft at the sudden abandonment of his warmth, she stuttered, "I...I am so sorry...I thought you wanted to...I should not have..." Shy and insecure for the first time that day, tears welled in her eyes, and she joined his serious contemplation of the ground.

For several agonizing moments, they stood apart, breathing heavily and collecting their befuddled thoughts.

"What you must think of me—" she muttered.

"Can you forgive me, my love?" he blurted at the same instant.

"Forgive you...what?" Wide-eyed, she looked upward and met his confused gaze.

His question tumbled over hers. "Whatever do you mean?"

"I behaved so wantonly—"

"I lost control of myself—"

Naturally, it was Lizzy who first saw the humor, smiling and laughing while he watched her in perplexity.

Gradually, his lips lifted in amusement. "You are laughing at me again."

"On the contrary, I am laughing at us. Mr. Darcy, let me see if I understand this. You are apologizing for enjoying kissing me, your betrothed, while I am apologizing for responding to said kisses?" He nodded, flushing brighter. "Therefore, in effect, we are apologizing for being in love?"

He opened his mouth and then snapped it closed, glancing away from her teasing face. "It does seem rather ludicrous when you state it thusly." His countenance turned serious. Clasping her hands, he spoke in a calm, reasonable tone. "Elizabeth, you surely understand that it is not merely the enjoyment of our love that concerns me but the appropriateness of it's expression before we are wed. It is shockingly improper for us to even discuss these matters, let alone experience them!"

"William, I appreciate your concern, although I submit that little about our relationship has been proper or appropriate, and yet here we are. You are correct, of course, in maintaining decorum until we are married."

"Elizabeth, please, I—"

"Mr. Darcy, I will not apologize for communicating openly with you! Nor will I hide my love for you. We have done far too much of both, nearly losing each other in our stupidity, misconceptions, and pride."

He stared at her silently as an expression of stunned happiness washed over his face. "You are amazing, Elizabeth, and I love you ardently. It remains a welcome shock that you love me at all, let alone feel the same... passion..." He sighed and ran one hand over his face. "It will take some getting used to, I suppose."

Before she could respond, he embraced her comfortingly and kissed her lips lightly. After another tender kiss, Darcy pulled away. "I shall leave you now, dearest Elizabeth. Extend my apologies to your mother, but I am not presentable, and frankly, my heightened emotions render me unfit for polite company. I will return this evening with Mr. Bingley."

He took a step to leave, but Lizzy gripped his hand to halt him. In a burst of enthusiasm, she wrapped her free hand around his neck, pulled him toward her as she lifted on her tiptoes, and kissed him soundly.

"From here on, I promise to behave as I should and not tempt fate. So, remember these kisses, Fitzwilliam Darcy, and do not doubt my love for you."

He nodded, his grin wide and eyes smoldering. Intent on holding to her promise, she propelled him out of the garden. They parted with formal salutations and proper hand kisses, Lizzy watching until he passed through the gate and turned for a breezy wave. She waved in return, laughed giddily, and performed a twirling dance of glee before skipping up the steps to the door.

CHAPTER TWO
Love Flurries and Fogs

*A*t the last second, Lizzy grasped the handle and closed the door quietly behind her. Briefly she leaned against the wood to catch her breath and still the fluttering of her heart—only a moment's respite, however, before she twisted about to look out the window.

There he was. His tall, sturdy frame was easily visible on the open pathway ascending the gradual slope. His coattails billowed with each stride, his long legs swallowing the yards. Lizzy leaned her forehead against the cool glass, eyes steady on the retreating figure of the man she loved. Suddenly he paused and glanced over his shoulder toward the house. Impulsively she jerked and pulled back from the window.

I am his betrothed and can stare at him as long as I want!

Chuckling at her folly, she stepped forward until pressed into the transparent surface. Unfortunately, he was too far away to see her through the glass, a fact she realized when unable to clearly decipher the expression on his face. She did not doubt his countenance was as sunny as hers, especially when he resumed walking. It took her a few moments to solve what it was that struck her as odd. After all, it was not as if she had been granted numerous opportunities to observe Mr. Darcy walking at a pace as brisk as the one he was currently setting. Yet somehow she knew that his normal gait was solid, each thickly booted foot planted confidently and with the hint of arrogant domination present in his bearing. Today, however, one would think he wore the lightest of house shoes or was seconds away from dancing on a slickly polished floor. She half expected his mincing feet to abruptly leave the ground in a balletic pirouette.

The vision was so ridiculous that she burst out laughing.

"Lizzy? Is that you? Jane, go see if that was Lizzy, and if so, bring her here. We have much to discuss!"

Lizzy's laugh was replaced by a groan at her mother's query. She wanted to bask in her happiness, not be subjected to an inquisition! She was already shaking her head and pleading with her eyes when Jane's face popped around the corner.

"No, Mama," Jane finally said, wincing at the untruth. "She must still be outside."

Thank you, Lizzy mouthed. She pantomimed climbing the stairs, pointed in the general direction of her bedroom, and then pointed at her sister and back toward the ceiling. Jane nodded, her face calm, as always, but Lizzy detected the confusion and colliding questions within Jane's blue eyes. *Come up soon. I need to talk to you.* Jane nodded once again before turning into the parlor to distract Mrs. Bennet so that Lizzy could dart past the doorway and escape to the stairs.

Once in the bedroom, Lizzy dashed straight to the window. It was ridiculous, of course. The angle from this corner of the house was inadequate to visualize the twisting pathway that led to Netherfield. Additionally, even if realities of geometric space and obstructing trees were not an issue, Mr. Darcy would have traveled beyond the reach of her eyesight by now. None of that kept her from trying anyway and then sighing forlornly when his figure was nowhere to be seen.

He still loves me! And we are to be married!

At her youngest and silliest age, Elizabeth Bennet had rarely been a girl known for flighty antics and addled brain. Vivacious and buoyant in spirit, indeed she was, but with a controlled demeanor differentiating her actions from those of foolish youths, such as Lydia and Kitty. Now here she was, at the mature age of twenty, giggling aloud and fighting an intense urge to twirl about the room or sprint down the trail until she had caught up to Mr. Darcy. In truth, she wanted to twirl *and then* run insanely after Mr. Darcy!

It was absurd in the extreme and should have embarrassed her into sobriety.

Instead, the ridiculous vision lead her to imagining catching her betrothed on the trail, which in turn lead her to imagining how pleased he would be and how he might express his pleasure, which in turn lead her to imagining—vividly—his kisses.

Lizzy pressed her palms against her flaming cheeks, closed her eyes, and inhaled several times. Finally, with a modicum of control restored, she moved away from the window. Inadvertently, her eyes opened to a reflection of her face in the vanity mirror.

The face staring back at her was a revelation.

Lightness and gaiety burst from within the chocolate depths of her eyes, startling her. It was a novel expression yet instantly recognizable as what she had detected within Mr. Darcy's eyes while gazing at her in the garden. There were a number of alterations to her mien that, if she were more her typical self and not overtaken by emotion, would cause her to laugh mockingly. Had she not just yesterday teased Jane for lips suspiciously plumper and ruddier than usual after her solitary walk with Mr. Bingley to the stables? Lizzy's lips were normally plump, but at the present, they were on the verge of swallowing her face!

Love, it has to be, and perhaps the residuals of physical desire.

This thought increased the warmth in her already burning cheeks, and hysterical giggling again threatened to burst forth. It did not help matters when she finally noted the condition of her hair. The pins and combs hastily placed earlier that day to restrain her heavy locks were loose and not at all where she had originally secured them. It was as if her hair had come alive, with whole clumps purposefully deciding to veer off into a different direction than nature, or her clips, intended. It was truly frightful, and even the echo of a resonant male voice declaring she was "incredibly beautiful" was insufficient to squelch the other voice that chided, "This is how the future Mistress of Pemberley presents herself?"

Before she could analyze why that second voice sounded more like Lady Catherine than her, the door opened. Relief flooded her body when only Jane entered and closed the door behind her.

"Oh, Jane! Your timing is perfect! I have much to tell you, but first you must help me with my hair. I am an utter fright!" She turned back to the mirror, pins and clips tossed haphazardly onto the vanity surface before attacking her snarled hair with a brush. "If Mr. Darcy were to return and see me like this, I am sure he would change his mind. You always were better skilled at arranging hair, and if only I had previously attended to your instructions, I would not now appear a bedraggled mess. I am mortified to recall how often I eschewed proper styling in my impatience. Somehow he saw past that, thanks be to heaven, but at the least I can henceforth attempt to *look* the part of a respectable woman worthy of being his wife and mistress to Pemberley."

"You *are* in love with him."

Lizzy paused mid-stroke and swiveled her head toward Jane. "Of course I am! Did you think I would consent to marry Mr. Darcy otherwise?"

"I never imagined you marrying Mr. Darcy under any circumstance, Lizzy! Consenting based on a mercenary inclination or a sense of obligation to help the family is unimaginable, and I have spent the past several hours arguing with Mama that this would not induce you to accept him. I assured her your opinion of Mr. Darcy improved after your stay in Derbyshire, citing this and perhaps greater appreciation for his character—and maybe a burgeoning affection—as plausible reasons for this stunning development. Never, however, did I entertain the notion that you might actually love him! How did this transpire, Lizzy?"

"Oh, Jane! I am indeed a wretched sister!" Lizzy crossed the room and clasped on to Jane's hands. "You would be justified to chastise and then never forgive me for being so secretive with my feelings—"

"I cannot chastise for that, Lizzy. Was it not I who so recently affirmed that I was indifferent to Mr. Bingley and quite over him? I suppose it is just that while I knew full well you did not believe my self-delusions any more than I believed them, I detected nothing indicating you thought of Mr. Darcy at all, let alone were in love with him! I suspect I am annoyed at myself more than I am you."

Laughing together, the sisters fell onto the bed.

"For sisters who care for each other as deeply as we do and have inhabited the same limited space for nigh on twenty years, we certainly can be ridiculous in keeping ourselves reserved. A lesson to be learned fortuitously before we are wed and carry the unhealthy attitude into our marital relationships, is it not?"

"I daresay it is, and"—Jane patted Lizzy's hand firmly—"you can practice your avowed newfound openness by telling me how it is that you came to love a man you once swore to loathe forever."

"It is a tedious story, Jane. Convoluted. Embarrassing in places. Dismaying in others. I hardly know how to make sense of it myself or how to comprehend that I came to love a man I once detested! I am not sure I can explain it."

"You must try. I refuse to fix your hair until you do."

Lizzy ran both hands through her snarled tresses. "I am a fright, yes?"

"Fairly so. But you are also radiant, flushed, and your eyes sparkle as I have never witnessed. So, no matter how convoluted the path you and Mr. Darcy have trod, I do not question that you love him. Does he love you as ardently in return, Lizzy?"

"Oh yes. I can confidently state that he loves me ardently." And even as she blushed bright red at the remembrance of *all* the reasons why she knew, beyond any shadowy doubts, that Fitzwilliam Darcy loved her, Lizzy launched into her story.

☙

Darcy covered the distance between Longbourn and Netherfield at a much faster pace than typical. Dimly he was aware of hunger pangs from having skipped breakfast, and the prospect of his quiet bedchamber where he could filter through his thoughts and emotions was appealing, yet neither was the reason for his rushed steps. It was as if his joyous heart and soaring soul lent buoyancy to his muscles, keeping his feet from touching the ground. Twice he burst into spontaneous laughter, four times caught himself whistling—and he *never* whistled—and he strongly suspected the only reason he did not stop to marvel at a flower or sun-kissed dewdrop was because he only saw Elizabeth's face. Under any other circumstances, such nonsensical behavior would have frightened him into seeking help from a professional versed in mental illness! Today, while he would not necessarily want anyone to witness his bizarre giddiness, he knew precisely the cause and relished the unique experience.

Elizabeth loves me! And she agreed to be my wife!

This time, a sort of dancing skip accompanied the thought, not that Darcy even noticed.

He paid no heed to the passing terrain, or the ground in front of him for that matter, and was startled to realize he was at Netherfield's north gate when he had just left Elizabeth's arms a moment ago. He could still feel her warm palms on his neck and the exquisite pressure of her lips, the sensations so vivid and acute that he groaned and turned around, as if she might actually be there.

"Get control of yourself, Darcy," he muttered, vigorously shaking his head in hopes of restoring clarity and control before entering the house. It helped to a degree, although he did stare at the gate's latch for a full thirty seconds before remembering how it worked. Fortunately he was able to slip in the side door and dash up to his suite without encountering anyone.

His manservant, Samuel, was straightening the bed when Darcy barged in. As if such antics were routine, Samuel lifted a calm face to his master and inquired after his needs.

"Coffee, please, and a breakfast tray if it can be managed. I left before eating."

For five minutes after the valet departed to carry out his orders, Darcy stood in the middle of the room. Always a person who craved solitude and the peace that comes from silence, Darcy breathed deeply and remained still for a purpose. He allowed the tranquility to infuse his body and clear his mind. As it did, he gazed around the chamber that had grown comfortable and familiar to him far more than any other temporary dwelling place ever had. It was not because this suite was particularly wonderful, but because it was while here, down the corridor from where Elizabeth Bennet had stayed when Jane Bennet was ill, that Darcy had fallen in love with her. Never mind that he had blindly denied his feelings. Netherfield, located in Hertfordshire, a mere three miles from Longbourn, would forever be associated with her. After today, and with the promise of happy moments inside these walls in the weeks to come, the connection would be strengthened.

So, while he yearned for the day when Pemberley and his bedchamber there would hold the premiere association with Elizabeth—and in a far more intimate way—Netherfield and this bedchamber were the current favorites. An odd sort of peace settled upon him in these rooms where his thoughts had been filled with Elizabeth nearly from day one.

Shrugging out of his coat, he tossed it onto the bed and sat on the chair near the low table, where his breakfast would soon be placed. He bent to remove his boots, the ordinary task occupying his hands while his mind sorted through everything that had happened. Attempts to gain perspective and latch on to a logical vein were difficult with his stomach growling like a caged tiger and Elizabeth permeating his being.

"Elizabeth." He whispered her name, a broad smile splitting his face. Leaning his head back and closing his eyes, Darcy succumbed to the irresistible euphoria.

There was an aspect to his euphoria that was unreal, like a beautiful dream so tangible that it stays with you even after you wake. How long had he been in love with Elizabeth Bennet? How many hours had he imagined kissing her? Was it possible to count the number of dreams in which she was his? Was this just another dream that he would awaken from?

His heart pounded in terror at the thought. Reaching one hand to press trembling fingertips to his lips, he relaxed. None of his dreams, as distinct and realistic as many had been, ever felt like this. Her taste remained on his tongue, her lavender-scented hair filled his nostrils, her passionate sighs rang in his ears, her adoring face floated before his eyes, and the softness of her flesh tingled the nerve endings on his hands. Darcy groaned and shifted in his chair, the irrefutably genuine sensations affecting him physically.

No, there was no doubt whatsoever that today was not a dream. It was a God-gifted miracle that he could never thank the Almighty enough for. He certainly would try, once he was fully able to wrap his mind around the reality of the miracle and accept that his dreams had come true.

Elizabeth Bennet loves me.

Months ago, when he first proposed in his arrogance and selfish comprehension of love, he had not given much thought to the importance of Elizabeth loving him in return. It still shamed him to admit how little he understood his own heart or the mysteries of real, soul-bonding love. Deep in the throes of ardent love for her, and sure that she would not refuse him based on his numerous qualifications— Darcy winced anew at *that* remembrance—he had not considered the emptiness, even if she had said yes, of marrying her without first winning her heart. Every word she had said to him, each sentence as clear today as it had been then, convicted him of his sins. Her truthful condemnation had taught him many things, not the least of which was the importance of mutual love.

Until the summer day when she had miraculously appeared at Pemberley, Darcy thought the lessons learned would never benefit him personally. Still grieving, the concept of finding another woman to take Elizabeth's place in his heart was impossible to fathom. He became convinced he had destroyed his one chance, and the logical, deserved outcome was a life alone. Forever a man of faith, though perhaps not as strongly as his grandfather, Darcy interpreted Elizabeth's surprising appearance at Pemberley as a message from God. Not that Elizabeth was destined to be his or that he was being handed her on a silver platter. Indeed, he immediately perceived that it was a chance. Nothing more. A chance to prove to her—and most importantly to himself—that he *had* learned the truth and was worthy of being loved by a woman of her caliber. If it took months or years, so be it. If in the end he failed, somehow he would accept she was better with someone else. The thought nearly killed him, but all that truly mattered, he eventually realized, was her happiness.

Her happiness—and to a large degree Charles Bingley's happiness—was what had prompted him to hunt down Lydia and Wickham. Guilt drove him as well, the sure knowledge that whatever might have prompted Wickham to seduce Lydia Bennet, whether a sensed awareness of her sister's importance to Darcy or not, the fact remained that it never would have happened if not for his abominable pride allowing Wickham to roam freely. If a solution were within his power, Darcy would have done anything to accomplish it so the Bennet family, especially Jane and Elizabeth, would not be adversely affected by a scandal. Fortunately, crossing a line into an illegal zone had not been necessary, but Darcy had prepared for that as well.

When it was finished, even after confessing his error in judgment about Miss Bennet to Bingley and seeing the positive outcome there, Darcy refused to allow himself to hope.

A knock at the door postponed further musings and ignited fresh rumbles in his stomach. Samuel entered with a heavily laden tray, sat it onto the low table by Darcy's chair, and proceeded to unerringly prepare his master's coffee the way he liked it.

"Do you have any specific instructions for me today, sir?" Samuel handed the hot cup to Darcy. "Should I unpack the rest of your bags?"

"Yes." Darcy winced at the scald to his tongue but took another gulp of the restoring beverage anyway. "We will be staying at Netherfield for a while longer after all. If I can have my bath drawn in an hour, that would be perfect. And I shall be dining at Longbourn tonight with Mr. Bingley. If my dark blue suit, and green and gold waistcoat are clean, I would like to wear them tonight."

He was staring directly at Samuel, so Darcy noticed the slight lift of his valet's brows. In a flash, the hint of surprise was gone, a smooth-faced Samuel assuring that all would be as he commanded. Once the door to his dressing room was shut, Darcy gave in to a smile and chuckle. He knew why Samuel was surprised. In his over ten years of service to Mr. Darcy of Pemberley, there was probably less than ten times Darcy expressed a preference for which garment to wear. Darcy honestly could not care less most of the time, as long as he was clean, properly attired in the latest fashion, and presentable. Darcy wondered if Samuel was thinking of the handful of particular clothing requests he had made, realizing that the majority of them were in the last year, when his day involved being in the presence of Elizabeth Bennet.

"Probably not," he muttered between bites of jam-smeared toast. Samuel was an excellent manservant, but his attention to Mr. Darcy's personal life did not extend past knowing his schedule so he could plan for the correct cravat knot and pocket fob. If Darcy had mentioned his engagement, the response from Samuel would have been something like: "Very good, sir. Congratulations. Would you like more salt on your eggs?"

The first plate was cleaned and refilled before Darcy resumed his musings.

Elizabeth Bennet loves me.

The thought was no less gratifying than before. The ridiculous grin and palpitating heartbeat continued unabated, even as he chewed.

Darcy knew she spoke the truth, Elizabeth never one to mince words or speak falsehoods. It was simply so astounding that he struggled to grasp how it had happened!

If he was being honest, the reality was that after spending time with Elizabeth at Pemberley, Darcy *had* believed her opinion of him had changed. He had not entirely trusted his ability to decipher Elizabeth's demeanor and actions after so hideously misinterpreting them before. Nevertheless, after nearly four months of constantly replaying every verbal and nonverbal exchange from the moment he saw her at the Meryton Assembly to that disastrous day when she vigorously refused his offensive proposal, he surmised his vision was clearer. While he had not thought for a second that Elizabeth had developed affection for him, her general disposition was not of a woman who actively hated him either.

So, yes, during their hours together at Pemberley, he had allowed glimmers of hope. *If* he was reading the sign from God correctly, and *if* he was finally interpreting Elizabeth's manner without bias, then perhaps they could start afresh. Tragically, there had been no time to anticipate or plan beyond that initial step. The letter from Jane Bennet reporting Lydia's affair with George Wickham violently destroyed everything, in Darcy's dismayed opinion.

How could Elizabeth ever forgive him? He who had the power to stop Wickham yet remained silent. It was a dramatic reminder of his pride and failure. The only bright spots during that whole sordid mess were a handful of vague comments by Mrs. Gardiner alluding to Elizabeth's favorable impression of Pemberley—and him. Darcy had tucked them away in his mind but prohibited his heart from dwelling upon them.

Upon the few, brief interactions when Darcy returned to Netherfield with Bingley, Elizabeth had not appeared angry or disgusted. His heart had lifted, but he clamped down on the tiny trickle. After all, her sister had just been proposed to! What woman would not be in a fine mood with smiles and cheery conversation?

Every day for the subsequent week—while Bingley danced with joy and gushed on and on about his great happiness—Darcy had remained torn. Not only had he felt the urge to throttle Bingley—purely out of his own heartache and not because he was unhappy for his dear friend and Miss Bennet—but he had also disliked the train of his thoughts.

He had never suspected that Elizabeth knew of his involvement with the Wickham fiasco but figured it obvious to her that he had played some part in bringing Bingley back to Hertfordshire—and to Jane. Add to that the natural romantic sentiments that revolve around an engagement and promised wedding, and it was not a leap in logic to imagine that, if he pressed Elizabeth, she may have been amenable.

While it made perfect sense on one level, and had been hugely tempting, Darcy refused to win Elizabeth's hand under any sort of leverage or artifice. Frankly, woman or not, he doubted her gullible enough to succumb to such emotional sentiments. Nevertheless, he preferred not to take that chance. The lesson painfully learned in the spring assured him that winning Elizabeth Bennet's heart, wholly and unreservedly, had to occur honestly. So he had decided that dwelling in London, rather than at Netherfield, at least for a while, was best.

A small voice inside had doggedly whispered *Fool!* and *Coward!* without ceasing. He had ignored it as best he could—aided by business endeavors and constant activity—and had remained determined to give her space to enjoy Jane's happiness before he returned to the area. Then, so his nebulous plan had went, he would proceed slowly and see where fate led as they found themselves together due to mutual connections to Charles and Jane.

Then, Lady Catherine descended upon Darcy House like a black tornado resolved to obliterate whatever positive headway had been made.

Darcy drained the cup of coffee and popped a fig into his mouth. Replaying yesterday's scene with his aunt actually made him smile. Envisioning what his cousin Richard's response would be to the scene broadened his grin. Darcy tolerated his mother's imperious older sister, ignored her attitude for the most part, and endured her rudeness for the sake of family stability. Richard, on the other hand, had a difficult time holding his tongue. He would thrill at the exchange, begging Darcy to describe her expressions in vivid detail.

Thinking of imparting his momentous news to Richard led Darcy to imagining the joy of telling of his great fortune to all those who were dear to him. The sudden vision of Georgiana's ecstatic face and Mrs. Reynolds' relieved pleasure supplanted any residual pique over Lady Catherine. Besides, it was her interference, as horrid and misplaced as it was, that prompted him to return to Hertfordshire immediately rather than waiting until closer to Bingley's wedding.

He had determined to speak with Elizabeth as plainly as possible, as soon as possible. Nothing had been certain, not by a long chalk, but the one irrefutable fact he clung to was that Elizabeth Bennet, above all, was frank and unafraid to speak bluntly. If she had decided absolutely and irrevocably against him, she would have promised Lady Catherine instantly, probably adding gleefully to the list of reasons why she considered Mr. Fitzwilliam Darcy the "last man in the world" she would ever marry!

Yes, hope had entered his heart.

Nevertheless, Darcy left the house on this fine morning without the remotest inclination that he would soon be engaged to Elizabeth Bennet. Even if an angelic whisper had hinted it was a possibility, never would he have presumed she loved him in return.

Elizabeth loves me.

Darcy closed his eyes and let the revelation sink deeper into his bones. The irrepressible joy bubbled under the surface of his skin, with every muscle and nerve alive as never before. Heated blood soared through his veins, and his mind raced with glimpses of their future.

Then, he sensed an influx of something profound steadying the euphoria. The reality of her love sobered him. He did not yet comprehend how Elizabeth had fallen in love with him, or when or even why, but that she had was an honor and precious gift he intended to treasure and respect for all eternity. After everything that had passed between them, Darcy fully appreciated how priceless her returned love was. He doubted there was enough time allotted him on this earth to ever express the entirety of his thankfulness and the breadth of his adoration. He refused to waste a single second.

The latter thought instilled a boost of energy. Darcy's eyes popped open at the same moment he launched out of his chair. A swift glance at the clock revealed only two hours had passed since leaving her on the doorstep at Longbourn. It felt like a week or more.

"I miss her." He spoke aloud, the words and sentiment a bit startling.

For close to a year, he had longed for Elizabeth Bennet whenever away from her. Nothing new about that. Yet after this morning, the sensation had altered. No longer was it a mystery whether he would see her again. No longer was it a one-sided desire that, if rewarded, would entail gazing upon her face from afar and nothing more. Suddenly he realized that while the pain of separation from her would grow as their relationship evolved into deeper intimacy, the joy of reuniting in mutual pleasure would be phenomenal.

He broke into a wide grin and strode briskly toward the door to his dressing room.

೮೦

Darcy exited his chambers no less buoyant or giddy than he had been before relaxing in a tub of warmed water and submitting to Samuel's careful attendance to his attire and grooming. A smile danced on his lips, even as they formed into a pucker for the whistle yearning to be released. Unfortunately, both the smile and whistle died at the sight of Caroline Bingley loitering not four feet away from his door.

"Greetings, Caroline." He inclined his head. "I thought you were in London."

40

"Indeed not! How could I remain there when desperately needed here? I raced to Netherfield as soon as my brother's letter arrived at our townhouse. I presumed you were with him and have been increasingly dismayed at your absence. I can only deduce you either returned to Town before his horrid blunder or have been devising a plan, but whatever the case, my relief at the news of your presence is immense. What *are* we to *do*, Mr. Darcy?"

"Forgive me, Caroline. Clearly you are distraught; however, I am ignorant as to what 'horrid blunder' you are referring to."

"Why, surely you know of his betrothal to Jane Bennet! Is that not why you are here?"

"Not primarily, no."

Darcy stepped past Caroline Bingley and continued down the corridor. After a stunned pause, she hastened to catch up to his long-legged gait. He was unsure whether to laugh or grimace at the dramatics that would ensue when she discovered Bingley was not the only gentleman at Netherfield betrothed to a Bennet.

"Mr. Darcy, I do not understand! You said you know he asked Miss Bennet to marry him—"

"I do."

"Well, how is this not the purpose of your visit? Are you not here to talk sense into him once again?"

"No, I am not. Bingley is a grown man, capable of making his own decisions."

"That was certainly not your opinion last year!"

"No, to my great shame, it was not. Now I am regretful of that judgment call."

"Surely you do not mean that!"

Her frantic clutch on Darcy's arm halted him, and with a sigh, he turned. Her face was creased with concern, and for a second, he experienced a stab of pity. With her next sentences, however, the pity was replaced by irritation and then downright indignant anger.

"By all that is sacred, we must not sit by and allow my daft brother to align himself with that family! What could he be thinking?

41

You have tremendous influence over Charles, Mr. Darcy, a fact I am thankful for, so he will listen to reason from you more so than me. I have tried to point out the severe deficiencies in Miss Bennet, to outline the consequences to his social standing if he marries her, yet he stubbornly refuses to listen. He walks around in a cloud of ridiculous emotion that I am sure will annoy and disgust you as much as it does me."

"Somehow I doubt I will be as annoyed or disgusted as you imagine."

Darcy managed to speak calmly and keep his facial expressions bland. Caroline stared at his impassive face in amazement, stumbling over her words as she continued, "Well…I applaud your forbearance, Mr. Darcy. Perhaps you are correct not to approach with a strong attack. We cannot waste time indiscriminately, or the news will spread, making his breaking the engagement a scandal in itself. However, you are correct that subtlety may be the best tactic in dealing with Charles in this matter."

"You misunderstand me, Miss Bingley," he countered, reverting to formality. "I am not suggesting any kind of attack in regards to Bingley's betrothal to Miss Bennet, subtle or strong. It is, to be frank, none of my business. Even if it were, I would not interfere. As it happens, I am happy for him. You should be as well. Furthermore, if you recall, I did say that was not my primary reason for returning to Netherfield."

And before he erupted in laughter at Caroline's bulging eyes and gaping mouth, Darcy pivoted and rapidly completed his jaunt to the parlor. Bingley was already there, sipping a glass of wine and staring bemusedly out at the front drive. His expression *was* rather ridiculous, Darcy had to admit, and if not for viewing a startlingly similar look upon his own visage the entire time Samuel was shaving him and trimming his hair, he probably would have felt as Caroline presumed.

Instead, he steeled his muscles and clamped down on any telltale signs of his joy. Prior to encountering Caroline unexpectedly, Darcy had intended to announce his betrothal to his friend. Dealing with

Charles's delighted surprise was no longer desirable, however, since it would be accompanied by goodness only knows what kind of reaction from Caroline Bingley.

"Bingley, is there more of that wine handy?"

"Darcy! There you are! I was beginning to worry that you were ill or on the run from the law, arriving late at night, so I was informed this morning, and then hiding in your room all day. Quite out of your normal routine, my friend, and that always worries me."

Darcy laughed along with Bingley. He took the glass of wine from the younger man's hand and lifted it in a toast. "I doubt I shall ever be as unpredictable as some, but here's too causing the occasional ripple of surprise."

Bingley clinked the edge of Darcy's glass with his, brows rising and eyes asking a question. After a large swallow, Darcy answered partially.

"I received news prompting my return, and I was not hiding in my room all day. I actually left early this morning to attend to some unfinished business. The weather was especially fine for a long walk."

"Walk? Since when do you prefer walking over riding your horse?"

"I cannot honestly say I *prefer* walking over riding my horse. Today it simple felt like the right choice, that's all."

"You are being irritatingly cryptic, Darcy. Not that you often aren't, of course, so I shall let it go. Whatever mysteries you have rattling around in that complicated head of yours, I am pleased to have you here. For many reasons, naturally, but especially since it means you can keep Caroline company for dinner."

He nodded toward his sister, Caroline having just then entered the parlor. She had taken time to collect herself, that much was obvious to Darcy. The cool, aloof gaze cast his direction was no different that it always was. At least for the moment, since she would again be spun in confusion by Darcy's odd shift in attitude.

"Alas," he began, eyes on Bingley and not Caroline, "I regret that I must disappoint. I intend to accompany you to Longbourn for dinner."

"Longbourn?" The amazed echo came from both Bingleys, Caroline a tad shriller than Charles. Darcy said nothing.

"Are you sure, Darcy? That is, the Bennets will welcome your unexpected addition with polite indulgence, of course." Darcy lifted one brow at *that* but continued to silently sip his wine while Bingley stuttered on. "It is just that...Well...I know the Bennets are not necessarily your favorite people in the world or...exactly the society you usually interact with...and the food, while excellent in its own way, is not on par with what Mrs. Langton serves at Pemberley."

"The Bennets are uncouth and lacking in the slightest hint of social graces, and Longbourn is barely a step above a hovel. Is that not what you mean, Charles?"

"Not precisely, Caroline," he countered testily. "Personally, I take no issue with the Bennets or Longbourn—"

"Only because you are blindly besotted by a pretty face! Otherwise, you would see the truth of it. Why warn Mr. Darcy if the Bennets are not an embarrassment to be avoided at all costs?"

"Why indeed?" Darcy's even tone cut through. Neither Bingley blurted the sharp words tickling their lips and instead turned their eyes toward Darcy, who had not paused. "No need to warn me of anything. I am well aware of what awaits me at Longbourn, and can assure you both that I am eager, *most* eager to visit, even if plain fare and humble surroundings are less than what I am used to. In fact, I have decided it is high time I cease looking at the world from the lofty heights that have thus far only served to stifle me and enforce an unhealthy sense of superiority."

He was staring straight at Caroline as he said the latter, and the thrill of perverse satisfaction at her astoundment was immense. Moments later, the crunch of wheels and horses' hooves on gravel drove all thoughts of Caroline's reactions from his mind.

Heart pounding at the sudden vision of Elizabeth that crystallized in his mind, he briskly set the wineglass onto the table and walked toward the door without another word.

CHAPTER THREE
Starlit Evening

*T*he long afternoon spent with Jane in candid conversation did wonders for calming Lizzy's overwrought emotions. Recounting her convoluted relationship with Mr. Darcy chronologically, in forthright language, and with Jane's insightful queries helped her understand the evolution of her feelings. At least to some degree. In truth, Lizzy did not care to analyze the hows or whens of her love for Mr. Darcy. That she *had* fallen in love with him, and that he still loved her, was all that mattered.

Leaving the sanctuary of their bedchamber was easier after hours laughing over romantic follies and dreaming of their futures. Lizzy discovered just how beneficial when she entered the drawing room.

"Lizzy! What an ungrateful child you are! Languishing in your room with no thought to my poor nerves! I have so many questions, and now there is scant time with Mr. Bingley and Mr. Darcy sure to arrive any moment! Mr. Bennet insisted I leave you be, and as difficult as it was, I did not defy his orders, a small bit of advice for a proper marriage I pass on to you two, for whatever good it will do when you especially, Lizzy, take pleasure in vexing me at every turn. I never thought I would say this, Mr. Darcy being a man I confess has not ranked high in my esteem, but I do pity him in dealing with your—"

Smiling all through her mother's reproach, Lizzy crossed the room and engulfed her in a firm embrace. That, along with a tight squeeze, a murmured "I love you, Mama," and kiss to her cheek, doused the flames of irritation. Mrs. Bennet relaxed instantly, and her tone shifted to one of teary concern.

"Oh! My dear girl! Are you sure you have chosen wisely?"

"Indeed, I am absolutely sure, Mama." Lizzy gave another squeeze, then laughed as she pulled away. "And here I thought you would be singing raptures that I have finally accepted a marriage proposal rather than rejecting them willy-nilly! No longer will you despair of me becoming an old maid with nothing left to claim as my own but a sharp tongue."

"Now, Lizzy, you know I have only wanted for your happiness and security. I daresay Mr. Darcy can provide the latter, but what of the first? Mr. Darcy is, well, somewhat pompous and disagreeable. If asked even this morning, I would have asserted you disliked him!"

"I know. Your confusion is justified. I have not meant to be secretive. It simply took me time to understand my feelings for Mr. Darcy."

"Do you care for him?"

"I love him. And he loves me."

"Well! That does change things! How *that* came to be is more than I can take account of at the present, but he is quite rich, as well as handsome, educated, and well-spoken when he does speak, and not a bad dancer at all, so even with his flaws, he has much to recommend as a husband. In time, I suppose I shall solve the mystery of it and be appeased that your personalities will balance and find their way to coexist. I am not, I admit, adept at understanding people, nor do I invest the time to do so in all cases, so I am glad of the weeks ahead to grow familiar with the man—"

"As am I."

All eyes turned to Mr. Bennet, where he stood in the doorway, leaning casually against the jamb. His expression was uncharacteristically somber, and his tone grim.

"Papa?"

"I have given my permission, Lizzy, but with reservations. In this area I am, surprising as it may be, in agreement with your mother. Mr. Darcy does indeed have much to recommend, and I am inclined to trust your assertions in regards to the other matters we discussed. Nevertheless, you are young, and while not remotely as puerile as Lydia, emotions can cloud one's judgment." He held up his hand when Lizzy opened her mouth to rebut. "I am not rescinding my permission, Lizzy, nor shall I say a word to Mr. Darcy. I am merely expressing a father's concerns. Pray, indulge my hesitation and wish to grow better acquainted with Mr. Darcy before I begin to sing any raptures."

Lizzy nodded. Truthfully, she could not fault her father's reservations despite her instinct to argue the point. Even Jane, who possessed the maddening habit of seeing only the good in everyone, and who on numerous occasions had defended Mr. Darcy when Lizzy ranted against him, was shocked and perplexed by the match. Frank conversation had gone a long way toward convincing Jane that Lizzy loved Mr. Darcy based on sound principles, as well as emotions. Yet she also knew that Jane would feel better as time passed and she witnessed their interactions.

Deciding that the whole situation was, in a strange way, rather humorous and a challenge, Lizzy laughed gaily. "As you wish, Papa. But when you are ready to sing your raptures, I get to pick the song."

"Knowing you, it will be an especially long one with complex notes and high octaves."

Further discussion was arrested by the entrance of Mr. Hill, who announced the arrival of Mr. Bingley and Mr. Darcy. Seconds after that the two gentlemen entered the room, and instantly upon laying eyes on her betrothed, Lizzy forgot the cautions from concerned family members.

He entered a step behind Bingley, paused when just over the threshold, and bowed politely before sweeping his gaze across the room until finding Lizzy. Warmth infused his blue eyes, his stoic features relaxed minimally, and a small smile lifted the corners of his firmly set mouth.

Lizzy's heart performed a strange fluttering dance before settling into a rapid pace. Then, in the subsequent minute, her heartbeat slowed until she feared it would cease pumping entirely.

After that fleeting glance, Mr. Darcy had smoothly looked away, his face once again the mask of cool indifference she was far too familiar with. Mr. Bingley was greeting her parents with his typical boyish hesitancy between frequent loving gazes toward Jane. Conversely, Mr. Darcy appeared cut from stone as he stared fixedly toward the far wall and remained silent.

Lizzy was baffled. Had she imagined his affectionate regard? Fear tightened her lungs, and uncertainty twisted a knot in her belly. Could he have changed his mind? Had he rethought her brazen actions while in the garden, seeing them now as an indication of her unworthiness? Was he here to undo the arrangements settled upon scant hours ago? Fighting the panic, Lizzy redirected her scrutiny from his blank expression to the rest of his body. As always he was impeccably dressed and groomed. Even in her alarm, Lizzy noticing what a handsome figure he presented. However, the finely cut garments did not hide the tense stillness of his posture. How was she ever to decipher the body language of a man so skilled in rigid control?

Provided I am allotted the chance, that is.

Anxiety rose another level. Then her eyes fell upon his left hand.

Two fingers curled tightly around the edge of his jacket, the fabric being rhythmically kneaded into tiny wrinkles, while the other two fingers and thumb twitched and tapped against his thigh. It was a peculiar gesture she had noted a time or two before, without consciously tying the mannerism to an emotional state. Could it be a nervous habit? His hands involuntarily acting in defiance of the tight rein placed upon the rest of his body?

"I pray the unexpected inclusion of Mr. Darcy for dinner is not a burden. He insisted on paying his respects to my future family, his desire such that he risked censure for lacking a proper invitation. For Darcy this is a major indication of his goodwill!"

Bingley's declaration and accompanying laugh startled Lizzy. She lifted her eyes just in time to encounter Mr. Darcy's penetrating stare before he jerked and swiveled his gaze toward Bingley and then Mrs. Bennet, when she replied with conviction, "Oh! We *were* expecting Mr. Darcy for dinner, naturally! Why, Lizzy made that clear, passing the information to Hill as soon as she returned to the house this morning. My apologies, Mr. Darcy, if you were not properly invited. Oh my! Lizzy can forget the proper way of things, although I am sure she will catch on quickly as to how the mistress of a fine manor should conduct herself in due time. Have no worries, Mr. Darcy, in that regard. Our Lizzy is a bright girl and—"

"I believe, my dear, that Mr. Bingley's statement is due to his unawareness of the situation rather than Mr. Darcy not knowing he was expected for dinner."

Darcy cleared his throat and visibly collected himself as he turned to address Mr. Bennet. "Indeed, I must apologize to Mr. Bingley for misleading. As it happened, our reception at Netherfield this afternoon was...unfavorable for imparting news of this nature. Afterward, I confess that announcing my great fortune while amongst all of you seemed appropriate."

"Plus, you are enjoying Mr. Bingley's confusion and relish the drama of his shock when he hears our news. Is that correct, Mr. Darcy?"

"I daresay, Miss Elizabeth, that vision did add to my decision to remain silent. Quite astute of you to analyze my true motives."

"Thank you. Although perhaps I am not astute so much as you are simply more transparent than you believe."

"Doubtful, otherwise you would have deciphered my sentiments some time ago, without needing outside interference."

"Point accepted. So now, the challenge is for me to discover where I went wrong before and why I easily gleaned the truth this time."

"I have never known you to fail a challenge, Miss Elizabeth, but I promise to assist in this particular endeavor, as it benefits me equally."

Six pairs of eyes flipped back and forth between Darcy and Lizzy, both of whom appeared to have forgotten they were not alone—and standing far across the room from each other. So focused were they that Darcy missed the drama of Bingley's confusion rolling into dawning enlightenment, and then the anticipated shock.

"Hold on! Is there an…understanding between you and Miss Elizabeth, Darcy?"

"I suppose it can be referred to as such, although I much prefer to state it plainly so as to leave no room for doubt. Today Miss Elizabeth Bennet accepted my proposal of marriage. Now you are in competition for who is the happiest man in Hertfordshire, Bingley."

Moderate pandemonium erupted at that point. Darcy said little else as he was congratulated by Bingley and lavished with praise by Mrs. Bennet. Lizzy was freshly engulfed by delighted sisters, all three of them—even Mary—acting as if news of her betrothal was revealed that moment. She never made it closer than five feet to her future husband before again being separated when called into the dining room.

Mrs. Bennet had been busy that afternoon, despite her claims of being overwhelmed by nerves and anxiety at Lizzy's choice for a husband. The dining room was polished until every last surface sparkled. Their finest china, tableware, linens, silver, and serving implements were in use, and the candles were brand-new. Freshly cut flowers and fragrant herbs were arranged in decorative vases strategically located around the room. The cook, Mrs. Price, who in Lizzy's estimation always served tasty dishes, had outdone herself with cuisine visually pleasing when served and divine when upon the palate.

Sitting catercorner across the table from Mr. Darcy—purposely assigned the chair to the left of Mr. Bennet—Lizzy covered her annoyance at being unable to easily converse with him by using the position to observe frankly. He ate with refined movements and precision pacing, but consumed every last morsel, as only a man with a hearty appetite and good food can manage. He spoke sparingly, as was his natural way Lizzy now understood, but seemed relaxed enough, even when conversing with Kitty, who sat beside him. Often he turned his eyes toward Lizzy. His gaze and expression were guarded in the mixed company, but he was unable to completely hide the love that sent tingles spiraling up and down her spine.

Taken together, Lizzy felt tremendous relief that his first dinner at Longbourn as her betrothed was not too uncomfortable for him—or an embarrassment to her. After dining at Pemberley, where Lizzy suspected ultra-formality was normal even if only Mr. Darcy and Miss Darcy were present, and at Netherfield where Caroline Bingley not only insisted on high dining style *à la Française*, but also commented on each detail to prove her cultured superiority, Lizzy knew the Longbourn dining experience would fall short. In this she was correct, just not as drastically as feared. She made a point of whispering her sincere appreciation to Mrs. Bennet.

Mary landed in the spot between Lizzy and Mr. Bingley and was the only person at the lively table who genuinely appeared miserable. She kept her head bowed as she ate and responded to the few direct comments from Mr. Bingley with nods of her head or monosyllables. Before the soup bowls were whisked away, he gave up and turned his attention to Mr. Bennet. The older gentleman devoted his conversation primarily to Mr. Darcy.

Kitty was clearly thrilled to be seated between Jane and Mr. Darcy. Her juvenile chatter and inane queries caused Lizzy to cringe and stifle a few groans, but aside from a handful of rapidly hidden surprised reactions from Mr. Darcy, he replied with serious deliberation and respect. Once deciding to ignore the somber Mary, Mr. Bingley became especially jolly. He laughed sunnily at Kitty's innocent quips, and gaily jumped in with answers to Mr. Bennet's subtle prods for information about Mr. Darcy. Lizzy saw through her father's casual repose and harmless promptings. She did not begrudge his mission, had agreed to it in fact, and was relieved to witness it unfolding in a nonchalant manner versus an inquisition.

Lizzy doubted Mr. Darcy was fooled by the carefree attitude from his future father-in-law. He replied succinctly and with traces of humor, although the bulk of the time he remained silent while Bingley and Kitty chattered on. The glances shared with Lizzy hinted of his comprehension and tolerance for Mr. Bennet's investigation. How long his good humor and forbearance would last was another matter entirely.

"Why, Mr. Bennet! I have had the most amazing idea!"

"If it is *amazing*, Mrs. Bennet, then by all means, do share it with the rest of us immediately."

"Jane and I have been discussing plans for the wedding, Lizzy too when she can remove her eyes from Mr. Darcy and pay attention"—Lizzy blushed and ducked her head—"and we were considering the practical benefits, as well as the romantic notion and delight to the community, if Jane and Lizzy were to be married in a joint ceremony. Is that not a fabulous idea? I think it best to avoid a date too close to Guy Fawkes Day, but shortly thereafter will give us plenty of time to prepare and announce the banns—"

"I see no reason to discuss the specifics at this point, Mrs. Bennet. There is no need to be hasty when Lizzy and Mr. Darcy have been betrothed for less than a day. Mr. Bingley has been promised to our Jane for over a week, and has yet to place demands upon wresting her away from the family. I am sure Mr. Darcy possesses the same patience and understanding of parental hesitation. And now"—Mr. Bennet stood, having not looked at either daughter or future son-in-law to verify their thoughts on the subject—"the gentlemen shall join me for a glass of port in my study while the ladies enjoy a respite from male conversation. I know it is fruitless to command you not to talk wedding folderol, so will merely caution against establishing concrete details as of yet."

Bingley and Darcy rose from the table after a slight hesitation, performed proper bows and expressions of thanks for the meal, smiled warmly at each fiancée, and moved to join Mr. Bennet where he had paused in the doorway.

"I promise not to keep them long, girls. Lizzy, if you can delay your ritual after-dinner stroll in the garden, I bet Mr. Darcy can be enticed to join you. With Jane and Mr. Bingley, of course."

₨

Mr. Bennet's study dually served as the Longbourn library. Open-shelf cases jammed with books covered three of the four walls, and encompassed the large desk sitting near the lone window. A narrow commode, overstuffed sofa, small wood-burning stove, and two worn chairs occupied the remaining area. Every inch of space was filled with a book or stack of papers. Odd personal items were strewn on top of or in between the books, adding to the impression of cramped disorder.

The room where Lizzy's father frequently retreated was a third the size of Mr. Darcy's spacious business chamber at Pemberley. In fact, the Derbyshire manor's library was so massive that a size comparison was ludicrous. Amazingly, while Mr. Bennet's study lacked the sophistication of expensive furnishings arranged with consideration for organization and pleasing presentation that Darcy's office possessed, the room was functional and well appointed.

Earlier that day, upon his first ever visit to Mr. Bennet's private sanctuary, Darcy's frazzled nerves prevented him from paying attention to his surroundings. On this night, with his happiness and inner calm at a supreme level, he was free to gaze with interest at a room he suspected Elizabeth passed substantial amounts of time in. In sharp contrast to what he might have surmised, based on his previous state of anxiety, Darcy realized with a start that the cluttered chamber was homey in an elemental way. Mismatched furnishings, many of which were worn and scraped, somehow blended to convey a sensation of comfort. The impressive volume of dog-eared books added to the ambience. Even the cluttered desk was soothing, but that was more due to familiarity since Darcy, despite his obsessive need for order, kept a cluttered desktop as well.

The biggest surprise, however, was the eclectic assortment of books. And, as Darcy discovered when he crossed the room to investigate—rather than sitting, as Mr. Bennet invited he and Bingley to do—a large number were rare publications. It was enlightening, and sobering, to recognize a kindred spirit in the elderly gentleman he had once dismissed as foolish and minimally educated. Clearly Mr. Bennet was a man who appreciated fine literature as well as educational books spanning a wide range of topics. Presuming he had read many of the books in his library—a logical conclusion based on the bent pages, finger smudges, and frayed bindings noted on nearly each book—and that Elizabeth had probably read a goodly number of them as well, Darcy's opinion of his future father-in-law started to shift.

Better yet, the information helped him formulate a plan.

"Your library is impressive, Mr. Bennet." Darcy used the glass of brandy Mr. Bennet handed to him to indicate the shelves as he spoke. "I see you have all of Mr. Wordsworth's volumes, including *Laodamia*, which I have yet to acquire, and this collection of Shakespeare is of a rare binding. I know because I have the same set, and it was a costly acquisition that took me six months to track down."

"I am fortunate to have certain connections at Oxford," Mr. Bennet said with a soft laugh. "All those hours passed in the library, when I should have been attending a boring lecture, proved invaluable in establishing a lifelong friendship with the master librarian."

"I attended enough boring lectures to know the truth in that. Not all professors or subjects taught were useless, of course. Nevertheless, I can attest to the ofttimes superior education gleaned from a well-written and researched book."

"*The reading of all good books is like conversation with the noblest men of the past centuries.*"

Darcy was not surprised Mr. Bennet could quote Descartes. The philosopher's writings were widely distributed and discussed, if not universally embraced. He did wonder how far-reaching the older gentleman's delving into philosophy was—especially in how deeply Elizabeth may have studied—so he returned the quote with another.

"Read not to contradict and confute; nor to believe and take for granted; nor to find talk and discourse; but to weigh and consider."

Mr. Bennet acknowledged his recognition of Sir Francis Bacon's words with a commentary. "Bacon's personal life was questionable, and I will argue some of his liberal philosophies. Yet one cannot deny he encouraged inductive reasoning. We are, to this day, seeing his influence as England enters an age of scientific experimentation." Mr. Bennet cocked his head. "Do you embrace progress, Mr. Darcy? Does the possibility of industrial advancements, with the potential for alterations to our society and class structures, worry you?"

"It is a double-edged sword to my way of thinking," Darcy answered carefully. He was loathe to veer the conversation away from Elizabeth and the subject of their wedding. Then again, sharing a discussion on philosophy was enjoyable, and it could lead to better understanding his future father-in-law, as well as his betrothed.

With that in mind, he explained, "England has established rules that have served us well for centuries. I trust in our heritage and, as a landowner, accept my duty seriously. I have also seen the adverse effects of this so-called progress in places, such as the coal mines and mismanaged mills. They harm the landscape and, in far too many instances, do not help the workers to improve their lot in life. Despite these facts, change is inevitable. Fighting the future revolution is a fruitless endeavor, in my opinion. It is better to work with the reality, doing what is wise to balance the old ways with the new waves that will come."

"I quite agree, Mr. Darcy, although I cheerfully leave the future to those such as yourself who are young and energetic. I do not have the stamina, bendable nature, or inclination to willingly change my ways." He laughed along with Darcy. "I do welcome your further thoughts on the topic, but as it is clear Mr. Bingley is not as fascinated, we can save our discussion for later."

Bingley flushed. "I do apologize, Mr. Bennet. Darcy has tried, without success, to ignite my passions for such matters. Alas, I am a poor student."

"Mr. Bingley has other passions," Darcy interjected, smiling warmly at his friend. "He has been an apt pupil in matters of farming and estate management. In time, with fortune leading him to an ideal property, Bingley will prove his capability."

Bingley's cheeks flamed redder. His expression conveyed pride at Darcy's praise, as well as a hint of anxiety, especially in the swift flicker of his eyes toward Mr. Bennet, who was frowning minutely. Instantly it dawned on Darcy that Bingley had not shared with Jane's family his plans to purchase an estate of his own. *Surely he has enlightened Miss Bennet to the fact that she may well end up residing far away from the Bennets?* Nevertheless, since none of it was technically any business of his—nor was he desirous to be in the middle of the conversation when it was broached—Darcy quickly changed the subject.

"Ah! Here is your copy of *Parzival* by Wolfram von Eschenbach." He drew the slim volume off the shelf, silently thanking the fates for drawing his eyes in a providential direction. "I named my stallion after this poem and confess to being quite startled when Miss Elizabeth instantly recognized where it came from. I greatly appreciate that your daughter is an extensive reader, Mr. Bennet, and clearly have you to thank for instilling that passion within her."

Mr. Bennet turned toward his desk, circling and relaxing into the chair as he replied. "Lizzy was always precocious in that way. No offense intended toward my dear Jane, Mr. Bingley, but none of my daughters have shown the intense interest in reading as Lizzy has."

"Not to worry, sir," Bingley assured, smiling dreamily. "I am not the rabid absorber of literature as Darcy is, so it matters little to me that Miss Bennet does not read to the extent of Miss Elizabeth. Darcy, on the other hand, would have a difficult way of it with a wife who was not the bookworm he is!"

Thanks for feeding into my plan, Charles. Darcy smothered his smile and nodded. "Indeed, Bingley is correct. It might surprise you, Mr. Bennet, but as lovely as Miss Elizabeth is, it honestly was not physical attraction that first drew me to her."

"I am not surprised, Mr. Darcy. After all, the people of Hertfordshire are aware that Lizzy was deemed 'not handsome enough' to tempt you into even a simple dance. I can only imagine the amazed speculation that will flitter throughout the countryside when your betrothal is announced."

Darcy stiffened and almost dropped the book from suddenly nerveless fingers. The citizens of Meryton thinking negatively about him was not a mystery, but he had no idea his rude dismissal of Elizabeth during that first Assembly over a year ago was common knowledge. Before the full impact of just how steep the hill he had to climb in order to improve popular opinion toward him—and clearly that of his future father-in-law as well—Bingley jumped in.

"Please do not judge Darcy harshly, Mr. Bennet! He is renowned for his gentlemanly behavior, most especially to the ladies of Society!" Darcy winced, not sure how *that* statement would be interpreted by Elizabeth's father. Bingley was not done, unfortunately. "His manners are normally of the highest caliber, I promise you that. So much so that he is sought by all as the perfect companion for dancing and the like."

Darcy fervently prayed the ground would open and swallow him.

"It is entirely my fault," Bingley rushed on. "I bullied him into coming to Hertfordshire last autumn. His heart's desire was to return to Pemberley and Miss Darcy. Then, I compounded the matter by insisting he attend the Assembly. His foul mood on that occasion was an anomaly, and his words were directed at me, not meant as a personal insult to Miss Elizabeth."

"Charles." Darcy halted his friend with a raised hand. "Your gracious rise to my defense is appreciated but unnecessary." He turned to Mr. Bennet, whose expression was unreadable. "There is some truth to Bingley's claims, insofar as my desire to be at Pemberley rather than here. Nevertheless, only I am responsible for my actions and words."

He paused to inhale, keeping his gaze level with Mr. Bennet's. "I am the master of my choices and my moods. Indeed, I was in a temper that night and confess with shame that I did scant to hide it. I also confess that my former prejudices blinded me—in many ways. I hope I can prove to you, sir, that my attitudes have severely changed since then, in large part due to your fine daughter. Yet, at that time and on that night, foul mood or not, when I said that I did not warrant Miss Elizabeth as a temptation to me, or as particularly handsome, I meant it."

"I see." Mr. Bennet nodded once. Then his serious expression faltered, a small smile playing about his lips. "Your honesty is refreshing, Mr. Darcy. And you need not worry at my displeasure in your confession. As I said, we already know the truth of your initial thoughts toward Lizzy. Others were appalled, such as Mrs. Bennet. Mothers tend to consider physical appearance and the ability to flirt with skill as the two most important attributes to ensnare a husband. Many fathers do as well, I suppose, so if one of those abilities fail it is a devastating blow!"

Darcy remained standing with *Parzival* and the glass of brandy clutched forgotten in his hands. Unsure whether he had salvaged matters or muddled them worse, he kept silent.

"In the case of Jane," Mr. Bennet resumed with a smile toward Bingley, "she was blessed with beauty outwardly and of the soul. Her fault, as seen from the standpoint of attracting a suitor easily, is her reserve."

Bingley diverted his eyes from Mr. Bennet. How true those words were! As admirable as Bingley considered Jane's modesty and gentleness, and as fully as he blamed himself for allowing others to persuade him rather than following his heart, if Jane *had* shown her favor toward him from the beginning, they might well be married long since.

"Lizzy is quite another matter." Mr. Bennet went on, studying Darcy's face as he talked, "She is clever, witty, and intelligent. She is also well aware of this. Some would and have argued that she is *too* aware and prideful of her cleverness." He shrugged, the gesture apparent to Darcy as a disagreement with this assessment of his favored daughter. "Her gaiety, humor, and frequent laughter is genuine, yet not as a means to entice or mask a dull mind." He chuckled. "You are not the first man, Mr. Darcy, to be mistaken about and surprised by Lizzy."

Abrupt, blinding jealousy surged through Darcy's body. *Not the first man? What in blazes did that mean?* Luckily, Mr. Bennet answered the questions Darcy was in no condition to voice without growling.

"Lizzy's handsomeness is often overlooked when compared to Jane, and because she rarely primps to feed her vanity, as most girls do. I have no problem with this, so long as my daughter's numerous internal attributes are recognized and appreciated. This appears to be the case with you, Mr. Darcy, as it certainly was not with Collins, thus I am pleased—"

"Collins?" Darcy blurted. "My aunt's rector, Mr. Collins?"

Mr. Bennet's brows lifted as he nodded. "The same, yes." Then he laughed. "I see Lizzy has not shared that information with you. Interesting. I suspect you may discover *that* rejected proposal rivals yours."

A multitude of emotions swirled through Darcy's head. Collins? Elizabeth married to that imbecile was a vision he could not begin to fathom. Of course, a woman as confident and wise as Elizabeth Bennet would never agree to marry a man like that! Still, the fact was Collins had asked, and she could have said yes.

Darcy shuddered. *How many other proposals has she received? What a fool to presume I am the first to be bewitched by her myriad charms!*

61

Assaulted by waves of relief, a fresh rush of consuming love, and a frantic urge to finalize their union so she would be his irrevocably, Darcy fell weakly into the nearby chair. Sifting rapidly through all that had been said since entering Mr. Bennet's study, Darcy latched on to the one point most pertinent.

Raising his head, he held Mr. Bennet's eyes and spoke in a voice remarkably steady considering the roiling emotions within. "I was, most assuredly and to my shame, monumentally mistaken in my initial assessment and dismissal of Miss Elizabeth. However, I promise you, Mr. Bennet, that learning of my error, identifying, as you stated it, the numerous internal attributes Miss Elizabeth possesses, has been nothing short of a miraculous development welcomed with all my being."

He paused to inhale, calming the residual turmoil before plunging ahead. "Of the assorted joys in being her husband, few, I venture, shall rival the joys of provoking debate, discussing literature"—he waved toward the stacks of books surrounding—"and witnessing her superb intellect in motion as Mistress of Pemberley."

"A fine speech. Words of truth, I can tell. Of course, if the library at Pemberley is as vast as Lizzy has told me, you may find it a challenge to pull her away for household duties."

Darcy relaxed at Mr. Bennet's lighthearted tone. "Fortunately, the harsh winter of Derbyshire translates to little happening with the estate and infrequent visitors, so our first months will allot hours for lounging in the library."

"Or, more likely now that it is apparent that you are, indeed, tempted by Lizzy's handsomeness, another chamber may hold a higher allure."

Darcy's jaw dropped and he felt heat flooding his cheeks. Whether this was primarily due to extreme embarrassment at such a subject even hinted at by Elizabeth's father—and with Bingley present no less—or due to the vivid visual of a semiclothed Elizabeth spread across his bed, Darcy could not honestly say.

Thankfully, Mr. Bennet made no additional references to marital relations, instead turning to the map of England pinned to the wall behind his desk. "Winter in Derbyshire," he murmured. "I forgot that fact. Roads are unsafe for travel, and foul weather is the norm. Too much time isolated alone, so far from family, may not be a wise choice for one as social as Lizzy. I think a spring wedding would therefore be best."

"Sir! You cannot be serious! That is five or more months from now!"

Bingley's verbal outburst, leap from his chair, and uncharacteristically choleric expression startled both Darcy and Mr. Bennet. Darcy was equally incensed at the idea of waiting until the following year to marry Elizabeth. He simply had not expected Bingley to explode first—or to launch into a tirade.

"I mean no offense, and respect your opinion, sir, but I protest vehemently! I have said nothing as yet on setting a date for marrying Jane, in all honesty content to enjoy our season of courtship. Also because it never occurred to me that a lengthy engagement spread before us. Nor has that been a concern of Jane's. In fact, we have discussed our plans and future with the presumption that well before Christmastide we would be husband and wife. Please do not—"

"Calm yourself, Mr. Bingley. I was referring to Lizzy and Mr. Darcy, not you and Jane. Unless Mrs. Bennet's idea of a double wedding was on your mind?"

"I cannot say I have had time to dwell upon the prospect, Darcy's engagement unknown to me until hours ago, but I am not averse to the idea, no. Nevertheless"—Bingley stepped closer to Mr. Bennet's desk—"whether our marriages occur together or not, neither of us nor our ladies should suffer the agony of waiting until spring. A handful of weeks, to organize the ceremony, announce the banns, and make preparations for our brides, is understandable and necessary, especially for Darcy, with Pemberley a distance away. Beyond that, I beg you, sir, do not insist."

Mr. Bennet stared at Bingley for another minute, then down at his hands clenched tensely on his lap, and eventually over at Darcy. "You are strangely silent, Mr. Darcy."

"Mr. Bingley has spoken succinctly, and since I agree with him wholeheartedly on each point, I see no purpose in elaborating."

Nor do I think a threat to abscond with Elizabeth straight to Gretna Green if not permitted to marry soon will help my case.

"The ardency of love." Mr. Bennet grunted. "I am not so old that I have forgotten what that feels like. And the paradox is that if ardency was not strong, I would be concerned as well. Hmm. It is clear I am overruled then. No question that Lizzy and Jane will agree with you two, but worst of all would be Mrs. Bennet's dismay if forced to postpone her visible triumph at marrying two of her daughters to such eligible gentlemen. Frankly, that prospect is more than I can bear. Very well then. Hand me that calendar, Mr. Bingley."

ஐ

As Lady Catherine de Bourgh had recently pronounced, the park surrounding Longbourn *was* small, especially compared to Rosings or Pemberley. It is also true that size is a relative measure, and any space can be utilized wisely and maintained.

Lizzy considered the gardens, graveled walkways, sheltered copses, cobbled patios, hedge-rimmed pond, lawned areas, and stable yard surrounding Longbourn more than adequate for childhood adventures—and mature pleasures. Prior to tonight, she had not thought to wonder whether Mr. Darcy's opinion would lean toward agreement with his aunt or be in line with hers. While Lady Catherine's dismissal of the garden bothered Lizzy not one whit, she did hope Mr. Darcy assessment was favorable. She foresaw them passing many hours strolling there in the weeks to come.

At least he has not said anything negative. She glanced upward at his serene face. *Nor has he said anything positive, as far as that goes!*

For fifteen minutes, since leaving the house, they had wandered in silence. The only sounds, aside from those of nature, were the soft tones of conversation coming from Jane and Mr. Bingley. They walked several feet ahead of Lizzy and her betrothed, and, she noted, were veering toward a tall elm tree under which sat a lone bench sized for only two people. Another swift glance at Mr. Darcy revealed nothing as to his thoughts on that development. By all appearances, he was content to placidly gaze at the starlit sky and passing foliage. Even his subtle leading in the opposite direction from the elm and newly occupied bench could be interpreted as sheer accident for all the obvious awareness he extended.

Lizzy bit her lip. She was undecided whether his silence was a sign of tranquility or if he was wrestling with weighty matters. After spending nearly an hour holed up with Mr. Bingley and her father, her imagination had run amok, leaving her unusually tongue-tied. That annoyed her more than anything!

"Mr. Bennet mentioned that you ritually stroll in the garden after dinner. Was he speaking literally?"

He spoke barely above a whisper, yet after a quarter of an hour yearning for him to break the silence, Lizzy jumped what felt like a foot in the air. "I...yes...I do...stroll, if weather permits, that is. If I sit still after a large meal I feel...weighted down, I suppose is one way to describe it. Unless engaged in active entertainment of some sort, I inevitably chafe to move and breathe fresh air."

"While staying at Netherfield when Jane was ill, I recall seeing you duck onto the terrace a time or two. Of course, I could not be certain if it was a need for air or to escape from Miss Bingley."

Lizzy's eyes opened wide. "Am I correct, Mr. Darcy, in that you are making a joke at another person's expense?"

He smiled and looked at her for the first time—that she was aware of—since their walk began. "It does happen upon occasion, Elizabeth. I shan't make a habit of it if humor from me is too shocking for your system to assimilate. As pleasant as it may be for me to perform tasks necessary to revive you, I still would not wish to see you faint at my feet."

"I think I can adjust well enough not to faint, but I appreciate your concern for my wellbeing."

"Always. Your wellbeing is my prime concern, Elizabeth." His timbre dropped into a husky purr, and for a split second, she thought he started to lower his head toward her. Then the moment passed, and once again he was smiling serenely and gazing at the skyline as they commenced walking. "I was pleased to hear Mr. Bennet mention your propensity for a nightly stroll," he resumed in a normal tone, "because it has, for as long as my memory serves, been a habit of mine."

"Truly?"

"Yes indeed. Depending on weather, as you noted, or if we have guests, I make it a priority to exit the house either immediately after dining or before retiring to my chambers. I will not go so far as to say I cannot sleep if unable to do so, but it is close."

They reached a low wall of mortared bricks that separated the cultivated garden from the wild meadow beyond. The elm-shrouded bench where Mr. Bingley and Jane sat was close enough to easily see them through the shadowy leaves of tall trees and shrub hedges, but far enough that distinct words could not be heard within the murmured voices.

Darcy continued to stare into the star-dotted sky. Lizzy stopped some four feet to his right and studied his relaxed posture and peaceful face while ostensibly admiring a flower picked randomly from a nearby pot. After a minute in which he showed no sign of speaking, Lizzy resumed the prior topic.

"Do you have a designated route to your nightly walks, Mr. Darcy, or does spontaneity guide your feet?"

He released a low chuckle and turned toward her. "I daresay the word *spontaneity* is not one you expect to be attributed to me, am I correct?" He chuckled again when she shook her head. "If in London, my choices are limited, as you will see eventually when I show you our house on Grosvenor Square. Pemberley is another matter entirely, the options myriad, as you might imagine having been there. The majority of my strolls stay close to the house, starting on the terrace, drifting through the numerous paths available, and not lasting a great length of time. I have, however, been known to embark on longer treks, planned and unconsciously done. The awareness of your pleasure in walking, day or night, is one of many traits I am delighted to discover we have in common."

Mr. Darcy had not moved during his speech, nor had she. Yet somehow the personal nature of his words, the halcyon atmosphere, and soothing resonance of his voice mingled to create an intimacy as powerful as if they were inches apart. Clearly he felt it as well, although instead of closing the gap and kissing her, as she desperately wanted him to do, he stepped back. Mildly disappointed, Lizzy was relieved to note the expression of peaceful happiness remained upon his face. Then, he perched upon the wall's narrow ledge, without glancing away from her face to check for breeches-staining debris.

That startled her more than his next question.

"I am curious as to why you have yet to ask me what passed during my hour with your father. I know we have much to learn about each other; however, past experience assures me that I could have wagered a substantial amount that your inquisitiveness would override reticence in this instance. In most instances, for that matter."

"I am not sure if I am ready to hear the secrets of manly conversation," she hedged. "Discourse on the best tobacco would merely bore me. Talk of politics or world events might begin an argument if I disagreed with you—"

"As you most likely would, honestly or with designs to test me," Darcy interrupted with a laugh.

Lizzy laughed with him. "True, I admit. And if the talk digressed to how best to gut a fish or skin a rabbit, I might fulfill your previous prediction and faint at your feet, Mr. Darcy."

Darcy pursed his lips, feigned serious consideration, and then shook his head. "No, that I doubt as well. Delicate and fragile you are, my Elizabeth, in all the feminine ways a man, especially this one, appreciates. Missish and squeamish? While I have no immediate plan to discuss animal gutting or skinning, I am not worried over an adverse reaction if I did."

He paused, still smiling and wearing the unguarded, playful expression Lizzy was learning to adore, even as it continued to amaze her. The eyes partially hidden in the dim light shone with humor and emotion such as she never imagined from him. The combination overwhelmed her senses.

"For the record, none of those subjects came up tonight. We spoke primarily of you, and Miss Bennet, as I am sure you suspect, and that is why I am curious as to your avoidance of the topic. Frankly, I was anticipating an interrogation. Instead, you are uncommonly taciturn." He cocked his head and playfully furrowed his brows. "I thought that was *my* failing and looked forward to being inspired by your fluency, not the other way around."

Lizzy stared at the flower in her hands for a minute before finally inhaling, tossing it over the wall, and then boldly meeting Darcy's eyes. "Would it surprise you, Mr. Darcy, if I confessed to being besieged by vacillating emotions all evening? Specifically nerves, confusion, and moments of fear?"

His body stiffened and, although still smiling, a sharp glint entered the eyes studying her face. Slowly he nodded. "Yes, I am surprised. Especially under the circumstances. All of us have our moments of lacking confidence or bravery. Nervousness I can readily comprehend, since I was nearly overwhelmed with anxiety several times today. For me this is not unusual, I am ashamed to admit. But you? Odd indeed. And worrisome. Tell me why you would feel any of those emotions, dear Elizabeth."

"It is your fault, if you must know!" She spoke with more vigor than she intended, the combination of irritation and absurdity in the situation imbuing her tone.

Darcy's left brow lifted. "It is?"

"Yes! You are a difficult man to read, Mr. Darcy, as I have tragically learned. Then, just as I begin to believe I am deciphering the subtleties of your body language, facial expressions, vocal tones, and the like, you change yet again! How am I to predict your reaction to a situation when you are inconsistent?"

"Perhaps I could aid in solving this serious dilemma if I had examples?"

Lizzy barreled on, completely missing his teasing inflection. "You entered Longbourn tense and cold as stone, yet fidgeting as you do when nervous. It frightened me near to death! I thought you had changed your mind. Then," she rushed on, not giving him a chance to reply, "you seemed normal enough through dinner, even flirting a bit with Kitty—"

"I certainly was not flirt—"

"—and it was a relief to see you comfortable with my family, but when my father all but forced an indeterminate delay on our wedding, I expected you to be angry. Heaven knows I was! Instead, you do not seem to care one way or another, staring at the stars and making jokes. Jokes! And your face..."

Darcy grasped her hands and pulled her toward him. Since he was still sitting on the low wall, they were eye level. Between the sparkling gaiety visible as he stared at her, the rumbling laughter passing through his lips, and the nearness of his body, Lizzy stuttered to a halt.

"Life with you will never be boring, that is for certain. And I mean that in the most wonderful way. What is it about my face?"

The whispered words, along with the rest, incited a deluge of tingles through her muscles. "I...I cannot place it in words. It is more than your face. Your entire being is...relaxed."

"I am happy, Elizabeth. You are seeing the man, the true me, who is deeply in love with you and ecstatic beyond words that you have agreed to share your life with me." He pressed his lips to each of her hands, the kisses barely brushing her skin yet sending jolts up both arms. "I suppose it will be a typical pose when with you, so try to adjust."

The teasing tone was not lost to her this time, although the second round of kisses, these a bit firmer, were extremely distracting. "So..."—she cleared her throat—"why so tense and cold when you arrived?"

"Do you *want* me to answer honestly?" The weighty undertone to his question gave her pause, but she nodded. "As you wish." He stopped kissing her hands and inhaled. His eyes, she noted, were again touched with a sharp glint. "The truth is, the moment I laid eyes on you, my desire to cross the room, enfold you in my arms, and kiss you unceasingly was so powerful it was necessary for me to clamp down on every muscle in my body and look away from your face. A second longer and I would have succumbed to the urge. I am not sure Mr. Bennet bashing me over the head or shooting me would have stopped me once I started."

"I...see." Lizzy was sure the blush had spread to her toes. "And now?"

"And now I have re-exerted my self-control. For the present. I shall have to be on constant guard." He smiled before resuming the tender kisses to her hands. "I pray that confession of my weakness, and my intensity, where you are concerned does not frighten, Elizabeth. Hopefully it eases your mind and convinces you that *nothing* will cause me to change my mind about us?"

"I am convinced, and I am not frightened, Mr. Darcy. I am shocked to hear such lengthy speeches cross your lips, however."

Again he laughed, the amused, low rumble initiating fresh flutters inside her belly. "The day of surprises and strange flipping of our personalities continues, it seems. Except for the flirting accusation. That is a skill I never mastered when it *was* acceptable, as you can attest, considering you are the only woman I *tried* to charm."

"Oh my! You must be awful indeed because I never detected behavior remotely flirtatious! Knowing you are a man who speaks truthfully, Mr. Darcy, assures me on that count as well."

"I am relieved at your assurance, Elizabeth. Do not doubt me or my convictions, please. Even...before, when I proposed so insultingly, as you were right to forcefully point out, my heart and soul belonged to you. I have never wavered in my feelings. Not once. Now"—he sighed and enfolded her hands between his palms—"if that is the extent of your vacillating emotions, then all is well. In general I am sensing favorable currents between us, Elizabeth, but persistently addressing me as *Mr. Darcy* is beginning to erode my peace."

Impulsively, as much to fulfill an inner yearning as to express a concrete assurance of her sentiments, Lizzy leaned in and pressed a closed-lip kiss to his mouth. She pulled back before he managed to overcome his surprise at her bold initiative and respond to the kiss. Then she withdrew her hands from his warm caress and walked away—she had to or it would be *her* losing control!

Best to instill additional lightness to the topic and maintain some distance. With her back to him, she pretended to examine the yellowing leaves of the elm. "Knowing your struggles, *William,* I am shocked you complacently agreed to my father's demand to delay our wedding indefinitely."

He did not reply immediately, and when he did, his voice was strained. "I agreed to no such thing. If allowed, I would marry you tomorrow, Elizabeth." She heard his cleansing inhale and exhale. "That being said, I cannot fault Mr. Bennet's reluctance in parting with his daughters, nor the understandable request for time to grow better acquainted with me. He needs the weeks to trust my love for you."

"Did he say that?"

"Not in those precise words, no. The implication was clear and, as I said, I do not fault him. I am willing to practice patience. Within reason, of course. Time, as painful as it is in one respect, is beneficial for planning a proper wedding and for me to make the necessary preparations for my bride."

"I see. It appears that my worrying over what transpired while you and Mr. Bingley were with Papa was wasted effort then. No climatic conclusion or dramatic confrontations to report. Pity."

"We did reach an agreement, and there were moments of drama and confrontation. Shall I relate our exchange as it happened, or would you prefer I embellish for greater entertainment?"

The notion of staid Mr. Darcy attempting to embellish made Lizzy laugh out loud. "A simple recounting will suffice. Or even a synopsis, in the interest of time."

"As you wish. First, we discussed the importance of reading..."

Lizzy listened intently, as much to enjoy the musical cadence of her lover's voice as to learn what was said in her father's library. Portions were difficult to hear, such as her father bringing up Darcy's rude dismissal during the Meryton Assembly. She winced at *that* revelation and cringed over Darcy's obviously feigned calm when informed of Mr. Collins's proposal. Otherwise, she delighted in his narrative, feelings of amusement and respect outweighing the embarrassment. A couple times, she sensed that he was omitting a comment or smoothly condensing, the prospect most notable because he repeated the conversations precisely, as if reading from a playwright's script. Adding further to her amazement were his occasional slips into a storyteller's rhythm, random descriptions of a facial expression or internal emotion, and twice an offhand mention of the scenery. The entire performance was so entrancing, and enlightening, that she nearly missed it when he revealed the date agreed upon for the joint Bennet daughters' wedding.

"November the twenty-eighth?"

Darcy smiled brilliantly and nodded at her stuttered repetition. "Truthfully, I believe Mr. Bennet randomly chose a day as late in the season as he could without risking Bingley or me bursting into another angry tirade. Fortunately, November twenty-eight is well before winter sets in. It is long enough from now to prepare as befitting my bride, yet not too long that I shall go mad with waiting. Does this please you, Elizabeth?"

"It pleases me to have a date established. It pleases me to be married in a ceremony with Jane and Mr. Bingley." She paused for a long moment before continuing in a firm timbre, "It pleases me, mostly, to be marrying *you,* Fitzwilliam Darcy, and since it cannot be tomorrow, November twenty-eight will do."

He stared at her silently for a full minute, his expression serious and eyes dark, and then he rose slowly from the wall. It could not have taken more than five seconds for him to cross the small space separating them, yet for Lizzy it was an eon during which her heart doubled in speed and her respirations narrowed to short gasps.

Will I ever not be astounded by his height and masculinity? Will the intensity of his gaze upon me ever cease to overwhelm my senses? Will the anticipation of his touch and kiss someday not cause my muscles to weaken?

The answer to each question was no—as she would have wished it to be—if she could have seen into the future. For the present she stood still, watched his approach, and gleefully allowed the sensations to wash over and through her. Not a word passed his lips, only a soft sigh as he engulfed her face gently between his palms and leaned to press his mouth against her uplifted lips—a light brush to begin, then a fleeting increase of pressure Lizzy knew would have lead to a glorious exchange if not for the interrupting voice of Mr. Bingley.

Lizzy felt a wild urge to strangle her sister's sweet fiancé. Judging by the grim expression on Darcy's face as he released her and pulled away, he entertained identical murderous thoughts. An instant later he was smiling calmly and offering his arm in a casual manner, the almost inhuman self-control Lizzy was starting to comprehend he possessed squelching his negative emotions before she managed to unclench her fists. If not for a remaining glint of burning passion deep within his eyes, she might have concluded she imagined the entire interlude.

SHARON LATHAN

CHAPTER FOUR
Flash Floods of News

*A*s slim as the odds were for Caroline Bingley to be in the Netherfield breakfast parlor at eight o'clock in the morning, Darcy breathed a sigh of relief to find the room empty. He had avoided telling her of his engagement before heading to Longbourn the prior evening, and his return with Bingley was after she had retired to her chambers. Fortune surely would not smile upon him much longer. He crossed directly to the buffet. She rarely descended the stairs before eleven, but on the off chance she did, it would be easier to face that conversation after a hearty breakfast and cup of coffee. Or maybe three.

Truthfully, he yearned to declare his joy to the world, Caroline Bingley included. In fact, Darcy intended to pass the morning at his writing desk, penning letters to people guaranteed to appreciate his engagement—and a few who may not be as thrilled, such as Lady Catherine. Pleasant or unpleasant, it was a task he anticipated. Perhaps writing the words, "I am betrothed to Miss Elizabeth Bennet of Hertfordshire," several times would erase the lingering fear that he was dreaming.

Once that duty was accomplished, he would ride to Longbourn for an afternoon walk with his beloved.

Darcy was unaware of his smile, or that he was staring into space rather than pretending to read the newspaper spread over the table, until it was pointed out to him.

"Mr. Darcy!"

He jerked and swung his eyes toward Caroline Bingley, who was standing directly beside him wearing an irritable frown.

"I entered the breakfast room, none too stealthily I might add, and spoke your name no less than four times. Being captivated by a news article of a riveting nature would be understandable and forgivable. But I am not sure how to explain the whimsical smile and vacant stare into the air."

Belatedly Darcy rose. "I do apologize, Miss Bingley. My mind was elsewhere." He executed a short bow before purposefully walking to the other side of the table to scoot a chair out for her.

She hesitated and glanced at the chair closest to him. When he did not move, she drifted around the table, taking the longer distance in what he supposed was an attempt to afford him plenty of time to observe her lush figure in graceful movement.

Then, as predictable as the sun rising, she shaped her face into what most men would agree was a beguiling expression and curved her mouth into a winsome smile. Brushing her fingertips lightly over his forearm, almost as if by accident, she murmured her thanks. After a precision-timed pause to allot him the opportunity to glance downward at her bosom, but not be caught in an ungentlemanly stare, she swiveled and sat into the chair.

The maneuver had less effect on him now than it ever had before, which was remarkable considering he had never been remotely attracted to her.

Darcy was a man, and thus not immune to a beautiful face, fine figure, and endowed breasts. Over time, he had done his fair share of oblique visual inspection and enjoyed the activity. Caroline Bingley's bosom was as fetching as other ladies within the ton, he could honestly admit, but beyond the standard recognition that any red-blooded man would have, his interest went no further.

So he kept his gaze level at a point over her left shoulder, pushed the chair in as expected, and returned to his seat. In his peripheral vision, he detected a flash of disappointment cross her face, although why she continued to play such games with him, or anticipate a different reaction, was incomprehensible. All attempts on her part to entice him—and there were many, constantly—had been rebuffed as pointedly and forcefully as he could manage while remaining a gentleman. Why she persisted he could not fathom. Another positive to his engagement would be relief from Caroline's uncomfortable advances.

He did not dislike Caroline. In fact, he thought her amusing, her gossip diverting and talents at the pianoforte entertaining. She was the sister to his best friend, and as such they were frequently in close company. At times, this was annoying, primarily when she was fawning over him or being gossipy and catty. Yet strangely enough, she was an excellent hostess, cultured, well spoken, and charming when she wished to be. Most of all, Darcy knew that she loved her brother. That love was often hidden behind self-absorption but revealed itself in small ways.

Taken altogether, Darcy rarely remained irritated toward Caroline for long. If only she would stop her vain efforts to ensnare him.

"I shall forgive your lapse, Mr. Darcy. After all, an evening spent in the uncivil company of the Bennets is sure to addle the brains of any man, especially one as cultured and intelligent as you."

"I do wish you would cease your harassment of the Bennets, Caroline. It is most unbecoming and unwelcome."

"Oh, come now! There is no need to pretend. Charles is not in the room—probably lying abed with unwholesome dreams of Jane Bennet lying with him."

She muttered the last statement while chewing a bite of scone. Darcy barely heard her and was momentarily stunned that she would hint at such a private topic. Unfortunately, his delay gave her a chance to swallow and resume.

77

"I admit to being flummoxed by your speech last evening, Mr. Darcy. You worried me greatly and almost had me convinced by your arguments. Upon reflection, I concluded that you must have a secret plan for saving poor Charles and salvaging the damage. You are too dear a friend of my brother to allow him to make such a mistake. I am unable to decipher your strategy, and as a mere female may never comprehend all the intricacies, but I want you to know that I am willing, most willing, to aid your endeavor."

Darcy's cold stare and pressed lips startled her into silence. Or maybe she thought he was agreeing with her. Whichever the case, it was past time to set the record straight.

"Miss Bingley, you insult me with your insinuations. I am not, nor ever have been, a man who would lie to a friend or, worse yet, plot against him while pretending kindness. I would act in such a manner to no one, friend or foe. Above all, I am a gentleman with honor."

"I meant no disrespect, sir, but last year you—"

"Acted in honesty. I spoke what I believed to be the truth. I meant no malice toward Charles, ever. I was mistaken myself, in the truth of Miss Bennet's affections. As soon as I learned of my error, from Miss Elizabeth, I instantly humbled myself before Charles and told him the truth."

"You told him? You are responsible for bringing him here?"

"I told him what I knew. Charles made up his own mind as to his course of action."

"But the Bennets are utterly unsuitable! Surely we agree on that? Did you not say as much and use it as further argument to persuade him?"

"I did. Guilty on both counts. Since then, I have repented and begged forgiveness from those I offended. As for persuading, I learned that this is not my place. Not with Charles or anyone, and that is why I left the decision up to him this time. Last year I did what I thought was best, but I was wrong. As for the Bennets, I have changed my opinion radically, largely because I came to realize that my vision was clouded by prejudices and my own emotions."

"I...well, I cannot believe what I am hearing. There must be something I can say to convince—"

"You will have to accept the reality, Miss Bingley. There is nothing to convince me of. My mind and conscience were clear on these matters weeks ago. Today it is a subject closed to any discussion and will only incite me to anger if broached in any way. I cannot speak for your brother's tolerance, but I will not endure the vaguest hint of abuse toward the people of Hertfordshire, and especially the family of my fiancée."

To her credit, Caroline grasped his meaning instantly. Her eyes widened and cheeks flushed as if slapped hard. When she spoke, it was a strangled whisper of astonishment. "Eliza? You asked Eliza Bennet to be your..."

"Wife, yes," he finished when she trailed off. "Miss Elizabeth accepted my proposal yesterday. We are to be wed, with Charles and Miss Bennet, at the Meryton Church on the twenty-eighth of November. Next week, I shall ride to London for the formal settlements, but Mr. Bennet has given his permission for our marriage, so the matter is settled. To my boundless joy."

He wiped his mouth on the napkin and rose from his chair. Caroline was staring into space, not unlike him when she came into the breakfast parlor, although he wagered his expression had been one of happiness rather than the blank shock on her face.

"Please relinquish your rancor, Miss Bingley. Our courses have been laid and will not be altered, trust me on that. Your unkindness toward Miss Bennet pains your brother. Pray his hurt does not turn to anger and exasperation. The consequences may not be pleasant. He is, remember, the man who provides for you."

∞

Several hours later, Caroline Bingley peered out her bedroom window, watching her brother and Mr. Darcy mount their horses and ride away. It was unnecessary to ask; they were heading to Longbourn. *To see their fiancées,* she silently sneered.

Releasing a highly indelicate sound, followed by a blistering curse and violent yank to close the drapes, Caroline stomped to the rumpled bed and fell across it. Screaming her frustration into the pillow, and adding a couple punches for good measure, offered some relief.

Eliza Bennet engaged to Mr. Darcy!

For the thousandth time, that one phrase sent floods of fury and misery cascading through her body. The urge to verbally rave or throw another breakable item against the wall was as intense as it had been when she first reached her chambers after leaving the dining room.

Somehow she had calmly finished her coffee and breakfast, not tasting any of it, sedately climbed the stairs, and traversed the long corridor at a casual pace. She had even closed the door behind her and silently leaned into the solid surface for a good five minutes before the roiling emotions exploded. The housemaid had dropped the pillow she was fluffing and bolted from the room. Caroline had barely noticed. She had already directed her rage at Anna, her personal maid, who had dashed from the dressing and bathing room the second she heard her mistress's voice.

Attempts on Anna's part to console lasted about thirty minutes before Caroline screamed at her to go away. Clearly Anna was relieved to exit the scene of madness, as was Caroline to have her gone. What good was she, anyway? It was unthinkable to confide in her, *a servant*, and if Caroline had done so, the result would be worse gossip circulating below the stairs than there probably already was. Not that a woman of Caroline Bingley's station cared what common laborers thought of her, but her humiliation being a source of amusement added to the insult.

Flopping over onto her back, she scowled up at the canopy over her bed and pondered the same question she had for hours: *How could this have happened?*

Eliza Bennet engaged to Mr. Darcy? It was impossible! All of Caroline's careful designs destroyed by a nobody from a backwater town. The Bennet women should marry men of their own class. Why steal men of substance far above their pathetic circumstances? What right did *she* have to pick the one man—*the only man*—that Caroline wanted? Who was *she* to come out of nowhere and, in a matter of seconds, snatch Mr. Darcy when Caroline had been cultivating their relationship for three years?

Upon her first introduction to Mr. Darcy, the same month as her debut into Society, Caroline made up her mind to have him. It was a simple, logical decision, and for two years, she had waited patiently. In truth, she was content not to rush into matrimony. The frivolity available to an unattached female of the *ton* was extremely enjoyable. She excelled in the flirting, delighted in seductive taunting, and adored the attention from both sexes. While having fun, she learned how the wife of a high-ranked gentleman of the gentry was supposed to act in every situation. Her brother's friendship with Mr. Darcy played to her advantage, the two of them invariably together for stretches at a time. A comfortable level of amiability grew, and since Mr. Darcy did not seem to be in a rush to find a wife or establish female relationships aside from with her, Caroline saw it as merely a matter of *her* deciding when *she* was ready to take the next step. When she did, the familiarity between them would make it easy for her to communicate her willingness to accept the proposal she confidently believed he would offer.

In fact, it was as they were traveling to Netherfield last autumn, at the end of an exhaustive but wonderfully successful season, that Caroline found herself staring at Mr. Darcy's handsome profile and contemplating the pros and cons of another year of unencumbered gaiety versus the prestigious amusements available as Mrs. Darcy. She was leaning toward the latter and, while not definitively decided, had been formulating scenarios that would make her intentions obvious. Then, suddenly, Elizabeth Bennet and her "fine eyes" entered the picture. Caroline's planned agenda was tossed into chaos! Between Charles's ridiculous admiration of Jane Bennet and Mr. Darcy's inexplicable fascination with Elizabeth, not to mention being in boring Hertfordshire in the first place, Caroline's temper had remained on edge for months. Luckily, she had her sister, Louisa, to offer comfort and guidance. Best of all, in the end, Mr. Darcy came around and agreed that the Bennets were unworthy. Together they convinced Charles and returned to London without a backward glance.

Or so she had thought.

Jumping out of bed, she commenced another furious pace around the room, her mind whirling over the months since then.

In all honesty, Caroline had recognized Charles's melancholy over losing Miss Bennet and experienced moments of empathetic sadness. She did love her brother and desired his happiness, primarily because his positive emotional state benefitted her. But she remained convinced that Jane was wrong on every level, and that Charles would come to the same conclusion in time. Gradually he seemed to emerge from his heartache, and as the season progressed, he embraced the activities as fully as in previous years. If not quite the effervescent young man as before, his temperance and maturity was regarded by many, particularly prospective fathers- and mothers-in-law, as advantageous. Caroline and Louisa agreed that in time he would fall in love with another, as he had dozens of times before Jane Bennet.

As for Mr. Darcy, indeed this past year he had been withdrawn more so than typical. He had spent the bulk of his time away from London, and when in Town rarely left his townhouse on Grosvenor Square. Charles visited with him, although not as often as previous, but Caroline had not once been invited. Their encounters at various social events in Town were few, brief, and in the company of so many other people that Caroline had spoken barely a word to him. Once she had pondered whether his strange behavior had something to do with Elizabeth Bennet, but despite his irritating infatuation, they had left Hertfordshire with no further mention of either Bennet sister occurring in the months subsequent, so she failed to account for a minor interest in a country girl being the cause. Then, distracted by balls, operas and plays, dinners, shopping, garden parties, and other endless festivities with her friends in London and elsewhere, Caroline ceased fretting over it. To her way of thinking, nothing had truly changed. Her plan to become Mrs. Darcy had merely been postponed. With the fall season of shooting and hunting, they would dwell at Pemberley as they had in the past, and everything could then be settled between her and Mr. Darcy.

Clearly she had been outrageously mistaken. Unbeknownst to her, Elizabeth Bennet had managed to evilly cast a spell over Mr. Darcy. Caroline did not know how or when, but somehow the chit had dug in her claws and tricked a man of uncommon intellect and sense into proposing. There could be no other explanation than a devious ploy. What could a country girl who had never set foot in London Society possibly have to offer a man of means such as Mr. Darcy? What did she know of managing a fine household or hosting a social function or conversing with a dignitary?

Caroline fell into the chair near the fireplace, shuddering at the vision of Elizabeth as the Mistress of Pemberley. A tragedy! Again she deliberated writing to Louisa. Just as the prior dozen times, she relinquished the idea. Her sister's sympathy would be soothing, and perhaps together they could work a miracle in devising a plan to break the two betrothals, but Louisa was in Bath on holiday with Mr. Hurst. Unfortunately, Caroline was alone in her misery.

Mr. Darcy engaged to Elizabeth Bennet. *How could it be?* Caroline frowned, honestly baffled. *What did he see in her?*

She possessed few discernible accomplishments and argued with him abominably. She was ordinary and unremarkable! She did not own a single fashionable gown, not one piece of fine jewelry, nor lone garment of fur. Half the time her hair resembled a bird's nest of coarse twigs, and it was unlikely a drop of cosmetics had ever touched her skin. How Mr. Darcy could claim Elizabeth Bennet the handsomest woman of his acquaintance was an unsolvable mystery, so it must be the result of an enchantment. Grudgingly, Caroline granted Elizabeth was not hideous to look at or utterly lacking in manners. Admittedly there were scores of worse examples within the eligible ladies of Society, even those with purest bloodlines. But in no respect could she compare to the majority of women in his circle.

In no way does she compare to me.

The thought knifed through Caroline's mind painfully, leaving in its wake an odd restoration of clarity. Shifting her gaze to the tall mirror propped in the corner she critically examined her reflection. High emotion of any type affected her fair complexion in a negative way—that being one reason Caroline had long ago fostered an icy core, to prohibit mood swings—so at the present her cheeks were blotchy and eyes red. This, however, did not hide the facts. Physical appearance was one measure of worthiness, accomplishments and elegance being among the others, and in every point imaginable, Caroline was simply stating the obvious—as anyone with a modicum of rationality would agree—when she claimed her superiority over Elizabeth Bennet.

Standing, Caroline walked leisurely toward the mirror. She gazed discerningly at her figure. Elizabeth, with her tanned cheeks, dull brown hair, small breasts, and skinny body hidden under drab gowns lacking style, could not hold a candle to the vision of feminine perfection seen in the silvery surface. Caroline did not understand why a lushly beautiful woman caused men to universally transform into drooling dogs incapable of thinking with a body part above the waistline, but it was a fact she intended to exploit.

The answer is simple, really. Caroline replaced her anger and despair with cold calculation and determination. Now was not the time to be depressed or wallow in pointless regrets. Impossible it may be to turn back the clock and remedy her error in not ensnaring Mr. Darcy when she had the chance; however, until he stood in the church and repeated vows before God, the tragic deed was not final. Caroline Bingley was, above all, a woman who knew what she wanted—that being Mr. Darcy—and she was willing to do whatever it took to get him.

Her superior attributes had been right under Mr. Darcy's nose for three years, figuratively speaking. All Caroline had to do was pointedly express her preference and blatantly remind him of her sophistication and exceptional qualities. If that involved placing her finest assets literally under his nose, she would do that too.

In the morning, she resolved to emerge from her chambers set on a course to steal Mr. Darcy away from the impertinent upstart wholly unworthy of him.

Caroline Bingley was a woman on a mission.

తో

Jane and Lizzy were waiting on the Longbourn porch when their two gentlemen rode into the yard. With bonnets, shawls, and gloves donned, their purpose was evident. After a rushed greeting and a brief time for the men to pay respects to Mrs. Bennet, arms were secured and they were steered down a winding path west of the house.

It was a trail Darcy had never walked, and normally he would have paid keen attention to the ground and passing terrain. Instead, he happily trusted Elizabeth's familiarity and awareness of any hazards.

What man of sound mind would inspect trees or flowers when the beautiful woman he loved was holding on to his arm and positioned inches away from his body?

"You and Miss Bennet appeared most anxious to begin your walk. Dare I presume our company was a significant factor? Or were you merely anticipating the delight of escaping the confines of Longbourn?"

"It is true that I prefer being out of doors rather than within, so I do look for any excuse, no matter how implausible, to escape. Today you gave me a decent enough reason."

"Decent enough? Well, I shall have to be satisfied with that!"

Darcy smiled at Lizzy's gay laughter.

"Will you be scandalized, William, to hear that I walk at my own pleasure, braving the elements if necessary, and facing the censure of others upon occasion for my wild ways?"

"I am not scandalized. I vividly recall your appearance after one such wild walk in the elements and confess I appreciated the picture far too much to censure."

"Did you?" Lizzy halted and glanced up at his face. She looked genuinely amazed at his confession.

"Indeed. Exercise becomes you, Elizabeth. Your eyes were bright and cheeks rosy. A soft sheen bathed your skin, making your face glow. Several tendrils of your hair had escaped your bonnet, and were dancing across your forehead and neck. You were…exceedingly fetching." *To state it mildly.*

"I recall only surprise, and what I interpreted as contempt. Granted, you were silent and grave rather than openly incredulous, like Miss Bingley and Mrs. Hurst, but I did not guess appreciation. I apologize for misinterpreting."

"An apology is not needed. I *was* surprised, Elizabeth, for I had never met a woman who would *think* of walking so far, let alone do it. I questioned your judgment in traversing muddy fields unescorted, in the early morning while the mist remained, and under the threat of further rain. I still believe it an unwise course under most circumstances and hope in the future you will appeal to me before setting out in such a manner. Nevertheless, I soon comprehended your level of comfort in the countryside and that I was wrong to question your capability. Most touching to me was the devotion to your sister. This I can readily understand."

"Yes, I suppose you can." She glanced away from his eyes, her gaze falling on Jane and Mr. Bingley as they disappeared around a bend in the trail. Suddenly she laughed. Darcy lifted a brow questioningly when she looked back at him.

"I was comparing Jane now, walking happily with Mr. Bingley and mindless of our existence behind them," she explained as she tugged on his arm and resumed walking, "to the Jane earlier, who argued with me about waiting on the step and whisking the two of you away seconds after arriving. She thought our behavior would be condemned as brazen and unladylike. I bullied her along, with help from mama, but did not successfully convince her that Mr. Bingley would be gratified to witness her enthusiasm. What say you, Mr. Darcy? Who was correct, me or Jane?"

"As I see it, Miss Elizabeth," he emphasized her formal name, as she had his, and spoke in an exaggerated, stilted manner, "there is a place and time for proper behavior, and one must take pains to never cross into vulgarity. Undue *enthusiasm* can be most unsettling. Nevertheless, in affairs of the heart, no one, not even a mature man of confidence, would reject an overt display of affection and—dare I say it?—*enthusiasm* from the woman he loves. As illogical as it seems, the greater one's feeling for another, the more he needs to be assured the sentiments are reciprocated."

His kept his tone of humorously dramatic instruction but hoped that she would detect the truthful revelation, especially in the last two sentences.

She held her teasing smile but nodded seriously. "I shall keep your words of wisdom in mind, William."

"Excellent!" he exclaimed in relief, and then attempted to lighten the mood. "And I shall remember that you have now confessed to desiring this time with me rather than for the single wish for a walk."

"Did I confess that?" She succumbed to laughter at his firm nod. "Yes, it is true. I enjoy every moment with you, and intend to make the most of it. I want to know everything about you, which, of course, means that you must talk freely and be prepared to argue with me if I disagree. Are you up to the challenge, sir?"

"Like you, I never back down from a challenge, my dear. How do you wish to proceed in this endeavor to know *everything* about me?"

"How about beginning with recounting your morning? You said you had letters to write, some announcing our engagement, I believe. Did you complete your task?"

"Nearly. I shall finish tomorrow. There are quite a number, and I am not the fastest writer."

"Oh? I heard you write uncommonly fast." Darcy chuckled at her reference. "Quite a number, was it? Endless possibilities to reveal the mysteries of Mr. Darcy!" The mischievous glint in her eyes was absolutely adorable, and Darcy resisted the urge to kiss her only with great effort. Luckily, to avoid an unseemly display sure to embarrass them both, she returned her gaze to the trail. "Were they primarily business matters then, or personal? I did not think your family large."

"My family is more extensive than you realize. Primarily the letters were personal, although I did write to my solicitor in London, Mr. Daniels, whom I am sure you shall meet someday. The Daniels firm has handled my family's affairs for decades. He will begin the necessary paperwork pertaining to our betrothal settlement. I sent detailed instructions on that and a few other matters I dropped when I rushed back to Netherfield."

This time, it was he who halted their steps, turning to Lizzy and grasping both her hands between his. For several seconds he could not breathe and forgot what he meant to say. They were not physically closer than when walking side-by-side, but the impact of facing her fully was striking.

"I have to warn you, Elizabeth, that as unappealing as it is for me, and as loath as I am to be parted during this special time, it is inevitable that I travel to London to personally discuss the specifics and formalize the legalities of the settlement. Additionally, I want to arrange estate business now, before our marriage. With proper planning, my steward and solicitor can keep Pemberley functioning after our marriage, for a time at least, with minimal input from me. Once at Pemberley for the winter, I do not wish our solitude disturbed unless a drastic emergency arises."

And since it is quite possible I'll keep us locked in my bedchamber all winter, they better handle it!

Visions of Elizabeth in his bedchamber were highly pleasant. They were also unsettling and inappropriate. The thought was a fleeting one, but with her standing directly in front of him, the abrupt barrage of emotions were as strong as they had been yesterday evening when entering Longbourn, and again while in the starlit garden last night. Both times his desire to kiss her overwhelmed his reason. Restraint honed over nearly three decades, and the gentlemanly breeding of generations, all but disappeared. Somehow, he needed to smother his baser impulses before his uncontrolled ardor frightened her into rethinking her choice in husband.

Your ardor did not seem unwelcome. She did not look frightened before, and looks quite willing to be kissed now.

Darcy silently concurred with the justifying voice in his mind. Then he shook his head and gulped past the lump in his throat. In matters of sexuality and romantic love, Darcy was not what anyone would label experienced. Nevertheless, he was educated on the subject—while surely Elizabeth was not—and as a man, it was his job to lead and set a proper example. Despite her assurances of love and trust, Darcy knew they were new developments harshly won. As such, they were fragile things, to his way of thinking, and he refused to allow any action borne from his weakness cause either her love or trust to shatter.

"I understand you have affairs to manage, William. I will miss you, of course, but you must not fret over my feelings. I recognize the sacrifice and appreciate why you are making it. How soon, and for how long will you be in London?"

Her soft voice and tender touch of gloved fingertips to his left cheek broke him out of his trance, Darcy only then realizing how close he had drawn to her lips. He straightened slowly, forcing a serene smile. "I will give Mr. Daniels a week or so to prepare. I cannot say how long, but trust me that it will be as short as possible."

Maybe it will be beneficial to separate for a short span. The thought was sensible but painful to contemplate, so he tucked her hand under his arm and resumed their stroll. Bingley and Jane were far ahead but had stopped to wait for them. Or perhaps they had paused for an intimate conversation of their own. Darcy waved casually, and Bingley waved back.

"We seem to have lagged behind, but at least we are in eyesight, so my promise to Mr. Bennet to remain as a group is not broken. Now, where was I? My letter to Daniels was complete, with assistance from my valet who has neater penmanship than mine. Fortified with coffee, I attended to the personal correspondence. First, naturally, was Georgiana."

"Miss Darcy is such a dear! She will be pleased, will she not?"

"Pleased? Indeed not! She will be overjoyed, Elizabeth. She has longed for a sister all of her life, dreams of the intimate friendship not possible with a brother over a decade older. I have wished for Georgiana to have this as well, and it is doubly gratifying that my tremendous fortune in earning a place in your life also means fulfilling her desires."

"If Miss Darcy were anything other than the sweet-natured creature she is, I might be daunted by the charge. As it is, my only apprehension is that my impertinence and quick temper shall frighten—or corrupt her good manners."

"The liveliness of your mind and sportive manner will be good for her, I am certain of it."

"And when I tease you? Or we argue, as we surely shall? Will her high opinion fade and affection cool in defense of a beloved brother?"

They had almost caught up to Jane and Bingley, so Darcy did not hesitate to once again stop walking. If not for his concern over the trace of strain amid her humorous tones, Darcy would have been gladdened to realize his improving ability to detect her emotions. At the present, his only thought was to console her.

"It is in large part *because* of her love for me that Georgiana's sentiments toward you spring, Elizabeth. She is one of a handful who knew my love for you and has seen the affect upon me when hope was lost. Rather than despising you as the cause of my...sadness"— *agonizing, soul-wrenching pain*—"Georgiana welcomed you to Pemberley with jubilation nearly as intense as mine. She supported my decision, that is true, and trusted my resolution that you alone could bring me happiness. Yet, Georgiana drew her own conclusions and grew to care for you because of your interactions with her. It is impossible for me to imagine your heart opening to me without my sister's influence as a portion of the catalyst. As for the rest"—he brushed the tip of one finger over her nose playfully—"Georgiana will soon learn the relationship between husband and wife is quite different than that of siblings."

They walked in silence for a while after that. Lizzy seemed deep in thought, and Darcy was content to quietly dwell on the rosy flush his touch had elicited. Soon their steps brought them to the waiting Jane and Bingley, the duo suggesting a rest beside the creek-fed pond visible behind a cluster of oak and elm trees. In short order, they were settled in moderate comfort on the flat tops of several rocks conveniently located under the shady branches. Slices of cheese, dried fruit, and soft rolls were pulled from the basket Jane carried, and Darcy bravely risked slipping into the pond to fill two pewter mugs with water.

Casual conversation flowed amongst the foursome, mixed with laughter and the occasional lull.

It was in one of the latter that Lizzy turned to Darcy and murmured, "We never made it past your letter to Miss Darcy. Is that as far as you got?"

Darcy chuckled. "No. I may be a slow writer, but not that pathetic. Next was a letter to Mrs. Reynolds. The staff must be alerted, of course, and there are a number of preparations necessary to conclude before we come home."

"Home," she repeated thoughtfully. "Yes, Pemberley will be home. I suppose I shall have to acclimate to that."

He squeezed her hand. "I am not insensitive to how difficult leaving Longbourn for Pemberley will be, Elizabeth. I shall do all in my power to ensure it is a smooth transition. As will Mrs. Reynolds. Most of my letter involved instructions to accommodate your personal comforts."

"Oh my! I pray you did not insinuate I require much! I do not wish to impose—"

"You are to be my wife and the Mistress of Pemberley. Nothing you want or need shall *ever* be an imposition. But, if it reassures you, I only ordered simple tasks, such as cleaning thoroughly, airing out my mother's chambers, resupplying the dressing room that shall be yours, and so on. Mrs. Reynolds would have done this whether I asked or not. She is phenomenally capable, and her happiness that I am finally to be wed will rival Georgiana's."

"You speak of her with great affection, as she did you during our tour of Pemberley. I sensed a caring beyond what one typically sees from a servant."

"I was four years of age when Mrs. Reynolds secured the position after Pemberley's previous housekeeper, Mrs. Sutherland, passed on. She never blatantly assumed a parental role, but due to my mother's illness, often she was the only female adult I could turn to during my formative years. She is warm and compassionate, and severely loyal to Pemberley and the Darcy family. I have learned to rely upon her gentle touch for myself, and especially with Georgiana."

"Then I shall try not to worry over Mrs. Reynolds being burdened. Her assistance in helping me adjust to life at Pemberley will be appreciated."

Unable to resist, he reached up and twisted an errant curl around his finger. "You will love living at Pemberley, I promise. Do not hesitate to tell me if there are any particular wishes or items you want purchased or, well, any supplies proper for a lady. My knowledge of feminine requirements is woefully inadequate."

"I will keep it in mind, thank you. So, were your letters of instruction completed? Or are there others in your employ to be raised to a dither and sent scurrying about?"

"The rest were family, although I cannot claim none shall soon be scurrying about. I do hope a few might make the journey to meet my bride."

"My interest is piqued, William. The only relatives I have heard mentioned are Colonel Fitzwilliam, his parents, and Lady Catherine. Oh, and Miss de Bourgh. I saw the family tree tapestries hanging in the foyer of Pemberley and was overwhelmed by the Darcy lineage. I guess the recent generations were lost to me amid the vastness of your ancestry. Have you so many kinsman close to you?"

Aside from the occasional comment by Mr. Bingley, who had met a few of Darcy's relatives, Jane and Lizzy listened in amazed silence as Darcy summarized his immediate family. He began with his father's four siblings, those whom he had written to first.

His father's favorite sister, Darcy's Aunt Estella, lived with her husband, Mr. Xavier Montrose, and their children and grandchildren, in Devon near Exeter. He was confident that they would attend the wedding, or at least make an attempt.

Dwelling in Manchester, his Uncle Phillip was not awfully far away, yet the likelihood of him or his family coming to the wedding was slim. Born when Darcy's father, James, was sixteen, the brothers had never been overly intimate. Darcy barely knew him or any of the cousins.

The eldest of James Darcy's siblings was Darcy's Aunt Mary, the Baroness Oeggl. Even though Mary had dwelt in Austria with her husband, Baron Oeggl, and their children and grandchildren for all of Darcy's life, they had managed to visit each other from time to time. Darcy was quite fond of them. While doubtful they would travel to England so near winter, it was possible a couple of his cousins might, so he had already dispatched the missive via private courier.

As for the last sibling, and the one who had been dearest to both of his deceased parents' hearts, his Uncle George was unquestionably the one most willing to move mountains to be at Darcy's wedding.

"It is strange that somehow I know this," he murmured. "The truth is, I am not close to my Uncle George. Nothing amiss or to be guilty of in that assessment, you understand. George has lived in India as a practicing physician with the British East India Company since I was a baby. His return visits to England, only three of them, have been under…unusual circumstances."

Deciding it was far too complicated and personal to dive into at the present, Darcy left it at that. "Suffice to say, our personal relationship has never flourished into true intimacy. He is brilliant and a good man, but eccentric and reckless. Over the years we have corresponded regularly, and as much as possible within letters, my fondness for my uncle has grown. George cares for me as well, although how much of that is based on my own merits or due to being the son of his favorite brother, I cannot say."

Darcy pointed out that no matter how swiftly dispatched, an invitation would reach India long after November the twenty-eighth. Dr. George Darcy would *want* to be at his nephew's wedding, Darcy was sure of this, and therefore would be the most heartbroken at missing it.

"All I can do is pray my lengthy letter rich with details will soften the blow." Darcy did not elaborate that the pages had been filled with gushing enumerations of his joy, praise for his betrothed, and rapturous assurances of how her excellence would, in countless ways, positively affect George's namesake, Georgiana, and Pemberley.

"Once finished with those, it was after noon. My desire to be here, on this path with you and enjoying the fine autumn weather, overruled the desire to inform my mother's side of the family of our engagement. Time enough for that tomorrow."

"Colonel Fitzwilliam will be top on that list, eh, Darcy?"

"Do you know the colonel, Mr. Bingley?" Elizabeth asked before Darcy could affirm his friend's query.

"We have met on several occasions, yes. Capitol chap. Dissimilar to Darcy in temperament, but the two are thick as thieves."

"Colonel Fitzwilliam is my cousin," Darcy clarified to a confused Jane. "He is nearly three years my senior, but our families live less than ten miles apart in Derbyshire, so we grew up together. His father, the Earl of Matlock, was my father's oldest and dearest friend. His lordship's sister, Lady Anne Fitzwilliam, and my father, James, fell in love when quite young. They married a few years after my Uncle Malcolm, that is Lord Matlock, married Lady Madeline Hamilton, one of my mother's dearest friends. Rather cemented the relationships, I suppose, but as Bingley said, Richard is a capitol chap, so my affection for him is based on more than shared blood—when he is not driving me insane, that is."

"Yes, I seem to recall an undertone of familiar sparring between you two." Lizzy laughed at Darcy's long-suffering sigh. Turning to Jane, she said, "I met Colonel Fitzwilliam while in Kent this past spring. A most amiable gentleman with a delightful humor." Darcy frowned, but Lizzy did not appear to notice. "We conversed a great deal, although he never mentioned his kinship to Mr. Darcy. It was a surprise to me when I learned of it."

She did not ask aloud if his cousin knew of their history, but Darcy could see the unspoken question in her eyes. He inclined his head slightly. "As Bingley intimated, I will write to my cousin later. He is currently away from London, on some sort of secret military assignment, and not expected to return for another week or more. I may wait until I am in Town to share my news. He will be pleased to see me settled, if for no other reason than to have something new to harass me about. He praised your amiability and humor as well, Elizabeth, and appreciated your company at Rosings more than you probably realize." He smiled at the blushing surprise crossing her face. "Our Aunt Catherine annoys him far more than she ever has me, and he hates it when I drag him along for my visits there. Your presence was...beneficial for both of us."

Darcy said no more. Best not to dig too deeply into all that had happened while at Rosings Park in Kent. And there was no reason for her to know that Richard's continual innocent effusions about Miss Elizabeth Bennet had brought Darcy closer to strangling his cousin than the worst of their youthful skirmishes ever had! Luckily, Richard was a confirmed bachelor, so his harmless flirtations had not been too worrisome.

Another topic he had no intention of discussing with Elizabeth now, or ever if possible, was how his Uncle Malcolm and Aunt Madeline might react to Darcy's choice of bride. Possible objections to the match mirrored the regrettable words he had spoken when he proposed at Hunsford in April. Richard's acquaintance with Elizabeth, and resulting excellent opinion of her, could prove beneficial in persuading his parents.

His Aunt Catherine's opinion on what constituted a marriage was absolute and forever had been. There was no question how she would take the news of his engagement to Elizabeth Bennet, and after her unforgivable offense in barging into Longbourn, Darcy had no intention of wasting his time with more than the briefest of letters.

Lord and Lady Matlock were altogether a different matter. For one, other than an occasional vague comment and the habitual introduction to unattached young ladies at any function Darcy happened to be at, neither of them had overtly seemed concerned about his marital status. Unlike Lady Catherine, the suggestion that Darcy marry their daughter, his cousin Annabella, had never been broached. Affection between them was genuine, so he knew they would desire his happiness. And, as he had told Elizabeth yesterday, he truly believed they would adore her once they spent time with her. How could they not?

On the other hand, Darcy knew his uncle to be, like most English aristocrats, exceedingly proud of his title and heritage. In essence, Darcy did not dispute this. He too was a man of ancient lineage, with roots firmly bound to his family's land and wealth. It was no secret that the obligation and expectation, even if never loudly vocalized by Lord Matlock, was for Darcy to marry well.

In Darcy's mind, he *was* marrying well, better than he deserved or could have found amid the polished veneer that comprised the vast majority of women in Society. Yet it had taken him a long while, and the indictment passing the lips of Elizabeth when he first proposed, to fully comprehend this meant more than a title or generous dowry. Hopefully his uncle and aunt would understand, but he honestly did not know.

"So now you know all there is to learn of my family—"

"All there is to learn? I can think of several dozen more tidbits to pick from your brain. For instance, you never mentioned your other cousin, Colonel Fitzwilliam's brother. The colonel is a second son, so I presume there is another?"

"Indeed," Darcy agreed while standing and extending his hand to help her rise, "there is. I recommend saving your dozen tidbits for another time or we shall have nothing to talk about on our next walk, thus left with scant to do but stare at the passing grass."

❧

On Monday and Thursday, in the minutes between three and four o'clock in the afternoon, a postal carrier crossed the bridge over the River Derwent and passed under the massive stone arch emblazoned with the name PEMBERLEY. He then veered toward the narrower avenue to the north, until reaching the gigantic graveled courtyard between the stable complex and the domestic wing of the great house. His presence was expected, and without fail, he was greeted near the kitchen entrance by Mrs. Reynolds, who exchanged the sack of incoming mail for an identical sack of outgoing mail. She also routinely handed him a flagon of cold water and a tin plate heaped with food. While the thankful young man enjoyed the nourishment, he and his mount resting in the shade for a spell, Mrs. Reynolds immediately retired to her office to sort through the mail.

The twice-weekly Royal Mail shipment primarily consisted of personal correspondences from friends and family members of the extensive Pemberley staff, as did the shipment leaving with the postal carrier. However, it was not unusual for letters to arrive via the general mail service for Mr. Darcy, Miss Darcy, or the Pemberley steward, Mr. Keith. Of utmost importance was ensuring these three individuals be given their mail before anyone else in the household.

This long-ago established post routine for Pemberley was rarely deviated from. Conversely, the arrival of dispatches sent by special courier was impossible to predict.

If able to afford private delivery, as Mr. Darcy of Pemberley certainly was, that avenue was preferred due to the frequent delays and mishaps plaguing the Royal Mail system. Pemberley's butler, Mr. Taylor, and the footmen who were under his jurisdiction never knew when a rider may gallop up to the front entrance of the manor, so there was always someone standing at attention in the vaulted, massive foyer just in case.

On the day Darcy's letters to Georgiana and Mrs. Reynolds arrived at Pemberley, the footman Rothchilde was on duty as sentry. Diligent to the serious task of delivering any missive from Mr. Darcy, Rothchilde enlisted the aid of fellow footman Phillips to hand carry the envelope addressed to Mrs. Reynolds. Neither footman knew precisely where she might be at that exact minute, but Phillips hunted her down to the main linen closet on the second story.

She and three maids were conducting the yearly inventory, literally knee deep in stacks of neatly folded towels, sheets, tablecloths, and assorted other linens. With a nod, Mrs. Reynolds took the letter from Phillips and tucked it into her pocket for careful reading in the privacy of her office later. While receiving messages from Mr. Darcy directly to her was not a daily occurrence, it was common enough not to warrant undue concern. How was she to know it was arguably the most critical and thrilling letter she had ever gotten from the man she loved almost as if her own son?

As for Miss Darcy, Rothchilde knew Mr. Darcy's sister was riding her horse, but with the immense size of the estate grounds, delivering the letter was impossible until she returned from her pleasure jaunt. Thus he was forced to maintain his assigned post hovering near the door, keeping one eye on the table where the letter to Miss Darcy was safely stowed. If he had suspected the momentous nature of the pages, he might well have saddled a horse and ridden out to find her.

Instead, it would be later that afternoon before either woman tore through the wax seal, and by happenstance they were reading the news of Darcy's engagement to Miss Elizabeth Bennet at the same time.

Mrs. Reynolds,

As always, madam, I open my correspondence with the warmest of greetings and sincerest regards. I am confident all is well with Pemberley, pray your health is superb, and trust Miss Darcy is thriving under your gentle, guiding hand. My faith in the validity of these three factors arises from my earnest desire, to be sure, yet is also due to the news I am writing to impart. The momentous, superlative nature of my announcement will undoubtedly be appreciated to the unparalleled degree it is worth if nothing is amiss at home. And now that I have, I hope, sufficiently piqued your curiosity and heightened your anticipation, it is time to communicate my joy—if it is possible to adequately do so in words etched onto paper without diverging into poetry. I shall attempt to remain sensible.

I suspect you have already leaped ahead to a conclusion. You have perceived my inner thoughts since a child and instantly perceived my sentiments toward a certain young lady upon meeting her at Pemberley some weeks ago. Indeed, I speak of Miss Elizabeth Bennet of Hertfordshire, the most exceptional lady who captured my heart once and forever. Now I am pleased beyond measure to report that Miss Elizabeth has acknowledged her heart is equally captured, and furthermore, to my continuing astonishment and thankfulness to God, she has accepted my proposal of marriage.

Such joy is unprecedented, my dear Mrs. Reynolds! To you I can uninhibitedly shout of my rapturous happiness as I can to few others on this earth. Long have I yearned for a relationship such as my excellent father and mother possessed. Only you, who knew them long and intimately, can fully appreciate this yearning. Rare it is in our world to find one's perfect match, and I know it is not a revelation to you when I confess that I was beginning to lose hope. My dearest, loveliest Elizabeth has fully restored my hope and renewed my heart. This alone would be a miracle and a gift to be treasured. Yet, in Miss Elizabeth—she who will ere long be Mrs. Darcy—it is not only me who will reap the bounty of hope and renewal. Pemberley, and all that the word conjures, shall be touched by the miracle. Not a particle of doubt exists within me that Elizabeth will be a fine mistress for Pemberley, and that our mutual love and devotion will be a boon.

Poetry surely is the only way to adequately express my feelings on the subject. Rest assured, madam, that as easy as it would be for me to pen a missive replete with nothing more than exaltations, I shall restrain myself. As you likely have surmised, much needs to be done to prepare the manor for Mrs. Darcy. Our engagement transpired yesterday, so the benefit of time and reflection I do not yet own. However, I wanted you to be informed immediately, for the obvious reason of our shared affection and also because I trust your judgment in proper necessities for my wife—a topic I am currently woefully ignorant of. I am confident your leadership, working in concert with Mr. Taylor and the servants, will accomplish what must be done before we arrive together in late November.

The remaining paragraphs covering the two sheets of paper contained instructions for cleaning certain chambers and rearranging furnishings, warnings to anticipate frequent messages and shipments of merchandise, and permission to spend estate funds liberally on anything deemed essential or desirable for his future wife. Mrs. Reynolds's smile broadened with each passing sentence. True to his pledge, Mr. Darcy restrained himself, writing in his typical straightforward manner with an economy of words. A person minimally familiar with a letter from Darcy of Pemberley might not have noticed the subtle alterations, but Mrs. Reynolds readily detected a relaxed style to his sentence structure with cheerful and optimistic word choices. While he never crossed the line into pure romanticism, stray phrases of love were numerous.

She read the letter through twice. Additional readings would be done, methodically, while taking notes to formulate a concise agenda for the weeks ahead. Discussions with Mr. Taylor and Mr. Keith and others of the senior staff were requisite and not to be unduly delayed. Already the housekeeper's businesslike mind was creating lists and plotting strategies. She wiped the moisture from her cheeks and tucked the folded papers into her pocket.

The butler was in the dining room, as he had been for most of the past week, overseeing the polishing and inventory of the silver. Like Mrs. Reynolds's task with the linens, it was during periods when the master was away that they were able to carry out time-consuming projects and perform extensive deep cleanings. Nicely coincidental considering they were now ordered to do precisely that!

"Mr. Taylor, a moment of your time, please?"

The butler, a distinguished man of roughly sixty years, accompanied her into the hall, saying nothing until they were alone. "The letter from Mr. Darcy contained news of substance, I take it. Was it the favorable report we hoped for?"

"I am most pleased to say that it was, Mr. Taylor. Mr. Darcy has secured the hand of Miss Elizabeth Bennet, and on twenty-eight November, they are to be wed. We shall soon have a new Mrs. Darcy." Mrs. Reynolds attempted to speak composedly, but her emotions could not be repressed.

"This is excellent news and a tremendous relief." Mr. Taylor's tone remained bland, despite his sentiments closely paralleling those of Mrs. Reynolds.

Mr. Taylor had worked at Pemberley since a young boy, rising through the ranks to the top rung as butler, a position he had flawlessly executed for over thirty years. While never establishing an intimate relationship with the family he served, as Mrs. Reynolds had, Mr. Taylor was fiercely loyal. Nothing was more important, to his way of thinking, than the prosperity of Pemberley, and that, naturally, depended upon the prosperity of Mr. Darcy. Having never married nor being a particularly romantic person by nature, Mr. Taylor had spared scant time considering his master's preferences on marriage. Mr. Darcy would do so eventually and produce the required heir to continue the Darcy lineage, was his opinion on the matter.

When Mrs. Reynolds confidentially told him that her suspicion as to why the master was distressed to the point of being ill during the past summer was due to a romantic heartbreak of some sort, Mr. Taylor had brushed her speculations aside. Surely they were the fancies of a sentimental female who was far too emotionally involved with the family. After witnessing Mr. Darcy's curious behavior while entertaining Mr. and Mrs. Gardiner and their niece Miss Bennet, Mr. Taylor started to believe the housekeeper's claims might have validity.

The concept of a man's happiness being wrapped wholly around a single woman was bizarre to the pragmatic butler. That being said, he had watched the previous Mr. Darcy mourn his wife, Lady Anne Darcy, until death was the only escape from the unrelenting pain. Despite his tendency to ignore the private lives of the Darcys, or his own staff if he could avoid it, he was not a fool. There was no denying the facts that pointed to young Mr. Darcy being akin to his father. As with the love between Lady Anne and James Darcy, apparently the love of Miss Bennet was critical to the wellbeing of Fitzwilliam Darcy.

Like it or not, and he assuredly *did not* like it, Mr. Taylor had spent the past several weeks anxiously praying for positive news.

"I presume Mr. Darcy has instructions for us?" he asked.

"He does. I need to speak with Miss Darcy, and then we can gather the staff to make a formal announcement. Perhaps you can come to my office at eight to discuss and plan?" Mr. Taylor inclined his head. "I think a glass of punch is in order, after dinner, of course." Mrs. Reynolds smiled at the butler's raised brows. "It is news worthy of celebrating, Mr. Taylor."

"As you wish, Mrs. Reynolds."

She saved her chuckles at his dry reply until around the corner.

Now, I must see Georgiana.

"Miss Darcy was given her letter and went straightaway into the main parlor," Rothchilde reported, directing his gaze toward a set of closed doors visible on the balcony level above the massive grand staircase where they stood. "Mrs. Annesley was already in there, and still is I believe. No one has exited the room."

Mrs. Reynolds tapped on the parlor door, and then laughed aloud when it flew open before her knuckles left the solid surface.

"Oh, Mrs. Reynolds! Is it not the most amazing and wonderful news? I am dancing with glee!"

"She means this quite literally," interjected an amused voice. "Your timely interruption has undoubtedly saved the carpet from being worn to threads by her twirls."

Mrs. Reynolds crossed the threshold, her laughter lifting at Mrs. Annesley's teasing remark.

Georgiana blushed but continued to grin and bounce on her toes.

"I only twirled once," she started, and then, at her companion's raised brow, laughingly amended, "or maybe thrice, but how could I not? William is to be married, and to Miss Elizabeth! My happiness is uncontainable! I cannot imagine how he must be feeling, although his letter reveals much."

She scanned the pages in her hands. "Listen to this: *'My heart is now whole and liberated, dearest sister, and my joy immeasurable.*

103

God has granted me a miracle, a divine gift in gaining Elizabeth's love and being entrusted with her heart. It is a fearsome responsibility, this I know and shall never forget. Ensuring her happiness, every day of the life God gives us together, is now my supreme purpose. In striving thus, my life shall be enriched and heart secure.' Is that not lovely?"

The response was a duo of sighs.

"There is more: *'This morning it appeared as if the sun had risen with brilliance unmatched at any other time. Or perhaps, with the awakening of my heart, my eyes now see the simple beauties of the natural world with a keener light.'* Who knew my brother was so poetic?"

Mrs. Reynolds opened her mouth to affirm, but Georgiana barged on.

"This is my favorite, where is it? Oh, here, *'...peace and contentment washed through me, Georgie. Hours after her acceptance, in a place unfamiliar to me, surrounded by people talking and plates of food, I experienced a profound flood of tranquility every time I met Elizabeth's beautiful eyes. I can only liken it to how I feel when at Pemberley, yet it was deeper still. I tried to envision gazing into her eyes while dining at Pemberley, as we once did, only this time as my wife, and the euphoria was too intense.'*"

"Mr. Darcy certainly writes as a man in the throes of passionate love," Mrs. Annesley murmured, her expression wistful.

Mrs. Reynolds wondered if the poetic sentiments sparked memories of the deceased Mr. Annesley. Heaven knows she was not immune from remembrances of new-love fervor, and she was twice Mrs. Annesley's age!

"I cannot claim to know him well," Mrs. Annesley added, "but I would not have suspected his romantic nature."

"Mr. Darcy is a dichotomy in many respects." Mrs. Reynolds sat across from Miss Darcy's companion, poured a cup of tea, and explained as she stirred the sugar. "Always a serious person, even as a boy, yet possessing a sensitive soul and playfulness as well. Ofttimes the balance between the two has been unequal, I fear."

"William needed someone to bring out his softer side, and who better than Miss Elizabeth? She is wonderfully lighthearted, compassionate, and beautiful too. Do you not agree, Mrs. Reynolds?" The housekeeper concurred, although her words were lost as Georgiana rushed on. "Oh, but it was evident how strong his feelings toward her! When at Pemberley, she must have noticed how he stammered and blushed, as I have never seen him do, and the expressions on his face were altogether tender. Quite revealing. I would have deduced his preference for her even if he had not told me."

"Yes, you have said this before, with the suggestion that Miss Elizabeth did not initially return his affection. Fortunately, her heart was swayed. The trauma of unrequited love is harsh."

"Indeed it is." Mrs. Reynolds conceded as her eyes darted to Georgiana, who was reading the letter again with an elated smile on her face.

Mr. Darcy had never divulged the finer details of what happened at Ramsgate, Mrs. Reynolds informed of the barest generalities only. Miss Darcy had never confided fully either. What she knew was deduced from offhand comments and reactions to the words of others. That Mr. Wickham had harmed her young lady's heart was evident, and such pain can be tortuous to overcome. Observing Miss Darcy's joy for her brother, and aware of the pleasant personality of Miss Bennet, Mrs. Reynolds was doubly thankful for Mr. Darcy's engagement. The benefits promised to ripple through all of them at Pemberley.

"Miss Elizabeth may not have instantly fallen in love with William, Mrs. Annesley." Georgiana flopped onto the settee beside her companion, clasping her hand. "I, of course, think William the handsomest, smartest, wittiest, kindest man on the planet, and believe every woman mad for him! I shall confess that I am extraordinarily prejudiced, however. Mrs. Reynolds, you agree with me, yes?"

"I do, naturally. That is not to say he is without some flaws, however minor."

"You do tease, Mrs. Reynolds! I suppose it is true, although I cannot name a one," Georgiana declared pompously, and then winked at Mrs. Reynolds.

Mrs. Annesley feigned wide-eyed shock. "Not even one flaw? My word. How is it Miss Elizabeth Bennet was able to withstand the lure? I would think no woman alive strong enough to resist such a supreme specimen of manhood."

"I cannot fathom it either!" A fleeting frown wrinkled Georgiana's brow, revealing to Mrs. Reynolds that underneath the dramatic fun was a hint of seriousness. "Whatever the reasons, Miss Elizabeth's feeling for William were crystal clear during her visit this summer. If her stay in Derbyshire had not been cut short, I bet their engagement would have happened then. William was hopeful, I know, and then terribly distressed. Something happened within her family, although I do not know the details."

"I only saw Mr. Darcy briefly during those days, before he left for London." Mrs. Annesley squeezed Georgiana's hand. "He was quite distraught. Praise God the obstacles were overcome and now the desired happy ending will soon occur."

"Yes! As they both deserve!" Georgiana sang merrily. "Oh! I cannot wait! Twenty-eight of November seems so long from now."

"The time will pass swiftly, especially since we have much to do to prepare for a new mistress. The staff, that is."

"Oh! Please allow me to help, Mrs. Reynolds!"

"I am sure Bonnie and Colleen would appreciate another strong arm beating the carpets. Thank you, Miss Darcy, for the kind offer."

Mrs. Annesley chuckled at the amazed expression that crossed Georgiana's face before she also laughed. "I suspect you are teasing me, Mrs. Reynolds. But if beating carpets or washing drapes is how I may best serve my new sister, then I will gladly do so."

"I am sure you would, my dear. Nevertheless, your unique talents are more valuable. I prefer your guidance in regards to decorating and stocking the new Mrs. Darcy's private chambers. Your taste and elegance are superior to mine, of that there is no question. The shelves of *La Belle Assemblée*, *The Lady's Magazine*, and Ackermann's *Repository*, the pages of which I believe you have memorized, qualify you for this assignment."

Georgiana flushed prettily at the high praise. "Thank you, Mrs. Reynolds. I accept the assignment. When do we start?"

"Right away, if you wish. Mr. Darcy is requesting a concise inventory of the contents and description of the rooms, as well as a list of furnishings in the manor that may do for Miss Bennet. Your skill in drawing might prove beneficial, Miss Darcy, and the more help I have in note taking, the quicker I can deliver the information to Mr. Darcy. He wants the list before he travels to London."

"My brother shopping for home furnishings and womanly things? Now that I would like to see!"

CHAPTER FIVE
Frosts of Jealousy

D o not dare slam the door, Lizzy!"

Jane's hissed warning was obeyed. Barely. Lizzy closed the haberdasher's door with a firm thud that did not rattle the glass unduly, and she expelled her anger with a growling exhale as she stomped down the steps, onto the wooden walkway.

"Feel better?"

"I would feel much better if I *had* slammed the door, preferably directly onto Lottie Thorne's face," Lizzy snapped at her sister's placating tone. "As if Mr. Bird, who resembles his surname uncannily, can be compared, on any level or point, with Mr. Darcy! Why, he is superior in every regard, as Lottie well knows, or she would not be reduced to grasping at Mr. Bird's sleight-of-hand abilities and dancing skills as the only proof."

"Mr. Bird has entertained with his excellent card tricks on numerous occasions, and many of us, you included, have delighted in dancing with him these past couple years."

"That is hardly the point, Jane!" Lizzy stopped cold and turned her furious face toward her sister. Then, seconds later, was joining her in laughter. "Oh my," she finally gasped, "I am quite testy today."

"Perhaps a little, and it is understandable, although unfair to blame poor Mr. Bird for it."

"You know I do not blame him. Mr. Bird is a fine gentlemen, his unfortunate name notwithstanding, and I am sure he and Lottie Thorne will be deliriously happy together."

She sighed deeply and gazed across the main street of Meryton. People bustled about, intent on their own business for the most part, but a fair number cast glances toward the Bennet sisters, some even going so far as to openly point.

Lizzy felt the irritation rising again. Jane must have sensed her returning tension because she placed one hand calmly onto Lizzy's arm and, with a gentle nudge, led them toward the butcher's shop.

"They only stare and whisper because our engagements are the most excitement seen hereabouts for weeks. What else would they gossip about? Mr. Epworth's prize hog? I did hear he was a stupendous specimen that brought a hefty sum at the auction in Hertford, the largest ever, so the story goes, but I doubt if even that compares."

"Jane," Lizzy giggled, "you do improve my spirits! But as usual you are being kind and painting a pretty picture when you should not. True, your betrothal to Mr. Bingley, of its own accord, would generate bounteous chatter. Every word would extol the virtues of the match, with the only argument being whether it is Miss Bennet or Mr. Bingley who is most fortunate to have won the hand of such a perfect mate. I, conversely, am subjected to pity for falling prey to a disagreeable and domineering man who must have hidden, nefarious designs that will be revealed in a heinous manner after the wedding, at which point I will be tossed shamelessly aside. Or I am condemned for abandoning all my morals to ensnare, by any improper or dissolute means at my disposal, the richest man to ever set foot in Hertfordshire."

"You do have quite an imagination, Lizzy. If ever you are bored during the cold winters of Derbyshire, I suggest lending your hand at writing a novel or two."

"Laugh if you wish, but you heard Mrs. Rusch talking to Miss Castell and Maria Lucas last night."

"All Mrs. Rusch said was that Mr. Darcy appeared clearly besotted and was unable to remove his eyes from you for more than minutes at a time for conversation. She thought it was sweet and romantic."

"She made it sound as if he were lost in an enchantment," Lizzy countered grumpily.

"Did you not tell me Mr. Darcy said you had bewitched him? Love is a sort of enchantment, do you not think so?"

"Not the kind that comes from potions stirred in black cauldrons or woven while dancing unclothed under a full moon."

"Your imagination running amok once again, and another plot for a potential book."

Lizzy rolled her eyes. "Ask Caroline Bingley, and I wager she would assert I did one of the two. Or both."

They reached the corner of the butcher's shop, where they were conscripted by Mrs. Bennet to ensure the two geese ordered for dinner that night were being prepared for delivery. Lizzy stopped, Jane obediently waiting at her side while she inhaled several times to quiet her frustration. Suddenly she felt a burning behind her eyelids, realizing with a mild start that it was the prickling of tears!

"Dear Lizzy…"

Jane's soothing, sympathetic voice only made it worse. Lizzy turned away from the road, busying herself by pretending to search inside her reticule. "Blast it all! Oh, Jane," she sobbed, "I know you are correct about Mrs. Rusch. And Lottie meant nothing vicious by her comments either. I am…I just hate the constant expressions of shock that accompany news of my engagement to Mr. Darcy. Perhaps I exaggerated a moment ago, but you know not by much. Few believe I accepted his proposal out of love and not because of his wealth. Those who credit affection to my decision and acknowledge Mr. Darcy's affection for me do so grudgingly. I have lost count of the insinuating comments. Even the well wishes for our future happiness are spoken with an edge of disbelief or desperation, as if none can imagine it possible in the slightest for me to be happy with Mr. Darcy."

"Lizzy, are you beginning to doubt your future with Mr. Darcy?"

Jane's hesitantly whispered question doused the flames of Lizzy's emotions swifter than a bucket of icy water to the face. She gasped, the idea so utterly unfathomable that for a moment she was too stunned to speak.

"No," she stated with conviction. Her eyes were steadfast and clear of tears as she met Jane's. "Not for the tiniest second. If anything, these past days have strengthened my assurance of our life together. The more time I spend with William, the more I love him and am sure that we are superbly compatible. Do you not see, Jane? This is precisely what is so, so…annoying! It is not for myself that the gossip and demeaning attitude pains…Well, perhaps to a degree as these are people who know me, so they should trust and be happy for me. No, I hurt and grow angry for Mr. Darcy's sake."

"*That* I do not believe you should fret over, Lizzy. Mr. Darcy seems quite impervious to what anyone says. Frankly, I doubt he notices, or cares if he does. His attention and concerns are directed solely toward you, dear sister."

Lizzy blushed, her smile automatic. "I cannot deny what you say, Jane, and daily count my blessings for having such a man. What I also see, and perhaps you do not, is how he strives to please me by ingratiating himself. Dinner at a different house each of the past four nights with an endless parade of people he barely knows, the bulk of whom span the spectrum between persistent rudeness to obsequious fawning. He has endured personal questions, not-so-cleverly veiled insinuations, and displays of ill manners and vulgarity, such as our Aunt Phillips's at Mr. Meldon's on Tuesday"—they both shuddered at the memory—"and has done so with forbearance and politeness that honestly astonishes me. At every turn he has made a concerted effort to be pleasant and conversational."

"Be patient, Lizzy. It has only been five days. Mr. Darcy's sincere affection for you, fine manners, pleasant conversation, and willingness to interact with Meryton's citizens will be noticed. In fact, they already are. He was invited personally to join Mr. Bingley at the Reading Room this afternoon, was he not? You know how ridiculous the men are about admitting strangers into their private club. They had yet to invite Mr. Bingley, and honestly I doubt they would have for another month if not for...Mr. Darcy!"

"You may have a point, Jane, but—"

"No. I mean, there is Mr. Darcy, standing by the pastry shop."

Lizzy twirled around, her hat flying off in the process and snatched by Jane when only inches from hitting the ground. Lizzy hardly noticed. "Where did he come from? And what is he doing?"

"Examining something in his hands, but I cannot see what from this angle. His pocket watch, perhaps?"

"He and Mr. Bingley are not expected at the club until one o'clock, and it is not yet ten."

"Mr. Darcy is obsessed with punctuality," Jane teased. "Although it is more likely that he had other business in the village," she added when Lizzy flashed a sidelong glower.

As they spoke, a woman with two children rounded the corner, making for the pastry shop door. Mr. Darcy hastily slipped the object into a pocket, patting it securely even as he bowed and tipped his hat.

"See how freely he engages Mrs. Larimer and how cheerfully she responds to him, Lizzy? He even speaks to the children, and they appear contented."

"Jane, go on to Mr. Trask's for mama, and give my regards to the Janssens. I will meet you by the fountain at noon."

Lizzy was off the curb and heading into the street, the instructions tossed over her shoulder. After pausing for a passing coach, dodging other pedestrians, and circumventing a cluster of men repairing a broken railing in front of the mercantile, Lizzy had lost sight of Mr. Darcy. A frantic sweep had her spotting him turning onto Poole Street, one block further down from Main. Unerringly, Lizzy diverted into a small alleyway traveling the same direction. Another turn down the alley between the bank and the mail office, a catercorner dive through the public garden, and a jag past the flower vendor brought Lizzy onto Poole Street just in time to see Mr. Darcy walk into the bookseller's shop.

Now that makes sense, she thought, smiling. Determined to surprise him, she approached the shop the long way around, rather than passing where he might glance out the window and see her. Her heart raced and butterflies danced in her belly as she imagined his unexpected delight to see her. Or maybe it was mostly her delight at the chance encounter well before the scheduled dinner at Netherfield that evening. Giddily excited, she was so engrossed envisioning sneaking up behind him inside the store, that she was taken aback when the door opened just as she placed her hand on the knob.

Lizzy emitted a faint yelp at the same moment Darcy released a surprised, "Pardon me, madam...Elizabeth!" He jerked to a halt, an inch away from bashing into her, and blinked his eyes in amazement. "What are you doing here?"

"I live here, Mr. Darcy, remember?" She giggled at his expression. "My intention was to surprise you, just not in the doorway. Although, on second thought, startling you while standing in an aisle between tall, unstable bookcases may not have been a wise action after all. You are quite jumpy."

"Elizabeth, I...am surprised, yes. I thought you and your sisters were calling upon the Parkholmes today."

"We were. That is, we did, however belatedly discovered that Inez, the youngest Miss Parkholme, is ill, so did not stay long."

"Nothing serious, I pray? She appeared hale enough at Lucas Lodge two nights ago."

"You remember Inez?"

"Indeed. Pleasant girl. She recited the poems with amazing diction and feeling. Why are you looking at me with raised brows? Have I said something wrong?"

"Sorry. No, of course not. I just did not realize you noticed her reading."

"I am comprehensive in my awareness, Elizabeth, or at least I try to be, particularly as it pertains to you and your homeland. I did not, however, notice that you were on the streets of Meryton—or following me. How long were you following me?"

His tone was neutral, but she sensed a hint of anxiety, and he unconsciously touched his left pocket. This is where he had slipped the item he had been inspecting earlier, and Lizzy suddenly wondered if it might be a gift for her. Unwilling to spoil his plans, especially in light of the tight set of his jaw and flicking fingertips, a known nervous gesture, she smiled sunnily and avoided glancing toward the visible lump in his pocket.

"We saw you opening the door for Mrs. Larimer and her children. A true gentleman you are, sir, and whatever you said caused little Marigold Larimer to blush. Do I now have competition from another young lady who has succumbed to your charms?"

"If she were but a dozen years older, you may, indeed. Alas, as sweet and adorable as Miss Larimer is, she cannot steal the tiniest fragment of my heart away from you."

"Pretty words, Mr. Darcy. I shall accept them as insurance that I am safe."

"You are safe, trust me. All teasing aside, there is not a woman in the world who could compete with you."

"That is good news, William, because if any woman did try to compete for my place in your heart, a fight would be in order. I may be tiny, but I am a country girl, so it could get ugly."

"Your place is as secure as gold in a vault, my Elizabeth. A fight will never be warranted."

Darcy had not moved from his position straddling the threshold, and Lizzy had not backed away either, meaning their bodies remained incredibly close. This alone amply magnified the flushing and tingles that played havoc on Lizzy's composure. Complicating her control further was the intensity of his declarations, the way his resonant voice dropped into a caressing purr, and the glimmer of wildness detected within darkening eyes. Frequently over the past five days, she had noted similar physical evidences of his zealous yearning for her. Then, each time, while she reeled from the emotional surge ignited by his fiery demeanor, it was as if the blaze was instantly snuffed.

The same happened this time.

Between one racing heartbeat and the next, between two blinks of her eyes, he was again the calmly restrained man familiar to her. Present was the soft smile and tender gaze only for her, but gone were the traces of something deeper, leaving her, as it always did, to wonder if she had imagined the rest.

In one smooth motion, he withdrew a pace and extended his arm, every ounce the urbane gentleman. Aside from the fact that he drew her slightly closer to his side than typical, they could have been nothing more than new acquaintances on a casual stroll.

"Our meeting is fortuitous, no matter how unexpected," he began, leading away from the bookseller's doorway. "I came to pick up a few items I needed, including this book"—he held up the wrapped rectangle in his hand—"and thought I would pass the time until meeting Bingley by drinking coffee at the inn. Instead, I would much rather fulfill a desire of mine, that being to have you escort me through Meryton. If you have the time, that is?"

"I will always make the time to be with you, William. Happily so. Why else would I dash crazily after you?" She met his warm eyes briefly and then lowered her head to hide the instant blush. "I shall do my best to conduct an encompassing tour of Meryton, although it is fairly easy to discover what is here without a formal guide."

"My hope was for a *personal* guide. I desire to see the village through your eyes, as it were. I wish to hear of your adventures on these streets, as I have enjoyed while on our walks near Longbourn. Then, perhaps we can share refreshments together, with your sisters too, of course. I presume you were not here alone?"

"Only Jane is with me. She is completing our errands and will meet me by the fountain at noon."

"You deserted her so you could stalk me?"

Lizzy laughed at his feigned tone of shock. "Jane understands. She would have done the same if it were Mr. Bingley we saw—after I forced her too, that is." Darcy chuckled and nodded. "And stalking is not entirely accurate, since I did loudly frighten a stray cat when I moved the mailbags he was sleeping behind in order to pass through the narrow alley by the postal office. And in my haste and worry over losing sight of you, I nearly plowed into one of Mrs. Jacques's flower baskets, which she was verbally upset about. So, any attempt to be stealthy was a dismal failure, my only success being that you were strangely unaware of your surroundings. Fortunate for me but quite odd, Mr. Darcy. The vision of coffee and reading this book must have been tremendously engaging!"

"Normally you might have a point, coffee and reading being two of my favorite things in life. In this case, it was you, ironically enough, who served as my distraction."

"I feel as if I should apologize!"

"There will never be a need for you to apologize for distracting me, Elizabeth. I quite enjoy it, if you must know. Ah, yes, this will work well, I believe."

His last sentence penetrated Lizzy's happy haze, belatedly realizing, as he walked them under the arched stone gateway, that he had steered them into the public garden. "Did you decide to start here because you suspected I had adventures in the park?"

"No, although now that you mention it, and as I am learning more of your youthful exploits, I would wager you had a few."

"Not an abundance, unless you count the numerous times I escaped while Mama was distracted. Inevitably I came here to play. Oh yes! There was the "elm tree fiasco," as Mama termed it," she laughed in sudden memory. "I was eight at the time. Donnie and Benji Rochester, who are now both respected surgeons in villages nearby, were twelve then, and asked me to climb that tree"—she indicated a tall elm—"to rescue a stranded cat."

"Quite unchivalrous of them. Were they afraid of the tree or the cat?"

"Neither, I am sure. In fact, their argument was sound. You are much lighter and smaller than us, they said, which was true as they were burly boys. They also pointed out that the cat would probably respond better to me." Lizzy shrugged. "Whether that was as much the enticement as merely seeing if I would do it, I cannot be sure, but I gave them the benefit of the doubt."

Lizzy sat on the wooden bench Darcy motioned to, tucked in a shady corner away from the street, surrounded by shoulder-height hedges and spaced shrubs, affording a measure of privacy in an otherwise public place. A few pedestrians roamed through the verdant pathways, and a dozen children laughed as they played on the lawn area in the middle of the square garden park. The people provided a sense of being chaperoned without being closely watched.

"So what happened? Did you save the cat?"

"Not exactly. I climbed the tree easily enough and reached the branch where poor puss trembled and stared with his wide, yellow eyes. I could not reach him, so I spoke softly, purred and meowed in what I thought a brilliant imitation of a cat, and even offered him pieces of my apple. The Rochester twins shouted encouragement and instructions, none of which seemed to be working. I was nearly in tears, sure that the animal was going to die if I could not save him, when all of a sudden, the ungrateful beast hissed and leapt, claws extended, straight at my face! If I had not been so startled and jerked aside, he would have left a deep scratch on my cheek. As it was, he gouged my neck, then bounded down the branches and to the ground quicker than lightning and as graceful as, well, a cat! He left me clinging for dear life. You see, you are laughing, same as those horrid Rochesters."

"I am sorry, but I cannot help it! Had no one ever told you that a cat will never remain stuck in a tree, or anywhere for that matter?"

"I do know that now, thank you very much."

"Were you wounded severely?"

"I was too angry at the time to feel any pain. And a good thing since my prevailing thought was to chase that stupid cat and wring his neck. I scrambled down that tree almost as fast as he had, but not as gracefully, to be sure. My dress was torn in a half-dozen places, my knees scraped, and I lost one of my favorite hair ribbons. Mama was absolutely horrified. Oh, and I punched Donnie Rochester in the nose for laughing the hardest."

"The other Rochester escaped your wrath?"

"Only because he tended to the cat scratch. Used his own handkerchief, which I thought rather nice of him since it was then ruined with my blood. I suppose his future profession was within him because he smeared the scratch with the sap from an aloe plant. See, I still have a small scar here."

She arched her neck and peeled her shawl away, not consciously thinking of her actions until Darcy leaned closer and ran a fingertip gently across the faint silver line. Instant ripples of fire spread, and her cheeks heated. "Yes, I see the scar," he murmured, a wave of breath adding to the flaming eddies.

"I was fortunate, considering what could have been." Amazed her voice sounded almost normal, Lizzy drew the shawl over her shoulders and smiled up at Darcy. "That is the most exciting story I have to tell about this park, I am afraid. My other memories involve harmless playing, as those children are, picking flowers and pausing here for restful interludes while shopping."

"It was a marvelous story, another one I am sure our children will someday love to hear. Between our various exploits, we shall keep them entertained and probably give them bad ideas."

It was the first he had referenced their future children. The warmth infusing his voice triggered a series of delicate flutters within her belly, almost as if her body automatically responded to the vision of babies favorably.

"It is not fair that so far the stories are of my past mishaps. You allude to a reckless youth, which I find difficult to fathom. I want to hear more of your childhood, William."

"You will, once at Pemberley. I daresay we have much more to cover while dwelling in your country. I am swiftly gathering that you were incorrigible."

"I did have my moments but have outgrown my reckless ways. For the most part." She smiled impishly, Darcy laughing and shaking his head.

"Before you feel the overwhelming urge to climb the elm again, I brought us to the park because I have something to give you."

"Something to further improve my mind?" She tapped the book balancing on his thigh.

"Not this time. I am replacing the copy from Netherfield's library, that one ruined when my cup of tea spilt onto it." Lizzy's brows rose. Darcy grimaced and diverted his eyes. "Miss Bingley...startled me while reading. She...bent over my shoulder unexpectedly. It was clumsy of me."

He trailed off, shrugging and turning away from Lizzy to place the book onto the bench space behind him. She noticed how his lips were pressed tightly together and how the creases between his thick brows had deepened. Those clues of his anger, along with the hard edge to his voice, negated his effort to wave off the tea accident as nothing of significance. Obviously Caroline Bingley had done more than merely sneak up on him unawares. Lizzy was quite confident that Mr. Darcy did not rattle that easily.

What could Miss Bingley have done to anger him so? A scathing remark about me? While that was entirely plausible, it did not fit with his explanation for this incident.

Abruptly, a vision seared through Lizzy's mind: Caroline leaning too close, her generously endowed bust brushing his arm as she murmured provocatively.

Did Caroline Bingley make some sort of intimate advance toward my fiancé? It was effortless to imagine the scene, since she had witnessed Caroline employing her seductive arts to ensnare Mr. Darcy on numerous occasions.

Those had occurred over a year ago, and at that time, Lizzy felt nothing but amusement when observing Caroline's subtle maneuvers. What Mr. Darcy had honestly thought of Miss Bingley, Lizzy never tried to ascertain. Based on his indifference, if she had given the idea undue consideration, she would have guessed he was unmoved by Caroline's beauty or charms. Then again, Lizzy had not suspected his strong regard for her, so who was she to claim insight into his sentiments toward Caroline? Whatever his inner musings might have been, or even if he had given Caroline Bingley a hint he might be persuaded, a sensible woman would accept that the coquettish games not successful after years of use would be utterly pointless once he was engaged to another.

In these past days, with not one but two Bennets engaged to Netherfield men, Lizzy and Jane had braced for an escalation of Caroline's rudeness and verbal harangues. Instead, she was surprising polite, even to the point of nauseating sycophancy. The sisters tolerated her, jesting when alone at home, and not once had Lizzy wondered what transpired when they were not around.

Had Caroline decided to increase her provocative advances and sickening flattery, hoping to turn Mr. Darcy away from the unworthy country chit? And how will Mr. Darcy respond to such invitations, from Caroline or any other woman?

Lizzy experienced intense waves of fury, jealousy, and humiliation. Physically ill from the wild emotions surging inside, she was unaware of him speaking until he firmly lifted her chin.

"Are you feeling unwell, Elizabeth? You are pale and trembling. I can run for some water."

"No, no. I am fine. Sorry. It is a bit warmer today than I thought, and this shawl is thick. I will be fine." She slipped the shawl down and pulled her fan from within her reticule. She made a show of fanning herself—it did help to ease the fire of her emotions—and smiled brightly up at Darcy's concerned face.

His eyes were scrunched, brows knotted, and jaw clenched tight enough to make the muscles twitch. The whole picture was one of near panic. Persistent niggles of jealousy ate at her, but his devotion was reassuring.

"I am fine, truly." She patted his hand, only then realizing that he held a small box. "Oh! Is this what you have for me?"

"Yes, but it can wait if you need refreshment—"

Lizzy impulsively planted a short kiss to his lips, surprising both of them. "I am fine," she repeated, a bit huskily, "and will be even better after a present."

"As you wish." He cleared his throat and stared downward at her left hand where it covered the box in his right. "I have been yearning to give this to you for days now. I was forced to wait until it was ready, and I planned to secure time alone with you later tonight. Our surprise encounter is, as I said earlier, fortuitous. I shall no longer feel a sense of something missing. And it is probably for the best we are in a public place."

He muttered the last sentence under his breath. Lizzy suspected it was a thought spoken aloud, and smiled when he again cleared his throat before raising his eyes to her face. All traces of concern vanished, replaced with tender love and a sliver of embarrassment.

"Maintaining decorum when near you is...trying at best...and nigh impossible upon occasion. I am fairly certain this will be one of those occasions."

Before Lizzy could think how to respond to such an admission, Darcy snapped open the box.

"William!" Lizzy gasped, her free hand covering lips parted in wonderment. Nestled amid a cushion of velvet was a narrow ring of gold with seven gemstones in a perfect row. Each stone was brilliantly polished and set into the band with an intricately woven design of gold.

Darcy slipped the ring onto her finger. "Elizabeth, it is important to me that you wear a tangible symbol of our engagement as a reminder of my promises to you. First is the promise to grow closer during our season of courtship. Second is the promise of my commitment to stand with you before our families and God on

November twenty-eight, at which time I promise another ring will be given to symbolize my commitment for eternity. This betrothal ring is not the one I most desire to place on your finger, and I will say no more on that for now, however, as soon as I saw this in Mr. Bijoux's jewelry case, I knew it was a splendid alternative."

"It is stunning, William. I cannot imagine another to surpass it."

"I am pleased you like it."

"Like it? No, I love it! Never have I seen a ring to compare, and all these stones—"

"It is a new design in jewelry fashion by Parisian jeweler François Mellerio. Normally I pay scant attention to such things, but this one did pique my interest, probably because I was thinking of you. See, the stones are chosen to spell a message."

He touched each one as he explained, "Diamond, emerald, amethyst, ruby, another emerald, sapphire, and topaz." He gazed directly into her eyes, voice rough and each word enunciated meaningfully. "DEAREST. To me, dearest Elizabeth, you are everything that the word encompasses: precious, beloved, cherished, valued, highly regarded and respected, and so much more. I…I do not wish to overwhelm or…frighten you with my fervor. I do, however, believe it necessary to reveal the earnestness of my convictions."

"I am not sure what to say," Lizzy ventured after a long pause. A tiny smile lifted the corner of her lips. "Strangely, you, the man with the taciturn reputation and claims to not converse easily, have turned out to be the one in this relationship better skilled at expressing emotions verbally."

"I am practicing."

His ready quip broadened Lizzy's smile. "I daresay the exercise has been effective. At times almost too effective." She tightened the grip on his fingers when he tensed at her words. "Thank you, William, for the ring and for being honest. Understand that I am not frightened by your feelings for me, nor am I overwhelmed, precisely. It is just…" Frustrated, she exhaled and shook her head. "See what I mean? You have become the eloquent one while I stutter and blunder my words!"

"Please, Elizabeth. You have no need to worry over trying to explain. I do understand, truly. Much has happened, and quickly from your perspective. I have the advantage of age lending maturity, I suppose, but primarily the difference is that my love for you is of long standing. Despite all that passed between us before, my affection continued unabated and grew. Your love for me is a newer development. I denied my feelings for you for months, so I can appreciate the strangeness of embracing the emotions and then learning how best to reveal them."

He glanced down at her hand, tracing the jewels on the ring encircling her finger and emitting a sound somewhere between a laugh and a sigh. "Considering how terribly I initially expressed my love for you, I cannot claim any expertise or be dismayed if you struggle. In time, I am confident that we will both improve in our eloquence. Now"—he patted her hand, smiled brightly, and stood to his feet, pulling her with him—"we have a village to explore and a short time left for you to tell me of all the ways you managed to get into trouble. I suspect it may well require more than one day!"

ဆ

Caroline Bingley stood before the tall mirror, turning side to side as she subjectively examined herself from head to toe. Her gown was a true work of art and the latest fashion, naturally. The underdress was sheer silk of iridescent cream, overlaid by a netted-lace sheath robe of silver, belted and edged in midnight-blue gilt braid intricately woven into a scalloped design. Sewn to her precise measurements, the garment fit her figure like a glove. Rather scandalously so, considering how the braided bodice cupped her bounteous breasts and dipped into an angle pointing to the deep valley in between. The gossamer skirt intentionally draped so as to cling to her shapely legs and curve above her slender ankles. Exquisitely tailored, and outrageously priced, it was a gown intended for an exclusive Society event. Caroline was certain her modiste would die a thousand deaths if she learned her masterpiece was unveiled at a private dinner in the inconsequential town of Meryton.

Fortunate for Caroline, none of the people coming to dinner on this night were likely to report her fashion infraction. Besides, if wearing the gown accomplished the desired outcome, Caroline would be able to afford dozens of expensive ensembles on a monthly basis, and there was not a modiste in the world who would turn her nose up at that!

For good measure, Caroline adjusted the sleeves to show a bit more of her smooth shoulders and added another drop of perfume to the crevice between her breasts, pausing to plump each one to maximum effect. What it was about a woman's bosom that made men go crazy she truly could not fathom. But it was a fact they did, and since she had caught Mr. Darcy's gaze drop to her décolletage upon occasion, it was sensible to emphasize what she knew to be one of her prime assets. Each of the items she wore tonight, from embroidered slippers to jeweled hairpiece, were chosen to accent her best features or camouflage her few flaws.

Her mission to entice Mr. Darcy away from Miss Elizabeth was proceeding. Not as swiftly as hoped, she cringed to admit. Opportunities to strike were limited, since catching him alone had proven to be nigh on impossible. To her chagrin, he passed most of his time away from Netherfield in the company of *that woman*. The handful of hours when the Bennet sisters were with the gentlemen at Netherfield, Caroline grit her teeth and forced polite words between her lips, hoping to persuade him by the contrast of her charm and refinement to theirs.

Mr. Darcy had forever been a man difficult to read, and she might have feared she was failing if not for his response on those fortunate encounters when she was able to attack—such as the incident in the library with Mr. Darcy so flustered by her close

125

proximity and pressure of supple breast on his arm that he spilled his tea all over the book he was reading.

Caroline laughed aloud at the remembered flush that had spread over his cheeks, how he had avoided her eyes, and hastily vacated the room. Indeed, like all men, Mr. Darcy was a slave to passions—hence the decision to bombard with her entire physical and sensual arsenal tonight. Elizabeth Bennet was no match for Caroline Bingley, of that she was certain.

Giving a final tug to her bodice, she headed downstairs to welcome their guests. As luck would have it, her prey was alone in the front parlor when she entered. He stood by a wide window, tall and stately, dressed impeccably as always, and gazed placidly onto the front avenue. Always she had admired his physical attractiveness and pronounced masculinity, yet it was his arrogance and self-possession that appealed to her more than the rest. The latter was evident in the way he glanced her direction, then after a flash of widened eyes and rapid second glance, resumed his calm contemplation of the graveled drive. His stiffened spine and tense jaw revealed he was not unaffected, however.

Hiding her satisfied smile, Caroline glided across the room and sidled as close to him as decency allowed. "Is there something of riveting interest, Mr. Darcy? Or are you merely enjoying the sunset?"

"It is a colorful sunset, although I would prefer it not transpire so early. Shadowy roads are treacherous."

"Your concern is commendable if unnecessary. Our guests have passed their entire lives within a radius of ten, twenty miles at the most, so I am sure the roads are familiar to them. If Miss Elizabeth can walk across open, muddy fields without mishap or losing her way, a carriage ride should contain no hazards."

Out of the corner of her eye, she saw him press his lips tightly together, but he said nothing. Hopefully her subtle jibes brought to mind how uncultured the residents were, particularly his betrothed with her ill-bred behavior. Letting the image of a mud-splattered, sun-browned, and wind-swept Elizabeth Bennet linger, and compare with

126

her refined beauty, Caroline turned until facing him. Again he glanced down at her, Caroline smiling seductively and catching his eyes before he looked back out the window.

"How well do you know the people Charles invited to dinner? I confess I cannot recall them at all, despite Charles assuring me they came to the ball last year. Frankly, I am divinely grateful to have largely forgotten that night of what passes for genteel society in Hertfordshire. Nevertheless, I have promised Charles, and you, Mr. Darcy"—she laid one hand onto his forearm—"to be hospitable to the friends of the Bennets, so I will be the perfect hostess. I even wore my newest gown for the occasion"—she slid her free hand provocatively along her torso—"a risk on my part since it is unlikely they will appreciate the nuances of high fashion."

"Your suspicions are undoubtedly correct, Miss Bingley. I fear wearing that ensemble will be a wasted effort." He walked away from the window, speaking in the same dry tone, "Mr. Denbigh is a barrister and a fine billiard player. We met at the Club when staying here last year, and then again yesterday. Pleasant gentleman, well read and educated. I have not met Mrs. Denbigh, so cannot say whether she is versed in modern fashion or not. Mr. Denniston owns a modest estate not far from Longbourn, and he is betrothed to Miss Desiree Stedman, a longtime friend to Miss Bennet and Miss Elizabeth. I have met both on several occasions lately. He is a gentleman, and Miss Stedman is sweet, although remarkably shy. In that respect, she reminds me of Georgiana."

Only half listening to his commentary on their guests, who she cared not one iota about, Caroline watched him walk to the sidebar and pour a glass of wine. Outwardly there were no signs of wound nerves, so she could only hope that his need to imbibe was due to her. Intent on testing the theory, she left the window, drifting toward him in a leisurely manner. Darcy, she noted, flicked his eyes her direction without turning his head—not the appreciative stare she would have preferred, but he also did not move away from the sidebar.

"I am surprised you do not remember Sir Giles Osteler. He is a baronet, unmarried, wealthy, and has a fine estate, Tawneywood, to the north near Boddenham. Excellent reasons for him to capture your interest, Miss Bingley. I knew him at Cambridge, ironically, although it never occurred to me that he might be on friendly terms with Sir William Lucas. Accompanying Sir Giles will be his sister, Miss Ada Osteler, who is, I understand, scheduled for her Court presentation this next year. Therefore, in my estimation, these two are likely the *only* ones here tonight to appreciate your choice of clothing."

"I suppose it is true that Jane and Eliza are sadly *démodé,* not being able to afford the best fashion magazines upon first issuance. Poor dears. Then to be at the mercy of a village seamstress and the limited number of merchants available in Meryton. I have checked for myself, and it is appalling the dearth of choices in fabrics and lace!"

"I suspect Miss Bennet and Miss Elizabeth are not limited by lacking knowledge or choices, but rather dress in apparel that is demure and practical as a reflection of their characters."

"There is a place for practicality, I suppose, but demure is not an attribute most women of Society find advantageous. Clearly modesty or plainness of dress is not desired by gentlemen, since they are the ones who establish the fashion styles for females."

"I cannot argue your logic, Miss Bingley. However, I am not now nor have I ever been a typical example of what most gentlemen desire from the ladies of Society. Fashion trends I do not follow, and too often what I see is ridiculous or bordering on tasteless."

A hard edge had entered his otherwise bland tone, and not once had he looked away from her eyes, even though she was standing inches away from him with her bosom generously on display. It was disconcerting. Not at all the reaction she expected. His words were ridiculous, and it impossible to believe he truly felt, since it was contrary to what was normal. The perplexing messages rendered her unable to formulate a response. Whether that was a good or bad thing, she never knew, because at that second Charles rushed into the room.

"So sorry I am late! I hope no one is here...Oh not yet, I see. Good...Caroline! What in God's name are you wearing? I can see your legs and your chest is practically spilling...Forgive me, Darcy, that was too personal..."

"No, no. Lecture away as you deem it necessary."

Caroline distinctly detected amusement in Darcy's voice as he walked toward Charles, adding to her irritation. "Charles, do not be a prig." She tossed her head and sighed in exasperation. "You may not attend to the dictates of fashion, but I do. Being a proper lady of a fine house requires looking one's best, especially when functioning as the hostess for a dinner party. You might want to remember this in regards to who you have chosen to be Mrs. Bingley."

"My Jane always looks perfect and stays properly covered in the process. Can you at least add a fichu? I suppose there is no time for you to change—"

"There is no reason for me to do either. As I was attempting to explain to Mr. Darcy, fashion is—"

"Yes, I have heard all the arguments." Charles waved his hand, voice testy. "A daringly dressed lady is fine under certain circumstances, I will admit. Personally, I prefer not to see so much of my own sister, but I am sure Sir Giles will be pleased."

Caroline opened her mouth to refute any interest in the baronet and add on a bold declaration that she had her mind set on a particular gentleman, but the chime of the doorbell forestalled. Minutes later, the foyer was filled with people, and in Caroline's estimation, the evening slide further downhill from there.

Mr. and Mrs. Denbigh were decent enough, even moderately entertaining and surprisingly versed on the theatre and other aspects of London society. Yet neither of them paid Caroline much attention. Not that she cared for the regard of a lowly barrister or his wife; however, the lack disclosed their dismal understanding of proper social grace, augmenting her annoyance.

Mr. Denniston was a quiet man, perhaps not as taciturn as Mr. Darcy, but close. When he spoke, it was with deliberation, his tone dull and ponderous. Caroline nearly fell asleep each time he opened his mouth and struggled against the inclination to ignore him completely only because Mr. Darcy appeared to respect his conversation. All the gentlemen did, in fact, to Caroline's bafflement. On top of that, Elizabeth Bennet, of all the women in the room, actively partook of the concourse between the gentlemen. Whether Eliza truly knew what they were saying and contributed intelligently, Caroline could not tell, although the fact that they replied seriously in turn indicated she did. Worse yet was the proud expression on Mr. Darcy's face whenever Elizabeth spoke. Caroline resisted grimacing or rolling her eyes with effort.

Miss Stedman and Miss Osteler were reserved creatures on the whole. They spoke haltingly, primarily with the women in the room, and said little to Caroline. Both their mouths dropped upon laying eyes on Caroline, as she anticipated and rather enjoyed, and thereafter they were intimidated, as Caroline also relished. Of all the women present, only Miss Osteler was gowned in anything close to what Caroline would consider the latest fashion. Her gown was simple and modest, as seemed to be the standard amongst the pitiable country folk, but of a quality taffeta well sewn with beautiful embroidery along the hemline. Guessing as to the cost of even that basic of a garment, and the jewelry pieces and high-caliber accessories, affirmed Mr. Darcy's assessment of Sir Giles Osteler's wealth.

Mr. Darcy's other prophecy proved true as well. Sir Giles took one look at Caroline Bingley and his eyes literally bulged! As soon as the formal introductions were made, he glued himself to her side. Caroline's emotions ran the gamut from egotistical pleasure at his adulation to nausea-inducing dismay when Mr. Darcy did not seem to notice. The latter gentleman's focus was entirely upon Elizabeth, increasing Caroline's stomachache.

Then, at one point, she noticed Mr. Darcy flick a rapid glance toward Sir Giles, who was babbling something to her while his eyes were firmly locked upon her décolletage, followed by a harsh glower and tight press of his lips. While it was entirely possible the reaction was not borne of jealousy, Caroline refused to accept it was sparked by any other emotion.

Hatching a new plan, Caroline smiled winsomely at the baronet and offered her hand for a glancing kiss. Sir Giles was handsome, Caroline admitted upon closer inspection, and his manners were impeccable. Under different circumstances she might have been interested in considering him a suitor. But for this evening, his purpose was specific: to make Mr. Darcy jealous.

Flirting, for Caroline, was as easy as breathing. With no other women vying for the baronet's favor, she was free to monopolize. Sir Giles was smitten within minutes, Caroline deftly playing the game all through the evening. There were the occasional disapproving glares from Charles, and indecipherable glances from Mr. Darcy, but she had no clue if her ploy was having a lasting impression. It was maddening!

The after-dinner hour with the ladies in the parlor was another low point to the evening. Caroline's hopes to embarrass the Bennet women and plant seeds of self-doubt with disparaging comments never seemed to have the desired effect. Elizabeth inevitably laughed, as if Caroline's jibe was meant as a joke, or nimbly redirected the conversation. Once or twice a strained silence fell, Caroline noting a troubled flicker cross Elizabeth's brow, but it passed too swiftly for assurance as to the lasting impact. It was enough to lift Caroline's sagging spirits and inspire more subtle attacks, until, that is, Miss Stedman noticed the ring on Elizabeth's finger. Cheeks rosy and eyes shining, Elizabeth recounted how Mr. Darcy had given the ring as a symbol of his affection and promise, the ladies oohing and ahing disgustingly. Caroline honesty thought she would retch.

The final insult came after the guests had left. Caroline turned to Mr. Darcy, who was staring wistfully at the closed door, and requested he escort her upstairs to her room. She wanted to scream when Charles jumped in, before Darcy looked away from the door, and offered his arm. The message was crystal clear, Caroline additionally shocked when her normally polite, meek brother reproached, "I will escort you, Caroline. I believe Mr. Darcy has had enough of you for one night. Come along, Caroline."

ॐ

Darcy waited with a glass of brandy in each hand, thrusting one at Bingley the moment he entered the library. "No need to say a word, Bingley. Take a big swallow and forget the whole thing."

Bingley smiled faintly at Darcy's light tone and did take a big swallow of the brandy, but then shook his head. "I must apologize for Caroline, Darcy. No, please, I must." He dropped into a plush chair with a groan. "She vexes me no end! But what am I to do? She is my sister, and as much as I hate her ridiculous attitude, I can appreciate where she is coming from. She is wrong, but I am trying to be patient and understand. Is this weak or foolish of me?"

"No, not entirely," Darcy agreed, albeit with hesitation and a wince. "I am painfully aware that Caroline's opinions are precisely as mine were not so long ago, and that you tolerate her expressing them, in part, out of deference to me."

It was Bingley's turn to wince. "That is not entirely true and you know it, Darcy. Never have you been as…mean spirited, God forgive me, as Caroline can be. You were restrained. She is openly vocal."

"If you recall honestly, my friend, I was not always restrained. Perhaps not as mean spirited, but I made no secret of my aversion to society here, or the Bennet family."

"That was a year ago, Darcy, and we both know why you reacted so strongly. Quit torturing yourself over the past."

Darcy smiled fondly at his friend. "Charles, can I say, without sounding condescending, that I am impressed by your…*maturity*, for lack of a better term?"

"As I see it, we have both been changed, in ways we may not yet fully understand, by events this past year."

Reclining into the chair beside Bingley, Darcy humorously raised his brows and grinned. "Touched by love? Rather cliché, is it not?"

"Indeed, it is. And best kept our secret." Bingley lifted his glass, Darcy toasting as they both laughed. Then Bingley grew serious. "I cannot honestly say I am thankful for all that happened…with Jane. Yet it did afford me an opportunity to mature, as you say, and learn to think for myself. I do believe I will be a better husband because of it." He shrugged. "I suppose I owe you thanks, Darcy, although I cannot go that far."

"If you thanked me I would question your sanity." Darcy swirled the amber liquid, his tone as serious. "I am unable to completely embrace thankfulness for the struggle and torment of this past year, Bingley. I know I am also a better man because of it, yet I would not willingly walk through the valley again."

"Best we put the past behind us, except for remembering the lessons, and face the future with happy hearts and hope."

"I can drink to that."

They sipped in contented silence for a bit, each man staring at the fire and lost in their thoughts.

For Darcy, those thoughts were centered on Elizabeth. He missed her, yet a part of him loved the night. Alone, mentally replaying every word and glance and stolen touch, he could allow his musings to drift. Sometimes they drifted into future imaginings, times when they would be able to freely express their love in highly intimate ways, but also in the simple joys of warm embraces or entwined hands. Other times, his private musings were for the present, listing all the topics he wanted to discuss so as to increase their bond, and planning a host of special moments to ensure their courtship was eternally memorable. It was amazingly easy for him to relax when thinking about Elizabeth, so much so that he nearly dropped his glass when Bingley's voice broke into his reverie.

"My hope has been that Caroline release her prejudices. I thought she would, at least to a large degree, the more she was around

Jane and saw her sweet nature and pure heart. Should not our love be so evident that, if for no other reason than a sisterly desire for my happiness, she would accept it?"

Darcy did not answer immediately. The subject of Caroline's behavior was uncomfortable for several reasons. Yet clearly Charles sought the discussion, so after another sip of brandy and deep inhale, Darcy answered, "Indeed it should. I suspect if it were only you and Miss Bennet, Caroline's attitude would be softening. Perhaps even resigned and happy for you by now."

"It is not right, Darcy. She has absolutely no business including you and Miss Elizabeth in her harangues! It is wrong for her to speak to me as she does, but I am her brother. While I know she is overstepping and being utterly rude, I practice tolerance because we are family. My choices are indeed mine to make, but they do affect her, so I am doing my best to maintain my calm. You are an entirely different matter, however. I am mortified by her behavior, and I confess rather flummoxed over how to deal with her."

"Caroline is playing a desperate game she is doomed to lose. I...mean no offense, Bingley"—Darcy shifted in his chair, eyes darting to his friend then back to the fire—"but I have never felt any attraction for your sister. I have been careful to never wittingly give her cause to expect more from me than friendship."

"Has *this* been your concern? That I would blame *you* for her actions because I believed you encouraged her? Lord! No!" Bingley scooted to the edge of his seat, forcing Darcy to meet his eyes. "My astoundment this past week is the result of incomprehension as to why she was so annoyed with *your* choice! Me choosing Jane, I could understand, as I said. But you? It made no sense to me precisely *because* it has been abundantly obvious from the first day you met Caroline that she did not interest you in that way! Hell, half the time you are barely civil to her! Not that I blame you, trust me."

Darcy was unable to halt the smile Bingley's words elicited. "Thank you, Charles. I did need to hear your reassurance. Mind you, I do not dislike Caroline, and it is my pleasure to welcome her as your

134

sister, as I do Mr. and Mrs. Hurst. I also cannot say I was wholly unaware of Caroline's interest, although until this past week I underestimated the extent. I feared I blundered in some way, or my hospitality was interpreted as personal."

Bingley was shaking his head. "Indeed not! If Caroline interpreted thusly, it was her own misguided purposes, and not in any way your fault. In fact, you are masterful at deflecting undesirable advances from women, having been subjected to it for so long."

Bingley freshened his brandy and then leaned to pour more for Darcy. "Whatever craziness is going on in my sister's head, we both know it will lead to nothing. Two questions remain: How far she will go? And how long I can be patient with her nonsense?"

Honestly, Darcy did not know how to answer either question. Until seeing her in that dress tonight, and then her shameless display with Sir Giles, Darcy had not been worried. Annoyed, yes. But it had never entered his mind that the controlled, cool Caroline Bingley would cross a serious line. Just how desperate was she to have him? His mind cringed at the possibilities.

As for Bingley dealing with Caroline, that opened up a host of variables.

"I can take care of myself, Charles, and can handle Caroline. She is not the first woman of my acquaintance to overstep," he asserted, the claim true. "She is your family, so naturally you desire accord for the future. This is proper and justified—to a degree."

Bingley frowned, his eyes questioning. Darcy did not move from his relaxed repose in the chair, but he turned the full force of his penetrating stare and commanding demeanor toward his young friend. "Never forget, not for a second, that your first and primary responsibility is to your wife. A formal betrothal is as binding as the final vows. Miss Bennet is the only one you completely owe your allegiance to. We pray our choices will never come to a disagreement or separation, but just as I had to take a stand with Lady Catherine, so too must you—if it comes to that."

They stared at each other in silence, Bingley finally nodding once. "Thank you, Darcy. You have given me much to meditate upon."

Darcy's reply was to swallow the last of his brandy, setting the glass onto the table with a clink, and then standing. "Now, I am off to bed. Pleasant dreams of my Elizabeth await." He clapped Bingley on the shoulder, exiting the room whistling softly.

CHAPTER SIX
Warmth of Autumn

*D*arcy woke the next morning wholly rejuvenated. Forever a person who slept deeply, if typically no more than six or seven hours at a stretch, Darcy had rarely been plagued with insomnia or restlessness. Therefore, waking invigorated was not uncommon. Lately, however, his slumber had taken on a new dimension. Sleep was no longer merely an empty span of time his body required to function. It had become a wonderful interlude, blissfully replete with dreams of Elizabeth.

A good number of those dreams were erotic, and while left with the physical ache of unfulfilled sexual desire, his heart and soul were buoyed. In a few weeks, they would be husband and wife, no longer with any barriers between them. The yearning to be with Elizabeth was overwhelming at times, and there were moments when the weeks ahead felt an eternity. Yet he knew these days were precious and that they would speed by, so he welcomed the dreams of loving Elizabeth as a means to prepare himself for the reality. *Practice sessions*, as he jokingly referred to them.

Not all of his dreams revolved around marital intimacy, however. More often they consisted of rehashed conversations and moments from their days together. Others were jumbled image collages that were illogical, but lovely nevertheless. Expressly delightful were dreams pointing to future possibilities, such as them surrounded by hordes of children while walking across the gardens and lawns of Pemberley. The sweetness of these placid, soothing dreams was surprisingly powerful and went a long way in easing the urgency instigated by the sensual dreams.

There was a beautiful balance to his dreams, leaving him renewed and eager for the day.

Darcy's valet, Samuel, assisted him in a truncated toilette. No need to shave or bathe thoroughly nor don a fine suit. Instead, he dressed quickly in one of his numerous casual ensembles designed specifically for riding his horse.

It had been over a week since he and Parsifal had embarked on one of their daring, wild races. Few activities delivered the freedom and sense of adventure as thoroughly as when bent low on the back of his stallion. Reins held loose in his hands, he and the powerful animal flying as one across an open meadow, leaping over or dodging around the obstacles in their path. Since a young boy, Darcy turned to his horses as the preferred outlet for his bottled energy, frustrations, grief, or merely the need to disengage. Physical exertion in various forms— fencing, hunting, swimming—were an essential aspect of Darcy's life, but none offered the complete gratifying experience as riding his horse.

Whistling, he bounded down the stairs and entered the empty dining room. The servants were setting up the pots of coffee and boiling water for tea, half of the additives not yet on the table. The Netherfield butler apologized, but Darcy waved it away, smiling as he assured the man he was early and would be more than content with coffee and toast.

Minutes later, both items were provided, and Darcy walked onto the rear terrace. Standing by the railing, he ate the raspberry jam–smeared toast and drank the hot coffee, taking his time with it despite his fervor to be riding, because the morning was simply too beautiful not to savor. The brisk air, hint of a breeze, lush smells of earth and foliage, and filtered beams of the rising sun casting shadows and illumination on the array of autumn colors augmented the sensations of health and joy pulsing through his body. Fresh from sleep and vivid dreams, and with the anticipation of another remarkable day with the woman he loved, Darcy almost felt as if he could fly. Not literally—although there had been a handful of odd moments when he swore his feet did not touch the ground—but in the sense that his spirit felt alive and invincible.

As a man noted by everyone, including himself, to be far too serious and somber, the sensations were surprisingly wonderful. Not for the first time, he recognized how akin his love for Elizabeth was to the euphoria experienced while racing his horse. Of course, with Elizabeth the euphoria was constant and penetrated into the marrow of his bones.

Tossing the last edge of toast onto the grass, Darcy's smile widened as three blue jays dove to the ground and commenced a heated battle over the delicacy. Indeed, even common acts of nature were now a source of amusement and joy. Shaking his head at the folly but still smiling, he headed toward the stable compound.

It was quiet inside the brick structure, or relatively so. The horses nickered and neighed softly, some munching hay and oats or shuffling lazily inside their stalls. Intermittent dull clanks drifted from the smithy to mix with the sporadic sharp ring of metal tools. Hushed conversation and laughter came from a trio of grooms sitting on a bench drinking coffee, none of whom noticed Darcy enter. Another groom glanced up from the bridle he was repairing, inclined his head respectfully, and then went back to his task without saying a word.

Within days of his first stay at Netherfield the year prior, the stable workmen learned Mr. Darcy was supremely particular when it came to the care and handling of his horse. Typically, he preferred to groom and saddle Parsifal himself, today no exception, so being ignored suited him just fine.

Stealthily, he walked directly to a large enclosure in the back where his faithful mount waited. It had unconsciously become a sort of game, Darcy sneaking as silently as possible, trying in vain to surprise. Parsifal, as always, poked his head over the wooden gate long before his master was visible, his welcoming nicker a combination of *Happy to see you!* and *It's about time you came!*

"Good morning, Parsifal," Darcy murmured, one hand stroking the horse's neck while the other offered a sugar cube confiscated from the breakfast room. "Plenty rested?"

Parsifal flicked his ears and released a snort. Darcy laughed, correctly interpreting the sarcastic *Of course I am.* Parsifal butted his nose against Darcy's shirt-no-waistcoat-covered chest, and then snagged the lapel of his plain jacket between his teeth, tugging once.

"Yes," Darcy answered, "we are going to race today. No need to avoid mud puddles to keep me clean. Happy now?"

Lifting his head in an exact mimic of a nod and swishing his tail vigorously, Parsifal expressed his happiness at the idea. The firm nudge into the locked gate was quite clear too, Darcy soothing him with another sugar cube and rub between the ears. "Be patient. Give me a minute to gather your gear."

Despite their mutual enthusiasm to run, Darcy took his time saddling Parsifal, the horse not minding the delay too much. The occasional jab with his nose or pawing leg revealed his impatience, yet the familiar routine was an enjoyable interlude for man and beast. For Darcy, raised with horses since birth, it was an ingrained necessity to run his hands over his mount's body, testing and examining for anything amiss, while simultaneously strengthening the bond established when Parsifal was a foal.

The last buckle was being cinched when Darcy heard voices. Paying minimal heed, his ears perked at the pitched tone of a female, and then he swore when identifying Caroline Bingley.

"Mr. Darcy! I am in luck. I hoped you had not departed as yet. Gorgeous morning for a ride, is it not?"

"It is indeed, Miss Bingley. If I may suggest, the trails through the east wood are wide, easy to traverse, and provide adequate shade." He tugged on Parsifal's reins, the horse all too happy to comply, but Caroline stepped directly into their path.

"Those paths are lovely; however, I am in the mood for a faster pace."

"The avenue skirting the wood is even, as is the track encircling the pond. Perfect for a moderate speed, yet safe."

"I prefer a bit of danger…when riding. Dare I challenge you to a race, Mr. Darcy?"

Parsifal tossed his head, apparently in agreement with his rider on the ridiculousness of *that* notion. Unavoidably smirking, Darcy said, "It would be a pointless endeavor to do so. Apollonia is a fine mare, but no match for Parsifal."

"Perhaps," Caroline countered, moving closer, "although until the end, nothing is certain. Besides, it is the race itself that thrills and heats the blood. Even if I lose the sprint, I will catch you in the end, Mr. Darcy."

Belatedly, Darcy realized that she was misinterpreting his discourse as an invitation to ride with him, and peppering her response with personal messages. Steeling his facial muscles, he moved to the right, placing Parsifal nearer to Caroline.

"Therein lies the problem, Miss Bingley. I have no desire to engage in a race with you today, or any other day for that matter. If you tried, I can assure we would not be caught." Pausing, he leaned forward, training his stony eyes on hers. "Take my suggestion. Stay to the safe pathways, where you will not run the risk of being hurt."

As if on command, Parsifal emitted a harsh blow out his nose and stomped his front hoof inches from Caroline's feet. She yelped and jumped aside, Parsifal accepting her submission and stepping past her. Darcy said nothing else nor did he look back. The second they were outside the stable, he swung into the saddle, one brush of a booted-heel the only signal Parsifal needed. Within minutes, they had cleared the compound and swiftly left the orderly areas of Netherfield Park behind them.

They ran hard for a good mile, during which Darcy steamed at the persistent advances from Caroline Bingley. He was not so foolish as to expect her to admit defeat so easily. Worst of all, her ploy that morning hinted at a determination greater than suspected, even after the scandalizing fashion exhibition the night before. In all his years of knowing her, never had she risen so early in the morning. Not to ride a horse—an activity she was not overly keen on in the first place—or for anything else.

And how had she known he was awake and heading to the stables? He had not mentioned his agenda the night before, except to Elizabeth, but Caroline had sat at the far end of the dinner table. Either she was talented at lip reading or a servant was spying. He rather doubted the first, and the latter, while not shocking, was disconcerting. Taken altogether, it increased his apprehension that a confrontation was inevitable.

Eventually the exhilaration of cool air whipping his face, the potency of flexing muscles charging over the earth, and profound unity with his mount as they moved together overcame his unrest. Caroline was forgotten. Anything troubling was forgotten. There was only the connection with Parsifal, their power and control synchronized as the terrain rushed by, hooves pounding a rhythmic beat in time with Darcy's heart.

They stopped to rest in a hidden dell, where a trickling stream formed a tiny pond. Discovered accidentally while here the previous autumn, it was a tranquil place to catch their breaths, quench their thirsts, and snack from the wild berry vines and two apple trees growing near the water. Darcy was unsure who owned this land. There were no markings, no dwelling places visible, and no signs warning visitors away, so he did not worry over it. Besides, just beyond this valley parcel was the extensive meadow that was by far his favorite place in Hertfordshire to run with Parsifal.

Also discovered last year, the grassy field was flat and uninhabited, so great speeds could be attained. There were also a number of conveniently located rocks, cattle stiles, bushes, and the like that were excellent for jumping. Unlike the land near the secret dell, he knew who owned the meadow, or at least a portion of it. The property lines were imprecise, so he was not clear on exactly when the northern pastureland crossed into Netherfield Park acreage, but the locale was perfect for finishing the circuit of their vigorous race.

He and Parsifal had ridden over the meadow a dozen times, never once speculating where the green veldt was in relation to Longbourn until encountering Elizabeth one morning shortly after her stay with Jane at Netherfield.

To say he had been stunned to happen upon her was a massive understatement! Never had it remotely entered his mind, even knowing how fond she was of walking, that he would meet the woman already burrowed into his heart and invading his dreams, in ostensibly the middle of nowhere. One of the prime reasons he had embarked on that particular furious race was to seek oblivion from the torment of wanting her, when logic told him she was utterly wrong. Yet there she had been, standing on the rungs of a fence near a remote copse of willow trees, watching him. Even after he had skidded to a halt, he had expected it to be a conjured vision sure to disintegrate any second.

Then she had spoken—"Demons chasing you, Mr. Darcy, or do you have a death wish?"—startling him further, but also restoring a modicum of clarity—only the smallest sliver of clarity, because to this day he could not recall their brief conversation with accuracy. Parsifal's name was mentioned, Elizabeth adding to his amazement, and respect, by knowing the poem by von Eschenbach, where he had acquired his stallion's name. Then something ridiculous about reading German and accomplished women, and a vague impression of his sister's name in there somewhere. It truly was a jumble, since all he vividly remembered was wanting, more than life itself, to wrap her in his arms and kiss her until neither could breathe. Hell, if being honest, he envisioned far more than simply kissing her! His dream from the night before had meshed with the living, gloriously beautiful flesh in front of him, and he could not say how he had maintained any control over his body. A certain part of his body had painfully resisted his harshest discipline, a fact best not shared with his betrothed until long after they married. If at all. How his innocent love would respond to his admission of such beastly, ungentlemanly thoughts he did not want to know.

How many times after that embarrassing encounter did he ride by the willow copse and look for Elizabeth Bennet?

Every. Single. Time.

Glancing at the rise, where the trees stood near the rickety, wooden fence bordering Longbourn estate, became a reflexive action he did not consciously register. Until he saw no one there, and then the sensation of sadness, while swift, was intense.

Today was no exception.

He and Parsifal dashed at their typical breakneck speed, Darcy enveloped by the incredible fluidic movement of his mount. The world was a blur yet queerly sharp at the same time. Together, as if seeing from the same eyes, they distinguished dips in the land, every rock or moldering log or bush. The deer grazing off to the right were noted, as were the startled rabbits and squirrels, and the hawk circling something delicious on the ground. Everything checked and then dismissed unless recognizable as a hazard to avoid or an object to jump.

Approaching the willow copse, Darcy's attention was on the small herd of cattle up ahead, trying to determine which direction they were going to veer as he and Parsifal rode closer, when his eyes automatically swept to the left.

For a split second, he wondered if love truly had bewitched him to the degree where hallucinations of Elizabeth were invading his waking minutes! After all, the fuzzy figure could be anything or anyone when seen in a flash peripherally from a distance.

No, it is a person waving at me!

Heart pounding harder than Parsifal's hooves striking the turf, Darcy smoothly steered them into a wide, arcing turn. By the time they reached the fence where Elizabeth stood, her smile brilliant and eyes shining, Darcy had gotten over his astoundment and was silently thanking God and the saints in heaven for this wondrous coincidence.

He slowed Parsifal to a trot well before reaching the fence line. He needed the time to steady his breathing and master his overloaded faculties.

She was as ravishing as she had been during their encounter last year. More so, actually, because rather than appearing annoyed or uncomfortable, as she had then, today she was bursting with delight. Darcy did not think it possible for his heart to beat faster without failing utterly. Pleasure was written on her flushed face. She leaned forward from her precarious perch on the second rung from the top, her chest rising rapidly with each inhale. The combination revealed, even to his untrained and dubious eyes, the full scope of her love for him.

The reality hit him square in the chest. Yes, she had told him of her love. Yes, she had accepted his proposal. Yes, she had expressed her affection in numerous small gestures. This Elizabeth Bennet, however, was displaying her ardency blatantly and vehemently.

God! How is it possible to love someone so fiercely?

He ached from physical desire beyond what had assaulted him before. Elizabeth was staring at him boldly, her eyes scanning his body in a frank manner that was as arousing as it was extraordinary. As much as he thrilled at her appraisal, under the circumstances, it was vital to shove those fixations firmly aside. Focusing only on the awareness of her love was heady enough—accepting that she could yearn for him sexually was dangerous.

Their trot became a sedate walk, Darcy leading Parsifal directly toward Elizabeth. Without preamble, he leaned in, cradled her face with his right hand, and kissed her—just a tender press of closed lips, yet enough to ignite a fire inside his veins.

"Miss Elizabeth, what a delightful surprise. Come here often, do you?"

Caressing her cheek with gloved fingertips, Darcy bestowed a second kiss before she could answer. The feel of her hand pressing his tighter against her cheek and the slight parting of her lips nearly sent him over the edge. Literally. Maybe Parsifal sensed his master about to topple out of the saddle, or maybe he was bored of standing still. Whatever the instigation, his sudden shift and loud snort broke the spell.

Elizabeth jerked backward, and Darcy grabbed her arm before she tumbled off the fence. "Hold up there!" he shouted, the exclamation for Elizabeth and Parsifal. Yanking on the reins, Darcy squeezed his legs around the horse and leaned back while steadying Elizabeth at the same time, causing an odd dance to ensue. Both laughed at the absurdity, which only served to increase the shakiness.

Once assured of her stability, Darcy let go and walked his restless horse in a series of prancing circles. He was still laughing, but stopped when he saw her face.

"My apologies, Elizabeth. Did Parsifal frighten you?"

"A little, yes. All my attention was focused on you"—she flushed and glanced down for a second—"and I almost forgot you were on a horse. His commentary on the situation took me by surprise."

"He is quite opinionated, I fear. Especially when his purpose has been interrupted." Darcy pointed to the wandering cattle when Elizabeth cocked her head in question. "I do believe he was anticipating scattering the herd when I changed our course. In that case, his pique is directed at me, not you."

"Well, I do apologize to Parsifal for spoiling his fun, although I imagine yonder cows would thank me. I pray my interruption did not spoil your fun, Mr. Darcy?"

"Indeed not, Miss Elizabeth," he teased. "While stampeding cattle is tremendously satisfying, the pleasure of meeting you transcends. I cannot fathom a better way to end my ride than with you."

"What a pity, then, that you are on that side of the fence. We are doomed to be parted unless I climb over the fence. I have done it before—"

"Yes, I imagine you have," Darcy interjected, laughing.

"If you imagine it, then I suspect you know what I mean when I say it is not the most ladylike of ventures."

"Probably not, by some standards. I tend to think I would enjoy the spectacle, not the least because of the possibility of seeing a bit of your legs." He grinned at the rosiness that infused her face, and loved it even more when she tossed her head and made as if to climb higher, her expression arch. *Gods but she is a minx!* "Save your dignity, Elizabeth. My solution to the dilemma is expeditious and does not involve either of us resorting to improper behavior."

Wheeling Parsifal about, Darcy left her with mouth agape and eyes wide. Galloping full tilt a good clip, he whirled around, and with a shout and added jab with his heels, launched into a barreling rush straight at the fence. A glimpse at Elizabeth's pale face, as he and Parsifal leapt cleanly over the top rung, did send a sharp stab of regret into his heart. By the time they slowed and came about, exhilaration from their acrobatic feat and the sheer delight of seeing her standing feet away under the trees usurped any regret.

Until, that is, he dismounted.

"How could you *do that* without warning me? My heart stopped, I swear it did! You could have hit the rail or fallen off when he landed! Or what if he decided the fence was too tall and stopped? Off you would go, flying through the air and—You think this is funny?"

"Yes—that is, no, of course not, but, well, you are overreacting, Elizabeth. None of those things were likely to happen."

"How can you be so sure?"

He dropped Parsifal's reins, the stallion immediately wandering off to graze without a backward glance, and crossed to where Elizabeth stood. She was pale and trembling, but she had also fisted her hands at her hips and glared at him furiously. Her anxiety for his safety was rather touching, a warm glow spreading through his chest, and he tried not to grin. Obviously he was not showing an adequate amount of contrition because her scowl deepened.

Grasping her fists and pulling them up to his lips, he answered, "I am sure because Parsifal and I have jumped all sorts of obstacles, including fences, and many were taller than this one. In fact, we have jumped this fence before, a bit further south. My mistake for not giving due warning or elucidating my expertise as a horseman. Your concern warms my heart, but there is no need to fret over my safety on a horse, trust me."

"Anyone can have an accident, Mr. Darcy, and I would prefer it not be my fiancé weeks before our wedding," she scolded. "I shan't argue your skill as a horseman. That is evident even to my untrained eye. Just try to show a bit of restraint, please? For me?"

"I promise to be cautious. Or at the least not to frighten with my exploits while you are watching."

"That is not the same thing, sir!"

"No, I suppose not," Darcy agreed, grinning. Then he kissed her forehead. "You really must trust me, Elizabeth. I can handle Parsifal, and he is my friend so would never do anything foolish to jeopardize my safety. At the risk of annoying you with my arrogant boasting, if there is one special talent I possess, it is as a horseman. My grandfather said it was in my blood."

He gently steered her to the shade of the willows, his voice pitched low and soothing. She seemed calmer, no longer scowled or trembled, and the color was back in her cheeks. Best of all, her curiosity had been piqued, not that this had been his intention, but better to talk about Pemberley, even with the painful memories attached, than receive an additional tongue lashing for his recklessness.

"You have hinted to an unusual affinity for horses but have never mentioned your grandfather. Was he a skilled horseman like you?"

A long-ago fallen willow tree served as a perfect seat, and Darcy joined Elizabeth there as he answered, speaking slowly. "I can only pray to someday be as skilled as my grandfather was. Horses were his passion. Of course, Pemberley itself was his passion, but with thoroughbreds a major aspect of the estate, his focus was there."

"I did not realize this—about Pemberley and thoroughbreds, I mean."

Darcy was startled, his brows lifting. "Have I never mentioned our horses?"

"No, Mr. Darcy, you have not. In fact, you are irritatingly vague whenever I ask about your past or Pemberley."

Darcy heard the edginess underneath the teasing tone and reached across the two feet separating them to clasp one of her hands. "Forgive me, Elizabeth. My greatest desire is to know more of you and your life, and you have expressed the same from me. I do not mean to be secretive, truly. I confess it is…taxing for me to talk about myself, especially areas involving my grief. Please be patient."

"You do not need to tell me anything you are uncomfortable with, William. We have plenty of time for that." She squeezed his hand. "Start with what is easiest. Tell me about your horses."

Darcy silently stared at their entwined hands. *Why is it so hard to share my innermost thoughts? Do I not trust Elizabeth?* He did trust her to never betray his confidence. She had proven to be trustworthy by never speaking a word about Georgiana and Mr. Wickham.

No, it was that, since a young boy, Darcy had kept his emotions tightly bound. He rarely exposed himself and grieved in solitude. He was an intensely private person, increasingly so as he grew into adulthood and assumed the responsibilities of managing Pemberley. The yearning for a bond like the one shared by his parents had weighed heavy upon his heart for over a decade, and certain as he was that his relationship with Elizabeth had the potential to be as cohesive, Darcy could not instantly overcome years of locked away emotions. Nor could he miraculously become an extrovert.

Perhaps it is a lack of trust, Darcy grudgingly admitted. He had given Elizabeth a large portion of his heart freely; it was a risky venture, as he had agonizingly learned when she rejected him, the pain crippling. Loving another person went hand in hand with vulnerability, and vulnerability was one trait a man in Darcy's position must steel against. Paradoxically, he was learning that love made one stronger.

To love fully, one must trust. So, he inhaled and plunged ahead.

"When we get to Pemberley, I will show you more of my family history. We have the tapestries, which you saw, that outline our family tree. But the library houses dozens of journals and ledgers, the scribblings of my ancestors that recount, in pieces, our past. Not the most riveting reading, but it can be interesting—or useful in putting you to sleep."

He winked and then stretched out his long legs. Keeping hold of Elizabeth's hand, he resumed his narrative. "Where to start with Pemberley? Well, like most English estates, agriculture and livestock form the basis of our wealth, and have since the beginning. However, upon occasion, a daring Darcy has delved into other enterprises.

"For instance, about a hundred years ago, my several-greats-grandfather, Antony Darcy, had a talent and passion for metal work and weapons. He crafted some of the finest blades in England and increased Pemberley's fortune considerably. We have a collection in the armory, and a few are priceless.

"Then there was Antony Darcy's grandmother, an extraordinary painter, of landscapes primarily. Several hang in honored places at home. Most were sold as she painted them, on commission or in a gallery, and for a high price. Recently one of my ancestor's rare portraits sold at Christie's for two hundred pounds. I know, because I bought it. She signed her unmarried name"—he paused, closely watching Elizabeth's face—"Clara Steen."

Her eyes popped. "Clara Steen was your grandmother?"

"Several generations removed, but yes."

"Her paintings are brilliant! We have one in our dining room!"

"Yes, I know. One of her early works, but, as you say, brilliant."

"Why did you never say anything?"

Darcy shrugged. "I presumed the subject would be broached naturally in due course, and it was. It is her claim to greatness, not mine. I cannot draw a straight line, so clearly that talent was not passed to me. I only brought it up now to show that the Darcys have historically been an eclectic bunch—unafraid to take risks when necessary, inclined to fulfill their passions, and, if possible, turn them into profit for the estate. Not all have been successful, mind you. Various crop ideas did not reap as hoped for, and certain investments never materialized favorably.

"Fortunately, every Master of Pemberley down through the centuries kept a firm grasp on the staples to maintain moving forward, no matter the losses. Because of this, the estate's yearly income and accumulated worth results from diverse sources. I have not memorized all the past financial ledgers, but there is little doubt that in the last century, it was my grandfather's foray into the breeding of thoroughbreds that impacted Pemberley most profoundly."

He went on to tell her how his father, after completing his Cambridge education, assumed the management of the estate, while his father, James Senior, devoted all of his energies toward their horses. Within a decade, their stock had doubled, and the wealth of Pemberley close to tripled.

"Any gentleman worth his salt can ride a horse," Darcy stated firmly. "If they cannot, well, pardon my prejudice, but they are lacking in character. For my grandfather, it was much, much more than that. It was as if he could read the mind of a horse. Any horse. I know it sounds fanciful, Elizabeth, yet that is the truth of it. His gift transcended the normal."

He shook himself out of dreamy memories of his beloved grandfather, smiling sheepishly at Elizabeth, who was softly smiling and stroking his hand in the most delightful way. "He always said I had the same gift. 'Born in a saddle,' he would say—not literally, fortunately for my dear mother, but close. In fact, my father told me that grandfather took me to the stables when I was only a few months old, propped me on the back of his prized stallion, Leonidas, and walked us around the yard. A right of passage, I suppose."

"It must have worked, because you obviously inherited his passionate love for horses. Can you read their minds too?"

Darcy chuckled at her jest. "Not in general. I do feel one with certain horses, especially my mounts." He gestured toward the wandering Parsifal. "Parsifal was sired by my first stallion, Pericles, and he was sired by my grandfather's, Leonidas. Only the best bloodlines for Darcy men. In each case, Parsifal and Pericles, I made their acquaintance shortly after they were born. A unique bond forms between a man and his horse when devoted entirely to each other. I ride other horses if I must, but I prefer Parsifal."

Elizabeth was staring at the black horse with an odd expression. Darcy lifted her chin with his fingertips. "What are you thinking?"

"Only that I wish I possessed even a tiny affinity for horses. I hope you are not disappointed, William, but I am somewhat afraid of them. I am not sure why—"

Her words were cut off when he kissed her. "There is nothing about you that is disappointing to me, Elizabeth. Nothing."

He hovered a scant inch away from her lips, which chose that moment to part. Then she nervously touched the tip of her tongue to the upper lip, and he almost snapped. He probably would have, drawing her into his arms and kissing hungrily until they were forced apart to breathe, but she pulled back and whispered tremulously, "I see the inner workings of Pemberley are more complex than I imagined. I have much to learn."

"I have no expectation that you understand the business side of things or be involved. Those are my responsibilities."

She gazed at him, eyes serious but sparkling with a hint of humor, perhaps it was—or maybe defiance? He was uncertain so remained silent.

"From the time I was very young, I would sit with Papa in his study. Usually I quietly read while he read or attended to business. Occasionally I would ask questions, always curious about something, and as I grew older, I started asking him what he was reading or working on. My favorite discussions were when we had read the same book, and we would argue some point or another. It took me a while to figure out that often he was disagreeing with me simply so I would formulate a rebuttal. Now you know how I developed that habit."

"I must thank Mr. Bennet, since it is a habit of yours I appreciate."

"Good to know, Mr. Darcy, as I intend to argue with you now."

Darcy lifted his brow. "Oh? Thank you for the warning."

"You see," she went on, ignoring his comment, "as I asked questions of Papa, he began to tell me about Longbourn. Bits here, pieces there. Our estate is nothing compared to Pemberley, and I regret to admit that Papa has not been a keen manager. His books are more important to him, so he trusts the day-to-day affairs to his men. Still, I learned as we talked about farming and the animals and finances. I suppose I was as close to a son as Papa had. I adored our discussions and debates, and a few times helped solved a problem for him. Eventually Mama realized Papa was teaching me the business, albeit somewhat unconsciously, and she became furious. She said he was filling my mind with useless nonsense for a lady. According to Mama, it was a detriment—too much knowledge, too much reading of books and newspapers, too much encouragement to debate. Unhealthy traits for a female, and unattractive to men of quality."

"That, you must know, is untrue for me."

"Yes, I believe it is important to you to have a woman of intellect and will. I did not see that at first, but now I do, and it is one reason I love you, William."

"Then we are not arguing after all," he grinned.

"Not so fast." She wagged her finger. "I have not finished. I think Mama *was* correct, in that a large portion of the male population thinks that way about women. What was the saddest revelation to me was that because she believed this to be true, she and Papa had little to talk about. I...it would be unkind of me to speak of my parents' relationship. All I know is that I have wanted more for myself. I vowed that if I married, it must be to a man who respected my opinions, maybe even sought them if it was helpful. I do not want a husband who is afraid or unwilling to let me be privy to his world. If not quite a partner, I want to at least understand your responsibilities, William, and be your support."

Darcy curled one palm over her cheek. "Elizabeth, as I said, *nothing* about you is disappointing to me. Listen carefully. I held no expectations, but I did have hopes. Your words have exceeded my hopes. I value your opinion and am amazed at your intellect. I need your support and welcome it. Thank you, for daily proving how perfect you are for me."

"You agree so hastily, sir, giving me no opportunity to engage in a serious argument. What a tragedy."

"Next time, I promise to follow Mr. Bennet's example and offer a differing opinion purposely to rile you. How does that sound?"

"Or we could rehash our debate over which is more scandalous, a woman reading Mary Robinson or Lord Byron."

Laughing, Darcy stood, pulling Elizabeth with him. "Perhaps another time. Today is far too lovely to spoil with an argument, especially one you are doomed to lose."

"Is that so? In that case, we are duty bound to resume the debate, but I shall acquiesce to postpone. It will allot you time to hone your defense."

"Thank you. I deem I shall need to do so. Stay here a moment." He pressed lightly on her shoulder, and then walked a few feet away. Suddenly a shrill whistle rent the air and Parsifal, grazing happily yards down the sloping hill, lifted his head. A brief toss and flick of his tail indicated his annoyance at being disturbed, but he swiftly galloped toward his beckoning master.

"Are you leaving?"

"Not unless you wish me to." Darcy glanced over his shoulder, pleasure radiating through his body when she shook her head vehemently. "I wanted to introduce you formally to Parsifal—I promise he will not hurt you—and I have apples and blackberries in my bag that are delicious. They grow wild in a sheltered dell about a mile from here, next to a creek. We stop there to rest and I always take a few extras with me. Parsifal likes the small, squishy apples the best. Come." Darcy extended his hand to Elizabeth, steady and patient as she hesitated before grasping it and stepping closer.

"The key is to advance slowly," Darcy explained as she joined him. Pitching his voice low and tranquil, he brought her close to his side, their hands laced together, while he stroked the stallion's immense neck with his free hand. "You want to approach from the side. Their vision is unique from ours, their eyes focusing independently and with a delay in processing. That is why they startle easily and become defensive, which is frightening if you are not expecting it. Remember, horses are prey animals, meaning that while powerful and able to inflict pain, it is not in their nature to attack. They are inherently gentle, not aggressive. Parsifal hates for me to tell others this, but he is a lamb under that gruff exterior."

"I shall not breathe a word to anyone, Parsifal. I promise."

"There, you hear that Parsifal? She can be trusted." Darcy scratched between the funnel-shaped black ears, each one twitching and twisting as he spoke. Fluidly, Parsifal turned his head toward Elizabeth, both eyes swiveling to stare at her face, and he released a mellifluous nicker.

"That is his form of a greeting," Darcy interpreted when Elizabeth jerked. "Parsifal, allow me to introduce Miss Elizabeth Bennet of Hertfordshire. This beautiful woman has agreed to become my wife and will soon reside with us at Pemberley. I daresay you will see her from time to time. Here"—he lifted their joined hands, Elizabeth's on top—"let him smell you. Like many animals, horses identify through scent more so than the other senses."

Darcy did not push Elizabeth much further. She was outwardly calm and ran her hand over the stallion's muscled neck and withers, but he felt her nervousness. After feeding Parsifal two of the overripe apples he loved, Darcy instructed him to go back to his wanderings and slapped him playfully on the rump.

"He is majestic, William. Powerful, handsome, and elegant. He...suits you."

Elizabeth flushed and lowered her head. If not for her embarrassed reaction, Darcy would not have realized her description of Parsifal was also meant for him. For several heartbeats he was tongue-tied. He swiftly searched his memory and concluded this was her first compliment addressing his physical attributes—unless he counted how she audaciously examined his body when he rode up to the willow trees. And it was best to deter his musings about that .

"This spot…with the willows and the…view"—he swept his arm in a general easterly direction—"is lovely. Secluded yet not dangerously so. How far is Longbourn from here?"

"A half mile or so, I believe. The road is over there." Elizabeth pointed to a distant line, proceeding to indicate landmarks familiar to Darcy, as he would have recognized instantly if not so flustered. The sudden recognition of just how secluded the area was, was provocative…and perilous. So much for the scenery being a mundane subject!

"And to answer your question when you arrived, yes, I do come here often. Willow Bench has been one of my favored hideaways since I was quite young."

"Willow Bench?"

Elizabeth laughed. "Not clever, I know, but apt. I was ten or perhaps eleven when I first walked this far and saw the willows. How the six trees grew in a circle with their limbs draped to the ground, forming a shrouded lair was, to a fanciful girl, a magical place."

They returned to the trees, many of the yellowing leaves fallen, so the lair effect was diminished, and Lizzy pointed to the dead willow log. "It was already fallen when I found this place, and my thought was, 'Oh, how nice, there is a bench for me to sit on.' So this place became Willow Bench."

She sat on the surface smoothed from unknown years of erosion and cushioned with a small, quilted blanket, and ate the juicy berries one by one. Darcy leaned against one of the willows, stared at the autumn landscape, and bit into an apple. He remained acutely aware of her presence and the effect she had upon him, but the peaceful atmosphere was hypnotic. Gradually he relaxed, realizing how uniquely gratifying it was to simply be with her in silent accord. A fleeting glance showed she too was staring placidly at the vista, not a hint of uneasiness apparent.

Later, upon reflection, Darcy would mark this time as a significant leap in their relationship. Bit by bit, they learned more about the other, and that knowledge created a growing comfortableness that warmed his heart. Oh, how he longed for the day when their minds, bodies, and souls were one!

"Elizabeth, I am not sure if I adequately apologized to you for...everything...that I said and did...before. I do, apologize, that is, down to the depths of my soul."

She turned her head and gazed at him steadily. She did not reply immediately, and when she did, her voice was tender. "Thank you, William. I do appreciate you verbalizing an apology, but not because I needed to hear it. You proved your regret by everything you have done since Rosings. I forgave you long ago. For some reason, *you* needed to say it. I hope you can forgive yourself now?"

"You never cease to amaze me, Elizabeth." Darcy shook his head and then sighed. "I think my guilt will never be repelled, and maybe that is beneficial. Your recriminations taught me a hard lesson, and thanks to your humbling, I am improving. I never want to forget how damned fortunate I am to have you in my life."

"Oh, you do not need guilt for that, Mr. Darcy, as I intend to remind you every hour of every day just how fortunate you are!"

"Please do," he laughed and tossed the apple core toward Parsifal.

"And, so we can lay this unpleasantness behind us once and for eternity, I apologize for my behavior. All teasing aside, I truly am sorry for misjudging you, for Wickham, for being endlessly rude, and—"

"No, Elizabeth, please. You were not at fault nor rude."

"I beg to differ, sir! If you recollect in all honesty, I was horrid to you at nearly every turn! Impertinent, uncivil, my sharp tongue seeking to cause you pain. How you bore it all is unfathomable, let alone loving me through it."

"I fell in love with you in part *because* of your liveliness of mind. Your wit is refreshing. If you were rude, I deserved much more for how ungentlemanly and unpardonable my behavior."

"So then, are we to end our lovely interlude at Willow Bench with an argument as to who shares the greater blame for our actions in the past?"

"There can be no argument, since I accept the blame is wholly mine to bear."

He meant it, but he spoke playfully and smiled. How could he not when she fixed her dancing eyes upon him and saucily cocked her head? She was utterly bewitching! Then she stood, casually crossing the shaded clearing toward him.

"We have two options, sir. The first is to add the topic of whose comportment was most abominable to the list of postponed arguments, after literature choices for women and the deficiencies in the justice system..." Elizabeth paused when Darcy laughed aloud at the last. He had completely forgotten their heated debate over London's crime problems, that one occurring while she was staying at Netherfield nursing Jane, as had most of their disputes.

"The second choice," she resumed when he regained control, "is for us to concur the entire matter is in the past. How about a treaty of peace and nullification? Does the latter sound preferential, Mr. Darcy?"

"Indeed it does, Miss Elizabeth."

"Very well then, we are in agreement. A sweet blackberry to seal the bargain." Abruptly she closed the space between them, the ripe berry held by her fingertips pressing against his mouth. Instinctively he opened, and the brushing touch of her downy skin over his sensitive lips followed by the burst of juicy sweetness sent a wild bolt of sensual pleasure through his body. It was all he could manage not to moan and crush her into his chest.

"As exciting as it can be to bicker with you, William, I am discovering harmony and obliging communication is richly satisfying."

A second berry entered his mouth, Elizabeth's fingertips lingering on his lower lip. *If she only knew how that simple touch,* and the faintly glazed expression in her eyes as she whispered about being satisfied, affected him!

"I conclude that our unexpected meeting today has been productive. We have forgiven each other and agreed that the misjudgments of the past year are behind us—"

Another berry passed his lips, Darcy barely tasting it with all his focus on her words, the close proximity of her body, and his struggle to remain composed.

"—we have agreed to move forward in honesty and accord—"

A caressing rub of her fingertips as one more berry was placed onto his tongue... *God! Please let it be the last!*

"—I learned more about you and Pemberley, and took a small step toward liking horses—"

Frantically he snagged the next berry from between her fingertips, and grabbed the handkerchief out of her other hand. Stuffing the latter into his pocket, Darcy masked his ragged inhale behind chewing the final blackberry and kissing her knuckles.

"Thank you for an extraordinarily wonderful morning, Elizabeth. It pains me, but we should say our good-byes for now. I do have some business to attend to before seeing you for dinner." Praying for tact and grace, no small request considering his raging emotions, he sidestepped away from the tree while tucking her hand into the bend of his arm. "How should I dress for the theatrical tonight?"

"Casual evening attire is sufficient. It is not a formal affair at all. I do hope you are not expecting too much from our community of actors, William. Miss Grant is gifted, but I doubt Mrs. Siddons is fretting in her sleep!"

"My expectations are for a charming country production that will, by its contrast to a Covent Garden play, be delightful. Do not mistake me, Elizabeth. I adore the theatre and prefer a serious, professionally rendered play or opera for the comprehensive experience offered. Nothing can compare, of course. Nevertheless, entertainments presented by traveling troupes or local groups have a value and pleasure that is unique. Wait until you view the plays enacted by the parish children at Pemberley, always for Easter and Christmas, as well as other special occasions. I daresay nothing is more adorable and amusing than children acting out Biblical stories."

"That sounds enchanting. I am pleased to hear this, and it eases my mind. I feared you would be bored or liken it to the worse torture imaginable."

"Not at all. I hope to be entertained, but in truth, it will matter little. I shall deem each act delightful whether I attend to it or not because I shall be with you, dear Elizabeth."

He kissed her knuckles again, added a florid bow and a tip of an imaginary hat, and ignored the frown flashing over her brow when he whistled for Parsifal rather than kissing her offered lips. If only she knew the battle being fought to resist! But it was definitely wiser not to initiate a kiss at this juncture and place.

He kept his promise not to jump the fence, riding on the Longbourn side until reaching the road and circling around. Once alone again in his chambers at Netherfield, he pulled the forgotten handkerchief from the jacket pocket where he had stuffed it. It was plain linen with narrow lace along the edge, and a red embroidered EB in bold script covering one corner. Inhaling, he could smell the blackberries as well as the lavender scent he long ago began associating with Elizabeth Bennet.

Smiling dreamily, he folded the square neatly and placed it onto the table by his bed. *A token for our surprise encounter at Willow Bench.*

ප

Lizzy brushed her hair absently while contemplating her dreamy face reflected in the silvery surface of the mirror. The dim candlelight and flames from the fireplace were the only illumination in the darkness of her bedchamber, but enough to reveal her beatific countenance. She sighed, the sound almost a breathy giggle, and closed her eyes as a euphoric shiver rushed through her body.

What a marvelous day.

Waking that morning to a gloriously colorful sunrise and vivid azure sky set the tone, and beckoned Lizzy outside as soon as a hasty breakfast was finished. There, she discovered the air as fresh and crisp as imagined, and walking the trails through tall waving grasses invigorating. Every leaf seemed sharper and brighter than normal. The willows at her favorite secluded spot swayed serenely in the breeze, the autumn-yellowed leaves a vibrant curtain and carpet. An hour of quiet reading with only the scurrying of tiny squirrels and chipmunks or the occasional cry of a bird added another layer of happiness.

Then, the distant sound of hooves registered, and her happiness tripled. An unexpected and delirious interlude in the solitary company of the man she loved surpassed any possibilities dreamt of for her morning. Walking home with the sensation of his lips tingling her hands and mouth was sheer rapture, and the feeling held all through the afternoon and up until Mr. Darcy and Mr. Bingley's arrival for dinner.

Sadly, the surprising inclusion of Caroline Bingley had dulled her joy. Invited to Longbourn several times since Jane's engagement to Mr. Bingley, Caroline had extended thinly veiled, contemptuous refusals each time. Therefore, no one anticipated her accompanying the gentlemen on the night of an after-dinner community theatrical. Lizzy's suspicions that Caroline was attempting to wrest Mr. Darcy away through seductive maneuvers were proven true by her outrageous display at the Netherfield dinner the night before. With her tolerance hanging by a thread, Lizzy barely hid her irritation, and even sweet Jane grimaced and greeted her future sister-in-law testily.

Assuming the evening was doomed to be ruined by Caroline's harping, sneering remarks, and simpering at Mr. Darcy, it was remarkably fantastic. Oh, Caroline did all that and more, but Mr. Bingley and Mr. Darcy deflected her barbs, smoothly interrupted, or humorously flipped the comment around. More often than not, they simply ignored her, the Bennets following suit. That alone was enough to lift Lizzy's spirits.

Best of all, Mr. Darcy held Lizzy's hand during the performance, whispered questions as to the people involved, and honestly enjoyed himself, just as he said he would. Caroline's pointless pursuit faded into oblivion.

A knock on the bedroom door brought Lizzy out of her woolgathering. It was Jane, as anticipated, and within minutes they were snuggled close by the fire with a blanket draped over their shoulders. A long-held routine after a particularly interesting day or evening, the eldest Bennet sisters gathered together in one of their rooms to talk and giggle. It was not unusual for one, two, or all three of their sisters to join them, but since Lydia's marriage and their engagements, it was typically just the two of them, and no matter what topics they covered, their lovers inevitably were the main subject.

So after talking about their neighborhood friends and the comedic farce enacted to enliven an otherwise humdrum season of the year, the gentlemen were mentioned, this time by Jane first.

"Mr. Bingley said it was the most amusing play he has seen in ages. Undoubtedly he was being polite more than factual, yet he did laugh often and comment relevantly."

"I suspect Mr. Bingley is amused easily compared to some. Not to imply his taste lacking or that he is less cultured. Rather that he possesses a gay heart and light spirit that loves laughter."

"As do you, Lizzy. Indeed, that is a trait you have in common with my Mr. Bingley to a greater portion than me. I do delight in humor, but I am not one to openly express, as you and Mr. Bingley so readily can."

"Perhaps in this we are mutually blessed. Mr. Bingley's ebullience touches you, as mine touches Mr. Darcy. You are not as reserved as previous, and to my constant startlement, neither is Mr. Darcy."

"I agree that Mr. Darcy appeared genuinely amused. His pleasure annoyed Miss Bingley profoundly. Her mouth pursed as if sucking lemons all night!"

Lizzy laughed out loud and hugged Jane. "Oh! How I do love it when an unforgiving commentary passes your lips! It is such a singular occurrence as to be noteworthy and of substantial weight. If you concluded Mr. Darcy's true delight in the evening's outing, then I can rest contentedly that my likewise conclusion was not merely the result of wishful thinking for it to be so."

"Not at all. It was obvious, Lizzy. In fact..." Jane paused, a faint crease marring her brow. "Correct me if I am wrong or overstepping, but I believe Mr. Darcy, in an odd way, is easier to interpret than Charles...that is, Mr. Bingley."

"Oh, Jane! I do think it is fine to address him by his given name, with me especially. I am curious what you mean, however."

Jane hid her flush by adding another log to the fire, finishing the task before responding. "Charles is lively and unreserved, easy with everybody, and unfailingly good-natured. I love these traits, you understand, so am not criticizing—"

"Indeed not! Jane never criticizes. Except for keen observances of Miss Bingley's puckered mouth, that is," Lizzy teased.

Jane's rosiness increased, and she went on as if Lizzy had not interrupted. "Charles's perpetual amiability makes it difficult to decipher if his mood is less than delighted at any given moment. Granted our lives are steeped in happiness at the present, but even at the best of times, one has occasion to be sad or irritated, yes?"

"Yes, of course that is true. However, my guess is that Mr. Bingley's natural disposition does not allow for sadness or irritation unless of a significant level, and then the negative emotions would be brushed aside or hidden behind a pleasant smile. In this, you and Mr.

Bingley are akin: neither of you wishes to displease others or be displeased, hence the enviable ability to view everyone, and everything, as delightful. You are the optimist whereas I am the cynic!"

Jane smiled at Lizzy's dramatic declarations, but she shook her head. "You are not cynical, Lizzy. You see the world and the people in it with a clearer vision and are unafraid to label accordingly. I cannot say I wish I were more like you, preferring to live in my sunny cocoon, as you once called it. Nevertheless, I now appreciate that shielding one's thoughts behind a placid face or gay smile is debilitating and has the potential for misunderstanding."

"My, you are full of deep intensity tonight, dear Jane. What has brought on this serious introspection?"

Shrugging, Jane answered, "Nothing untoward or of tremendous significance, merely honest observance. I wonder if my relationship with Charles might have followed a smoother path if I had been able to overcome my modesty to convey the depth of my sentiments. I truly never thought to do so and refused to heed Charlotte's advice, or listen to your assertions of his affections, because my retiring nature insisted on interpreting Charles's congeniality as universal and not special toward me."

"In regards to events from the year past, we could forever point to our errors in interpretation and judgment, all four of us. Best for you and Mr. Bingley to leave it be, as William and I have agreed to do. Learn from mistakes, to be sure, then carry on. That is my advice, and since you once before chose to ignore your sister's remarkable wisdom, you must do so now."

Lizzy kissed Jane on the brow, both of them giggling like silly schoolgirls. Then Lizzy jumped up, crossing to a small table where a plate of cookies sat. Pouring two glasses of water and grabbing the plate, she returned to their roost by the fire. Two cookies and some idle chitchat later, Lizzy resumed the previous topic, "I do understand what you meant by Mr. Darcy's moods being easier to interpret than Mr. Bingley. It was not always so, of course. Preconceived conclusions and erroneous translations were the hallmarks for both our relationships, Jane. Yet there were those, myself included, who knew Mr. Bingley cared for you. No one, however, had any idea that Mr. Darcy regarded me with special interest. Least of all me."

"You did tell me that Charlotte hinted at it."

"Yes," Lizzy answered slowly, "she did. Although at the time it seemed highly incredible. I laughed the concept away, and Charlotte came to agree that Mr. Darcy's demeanor was not consistent with a man in love."

"Obviously you were both wrong."

"I daresay we were." Lizzy chewed a bite of cookie and picked at the crumbs on the plate. "As I grow more familiar with William, I realize his cool demeanor is normal, yet also a façade erected to control, and perhaps hide, his spirited nature. He is a man of uncommon feeling, Jane. Far more passionate than he appears."

"Why does he hide, do you think?"

"For similar reasons as you, Jane. William is shy, although not to your degree, and he does not desire having attention called to him. Largely I think it is because he despises artifice. Rather than acting contrary to what he may be feeling about a person or situation, he has perfected a neutral, aloof mask. Obviously this has served him well for nigh on thirty years, while also causing troubles. I see this as why he now strives to be clearer."

"Precisely my point. He is impassive a great portion of the time. Thus, when he baldly expresses an emotion, it is transparent. When it comes to you, he makes no effort to disguise his delight and love. He is permeated with good humor and it colors everything, even a county theatrical. No wonder Miss Bingley was annoyed!"

Lizzy emitted a rude sound. "Caroline is an irritation I am fighting to be patient with. You have no idea how often I bite my tongue, and the urge to respond violently is harder to suppress with each passing day. If not for my promise to you and my sympathy for Mr. Bingley, I would have shoved her onto the floor when she sat next to William at the play tonight. The nerve!"

165

"You have a right to be angry, Lizzy. If it is any consolation, Charles is vexed by Caroline's actions. I fear his tolerance may soon end."

"Has he said this to you?"

"No. I do not discuss Caroline with Charles. I have no wish to hurt him, so remain serene and do all I can to assure that I am unfazed by her bitter words."

"Are you? Unfazed, that is?"

Jane sighed. "For the most part, yes. It is not her actual words that distress, but what they portend for our future tranquility. I harbor no concerns over Charles's dedication and commitment to our marriage. Caroline is doomed to fail in her attacks on me, and you for that matter—just as she is doomed to fail in changing Mr. Darcy's mind. So I pray daily her heart will soften before Charles—or Mr. Darcy—is forced to confront it directly."

"Well, you continue to pray for Caroline while I continue to pray for personal restraint. Frankly, I do not think either of us will have our prayers answered before one of our fiancés takes action. God help her if it is William."

CHAPTER SEVEN
October Showers

*E*xactly one week earlier, Darcy had awoke from a troubled sleep well before the dawn, his heart heavy and confused. As it turned out, that was the last morning for a long while that Darcy would wake in a depressive state. Within hours, his heart had soared and all traces of confusion evaporated. Elizabeth Bennet had declared her love for him and accepted his marriage proposal. The brilliant sunrise and richly blue sky on that October morning had been unable to compete with the resplendence inside his soul.

Today he woke after a deep, restful sleep long after the scheduled sunrise. As on each morning since his betrothal seven days ago, his heart smoothly transitioned from the rapture of dreams with Elizabeth to the blissful anticipation of spending the day in her company. Parting the drapes confirmed what he had presumed by the room's gray dimness: a sky dotted with dark clouds, and a sun that failed to break through them. It was not raining yet, and from the looks of things, it could go either way, but weather had no impact upon his mood. All it meant was their afternoon together would be spent inside rather than outside, and as long as he was with Elizabeth, it mattered naught.

Shortly after noon, the carriage sent for the Bennet sisters arrived. Darcy and Bingley welcomed their ladies with reserved affection, ushering them quickly into the warmed parlor. For the first day since the announced Darcy–Bennet engagement, and even longer for Mr. Bingley, the couples had no set agenda for the afternoon and no social appointments for the evening. All four of the persons involved were relieved to be free and, in light of this astounding development, had jokingly vowed to let whimsy and spontaneity rule.

Caroline Bingley was present when Jane and Lizzy arrived but remained oddly subdued throughout the afternoon. Not that anyone paid her much heed, which may have been one reason she was sulky. Then again, sulky and Caroline went hand in hand, so who could say for sure? Certainly not Mr. Darcy, or even her own brother, and since their attentions were largely captured by their fiancées, efforts to diagnose Caroline Bingley were nil.

The first two hours flew by. Luncheon consisted of finger sandwiches, fruits, assorted cheeses and breads, bite-sized cold meats, and sweet cakes for dessert, food easy to nibble in gradual intervals between conversation and laughter.

"We received a letter from our Aunt Gardiner this morning," Jane quietly interjected at one point. "She confirmed that she and our uncle will return to London by the twentieth or thereabouts. As we anticipated, they insist Lizzy and I come to Town to shop for our wedding dresses and trousseau."

"It makes perfect sense." Darcy nodded. "Your choices are ample in Town. No point in being limited to what is available for ladies of your class here in Meryton."

Darcy noted Lizzy hiding a smile by biting into a sandwich, belatedly realizing he spoke in his lofty, arrogant tone laced with condescension. Of course, what he had said, strictly speaking, was the truth, so she could not fault him for that. Still, he waited for a teasing rebuke and was surprised when she kept on chewing. More startling was that Caroline did not jump on the unintended slur with her own pointed one. But Caroline was staring out a far window and did not seem to have heard.

Lizzy cast a glance in Caroline's direction, apparently expecting a comment as Darcy had, but when nothing came, she shrugged. "We are making our lists so we will be prepared, and Papa is already cringing."

"Only because you add items that we would never buy, the sole purpose being to watch Papa blanch and splutter," Jane accused.

Darcy chuckled while Bingley's mouth dropped open.

"What are you requesting, Miss Lizzy?" Bingley had loosened enough to use her family pet name, but refused to relinquish the *Miss* appellative.

"Oh, nothing too terrifying or unreasonable really," she answered airily. "Only that I wanted my gown to be spun silk with a four-foot train. That I needed a fan of white dove feathers in case I feel faint at the altar. And that I have always dreamed of yellow daisies for my bouquet."

"I do believe it was the tiara that finally tipped Papa that you were jesting."

"A tiara? Along with a four-foot train? That is ostentatious even by my standards!" Darcy choked out between laughs. Lizzy winked at him. "If you really want a fan of dove feathers, my dear, I can find one for you. Yellow daisies this time of year are a tall order, however, so you must suffer the disappointment."

"I shall try to bear it," she sighed dramatically. "Actually, my ridiculous requests are not solely for the purpose of testing the limits of Papa's gullibility. I was hoping the fright of us emptying his coffers willy-nilly would encourage him to insist on chaperoning Jane and I to Town in lieu of Mama."

Darcy could readily imagine that intensive shopping amongst the crowded streets of London would not be a pleasant chore with Mrs. Bennet complaining every step of the way. He shuddered inwardly at the thought but, out of kindness, said nothing. Bingley, however, did not tie the pieces together.

"I would have thought your mother a preferred companion for purchasing gowns and...other female necessities. Mr. Bennet surely would be of little assistance."

"Papa is wiser with money than Mama, Mr. Bingley," Jane explained in her soft voice, a hand placed onto Lizzy's arm signaling her wish to respond rather than her sister. Considering Lizzy would undoubtedly be a bit more blunt, Darcy had to agree with Jane. "He can appreciate the quality and cost of products better than Mama. And of course, Mr. Gardiner is familiar with many of the merchants, and our aunt as well. Above that, Papa has traveled to Town frequently over the years, and lived there for a time while young and at Oxford. Thus, he is comfortable with the streets, traffic, rules, and the like."

"Indeed, Mr. Bennet does sound a wiser choice," Darcy agreed, sincerely meaning it for a host of reasons. "Aware as I am of Mr. Gardiner's professionalism and connections and Mrs. Gardiner's fine taste, I trust they will excellently fulfill your needs. Bear in mind that Bingley and I are residents of London as well. If there are any specific items either of you ladies require or want, enlighten us and we can more than likely point you in the right direction or acquire it for you."

"Oh yes! Absolutely! Say the word, dear Jane, and it shall be yours! Anything at all!"

At Bingley's ardent promise, Jane flushed and stared into her lap. Lizzy's eyes widened and darted to Darcy. For a moment he could not understand their reactions. Then it hit him. Long used to living within the modest means Mr. Bennet was able to provide, the concept of another substantially wealthier man buying, almost literally, anything they might desire was foreign and uncomfortable. Moreover, he gleaned they were embarrassed over either gentleman presuming the innocent topic was a devious ploy to acquire costly baubles.

Marrying advantageously was nothing to be ashamed of. Men, as well as women, were expected to obtain mates with prospective benefits as the impetus. The majority of people probably did presume the Bennet sisters had chosen Darcy and Bingley based on their wealth, without casting a negative aspersion upon them for doing so. It was wise for a woman to secure a stable future and better her place in society in the process if able. Neither Darcy nor Bingley would have condemned Lizzy and Jane if good sense influenced their decision.

Nevertheless, the joy in being accepted for their character and personality, to be loved as men rather than a name or bank account balance, was a priceless gift. Privately, they had spoken of this blessed reality, both men humbled by their great fortune. They were also thankful to be capable of ensuring the women they loved would forever be financially secure. Furnishing them with trinkets and finery was merely a bonus they hungered to do.

Darcy and Bingley shared a comprehensive glance as they silently considered how best to defuse the awkward tension and reassure their fiancées. Unfortunately, Caroline rallied first.

"How happy you must now be, Jane dear, and you as well, Miss Eliza, to have your whims and fancies eagerly fulfilled. Ensnaring rich gentlemen has such delightful perks, does it not? But of course, this is surely not a revelation to either of you." Caroline smiled her standard cold smirk and glanced from her brother to Darcy, one brow raised and an obvious, *Did I not tell you they were opportunists, stupid men?* message written on her face.

"Caroline—" Bingley began in a strained tone but was interrupted by Lizzy.

Ignoring Caroline, she lifted her chin and looked directly at the two men, "You are kind, Mr. Bingley, Mr. Darcy. I know I speak for Jane when I say that we appreciate your offers in recognition of the generous spirit they were extended. However, for the present, we are content to trust Mr. Bennet's excellent provision, as we have for over twenty years. We want for nothing and never have; thus we are confident that whatever we require for the wedding and entrance into the matrimonial state will be procured sufficiently."

"The only fancy I have ever been eager to have fulfilled is mutual regard and affection with a worthy gentlemen." Jane smiled demurely at Bingley. "In this alone, I am richer than a queen. The costliest object imaginable is worthless in comparison."

Bingley beamed.

Caroline huffed.

"As always, my sister expresses with poetic phrases superior to what I can manage," Lizzy laughingly proclaimed. Gazing playfully at Darcy, she qualified, "I would have said that my fancy was for a man to argue with, provided he allow me to win at least some of the time. And if he is an adequate dancer and with faults I can tease him about, then I am indeed rich beyond measure."

After that, Caroline retreated back into her sulkiness, saying little, and excused herself when the men returned to a previous chess match while Lizzy and Jane chatted softly over their needlework. Jane was the only one who acknowledged Caroline's comment, nodding her head and smiling pleasantly until she was gone. A drizzling rain had begun, but the fire-lit parlor was cozy, and the foursome contentedly settled into the domestic interlude.

It was nearly four when a footman entered the room, quietly crossing to the chessboard and delivering the day's post. Bingley's bundle consisted of three or four envelopes and one small package. He rifled through the letters, not opening any of them, and with a surreptitious glance toward Jane, who was intent on her embroidery hoop, shoved the package into his pocket.

Darcy's stack was thick, one bunch of envelopes tied together with twine. Like Bingley, Darcy flipped through the stack. He smiled at the second missive, that being from Georgiana, and hesitated. Deciding to wait and read it with Elizabeth, he pulled out the tied group. As suspected, these were from his solicitor, Mr. Daniels. Some, he knew, would pertain to various estate business matters and the monthly financial updates. The rest would be the betrothal settlement documents. All of them meant one thing: he could no longer delay a trip to London. It had been inevitable, of course, yet he still frowned as he resumed his survey of the mail.

One letter was from Mrs. Reynolds, quite thick, so hopefully containing the requested information vital to begin shopping for his bride. A slim, dirty envelope came from Colonel Fitzwilliam, who Darcy prayed was announcing his imminent return to London. The larger envelope, with multiple stamps and markings indicating the long distance traveled, Darcy recognized as from his Uncle George even before looking at the scrawling penmanship. The last was a letter from Lady Catherine de Bourgh.

At the latter, his frown increased. In no hurry to deal with his aunt, he had waited to write her of his engagement, doing so only four days ago. His letter had been formal and as unemotional as possible. He had reiterated his condemnation of her inappropriate abuse of Elizabeth Bennet, and clarified that her presence at their wedding was not desired. Knowing his aunt well, Darcy had anticipated a rebuttal, just not so soon.

Darcy broke the seal and started reading. By the end of the first page, anger blinded him and erased the awareness of where he was. Bolting up from his chair, a vile curse passed his lips, and rage jerked him into motion as he stormed out of the room. Incoherently desperate for solitude to deal with his wrath, he made for the library. Once there, he paced and read.

...Tragically wrong I have been to esteem you highly. You are selfish, Darcy. A spineless, weak fool enslaved to base whims and pathetic desires. Blinded to the consequences of your actions and irresponsible to your birthright...Infinitely unworthy of the revered Darcy name, and now a black mark on an ancient, respected house. The woe that shall fall upon Pemberley with this horrendous marriage is too catastrophic to fathom...Callously tossing aside Anne, whom you claimed to love and promised security, abandoning her to spinsterhood and a shattered heart...I beg God's forgiveness while also thanking Him for taking your sainted parents from this

earth before they could witness this unspeakable degradation. My dear, beloved Anne, who desired with all her heart to see our great houses merged, has been betrayed and her memory tainted by her only son's selfish choice...

Appalling! Damnable! The future forfeited by marrying a woman of low circumstances. How can you not see, Darcy? This scheming, sharp-tongued, classless girl as Mrs. Darcy? Oh, how it pains me! Elizabeth Bennet lacks beauty or grace, is devoid of style or wit, is uneducated, crass, and unaccomplished! This is to be the next Mistress of Pemberley? And Georgiana's sister? Mark my words, Nephew, you will regret your decision in short order, Pemberley crumbling into a hovel while you escape the prison of a hellish union by living in Town...

On and on she ranted, using different words to repeat the same dire prophecies and vicious attacks toward him and Elizabeth. He saw nothing humorous in the three-page harangue, other than a commendable command of adjectives, and that was insufficient in overcoming his fury. References to his parents' shame and Anne's tragedy were easily disregarded, since he knew those claims were blatant falsehoods.

The reminder that his parents were gone, and therefore unable to be present at his wedding, caused the greatest pain. At the same time, it strengthened him. Darcy was absolutely certain his father and mother would have adored Elizabeth and rejoiced in his choice of wife. Knowing how utterly wrong Lady Catherine was on this count, and irrational to assert her knowledge of James and Anne Darcy was greater than his, revealed how preposterous all her opinions.

Insane claims of woe and calamity were almost too laughable to be angry over. The slurs against his character he was far too self-confident to warrant, but it did hurt to have kin demean him so vociferously. This letter proved how dismal the prospect of repairing the rift, and his sadness blended with his animosity.

As horrid as the rest, worse were the rabid attacks against Elizabeth. In his heart, she was his wife, and thus his responsibility to protect and defend. A gentleman of honor did not allow *anyone* to harm the people placed under his care. The feeling of impotence in this situation was galling. Sightlessly, he stared out the rain-splattered window, fighting to calm the tense fury suffusing his entire body.

His head began to pound, the hammering rhythm ringing in his ears so that he heard nothing else. The gentle pressure on his arm might as well have been a fisted punch in his heightened state. Darcy jolted in surprise, swinging his glower to the offending interrupter.

It was Elizabeth, and clearly his thunderous expression alarmed her. Flinching, she stepped back a half pace, and a flicker of remorse shot through him. Immediately it was gone, swallowed by his rage.

"Leave me be, Elizabeth," he commanded flatly.

"No. Talk to me, William."

Darcy was flabbergasted at her direct refusal. No one dared ignore his orders—ever—especially when he was speaking in his authoritative voice. Yet there she was, petite hand lightly squeezing his arm, eyes tender and determined at the same time, and face boldly lifted toward his. She was so small and frail compared to him, but he had the distinct impression that he would fail if he tried to throw her over his shoulder and toss her out of the room.

He clenched his jaw and turned back to the window. Fluttering the letter in the air, he snapped, "My aunt is not pleased about our engagement."

Well, there's a massive understatement!

Astoundingly, Elizabeth started laughing.

"I find no humor in this, Elizabeth," Darcy snarled.

"Really, William! Did you imagine she would embrace me with open arms and host a party? Lady Catherine made her opinion of me quite clear at Longbourn, an event that we should essentially be thankful for since, left to your own devices, you may not have gotten up the nerve to propose again." She said the last bit teasingly and rose onto her toes to kiss one cheek while caressing the other.

Darcy was torn between crushing her into his arms and lashing out by reading the contents of the letter. Neither was a sensible option. Growling in frustration, he stomped several paces away. He needed the distance, and time, to gain control over his tumultuous emotions.

"William, I am indifferent to what your aunt has to say about me, or us. I love you with all my heart, and you love me. She cannot alter that, can she?"

"Of course not!" he choked.

"Then there is nothing to fear. Lady Catherine is angry at her dashed hopes for you and Anne. I am not a mother yet, but I can partly sympathize. It in no way justifies her actions or words, but you must try to understand a little."

He gripped the wooden edge of a chair back, jutting his jaw and frowning. "Elizabeth, it is more than that. She slandered you personally, your character and virtue and qualifications as my intended. This I cannot forgive!"

Deliberately stepping toward him, she whispered, "Did you not initially doubt my qualifications and connections, beloved?"

Darcy felt the blood drain from his face and his mouth drop open. Vaguely, he registered her calling him *beloved*. The wondrous development of hearing her first such endearment was sadly unable to offset the flood of shame and regret weakening every muscle in his body. For perhaps the first time, he fully comprehended how she felt during his offensive proposal in April.

Before he drowned in pain and guilt, she closed the gap between them. Then she cupped his face with her warm hands and her glorious eyes were inches away, staring intently into his.

"The difference, my dear William, is that *now* you know my character and virtue. The only truth that matters is you and I, and our love. The rest will be resolved, or it will not, but it is inconsequential as long as we are unified in our commitment."

As swiftly as it came, his anger, shame, pain, and guilt evaporated. Elizabeth was correct. Only the truth of their love mattered.

Only she matters—nothing and no one else.

Darcy released a cleansing exhale and enfolded her in his arms. Resting his forehead against hers, he murmured, "How are you so wise, my love, for one so young?"

She smiled impishly and kissed him. "It is a secret, Mr. Darcy. You cannot expect a girl to reveal herself too soon. Then where would the mystery be?"

"I do love you, my Elizabeth. Heart and soul."

He returned her tender kiss, then pressed her head against his shoulder, his chin resting atop the loose curls and hands lightly caressing her back. *Perfect. She fits me perfectly.* It soothed him to hold her, to feel her warm and alive in his arms.

"Very well then. I shall let Lady Catherine stew and rage if she must. I refuse to listen."

"Hopefully she comes no closer than Rosings, or we may hear her raging. Poor Charlotte! I wonder if even Mr. Collins's praise will appease."

Darcy did not reply. Truthfully, he cared less about either Collins—not that he held any unkind thoughts toward Mrs. Collins, but he did not know her well enough to muster sympathy. Elizabeth's remarks, which he knew were designed to lighten his heart, only reminded him of his cousin Anne.

"What is it, William? There is something else troubling you. Talking to me may help."

Darcy inhaled the sweet aroma of lavender embedded in her silky tresses, and then exhaled in a breathy chuckle. "You will never cease to amaze me, Elizabeth." He placed a lingering kiss on her forehead and led her to a sofa.

"Your jest brought to mind Anne. We are close friends, Anne and I, and have been since children. Our mutual affection is real, and precisely why we know how wrong we are for each other as marriage partners. Furthermore, imagining being...intimate...as husband and wife"—he cleared his throat—"well, it is incestuous, to be honest."

Evading Elizabeth's eyes, Darcy nervously smoothed his palm across his right thigh. "Despite Lady Catherine's insistence, Anne and I would never have agreed to marry, so this eventuality was destined no matter whom I chose to marry. I know Anne is thrilled for my happiness. What I abhor is her being alone at Rosings, forced to bear the brunt of her mother's ire."

"Oh, William, I am sorry for this! I regret that while in Kent, I paid scant heed to Miss de Bourgh, although she seemed pleasant enough. To be honest, I presumed that your not marrying her, when Lady Catherine claimed it a foregone arrangement, meant you were not fond. I apologize for my error."

"There is no need. I can see the logic in your conclusion. In truth, over these past half-dozen years, Anne and I have consciously inserted a distance between us when in Lady Catherine's presence. Her badgering worsened when we displayed our affection. As is obvious, our strategy of pretended dislike, or at least disinterest, did not thwart her intention, but it did allow us to experience some peace."

"Poor Miss de Bourgh."

"Yes. Of course, Anne is familiar with her mother's...temper and manner of speech, shall we say. She has developed techniques to deflect, or avoid when necessary. A fortuitous fainting spell or onslaught of fatigue will do the trick if nothing else works."

Darcy chuckled, a smile touching his lips. But Elizabeth was frowning. "Is Miss de Bourgh's illness feigned then?"

"Sadly it is not. She has suffered from a heart ailment since an adolescent. I only meant that her illness provides a ready excuse to be left alone. Under the circumstances, I cannot fault her for the occasional deception. And, regardless how it may appear, Lady Catherine does love her daughter and is overly solicitous to her fragile condition. Nevertheless, strain is not healthy for Anne, so I worry. Perhaps I can induce Richard to take a trip to check on her. I would need to promise him the moon since enticing him to visit Rosings under the best of occasions is a chore. Speaking of which…"

Darcy rose and retrieved the stack of mail from where it had been dumped onto a random table when he stormed into the library. "You, my lovely Elizabeth, have accomplished a miracle in defusing my fury and lifting my spirits. These letters will surely add to my tranquility and happiness."

He ripped open the one from Colonel Fitzwilliam first and scanned the practically unreadable penmanship that only decades of deciphering made it possible for him to manage.

"Excellent! As I hoped, Richard says he will be returning to London early next week. I cannot wait to tell him of us."

"I thought you wrote him already."

"I decided to wait to see him in person. By the time a letter reached him after bumping hither and yon, he would be in Town anyway. And, with that in mind"—he tapped the twine-tied bundle with one finger—"these are from my solicitor. I shall look through them tonight, but I am certain this means I need to leave for a short time. I am sorry, Elizabeth."

"You warned me, and I understand. Your business cannot be ignored. In a few weeks, Jane and I will be in London, so we will visit with you then, yes?"

Darcy stroked her cheek, smiling as he answered, "Yes, when you are in London, I will surely be there. However, I have no intention of tarrying in Town for weeks. Forgive another display of my ardency for you, Elizabeth, but I truly believe I would go mad if separated for so long." She flushed prettily and lowered her eyes. Darcy continued his feathering caress of her cheek. "I will attend to my business, some of which concerns you…No, do not ask, Elizabeth"—her mouth snapped closed—"because I will not tell you. Marriage to me, you may as well accept, entails being pampered and surprised upon occasion. So, I will do what I must, including visiting with my cousin, and return to Netherfield as soon as possible."

"When will you leave?"

"Tomorrow, early. Best to get it done with. Fortunately, Mr. Daniels and his staff are extraordinarily competent, so that portion of the journey will be swiftly accomplished. The rest may take a bit more time and effort, but I shan't be gone more than a week, I promise."

"This is all quite mysterious, Mr. Darcy. Now my mind is whirling with intriguing scenarios!"

"Good. It shall occupy your time while I am away. Of course, you will undoubtedly enjoy the solitude and reprieve from my selfish monopolization of your day."

"Indeed, it *has* been an exhaustive week, catering to the whims of such a demanding gentleman."

Darcy chuckled, knowing she was teasing but also suspecting she would not suffer without his company to the degree he would. Not wanting to think about it, he turned to Georgiana's letter. He held the pages so Elizabeth could read along with him, a move that startled her, judging by the expression on her face and hesitation before leaning closer. He doubted Georgiana's letter too personal or private. Moreover, the importance in Elizabeth reading of Georgiana's delight in their betrothal transcended any possible embarrassment on his part.

As it happened, the references to Darcy's "poetic phrases of love" and "heart-fluttering descriptions of his Elizabeth" as well as a lengthy commentary on how enraptured she, Mrs. Reynolds, and Mrs. Annesley were by his "ceaseless expressions of joy"—indicating his letter was apparently shared with them and goodness only knows who else among the Pemberley staff—did cause his cheeks to color.

Elizabeth merely smiled and murmured, "How sweet," but said nothing more on that topic. Instead, she focused on Georgiana's gushing delight, saying, "You were correct. Miss Darcy does seem stupendously pleased about our engagement."

"If I had to guess, the only reason she did not beg me to fetch her forthwith was to partake of the preparations for your arrival."

"There you go again, speaking of my joining the household as if a tremendous undertaking. Seriously, William, I hope you have not gone to extremes. My needs are simple and the only wish I have is to be with you. My embarrassment would be acute to think everyone at Pemberley was being put upon, or you were spending exorbitant amounts of money for objects or furnishings that are unnecessary."

Darcy listened to her carefully but did not hasten to respond. Slowly, he nodded and clasped her hands gently. "I believe this area is one where we need to shift our thinking."

He filtered through the correct phrases while she stared at him with a faint frown. "Elizabeth, I cannot begin to convey how marvelous it is to find a woman, a quality woman, who loves and wants me for who I am inside, the man Fitzwilliam, and not only for what I can provide as Mr. Darcy, gentleman of fortune and prestige. It is a gift. You are a gift. We are blessed to have found each other, are we not?"

"Yes...yes, we are. And I do love you. You, William. The rest is nice, I am sure, but not important to me."

"Therein lies the irony, my love. The rest, as you put it, is also who I am. Good and bad, I suppose. I am the product of my upbringing, heritage, station, and wealth. Thanks to you, I am learning to be a better person, but I shall always be Darcy of Pemberley. As such, I will forever, God willing, be able to provide for you abundantly. As I will for our children someday.

"To me, it is not merely a matter of having the wherewithal to do so, but it is also that my heart *desires* to take care of you. This includes your physical comforts and surroundings, and the pretty trinkets. It brings me joy to express my love in this way."

To emphasize his statement, he twisted the sparkling ring on her left hand and then planted a kiss on the knuckle above it. "All that being said, I am aware of how uncomfortable this is for you. I am not sure exactly why, but I never want you to be uncomfortable with me or about our future together."

Elizabeth was staring at their linked hands in her lap, making her face unreadable. He was unsure if he should say more or give her a chance to respond. Luckily, Elizabeth Bennet, even if taken unawares or nervous, was quick witted and rarely backed away from open conversation.

"It is uncomfortable, William, although I confess I cannot say why precisely. I suppose it is a residual fear that you might wonder, however slightly, if my change of heart was because of…the rest."

"Considering you knew about 'the rest' from the moment I walked into the Meryton Assembly and still have a difficult time calling it what it is—my money—you are safe from me doubting your motives."

"Good to know," she said, smiling but still gazing downward. "Honestly, I am not too worried, given all we have been through and how I abused you. Not the smart move of a woman after a man for his income. I know this, and you know this, and a handful of others as well, but…"

"But," he finished when she trailed off, "too many others *do* think that is why you are marrying me. Is that what troubles you?" She looked at him, tears filling her eyes as she nodded once. "Ah! My darling Elizabeth!" He kissed her lightly, brushing the tear that fell. "If you refer to Lady Catherine or Caroline Bingley, they do not matter. You said it yourself! People will presume and speculate, primarily because that is what bored people do. We know the truth of our relationship, and in time it shall be evident."

"It is not just Miss Bingley with her insinuations or Lady Catherine with her accusations. Nor do I dwell upon the opinions of strangers. It is the people here, in Hertfordshire, most whom I have known all my life. It is humiliating, and maddening, to hear the comments and whispers, answer the same questions, see the surprise or indicting smirks. How can they think so poorly of me?"

Darcy could easily answer that question but preferred not to remind her of Mrs. Bennet's unsubtle maneuvering and loud declarations regarding her daughters, especially Jane, and the two new gentlemen in town. As greatly as Darcy regretted his rude behavior during those initial weeks of their acquaintance, it undoubtedly spared him having to contend with Mrs. Bennet and her matchmaking. Not that most mothers and fathers think differently; they simply have a bit more tact as they go about finagling their children's futures. The reality is that wealth and rank *are* the driving forces behind a large percentage of unions. Marriages for love are the rarity, and even then the anticipation is that practicalities play a role. The prevailing judgment is to applaud a joining for practical purposes, not to condemn it.

Not wishing to point out facts connected to past troubles, Darcy answered with a less inciting response to her query. "Dearest, I believe you are mistaken. Surprised, yes—I am sure many of the local citizens are. That, however, is a reflection on me, not you."

"What do you mean?"

"Elizabeth, your friends know you are independent and intelligent. And as I am now painfully aware, they were privy to how intensely you disliked me. Furthermore, they disliked me as well, for some good reasons—"

"Because of Mr. Wickham—"

"He would not have been believed if I had not given them reason." He pressed two fingers against her lips to forestall the rebuttal he sensed coming. "That is past. The relevant point now is that because of their familiarity with you, the citizens I have encountered thus far at our gatherings are curious more than anything. My impression from the majority has been an honest willingness to ascertain what persuaded the esteemed Elizabeth Bennet to accept arrogant, reticent Mr. Darcy. Perhaps he does have a few decent qualities, they think, if Miss Eliza has agreed to risk shackling herself to him!"

"Do not say that," she scolded, but with a hint of a smile at his colorful speech. "You are wonderful, William, and they should be able to determine this immediately. You have been polite, conversational, generous with your time, and patient with their boring stories and fawning. I know how stressful it has been for you, yet you never complain or back away from any invitation or annoying person. I hate that you are striving to please while they do not recognize *this* incredible person I am marrying. Not the single man in possession of a good fortune, who was once considered the rightful property of anyone in Meryton with an eligible daughter!"

"That is one way to state it." Darcy laughed. "It is also the relevant point. I went from being…sought after, if you will, to summarily dismissed due to my surliness, to engaged to the one woman with the best reason to loathe me. Naturally they are flummoxed! But again, the response is not as dire as you perceive. I rather doubt they shall universally determine my wonderfulness, as you have"—he flashed a comically smug grin, earning the giggle he wanted—"nevertheless, my efforts to present myself in a gracious manner are paying off. And it is not stressful at all."

Elizabeth's eyes narrowed, and Darcy sensed a scold was coming. "Did we not agree to be truthful to each other, Mr. Darcy? Do not look me in the eye and fib that socializing to the degree we have this week has not been difficult. You, who has not the talent to converse easily with strangers?"

Darcy frowned. Standing, he paced to the window, rubbed the back of his neck, and then tugged on his cravat. They did agree to be truthful, and it was a promise he intended to keep. That did not mean it was easy, however, when the risk was damaging their newly established harmony.

Inhaling deeply, he turned but stayed near the window. "As you wish, Elizabeth. The truth. Yes, it is arduous for me. Largely, this is because I am not relaxed in unknown company. It is a fault of mine, I am well aware, and my position often requires me to step into situations and conversations that are trying. I do it because I must, but I also avoid it if possible. In this case"—he gestured between the two of them—"I gladly accept the necessity because I love you. I shan't deny that it is a sacrifice, of a sort, but one I am willing to make to please you."

"This is not right, William. You should not have to—"

"Yes, Elizabeth, I should. As will you, from time to time. Being unified means giving and sacrificing. Besides, in my case it is beneficial to socialize with people I would not normally entertain or if I did, would look down upon. Fulfilling my promise to be truthful, I have discovered some of your friends to be enjoyable."

"Some?" she asked, brow lifting and corners of her mouth curling slightly.

"Some," Darcy repeated, holding his serious expression. "I will not lie and claim to delight in the company here. I am sorry, but as I said, I am Mr. Darcy of Pemberley. My eyes have been opened, thanks to you. Yet I cannot change overnight, and the truth, again, is that as a matter of course, the society I prefer is…different and always will be. My standards are exacting, I admit. It is my upbringing, pompous pride if you wish, yet there it is."

He stepped to where she sat silently on the sofa, one hand clutching the cushioned armrest as he gazed into her beautiful eyes. *God, help me express myself and help her to understand.* "Elizabeth, in this, we are not akin. I am in awe of your ability to converse and easily connect with literally anyone. I do not have that gift, and I never will overcome my native reticence. If possible, I would only interact with family and close friends. I know that is impossible, but I do not like moving beyond my comfort."

Remaining still, he watched her stand and approach. "What was it you said earlier? That we needed to shift our thinking as we learn to understand each other?" Darcy nodded. "I am finding this to be an exhilarating exercise, Mr. Darcy. How boring would it be if we were precisely akin in everything?"

"Exceedingly boring."

"And were you not drawn to me because I am refreshing and, upon occasion, shockingly unlike the women you have been surrounded by?" She laid her hand over his on the sofa armrest, Darcy finally choking out a husky yes. "Similarly, I was drawn to and fell in love with Mr. Darcy of Pemberley as much as the man William. That is the truth."

No power on earth could have stopped him from kissing her at that point. He restrained his urgency to carry the kiss to a deeper level, yet even the tender exchange left them both breathless. Teetering on the edge of consuming desire, Darcy managed to withdraw from the intoxicating sensation of her lips, suggesting in an unsteady voice that they return to Bingley and Jane.

The last words on the subject were an agreement to forego fretting the opinions of others, from his world or hers, and to focus exclusively on strengthening their relationship. Then, as Darcy collected the stack of letters, Elizabeth indicated the one from Georgiana.

"William, may I request permission to write directly to Miss Darcy?"

"That depends," he said, feigning suspicion. "Are you wishing to establish a sisterly bond or ferret information on me that only a sister would know?"

"Both," she promptly replied, the smile dancing on her lips at odds with the stern tone.

Darcy sighed resignedly. "It was bound to happen. Yes, you have my permission. God help me."

೮ᗴ

Leaving Netherfield the next morning was harder than Darcy had anticipated. Especially trying was passing by the lane that led to Longbourn. If mounted on his horse instead of seated in a carriage, the impulse to turn in for another farewell—with perhaps another kiss or two—might have been impossible to resist.

Six weeks until we are married. God grant me the strength to remain a gentleman!

Arriving at Darcy House on Grosvenor Square by midmorning, Darcy crossed the threshold briskly. One arm remained inside the greatcoat actively being doffed when he requested an immediate audience with the townhouse's butler and housekeeper. Mr. Travers and Mrs. Smyth filed into his office less than five minutes later and, after the briefest of greetings, were informed of his impending marriage. Other than Elizabeth's name, and that she would be visiting London later in the month, no further details were given. For the present, it was not vital, and as servants, the facts were not warranted anyway. It sufficed that they understood the changes to come and began preparations of the townhouse accordingly.

Trusting they would pass the development on to the remaining staff, Darcy set to the task of writing notes to be delivered immediately.

First was to Mr. Daniels, requesting a preliminary meeting to discuss Elizabeth's betrothal settlement as early as possible. The reply, written in the solicitor's impeccable penmanship, slated him for the following morning.

The second short note was for his cousin Richard. Darcy said nothing about Elizabeth, only alerting him that he was in Town and anxious to visit. A swift response from the landlord informed that Colonel Fitzwilliam had not yet returned from his mission, but with the assurance that Mr. Darcy's letter would be delivered forthwith into the colonel's hand when he entered his building. Darcy could do nothing but wait and hope Richard was not delayed.

Next was a missive to Mr. Kennedy, one of several trusted contacts Darcy enlisted whenever he needed furnishings or unusual merchandise. It was far more efficient to pay an expert rather than troll shops or craftsmen's studios himself. By the end of the day, an appointment was arranged for the morrow in the afternoon.

Lastly was another request for an appointment, this one with his tailor. Darcy owned an outrageous number of suits, a dozen of which were formal, constructed with quality fabrics, and superbly adequate for one's wedding. Despite that fact, Darcy intended to honor his beloved Elizabeth by dressing in an ensemble specifically designed for the day she would willingly bind herself to him. She would always deserve the best, including the groom waiting for her at the holy altar.

Once those chores were done, the evening was his to enjoy in solitude. It was refreshing to dine in relaxed style in the parlor, coat and cravat removed, with only the faint murmurs of the servants and muffled street noises heard. Yet no matter how often he told himself how wonderful the tranquility was, his mind and heart traveled the miles to Longbourn.

How had her day passed? Had her mind drifted to musing of him? What activity was she engaged in at this moment? Was she breathing in relief to have a quiet night with her family?

Dare I hope she misses me and wishes I were there?

ॐ

Until dinner, Lizzy had gone about her day with only occasional flittering thoughts of Mr. Darcy.

In the early morning hours, she had helped her mother with a few domestic chores, after which she had visited Mr. Beller in the barnyard. The cows and other animals were longtime friends, of a sort, who appreciated special treats and gentle rubs. Rather than walking during the warmest part of the day, Lizzy had chosen to write a letter to Miss Darcy. She enjoyed teasing her betrothed, but truthfully, she had no intention of asking Miss Darcy to reveal secrets about her brother. Lizzy preferred learning from him rather than a secondary source. Indeed, her only instigation was to strengthen the tenuous bond she and Georgiana established during their brief company at Pemberley. Therefore, her letter was short and consisted of scant more than expressing her happiness with Mr. Darcy and anticipatory joy in another sister.

It was while writing to Miss Darcy that Lizzy initially speculated on Mr. Darcy's activities in London, a vague contemplation rapidly shrugged away. Then, as she had sealed the envelope, the name *Darcy* speared her, surprisingly, with a swift stab of sadness that required several seconds to recognize as missing him.

Honestly, Lizzy had not expected to mourn his absence greatly. After all, he had only been a serious part of her life for a week. It defied logic to pine for him a mere fifteen hours after last in his presence! She had shaken off the foolishness, the remaining hours before dinner serenely ticking by in mindlessly repairing the pile of garments with rips or frayed seams.

Further sentimental pangs had not intruded, even with the dining table space previously occupied by Mr. Darcy sitting empty. Conversation was abundant and gay throughout the meal, and on into the after-dinner socializing in the parlor. When a game of cards commenced, Lizzy opted to read instead. Curling into a chair near the window, she opened her novel to the marked page and glanced swiftly out the window to gauge the fading light.

William would love this sunset. I wonder if he is watching this same sunset in London.

Unexpectedly, melancholy was triggered and the tone of the evening instantly altered. Book forgotten in her lap, Lizzy watched the sun lower below the horizon. Mr. Darcy on her mind, she admired the dance of colors and shadows frolicking over the autumn-hued leaves, bare branches, and dying grasses. The cloudless sky was lit brilliantly with oranges and gold, gradually dimming until a mere sliver of yellow light skimmed along the edge where land met sky, to then be lost in darkness.

She sighed, the sound muted and forlorn.

Somehow the vision of him sitting in a window seat, or perhaps standing on the rear terrace of his townhouse, while observing the slipping sun was comforting and depressing. *If not gazing at the sunset, what else might he be doing right this second?* The vision of him relaxing in some fashion, alone in a silent room, reading or writing a letter, made her want to smile and frown simultaneously. *Undoubtedly he is delirious with joy to be away from my noisy family! Yet is he missing me? Or is he too happy in his solitude to wish for even my disruptive presence?*

She was incapable of deciphering the converging emotions. She loved Fitzwilliam Darcy unquestionably. The depth of her love and how it affected her were the weighty implications she hesitated to dwell upon.

Sleep provided oblivion from the chaotic emotions.

By morning of the second day without Mr. Darcy in Hertfordshire, a refreshed Lizzy woke determined not to mire in such ridiculously maudlin behavior. The weather was perfect for a long walk, Lizzy setting out immediately after breakfast with a small basket of food and her novel. Willow Bench sparked a multitude of Mr. Darcy associated reveries—more, in truth, than she expected based on two encounters out of the hundreds alone at the copse. Fortunately, the reminders of him were amusing and comforting rather than heart-rending, and the hours passing happily.

It was late in the afternoon when Lizzy approached Longbourn and spied the unfamiliar, plain black cabriolet parked on the drive. Any question as to the visitor's identity disappeared the second Lizzy opened the door and heard Mr. Collins's voice. Hoping Charlotte was with him, Lizzy hastened toward the parlor but stopped abruptly when he mentioned Lady Catherine de Bourgh. Pausing, hidden in the corridor, she unabashedly eavesdropped.

"...Lady Catherine's anger is intense. It is imperative that you understand, my dear Mrs. Bennet, that under the circumstances, from her perspective, Lady Catherine's dismay is justified. Her heightened emotions are completely comprehendible. I cannot find it in my heart to fault such a great lady as my esteemed patroness, and would never dream of saying a single word of criticism, not that I *do* criticize, you understand. Miss Elizabeth is a respectable young lady, and you know my impressions were once favorable, if proved to be adverse to my personal requirements, those being superbly satisfied by my dear Mrs. Collins."

"Precisely so, Mr. Collins. All is as it was meant to be. Charlotte for you, and my Lizzy for Mr. Darcy. I fail to see what Lady Catherine has to be angry about!"

"It is as you once said, Mrs. Bennet. Miss Elizabeth is headstrong, foolish, and, forgive me for repeating the words, not keen on what is best for her. It pains me to imply that Miss Elizabeth is an unfavorable choice for Mr. Darcy, an excellent gentleman I have no right to censure. Lady Catherine, however, judges the match most adamantly disadvantageous and unwise. As to this, I must admonish that as a woman of experience and superiority, her ladyship's judgment should be given due consideration. Furthermore, Lady Catherine is rightfully distressed that Mr. Darcy forsook Miss de Bourgh rather than adhering to his promise—"

"A promise, Mr. Collins, that I have great doubt was sworn with all parties in agreement." Charlotte's demure interjection provided Mr. Collins time to audibly inhale, but the comment fed into the focus of his speech rather than diverted it.

"Indeed, I cannot warrant a gentleman as highly praised as Mr. Darcy would baldly repudiate an avowed oath. Nor could I ever believe that noble and honorable Lady Catherine claimed falsely. Logical deduction asserts that there is a misunderstanding or complexity to the arrangement that we of lesser rank are not privy to, with no one party completely at fault. Nevertheless, Lady Catherine is distraught for her daughter and of the opinion the arrangement between Mr. Darcy and Miss Elizabeth is violating a prior commitment."

"This is all too much for my nerves! If there are impediments, Lizzy should break the engagement with Mr. Darcy immediately!"

Lizzy winced at the strain in her mother's voice, even as her heart stopped and her anger flared.

"There is no need for that, I am sure, Mrs. Bennet—" Charlotte's second calming attempt to downplay her husband's assertions was drown by further sermonizing.

"For the sake of a harmonious parish, I must appreciate the perspective of my patroness. As Lady Catherine's clergyman and a sworn officer of the Church, it is my duty to pacify, intervene, and advise. I have done so to the best of my abilities and with a clear conscience. Unfortunately, my connection with Hertfordshire and the Bennet family added to Lady Catherine's distress, and my spiritual services were no longer sought. My decision to quit Hunsford temporarily was to ease Lady Catherine's pain, not to cause discord amongst the family here, Mrs. Bennet. Nevertheless, Mrs. Collins and I agreed that the situation should be reported."

"Well, it is quite a distressing report, Mr. Collins! I do wish Mr. Bennet had not chosen today to tend to business with Mr. Phillips. You must inform him immediately upon his return! I am sure he will know what is best to do."

"But my good lady, I did alert Mr. Bennet! Some weeks past, in fact. Evidently he chose not to share my warnings with you or my cousin, the latter rushing into the precipitous closure with Mr. Darcy I expressly counseled against to avoid this very outcome! Now Lady Catherine is loudly proclaiming her opinions on the matter to anyone within proximity of Rosings Park, including the fact that she does not sanction the marriage, her permission expressly denied. Such woeful tidings are not auspicious for a happy union, I fear."

"Oh dear! Oh dear, oh dear…" Mrs. Bennet moaned in between sniffles.

Lizzy had heard enough. Determined to put an end to Mr. Collins's tirade, she moved toward the portal, but her steps slowed when Charlotte spoke, more forcefully this time.

"Do not be troubled, Mrs. Bennet. While I agree Lady Catherine's response to Lizzy's excellent news should be conveyed, I have a differing outlook than my fine husband. These personal, family matters are beyond the scope of our understanding. We are outsiders and only privy to one perspective. Undoubtedly Mr. Darcy's perspective is vastly different, that apparent by his actions. He is an honorable gentleman with a reputation for honesty and integrity, with nary a whiff of scandal or misbehavior, so I see no reason to distrust his relationship with Lizzy."

Not giving Mr. Collins a chance to rebut, or her mother an opportunity to launch into fresh hysterics, Lizzy spoke loudly as she crossed the threshold. "Thank you, Mrs. Collins. It is a relief to finally hear a sensible statement uttered within the walls of this room. Based on the ridiculous speculations, blatant falsehoods, and dramatic declarations I have overheard in the past ten minutes, I was beginning to lose hope that wisdom existed in Longbourn."

Mr. Collins—who was staring at his wife in what appeared to Lizzy as stunned amazement that she would dare to verbally disagree with him in front of others—lifted his gaze to Lizzy when she entered the room. Piercing him directly with eyes hard and condemning, Lizzy watched his astoundment mix with confusion and embarrassment. As she knew, Mr. Collins prided himself on his ability to dominate a conversation, humble phrases passing his lips even as he exalted his perceived superior intelligence. Most of the time, Lizzy was amused by him. Not so when he ignored her refusal of his marriage proposal, and definitely not at the present.

"It would behoove you, Mr. Collins, to hearken to Charlotte's reminder. Despite what Lady Catherine has shared with her rector, there is indeed more to the issue than her biased opinion and skewed facts. No"—she held up her hand when Collins opened his mouth—"I am not going to say more. You have done your duty, Mr. Collins, in giving advice and warning. I do appreciate this in the spirit intended, and thank you." *Never hurts to be magnanimous,* she thought, hiding the cringe inside. "However, now you must heed my advice and warning: exonerate yourself from being the watchdog over my relationship with Mr. Darcy."

"But, Cousin, how can I do that when it is my obligation to attend to the needs of my flock, especially Lady Catherine!"

"I daresay you have done an admirable job for your flock and Lady Catherine, Mr. Collins, and will continue to do so. Just not in regards to the matter of Mr. Darcy and me. We are to be married. There is nothing else to be said, and I refuse further discourse, other than to stress what Mr. Bennet wrote in his letter. You did receive it, yes?"

"We did," Charlotte answered when Mr. Collins flushed and looked down at his shoes.

"Then, as my father suggested, console your patroness as best you can, sir, but without offending Mr. Darcy in the process. *That* would be most unwise."

Saying nothing more to Mr. Collins, Lizzy turned to Charlotte. Smiling brightly, she grasped her friend's hands. "Come walk in the garden with me, Charlotte. The autumn flowers are blooming, and we extended past the row of lilacs since last you were here." Chatting warmly, Lizzy led Charlotte out the door in seconds, neither glancing backward.

Lizzy prattled gaily as they walked away from the house. Perfectly content to leave the subject of her engagement alone, she did smile when Charlotte interjected with her congratulations.

"Lizzy, you must know how delighted I am for you and Mr. Darcy. I think it is wonderful news, if surprising."

"And here I thought you, of all people, would be the least surprised! I do believe you were the only person who suspected Mr. Darcy held affection for me."

"I did, for a short time. But you felt sure that it could not be, that he disliked you even. Then, when nothing came of it while you visited us in the spring, I was sure I had been mistaken."

"Being mistaken was an epidemic last spring," Lizzy admitted, laughing halfheartedly.

Charlotte's pace slowed, her eyes on the ground. "Lizzy, I owe you an apology."

"Nonsense, Charlotte. You are not responsible for Mr. Collins's interference or attitude. In fact, I am in your debt for speaking up just now. I fear Mama was near to fainting!"

"I only spoke the truth as I see it, Lizzy. Yet that is not what I refer to. Regrettably, if not for me, Mr. Collins may never have gotten involved in this matter at all."

Lizzy quizzically knit her brows. "Whatever do you mean?"

Charlotte sat on a nearby bench and patted the empty space beside. "One night, during those weeks when Mr. Darcy called at the parsonage so frequently," Charlotte explained, "I mentioned the possibility of Mr. Darcy being in love with you to Mr. Collins. He was quite distressed by the idea, which greatly surprised me. I told him you laughed at the notion, convinced that Mr. Darcy disapproved of you far too much to be partial. This seemed to satisfy him, and we spoke no more. Nor did I speak of it with you, Lizzy." She squeezed Lizzy's hand, her smile warm. "I feared pressing the idea might endanger you by raising expectations, if indeed your feelings began to change toward Mr. Darcy, ending in disappointment if you were correct in his disliking you."

Charlotte shook her head, Lizzy detecting confusion within her friend's eyes. "Honestly, the behavior of you both puzzled me tremendously, more so when the gentleman left so abruptly, leaving you clearly depressed. Mr. Collins noted your distraction and wondered if Mr. Darcy's departure contributed. The truth is, Lizzy, I wondered the same! With nothing substantial, Mr. Collins and I said scant more about it.

"Until, that is, last month when my mother wrote of Jane's engagement to Mr. Bingley. She wrote that Mr. Darcy was again in the area, paying particular attention to you, and presumed a proposal was eminent. It was then, unbeknownst to me until afterward, that Mr. Collins reported to Lady Catherine. I am still unsure precisely what transpired afterward, but am aware she took action in a most unpleasant manner and continues to be furious. The blame rests on my shoulders for discussing with Mr. Collins in the first place. Can you ever forgive me?"

Lizzy did her best to maintain a neutral expression when what she wanted to do was scream. Not out of anger, however. She could hardly be angry with Charlotte for talking to her husband. That is what married couples were supposed to do. Nor could she honestly be mad at Mr. Collins's role in spreading rumors from the Lucases to Lady Catherine. Her temper prompted the confrontation with Lizzy and then Darcy, which eventually brought them together.

No, she wanted to scream from frustration. Continually being placed on the defensive in regards to her engagement with Mr. Darcy was maddening. Too many people, from Lady Catherine to Mr. Collins to Caroline Bingley, were hell-bent on darkening their happiness or destroying it completely.

Somehow she mustered a smile convincingly gay and amused. "Really, Charlotte, it no longer matters. Mr. Darcy and I have hashed over the past misconceptions, and are deliriously happy. Lady Catherine would be furious no matter how she heard of our engagement, and trust me when I say that Mr. Darcy can handle his aunt. I do regret that her attitude has filtered down to you, but it brought you to Hertfordshire for a spell, so I cannot be sorry even for that."

They talked then of pleasanter topics, catching up on local gossip mainly, as well as some female tittering about the wedding. Lizzy relaxed, she and her oldest friend gradually settling into their familiar companionship. She forgot Mr. Collins was still in the house until he appeared on the back porch calling for Charlotte.

"No, stay here, Lizzy." Charlotte waved at the garden as she stood. "Mr. Collins and I will be staying at Lucas Lodge for a time, so I shall have plenty of opportunities to visit." She bent to plant a soft kiss on Lizzy's cheek, whispering, "Preferably alone or with Maria," which made them both laugh. Turning away, Charlotte walked several feet before abruptly stopping and pivoting about. "Oh! I nearly forgot! I have something for you." She withdrew a folded paper from her reticule and handed it to Lizzy.

"A letter from Miss de Bourgh! But...why?"

"Mrs. Jenkinson brought it to me three days ago. Miss de Bourgh was unsure of your residence and asking Lady Catherine was out of the question. In fact, according to Mrs. Jenkinson, Miss de Bourgh feared for the letter if Lady Catherine knew of it, so trusted me to deliver. Since by then we had decided to leave Hunsford, I carried it rather than mailing. I do not know what she wrote, Lizzy, but based on what I know of Miss de Bourgh, it is unlikely to be unpleasant. Quite the opposite, I think."

Lizzy stared at the sealed paper for a long while after Charlotte left. Considering Charlotte's words and William's deep affection for his cousin, Lizzy had no reason to fear the contents of Miss de Bourgh's letter. Yet, in light of the harsh sentiments that persistently came, she hesitated.

"Oh bother!" Lizzy muttered and ripped the wax angrily.

Dear Miss Elizabeth Bennet,

Undoubtedly this direct dispatch from me will be met with trepidation, so please allow me to immediately ease your mind. My only purpose in penning these words is to convey my rapture at your engagement to my cousin. Aware as I am of his compulsory demand for honesty, surely you are now privy to our special relationship, and that our affection, while true, has never been of the romantic nature. Long have we humored Lady Catherine, certain that in time she would surrender the designs for us to marry. Alas, we erred in estimating the strength of her resolve. I must not speak as an unfaithful daughter, so cannot write extensively of my anguish over mother's reaction to this most blessed news. I pray you believe how deep my regret at being the center, however unwillingly, of any clouds obscuring the happiness of this precious time for you and Fitzwilliam.

We spoke only briefly during the spring, Miss Bennet, yet it was enough for me to hold you in the highest regard. To me it was apparent that Fitzwilliam cared for you, and I sensed that you were perfect for him. He is a complex man but has a tender soul and the kindest heart. With every breath and beat of my heart, I thank the fates for bringing you to each other, and wish for eternal joy in your lives together. I have faith that somehow, someday, we will overcome the troubles causing this tragic rift and will become friends. Until then, trust in your love to sustain, and know that my thoughts are of nothing but delight.

God's richest blessings, now and forever, Anne de Bourgh

Lizzy was unaware tears were slipping down her cheeks until one fell onto the paper. The balm, today of all days, in hearing delight expressed over their engagement was worthy of tears. Anne de Bourgh had perceived their rightness for each other at a time when no one else could, not even Lizzy. They were hopeful tears. Miss de Bourgh's endorsement, along with the delight of Miss Darcy, instilled a measure of hope that their union would not be universally snubbed by Mr. Darcy's family.

The tears were also the result of relinquishing traces of fear that by marrying Mr. Darcy she was hurting his cousin. Indeed he had explained their relationship, and Lizzy did not doubt his honesty, but he would not be the first man to misread a woman's feelings. What if Miss de Bourgh had loved him and wanted to be his wife? The fact that William never would have married her—and that it was in one respect no different than Caroline Bingley wanting to marry him—did not erase the vague pinch of remorse over dashing a decent, kind lady's dreams. Miss de Bourgh's reassurance was surprisingly liberating.

Sighing, Lizzy refolded the letter and wiped the wetness from her face. "What a ninny," she muttered and then chuckled. More than anything, she acknowledged that she missed William.

No, I actually ache for him...for William.

Her heart felt weighted, as if each beat struggled to pump the blood. An odd stupor invaded her muscles—not exactly paralyzing her limbs, but as if they required an external force to excite the nerves into motion. Or rather that her entire body was impatiently waiting for the impetus of a specific entity to move toward.

Of all the times in her life when parted from members of her family, missing them greatly while being entertained, Lizzy had never experienced this degree of gloominess. She suddenly suspected that if Mr. Darcy were to walk around the corner this second, she might literally dance and sing. Loving a man to this degree was disconcerting—but also wondrous. Either extremity would take more than one night to adjust to, Lizzy logically understood, so she shrugged off the unnerving melancholy and lassitude.

Stepping briskly toward the house, Lizzy vowed not to mope or brood stupidly during the remaining days until Mr. Darcy returned. So why did she pause on the threshold, peer into the dimming sky, sigh wistfully, and inquire of the moon, "Does William ache for me?"

SHARON LATHAN

CHAPTER EIGHT
Sun Shines on London

*D*arcy sat at the large mahogany table in the conference room of his London solicitor's offices, a single paper in his hand. He silently read the final paragraph, added the paper to the stack by his elbow, and neatly aligned the pile. "Precisely as stipulated, Mr. Daniels. As I wrote, it is imperative the settlement be generous and Mrs. Darcy's security firmly established no matter what the future holds. Thank you for the experienced suggestions. I can think of nothing further to add."

"You have been far more generous than most gentlemen, sir. I am sure Miss Bennet will be pleased and Mr. Bennet confident that his daughter has chosen wisely. Fathers can be demanding in their paternal concerns."

Darcy smiled at the dry statement. "Indeed, as I suspect you would know. How is your daughter faring?"

"As one expects from a young lady newly married and in love. Mrs. Daniels and I are content in her choice."

"Glad to hear it." Darcy handed the sheaf of documents to his solicitor. "Notify me when those are ready for my signature."

"I will have my clerks compile today. Would tomorrow morning at eleven fit into your schedule?"

"My schedule is loose, so I shall be here at eleven. I appreciate your expeditiousness, Mr. Daniels. I do wish to return to Hertfordshire as soon as possible."

The solicitor merely nodded.

Once outside, Darcy entered his carriage and sat back into the padded bench. It was a fair distance to the Royal Exchange on Cornhill, and with traffic in London inevitably heavy during the daylight hours, he might be in for a lengthy drive. Rather than daydream of Elizabeth, which would be pleasant but also increase his urgency to quit Town, he passed the time by shuffling through the papers sent by Mrs. Reynolds and his sister. He had memorized them, but it did not hurt to check again, just in case he missed something.

Armed with the papers, Darcy entered the recessed door on the west side of the massive building housing the Royal Exchange. This entrance led to private offices on the upper floor, bypassing the main areas where the merchants dealt with customers, so was less congested and noisy but far from vacant or silent. Instantly greeted by acquaintances, Darcy avoided extensive conversation by claiming an appointment, which was true. Nevertheless, making his way to the plush offices of Mr. Kennedy and his associates took some time. Luckily, the rotund, jolly Mr. Kennedy was used to the ways of the Exchange, so he laughingly brushed aside Darcy's apologies and extended his hand to the empty chair across from his desk.

"You have braved the streets and then the aisles of the Exchange, Mr. Darcy, so I have tea and coffee on the way. Or perhaps you prefer a nip of something stronger?"

"Coffee will be fine, thank you, Mr. Kennedy. And thank you for arranging time to meet with me on short notice."

"My pleasure. And I mean that literally, Darcy. A man on the hunt for refurbishing and provisioning for a new wife is my bread and butter!"

"I imagine so. And then yearly thereafter, when redecorating occurs, am I right?"

Kennedy laughed heartily, smacking his fleshy hand onto his desk. "For a man newly entering the married state, you are wise in the ways of it."

"I am learning, yes, but open for advice." Darcy unfolded the papers, explaining as he pushed them toward Kennedy, "My betrothed, Miss Bennet, is the daughter of a gentleman landowner in Hertfordshire. She is a lady, but not of London Society. If left to her own devices, she would ask for nothing to be done for her at Pemberley."

"But you have other ideas."

"I do." Darcy leaned forward, explaining each point, room by room, as Kennedy added his notes to the ones Darcy had jotted.

"The main focus is your wife's suite. I see you want the lavatory, bathing room, and dressing area modernized and refurnished completely. This you will find interesting, Darcy, being a man fond of modern inventions." Mr. Kennedy launched into an extensive lecture on the latest advancements in bathing tubs and other personal hygiene hardware, which Darcy *was* fascinated by. Sketches to revamp Elizabeth's toilette, floor to ceiling and wall to wall, with nothing overlooked and everything new, occupied a generous portion of the appointment. Once satisfied, Darcy tapped the next page sent by Mrs. Reynolds.

"The bedchamber once belonging to Lady Anne is in dire need of a transformation, but the decor must be as Miss Bennet desires. She has never seen the rooms, unfortunately, and has reservations regarding my...spending money on her at this juncture." Kennedy's brows rose at that, but he said nothing. "So, I am at a loss as to the best way to solve this dilemma."

"I can arrange for a designer to travel to Pemberley at a date after the new Mrs. Darcy has settled in. Or, I can recommend Mr. Price in Derby. He does brilliant work and has an exceptional staff. We have worked together a few times, including a job some three years ago at Rivallain for Lady Matlock."

"Oh yes, I do remember when Lady Matlock redesigned several of the lower level rooms, mainly from my uncle complaining at the cost! The interior was marvelously done, however, as his lordship grudgingly agreed." Darcy smiled in recollection. "Considering the time of year and weather concerns, and in light of your trusted recommendation, let's arrange for Mr. Price to come to Pemberley in early December."

"For the immediate, I can ensure the bedchamber is properly outfitted right away with the essentials. A new mattress, for example, with pillows, blankets, and bed linens. Mrs. Darcy must at least have a comfortable place to sleep."

Discussing mattresses and bed linens was mildly uncomfortable for Darcy, even though he anticipated skirting the edges of intimate subjects as an unavoidable consequence. It was vital to ensure Elizabeth's private chambers were cozy and to her taste, so despite his unease, he joined Mr. Kennedy in serious contemplation of the colorful drawings in the latest trade catalogs. Frankly, as he most definitely could not say to the merchant, his fervent hope was that his wife never slept there.

Darcy could only guess the nightly sleeping arrangement between his parents, but based on the intense love they had shared, and many clues not comprehended until he matured, in all likelihood they had slept together in the master bedchamber for the bulk of their marriage. Indeed, his greatest wish was to attain the same level of intimacy with Elizabeth. He dared not presume she would choose to stay with him in his room, or even visit him there in the first place. Where or how they would love each other was not a topic they could discuss beforehand.

He could dream, however, and the thought of sleeping with her body in his arms, or close enough to touch, sent sharp pangs of longing through his heart. With this hope in mind, he planned to redecorate his bedchamber as well. The masculine style and furnishings were fine for a single male inhabitant, and he could not bear to sleep in a room garish with pink ruffles and lace, but a compromise appealing to a female aesthetic was doable—and, perhaps, enticing.

Another two hours sped by. Darcy looked at samples of fabrics until his eyes were crossed, and settled on three new rugs from the rows of hanging carpets in one warehouse. A plethora of fine bed linens, towels, washing cloths, pillows, and cases, all per Mrs. Reynolds's knowledgeable specifications—which Mr. Kennedy concurred with—were purchased. A few select pieces of furniture were commissioned, Darcy examining a thick book of drawings until satisfied with his choices.

Darcy was pleased with the accomplishments and content that every single item purchased or ordered would be delivered to Pemberley well before his wedding date.

Out on the street, Darcy paused before seeking his carriage. He was done with his appointments, so considered visiting White's before returning to Darcy House. Between being out of Town for over a week and living as a relative recluse for weeks before that, he was quite behind in current events. Granted the city was in a lull, with most of the aristocracy and gentry retired to their country manors, but there were always people who stayed in London, and the men's clubs were never deserted.

There was also the call of Angelo's. Drawing his pocket watch, he flipped the cover up, his mind quickly figuring the drive to the fencing academy versus White's and whether he would have adequate time for a couple rounds. He was debating the issue when a voice called his name.

Glancing up, Darcy instantly doffed his hat and conducted a smooth bow. "Lady Buckleigh. Delighted to see you, although I confess to surprise that you are in Town rather than Suffolk."

"Only temporarily, Mr. Darcy. Lord Buckleigh and I are soon leaving for Yorkshire. We will pass the winter months and Christmastide with our daughter. You heard that Lady Celia wed Viscount Wyllis this past spring?"

"I did. Congratulations. I pray she is well in her marriage and new life up north?"

"It has been an adjustment, as you can imagine, living in a region to the north as well. Poor Celia was not thrilled with the idea of snow and cold, but sacrifices must be made for the sake of domestic peace and social prosperity. You shall discover this in due time, I daresay."

"I am sure I shall," Darcy nodded, keeping his face neutral. "Then my guess is you came to London for early Christmas shopping?"

"Quite so. Blythe Gallery is holding an auction, and has a new exhibit of Gainsborough and Richard Wilson, to name only two. I hope to find a summer landscape to cheer Celia. If I recall, you are fond of Gainsborough, Mr. Darcy."

Indeed he was, and suddenly the prospect of browsing through a gallery replete with beautiful art pieces displayed for hushed observation sounded better than White's or Angelo's. Best of all, Blythe was two blocks away, so easy to walk to.

Sitting beside Lady Buckleigh, the witty baroness a distant cousin of his Aunt Madeline, the Countess of Matlock, and thus a longtime acquaintance of his, enhanced the enjoyment of the auction. Within half an hour, a brightly painted landscape was obtained for the homesick Viscountess Wyllis, and Darcy bid successfully on a Gainsborough and two of William Blake's relief etchings. Darcy and Lady Buckleigh joined a group of Society friends for a glass of wine, the talk casual and centered on art, before the two fondly parted ways. Darcy was weary, but the hushed atmosphere of the gallery with marvelous paintings thick on the walls called to him.

Strolling leisurely around the spacious rooms and nearly empty corridors for some twenty minutes, Darcy was about to head for the exit when he saw it.

Hanging in a line of seascape paintings with an unmistakably nautical theme was an enormous, ornately framed canvas depicting a pastoral landscape. The artist was unfamiliar to him, and the title was simply *Tranquility* without any indication of where in England the real meadow was located, yet it stunningly resembled the scenery surrounding Longbourn—specifically the grassy moor where Elizabeth had accepted his marriage proposal.

Exquisitely painted in oil, the field of knee-high green grasses almost appeared to wave in the sun-kissed air. A small stream cut crookedly through the middle with a narrow, stone bridge spanning one edge. In the distance stood a house of red brick obscured by clusters of trees and the faint wisps of English mist hugging the ground. He could easily envision their figures inserted in the scene, hands clasped as they declared their love for each other.

Breathless and immobile, Darcy stared, transfixed as memories sprang into his mind—vivid ones of her warm hands encompassing his cold one, her sweet breath wafting over his cheeks, and honeyed voice declaring her love. Fiery emotions swept through him. The powerfully evocative sensations of her lips moving under his, her hands tangled in his hair, and soft body pressed against his chest fanned the fire into a blaze. Thank God no one else was in this part of the gallery because Darcy was sure he moaned aloud. Desire electrified every nerve. Yearning for her overwhelmed, it undoubtedly prudent she was not standing beside him.

Finally he calmed, at least enough to take the painting off the wall. Normal procedure was to ask an attendant to retrieve the piece, but he was not going to take a chance on anyone else claiming it before he could find someone.

Later that night, once again alone and relaxed in casual attire after a solitary dinner, Darcy sipped hot cocoa and dreamily gazed at the framed painting propped on a nearby settee. Tomorrow promised to be another busy day, beginning with meeting Mr. Daniels to sign copies of the betrothal agreement and tend to a number of estate business matters. After that was the appointment with his tailor, and with luck the items requested from Pemberley would arrive as well, so he could attend to those final tasks. Then it would be a matter of waiting for Richard's return, which better happen soon because Darcy had no intention of tarrying in London indefinitely.

Pushing tomorrow's plans aside, Darcy closed his eyes and rested his head back onto the cushioned chair. Envisioning Elizabeth, he freely indulged in the love and passion she roused within him. The sensations were unique and growing daily. As he had speculated on the day of their engagement, being separated by distance was painful in a manner it never had been before. Yet, as he had also speculated, there was an odd joy to the ache because it was a sign of their increasing bond, and being reunited would be especially sweet. Is this what Roman poet Sextus Propertius alluded to with the line, "Always toward absent lovers love's tide stronger flows," in *Elegies*? Perhaps, although Darcy preferred strengthening their "love's tide" in her presence!

Whatever the case, if he had to be away from her, as was bound to happen even after they married, he could use the time to dwell upon the marvelous feelings her existence generated. Already he could instantly conjure her face in all its myriad expressions, and hear her protean voice and laughter as vividly as if she were sitting next to him. Imagining her in this room was enough to warm his heart and fill the vacant areas of his soul.

Elizabeth Bennet.

Thinking of her and the love they shared was soothing. It was also stressful and, at times, downright physically excruciating. Wanting the release found only with a woman was not a new phenomenon for Darcy, naturally, but never had the ache of unfulfilled arousal affected him as acutely as it has since she kissed him in the garden at Longbourn. The ardent longing for her, amplified each month over the past year while dreams haunted him, had not remotely prepared him for the overpowering sexual desire her touch awoke. It was as if a dormant beast had come to roaring life. Not one completely unwelcome, he honestly admitted, but the wildness was contrary to the controlled temper he prided himself on possessing.

And then there were the inevitable questions he struggled to answer. Was allowing free rein to his passionate musing while alone a wise move? Was self-gratification while dreaming of her proper and enough to appease? Would it then be easier to regulate the limited intimate exchanges with Elizabeth? Or was he only baiting the beast with partial satisfaction and tasty samplings? Was he capable of restraint for another six weeks and then, a horrid scenario to contemplate, fail to be gentle on their wedding night?

If there was one thing Darcy hated above all else, it was not being able to intellectually and rationally work through a problem and come to a sensible plan. Methodical and confident in the extreme, being at a loss as to how best to proceed with Elizabeth was galling. Of course, as he had to concede, even if it did conflict with his need for disciplined logic, love was, by its nature, fluid and variable. As an emotion, love did not follow set rules, could not be forced to behave a certain way, would refuse to be contained, and gave no guarantees it would flourish.

At the end of the day—as the chiming clock alerted him it literally was—Darcy trusted that somehow, like every man down the corridors of time who waited to wed the woman he loved, he would survive, rejoice in their happy after, and laugh at his current anxieties.

At least that is what his intellectual, rational mind grasped on to.

 споры

The lower edge of the sun had dipped behind the roofs of neighboring townhouses when Darcy's carriage halted before the polished white stones of Darcy House on Grosvenor Square. Waiting for the footman to open the door, Darcy exited with the bundle of signed papers from Mr. Daniels tucked under one arm. Gesturing to the bags and boxes arranged neatly on the bench opposite where he had sat, Darcy said, "Peters, please see that these are placed in my chambers. Thank you."

The footman acknowledged his employer's orders, but Darcy was already heading toward the entrance. It had been a long day, and while satisfying in that he had accomplished much, he was more than ready to relax.

Mr. Travers took his coat, welcoming the master home as he did, and added, "A package arrived by private courier from Mrs. Reynolds at Pemberley, sir. I placed it on your desk."

Darcy inclined his head and thanked the butler. Heading straight to his office, which served as the townhouse's library as well, he opened the door and crossed the dimly illuminated room to the large desk. Plopping the tied bundle of documents on the surface, he nearly jumped out of his skin when a deep tenor spoke from behind him.

"About time you finished gallivanting about Town and wandered back to the house. I was beginning to think I would be dining alone tonight."

Darcy whirled around, a delighted smile already forming as he exclaimed, "Richard!"

Colonel Fitzwilliam was sprawled on the sofa, his booted feet crossed at the ankles on a pillow laying over the armrest. He was grinning smugly, an anticipatory gleam in his eyes even as he raised one brow quizzically.

"Richard? That's it? And why are you smiling like that? Where's the tongue lashing about my boots on the cushion?"

Darcy leaned against the desk and crossed his arms over his chest, his smile widening. "My humor is too high to chastise about a piece of furniture."

"Are you sure it's not a fever? There is a frightening radiance about you, and that smile is suspicious. Plus, you may well be delirious because you have yet to notice the tumbler in my hand filled with your private stash of Scotch moonshine. The second helping, I should add."

"Oh, I noticed, rest assured. I simply do not have a problem with your unwholesome proclivity for pilfering…this time. In fact, I intend to have a glass with you."

Richard frowned, only partly feigned, as he asked, "Who are you, and what have you done with my fussy cousin?"

Darcy laughed. Grabbing one of the empty tumblers, he snatched the open bottle from Richard's hand, pouring a healthy shot of the whiskey while answering, "Oh, never fear. I am still 'fussy,' as you put it, with admirable restraint considering the adjectives you could have chosen—"

"Uptight? Persnickety? Fastidious? Punctilious?"

"I have always preferred *meticulous* or *proper*, but I know those are words you do not comprehend the definition of."

"Aha! There it is! The bite I was waiting for. Thank God. I was beginning to think you had suffered a head injury while I was gone. And here I thought I was the one with the life-threatening occupation."

"Please!" Darcy snorted. "You sit in a tent and bark orders to your soldiers. Hardly life threatening."

"Now that hurts, Cousin. Truly. I'll have you know I stay in my tent only if I have to. I prefer to be on my horse giving those orders."

"On a bluff well away from the intense action."

Richard shrugged, ignoring Darcy's grin while swallowing a mouthful of the illegal liquor, and then adding airily, "It is called the burden of command. Someone has to make sure they do the job correctly. So what have you been up to, besides pining away from missing my charming personality? I was surprised to have a note from you at my house. I thought by now you would be holed up at Pemberley, ready to hibernate like a bear."

"I would be, and shall be by the end of November, but other concerns diverted my usual agenda."

"Sounds messy, especially knowing how you abhor anything upsetting your regulated agenda. What drama has addled your brains this time?"

"Stand up so we can toast, and then I shall tell you."

Darcy waited silently as Richard complied, grousing all the while and shooting strange glances his way. Rarely did Darcy ever do anything that was overly unusual, so startling his cousin when he had the opportunity was a treasured event. This promised to be one for the record books.

"So what are we toasting to? Did Anne finally have enough of the old battle-axe and lock Aunt C in the cellar?"

"Even better." Darcy lifted his glass. "Congratulations are in order, Cousin. Standing before you is a newly engaged man."

"Engaged!" Richard spluttered, so surprised he nearly dropped the whiskey. "You must be joking?"

"I would not joke about a serious matter such as this. I am betrothed and will be a married man come the twenty-eighth of November."

"How long was I gone? Did I suffer a head injury and no one told me a couple years went by? How did you…When…Who…?"

"How is a lengthy story. When was last week. And who is a woman I have admired and adored for a long while now—"

"You *never* showed interest in any lady! Lord knows Mother has shoved innumerable Society debutantes your way, and of course there is…Oh God! Please do not tell me you caved and are marrying Anne! I will not allow it, Darcy—"

"Rest easy. It is not Anne. She is safe from me forever, much to Aunt Catherine's chagrin. But that is another story for later."

"Thank goodness. Guess I should have known, since I doubt the prospect of marriage to Anne, dear as she is, would cause you to grin like a deuced idiot."

"I am grinning because I am supremely happy. You are incorrect that I never showed interest in a lady, as I am sure you would recall if you thought about it long enough."

Richard frowned, Darcy observing as he mentally filtered through the women they were acquainted with. Darcy suspected Richard had perceived his attraction toward Elizabeth Bennet while at Rosings Park in the spring, and so would eventually recall her.

However, before he started blurting out the names of any woman Darcy had ever spoken to or danced with, Darcy announced, "The woman who has made me the happiest man in England is Miss Elizabeth Bennet of Longbourn in Hertfordshire."

An indecipherable series of expressions crossed the colonel's face, and for a handful of seconds, Darcy wondered if his cousin held romantic feelings for Elizabeth. During the spring interlude at Rosings, Richard and Elizabeth had established a friendly relationship, their easy natures and witty humors similar. At the time, Darcy was caught up in his own confused emotions and so sure that Elizabeth would rush to accept his marriage proposal, he had spared scant thought as to whether there was something more happening between the two. Another symptom of his towering arrogance, perhaps in part, but Colonel Richard Fitzwilliam was confirmed in his bachelorhood and wildly adverse to the prospect of marriage. Darcy was a romantic at heart, but convinced nevertheless that his cousin was the last man on earth to swiftly succumb to love, even with a woman as beautiful and charming as Elizabeth, so any stabs of jealousy had been brief and faint.

Thus it shocked him how rapidly and intensely the present blaze of jealousy fogged his vision and choked his airway. Colliding with the jealousy were sharp pangs of regret for causing Richard any sadness, however unlikely or unpreventable.

"I knew it!" Richard's loud whoop jolted Darcy out of his tumultuous rumination, and he was further caught off guard when Richard clapped him hard on the shoulder. Darcy staggered, but the negative sentiments evaporated instantly by the combination of his cousin's jubilant grin and next words.

"I was right! I could tell you were attracted to her, maybe even in love." The last was spoken gaily and without his typical dramatic shudder or feigned retch. "But then figured I was wrong when you did nothing about it. I'll be damned! Congratulations are indeed in order, Cousin. Miss Bennet is a fine woman, probably better than you deserve," he laughed gaily, "so I am pleased you got over your insane struggles to accept your feelings for her. Would have saved you months of self-imposed torment if you had been less dense."

"As much as I want to argue your assessment of my intellect, I cannot. I did struggle, for a long while, as stupidly as you intimate.

Where you are wrong is in the when and why of my struggles and torment."

"Come again?"

Darcy chuckled, holding up his glass once more. "Before story time, toast to my superb fortune in winning the hand and heart of the most incredible woman I have ever been privileged to know—my intended, the beautiful Miss Elizabeth Bennet."

Richard held up his drink, adding before he clinked Darcy's, "To Miss Bennet and Mr. Darcy. May they love each other eternally, beating the odds by having that rarest of treasures: a happy marriage."

They knocked their glasses, each drinking deeply before Darcy responded. "That was an uncommonly saccharine speech coming from you, Cousin. Downright poetic. I do thank you for it."

"The benefits of a classical education and noble birth do show through from time to time. I shan't make a habit of it." He winked, smiling sunnily, and then shook his head. "You and Elizabeth Bennet. Truly the best of news, Darcy, my opinions of marriage notwithstanding. Aware of your longing for matrimony, I frankly expected you to tie the knot years ago."

"It was not being married that I wanted, Richard. If it were that simple, I *would have* 'tied the knot years ago,' as you eloquently stated it."

"True. I feared it, actually, that you would grow desperate enough to marry Anne or, worse yet, Miss Bingley." Both men shivered at the latter vision, gulping more whiskey to wash away the bitter taste left behind.

"I doubt I would have ever been that desperate, as much as it pains me to be unkind about Bingley's sister."

"How is she taking the news?"

"Not well, but that too is another story."

"With all these stories, it's fortunate I planned to impose upon your hospitality for tonight. Might be wise to get some food into my belly before drinking further, so I can remain coherent for the whole saga. Besides, knowing you as I do, and judging by the drippy expression, I am in for a nauseating recounting. I better eat *before* my appetite is ruined."

"Trust me, there are portions sufficiently riveting to stave off nausea or incoherency. As for the rest, I promise restraint."

"Normally restraint and Darcy go hand in hand. Now?" Richard shook his head. "Challenging with a belt of whiskey each time you blurt a romantic word is tempting, except I doubt even my famed resistance to inebriation would persist beyond the first chapter or two."

Darcy rubbed his chin and furrowed his brow. "Perhaps you have a point. Sonnets have spontaneously burst forth while in public, and today I was nearly trampled by a coach and six while crossing the lane to pet a lady's puppy."

"Good God! Seriously?"

Rolling his eyes at Richard's appalled expression, Darcy snatched the empty tumbler from his hand. "Of course not, you ninny! I am in love, not a brainless idiot."

"I have always been of the opinion they are one and the same."

"Someday, cousin. Someday. Now," he boomed crisply, ignoring Richard's grimace, "let us hustle the staff to serve our dinner. I am famished."

Luckily for them, no hustling was required. The unembellished, informal-style meal Darcy preferred when alone or with the colonel was ready to be served. Not bothering to change clothing for dinner, they sat at one end of the enormous table and within minutes commenced dining. Between sips of wine and feasting on the simple but delicious fare, Darcy chronicled the past months to his spellbound friend.

Segments were glossed over, or deleted from the narrative entirely, and as a man uncomfortable with baring personal sentiments or discussing private topics, he was characteristically succinct. Nevertheless, in light of the tumultuous course trod and his intense happiness at the outcome, Darcy's temperate delivery was remarkable. Richard made a point to comment on his impressive

215

scarcity of melodramatics, adding with a wink that he was keeping a mental tally of how often Darcy dropped the word *love* into the accounting! Twelve utterances were noted by the time the meat course was carried in, and it was then that Darcy reached the scenes involving Lady Catherine de Bourgh.

"I suppose it should not shock me that our aunt barged in on the Bennets and attacked Miss Elizabeth," Richard said near the end of that part of the tale. "I *am* shocked though. Not because it is especially out of character, mind you. It's the extremity involved that amazes. The desperation and...absurdity, really. Anne is sickly and nearing thirty, for heaven's sake! How could a woman as intelligent as Lady Catherine cling to the irrational idea that you, of all people, would marry Anne now when you have refused for the past ten years?"

Darcy shrugged. "Indeed I asked the same question. Hundreds of times. Obviously I underestimated her resolve, and erroneously believed she knew me better."

"Yes," Richard drawled, staring into the wine as he gently swirled the glass, "I think you have hit the nail's head. Do not take it personally, Darcy. I doubt she knows anything about me outside of my rank and surname."

"Aunt Catherine inhabits her pomposity utterly, and defines people based on predetermined categories. I am not unique in her pigeonholing me, that I am aware. How well does she truly know her own daughter, for example? The irony is that in defining and then dismissing me, she underestimated *my* resolve."

"Quite so. As I know from experience with more than a few generals and high-ranking officers, intelligence is often not linked to wisdom or basic sense. Whatever the case with our dear aunt, you turned her interference to your advantage. Now you are bindingly betrothed to Elizabeth Bennet. Nothing more she can do about it."

The servants interrupted the conversation momentarily to whisk the soiled plates away and deliver the vegetables. The colonel promptly scooped a mouthful of sliced carrots. Darcy stared at the steam rising from the mound of mashed yams on his plate while creating valleys with his fork tines.

"I can live with Lady Catherine's disappointment, although our estrangement does pain me," Darcy said. "What I wonder is how Lord and Lady Matlock will respond to my engagement with Miss Elizabeth."

"My parents?" Richard's surprised mumble filtered through half-chewed carrots. Swallowing, he wiped his mouth and gulped some wine before speaking further. "Are you seriously subscribing to Aunt Catherine's wild allegations of father being of like mind? You know him better than that!"

"I do. I also remember the affair of Jonathan's."

"That was a completely different situation, Darcy, if you recall."

"Actually, I was young, at Pemberley, and never learned the details. All I remember is my parents talking about it in vague terms, and that Lord Matlock was furious Jonathan wanted to marry someone deemed unsuitable. How was it different?"

"For one, my brother is the heir to an earldom. Secondly, he was barely nineteen. The girl was seventeen and the daughter of one of our tenant farmers. I may not agree with every social rule and law of the land, especially the ones that limit my inheritance just because Jonathan was born a year before me, but if Father had allowed him to marry a farmer's daughter, the consequences would have been catastrophic. Jonathan was a fool, brash, and, let us be frank, thinking with his groin more than his head."

Darcy continued to pick at his food when Richard fell silent. Clearly the affair with his cousin Jonathan was incomparable to his own. Elizabeth Bennet was the daughter of a gentleman landowner and not a poor farmer for beginners. Nor was Darcy a green youth or the heir to a peerage. That still did not guarantee Lord Matlock would be overjoyed, and while true that his lordship's approval was not required, Darcy cringed at the possibility of another family squabble.

As if reading his thoughts, Richard explained, "What you also must not know, Cousin, is despite Father's fury and refusal to sanction a marriage, he did not forbid Jonathan to be with Alice. That was her name," he clarified when Darcy glanced up. "He knew better than that. My brother is not quite as stubborn as you, but close, and Gretna Green is temptingly nearby."

They both smiled at that, Darcy adding a short chuckle. "This is interesting family history I never heard. What happened to Alice anyway?"

"Jonathan secured her a house in Arborville, with Father's financial help and approval." Darcy's brows rose even as his lips pressed together in reproof. "Jon did love Alice, Darcy," Richard insisted in defense of his brother, "and neither of my parents wanted him to be miserable. The relationship carried on for a year or so, until she married a surgeon from Derby. That was the end of it. Three years and numerous love affairs later, he met Priscilla. I doubt he is passionately in love with her any more than he was the others, but they do care for each other and, like it or not, she was born to be a countess. The point is"—he leaned forward, stabbing his fork Darcy's direction—"your relationship with Miss Bennet is perfectly respectable and she is an excellent lady. Just because you were too stupid to comprehend this from the start does not mean my father will be."

"Thanks," Darcy intoned dryly.

"You are welcome! Glad to help," Richard responded gaily. "The ace in your pocket, Darcy, is that you love her. If my gruff father, with his lofty airs and staunch conservatism, can soften in Jon's affair, he will be a marshmallow with you. Hell, you are the only son of his dearest friend and beloved sister! You probably *could* marry a farmer's daughter. Besides, if he does grumble or gripe, my mother will slap sense into him."

"Here's to hoping you are correct in your assessment." Darcy raised his wineglass, Richard doing the same but halting before touching the rims.

"My assessment that my mother will slap Father? Because that would be entertaining to witness!"

Laughing, they drank to the toast—whatever it encompassed—and commenced eating without further interruption. Darcy inquired as to when Lord and Lady Matlock were expected to return from their holiday in Bath and if they planned to pass through London. Based on a letter written two weeks prior that had been waiting at his house along with Darcy's, the colonel answered that they should be in Town within the week.

"I will be here and shall sing the praises of Miss Bennet. Fortunately, that is a painless task. By the time you return to Town later in the month, they will be rapturous over your engagement and dying to make the acquaintance of your beloved Elizabeth. Trust me."

"Why do those two words passing your lips instill shivers of trepidation rather than comfort?" Richard grinned and said nothing. "Well, Colonel Trustworthy, I have another task for you. If possible, I would greatly appreciate your superb guardian and militant services in escorting Georgiana from Pemberley."

"Stated like that, how can I refuse? When do you want her here? Or do you prefer I escort her to Netherfield?"

"That depends, I suppose. If you can get away in the immediate future, then it would be best to bring her and Mrs. Annesley to Darcy House."

Richard assured Darcy he could manage the journey soon, and Darcy trusted his cousin's promise and capability explicitly. Thereafter, they spoke mostly of topics wholly unrelated to romance. Darcy did tell him of Caroline Bingley's maneuverings, those descriptions ridiculously embellished thanks, in part, to the drained bottle of whiskey. The one time Darcy again mentioned his wedding, Richard stayed him by holding up his cue stick—the men battling sloppily over a billiard table—and opined, "Darcy, all I need to know about your wedding, or any wedding for that matter, is the date and place. I will arrive on time, smile cheerfully, offer my congratulations rather than sympathies, and happily eat the breakfast after."

If Darcy retorted, neither remembered. In fact, they remembered little else after that!

SHARON LATHAN

CHAPTER NINE
Fall Pruning of Prickly Debris

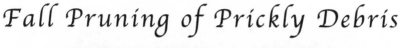

O n the sixth morning after Mr. Darcy's departure to London, Lizzy tied open her bedroom curtains and slid the window open. A cool breeze wafted inside, triggering a flood of goose pimples over her arms, but the sun shone brightly from a cloudless sky, promising a temperate day. The daily ritual of assessing the weather immediately upon rising enervated her mind as well as a splash of cold water or a cup of strong coffee. Rather than drifting off to the fields away from Longbourn, today her gaze fell on the arbor of unpruned climbing roses in the garden. Mr. Bennet employed sufficient persons to complete the vital chores for Longbourn's maintenance, but ofttimes less important jobs went undone. Cognizant of the necessity in properly snipping roses before winter, and equally aware that she was an excellent pruner, Lizzy's plan for the morning hours was decided.

Always the Bennet daughter who delighted in being outside and interacting with nature, Lizzy had dogged the steps of the grooms and farmhands since a little girl. Asking ceaseless questions of the workmen grew tiresome quickly, so in desperation, trowels, brooms, seeds, or anything handy had been thrust into the curious girl's hands in an effort to silence her. The tactic worked in part—Lizzy far too insatiable for knowledge to completely halt her queries—and her becoming skilled at dozens of jobs rarely imagined by the average upper-class female the result. "Digging in the dirt like a peasant," as her mother labeled it, was not a passionate hobby, but one she enjoyed upon occasion, especially when feeling a bit out of sorts.

Mr. Darcy is away in Town.

That glum reality influenced Lizzy's urge to seek the garden. The soothing combination of being in the out of doors where the air was fresh and abundant with earthy aromas and performing tasks that were pleasurable—and in the case of the roses also helpful—was an irresistible draw.

After breakfast, Lizzy dressed in an old gown with a grubby apron, worn ankle boots, a floppy-brimmed hat with a yellow ribbon tied under her chin, and stained leather gloves. Admittedly she *did* resemble a peasant laborer, as Mrs. Bennet claimed. Ignoring her mother's stream of dire consequences should Mr. Darcy discover dirt under her fingernails or a tanned tint to her cheeks, Lizzy exited the house and hastened to the solitude of the flower garden.

For a blissful hour she hummed and pruned. Frequently her mind strayed to her betrothed, wondering what he was doing and when he would return, but the business of precise rose pruning required enough concentration to shield against undue melancholy. In fact, her focus blocked the crunch of booted feet on gravel, Lizzy jumping slightly when a voice spoke behind her.

"Mornin', Missy Lizzy. 'Tis a fine day for workin' in the garden, sure 'nuff, though 'tis a mite on the warm side. Mrs. Hill sent me fetch a pail a water for ya. Should a thought it myself…Papa like ta tan my hide for being simple-headed agin."

Lizzy stood, brushed the loose dirt off her apron, and turned to the young farmhand. Smiling affectionately, she asked, "Matty, how many times have I scolded you for calling yourself simple?"

"Lotsa times, 'spose, Missy Lizzy," the blushing Matty mumbled into his chest.

"Indeed I have. Probably hundreds, and that is more than a lot. Remember what I remind you each time?"

"That I is kind and gentle, and those are ta best of all." The blush deepened, but he spoke in a slightly firmer tone, cocked his head, and peered upward.

"Yes. And what else?"

"That no one is smart as me with fixin' broke parts." This time he added a bashful grin and lifted his head a bit higher.

"It is the truth, so never forget it. If Mr. Beller says otherwise, you tell him Miss Lizzy will be tanning *his* hide!" Matty guffawed loudly at that. The image, as she intended, was an amusing one for a host of reasons, not the least of which because Mr. Beller, Longbourn's gamekeeper and Matty's father, was well over two hundred pounds of solid muscle. "Thank you for the water, Matty. I do appreciate it."

He was still snorting at Lizzy's jest so merely nodded. Then, as he started to turn away, he stopped and gestured at the pruning shears she held in her gloved hand. "You gotsa loose spring there, Missy Lizzy. I can fix that quicker than lightning, iffin' you want?"

Sure to his word, Matty returned in twenty minutes with pruning shears not only mended with a new spring, but also cleaned and oiled. A grateful Lizzy praised the beaming Matty, her effusiveness unequal to the minor repair but bolstering to the young man.

All the Bennet sisters, even Lydia, surprisingly, were fiercely protective of Matty Beller.

His age was unknown precisely, the orphaned boy taken in by the gamekeeper and his wife twenty years prior. The nuns at the Derby Home for Lost Children had found him abandoned, huddling in an alley and near death. They estimated he was three to four years, although it was impossible to be sure due to his extreme malnourishment. The Bellers brought him to Longbourn, Matty joining their family of five children who had similarly been saved from parentless situations. For two years he did not speak, and by the time he did, it was obvious that Matty was mentally damaged. Whether from birth or as a result of the deprivations afterward, none could say. Matty's innocence enhanced his innate gentleness and sunny disposition, everyone pampering and adoring him. An instant favorite with his siblings and every child on the estate, to the Bennet girls, he was beloved as if their own little brother.

He was twelve years or so, healthy but still small, and with a mind stuck at a rough ten-year-old level, when a broken piston water pump left in a heap of parts captured his attention. Suddenly, as if magnetically drawn, Matty knelt on the ground, and with unwavering focus, repaired the pump as if a trained master. From that moment on, his mystifying talent to comprehend the construction of anything remotely mechanical earned him respect and a place of honor amongst Longbourn estate's workers. No one was prouder than his father, thus the tease of Matty's "simple-headedness" was an affectionate banter purely to induce laughter. Matty, even with his diminished intelligence in most aspects, knew he was special and a valued asset to Longbourn.

"Are you assigned chores today, Matty? Or are you free to help me with the roses? I could use the assistance in reaching the top of the arbor, and your company would be appreciated."

The subsequent hour passed with an agreeable mixture of laughter and work. Lizzy explained why the branches must be trimmed at specific places and angles, demonstrating the techniques while he nodded seriously. How much of the science to pruning roses he understood was questionable, but his observational skills were keen. Once shown a procedure, Matty would mimic it precisely without fail for as long as the work continued. By the following day, more often than not, he forgot the process entirely. No one was disturbed by this, however, because being in young Matty's presence was a true pleasure.

In his halting manner, with faulty English, Matty chatted as they snipped the dead flowers and withering stems, entertaining Lizzy with tales of his nieces and nephews primarily. Another favorite subject was the antics of the rabbits he was allowed to raise. Matty called them *bunnies* with individual names and personalities, and at times, as he rambled, it was unclear if he was talking about humans or animals!

Finally they neared the end of the arbor. Lizzy and Matty stood side by side on ladders, supporting each other as they reached to the branches curving over the arbor's latticed ceiling. He cut the dried flowers, laughing as the petals fell onto his head, and Lizzy used the excuse of brushing them away to make his coarse hair stick up in wild spikes.

"Now you look just like a porcupine! No, wait, a hedgehog! Or maybe a skunk with these white petals," and so on she teased, to his delight.

"All done, Missy Lizzy," he announced with a last snap of his shears. "Lemme help ya down." Jumping to the ground, he reached up to steady her descent, one hand raised to take her hand while the other grabbed the body part closest to his eyes, that being her right shin, skirts and all. Seconds later, she was safe on the graveled pathway beside Matty, both of them satisfactorily scanning the perfectly pruned roses.

"An excellent job, Mr. Beller," she declared, the formality topped with a wink and pat on his shoulder. "I could not have completed this without you, kind sir. I shall be eternally in your debt." Dropping into a deep curtsey while Matty flushed scarlet, movement in her peripheral vision captured her attention.

Standing in the shade of an elm at the far edge of the garden, close to the house, was Mr. Darcy. His face was obscured, but of course she knew who it was. Straightening from her playfully dramatic curtsey, Lizzy broke into an even wider grin and dashed down the pathway toward him.

"Mr. Darcy! You have returned. How absolutely wonderful! I hoped today, but could not be certain so came into the garden—Oh my! I suppose Mama was right this time. I must look a fright in this dress, and the gloves—Heavens!" Laughing, she tugged on the frayed gloves while trying to remove flakes of rose petals from her clothing at the same, which was impossible and increased her mirth. "Bother!

Nothing to be done about it. You have caught me, sir…" She trailed off when an unhindered view of his face revealed a serious expression bordering on anger with traces of distress.

Frowning, she stepped closer. "William, whatever is the matter? Did something happen while you were away?"

Instinctively, she reached out to grasp his hand, startling when he jerked away. Then she flushed, assuming he was reacting to her grimy hands, although the severity etched onto his face felt extreme for a bit of dirt. Her happiness to see him and concern over some unknown tragedy mingled with vague irritation at his silence and behavior.

"My apologies," she mumbled. Tossing the gloves to the ground, she attempted to find a clean area on her apron to wipe her hands. "If you wish to wait in the parlor, I will wash and change quickly. Then I can greet properly and we can talk—"

"Who is he?"

"What?" She swung her eyes to his. "Who?"

"That man. Beller, was it?"

For nearly a full thirty seconds, she stared at Mr. Darcy, clueless as to what or who he was growling over. Matty was Matty. Even her "Mr. Beller" jest was a rarity, so it did not immediately register Mr. Darcy was referring to him. Mainly, however, it was simply that *no one* thought of sweet, innocent Matty as a man! Chronologically he was, of course, being three-and-twenty at least.

Lizzy turned back toward Matty, who was raking the rose debris and paying them no heed. For the first time, she examined him with fresh eyes, astounded to note that despite his short stature and thin physique, Matty had indeed physically matured. Adding to her amazement was the realization that he was quite handsome. *How extraordinary!*

She laughed aloud, capturing Matty's attention. He smiled and waved, Lizzy returning the bright smile and wave automatically.

"Clearly the two of you are *extremely* well acquainted."

Caught up in the epiphany about Matty, Lizzy reacted slowly to her fiancé's inference. When she did, the urge to dissolve into hysterical laughter was intense. Instead, she chose a different tactic.

Cocking her head, she replied innocently, "Yes, one could state our relationship in those terms, Mr. Darcy. I prefer to think of Matty as a *special* friend."

Darcy had balled his fists onto his hips and was glaring at her through dark eyes. Perhaps she should have spared his distress, but the idea of jealousy over Matty was so ludicrous that teasing him was irresistible!

"Matty, is it? Very interesting. Tell me, Miss Bennet, are there a profusion of gentlemen you refer to familiarly by their Christian name?"

Tapping her chin with one index finger, she gazed vacantly to the left. "Let me think for a moment. Hmmm....There are Abner and Percy"—two of her nephews, and not technically of adult age, but Mr. Darcy did not know that—"Gil and Keefe"—twin stableboys who, much like Matty, had grown up at Longbourn and had been playmates all through her childhood—"and, of course I cannot forget Stanz"—the elderly Russian newspaper seller whose surname was so difficult to pronounce that he had been Stanz since long before she was born—"and...No, I believe that is all. Why do you ask, Mr. Darcy?"

Lizzy arched her brows, relaxed her face into a guileless expression, and waited. His penetrating focus might have unnerved if not for the absurd circumstances. In fact, the longer he glared at her, the less she wanted to laugh.

"I distinctly sense you are mocking me, Miss Bennet, and do not appreciate flippancy after being subjected to witnessing my future wife cavorting with another man. A man you touched, and who touched you, several times, including, to my horror, on your leg!"

Now she was angry.

"As I see it, *Mr. Darcy*," she emphasized, matching his stern expression, "you interpreted what you witnessed and drew conclusions as you chose to rather than with a trusting, unjaundiced heart. Therefore you deserve to be mocked. Or worse. Instead, I shall ease your distress, but not for your sake. Matty is too kindhearted to have anyone misjudging him. Matty," she called, "come here please. I want to introduce you to Mr. Darcy."

Dropping the rake as if on fire, Matty rushed over, his hands scrubbing through his unruly hair and patting over his clothing in a vain attempt to compose himself. "O'course, Missy Lizzy! Iffin' you wish. Meetin' Missy Lizzy's gen'leman is special, yes, sir, it is!"

Lizzy clasped one fidgeting hand between both of hers, smiled at her childhood friend, and then pierced her fiancé with chilly eyes. "Mr. Darcy, allow me to introduce Mr. Matty Beller—"

Matty interrupted with a snorting laugh. "I not a mister, Missy Lizzy! Jus' simple-headed Matty Beller. That's me. Your fine gen'leman is a mister. Very special meetin' simple me, I say!"

"No talk of being simple, Matty, remember? You fixed my shears, and how would I have finished the roses if not for your excellent assistance?" Matty blushed and stared at his toes. "In fact, Mr. Darcy was just commenting on how helpful you were to his future wife—entertaining me while we pruned the roses, steadying me so I would not unbalance on the ladder, and aiding my descent so I did not fall. Is that not so, Mr. Darcy?"

"Yes." Darcy cleared his throat gruffly. "I...I was. Thank you, Mr. Beller. Miss Elizabeth's wellbeing is important to me, and I am pleased to know her safety is assured when I am absent."

"You like bunnies, mister?" Darcy blinked at the unrelated query, stammering a vague affirmative. "I gots pretty bunnies at home. Soft and fuzzy. You come by anytime, pick any bunny ya want, 'kay?"

"That is very kind of you, Matty. Now, can I impose upon you to return the tools to their proper place? I wish to speak with Mr. Darcy alone."

Lizzy watched Matty stack the equipment into the wheelbarrow and ignored Mr. Darcy until the young man was gone. Then she broke the silence, speaking coolly while gazing toward the empty pathway under the arbor. "Later, if you wish, I can recount Matty's story and why he is like a brother to us. I presume it is now apparent that Matty is harmless. That is why your comments amused me initially. No one has ever been jealous over me, so for a moment it was flattering— until you insulted me with your insinuations. Do you trust me so little, Mr. Darcy?"

She turned around as she asked the question, fully expecting to see embarrassment at the least, preferably deep remorse. To her surprise, Mr. Darcy's expression was largely unchanged! His face was stony, with furrowed creases between his brows and eyes hard as agates.

"Trust must be earned, Miss Elizabeth. Until this, I had no reason to distrust you."

He spoke bluntly, as if stating the obvious. Astonished, Lizzy asked, "And now?"

"Now I know my interpretation was erroneous."

"Quite magnanimous of you, sir. Is that to be the extent of your admission of guilt?"

Mr. Darcy pressed his lips together and she saw his jaw muscle twitch. Again speaking in that maddeningly icy, clipped tone, he said, "It is a statement of fact, not an admission of guilt. The advantage of knowledge was not in my possession, thus I interpreted based on what I saw. Yet rather than enlightening me immediately as to my error and easing my heart, you responded with mockery."

Ouch! That hit a nerve. Still irritated, Lizzy crossed her trembling arms over her chest, lifted her chin, and scowled. "Dealing with the ridiculous provokes me to mockery, Mr. Darcy. Be prepared for the consequences if irrational jealousy is to be your standard reaction."

"Jealousy, by definition, is ofttimes irrational, no matter how strongly one attempts to maintain control and a clear vision."

"Is this a warning, sir, to beware of smiling or talking to any other man?"

"If the talking and smiling includes that man touching you, then yes!"

With each sentence, their voices grew louder and their bodies stiffer. The space between them had narrowed to a mere foot. For several seconds the only sound was angry breathing. Then Darcy sighed, squeezed his eyes shut, and pinched the bridge of his nose between two fingers.

"Elizabeth, I cannot apologize for my jealousy because it is, and always will be, my natural response where you are concerned. Maybe a man who felt less for his betrothed would not experience possessiveness. I am not that man. The intensity of my love for you prohibits me from reacting complacently to what I saw today. Perhaps it is too soon to hope for, but I would like to imagine that if the situation were reversed, you might feel a glimmer of jealousy as well."

Lizzy gasped as a weight abruptly slammed into her chest. Instantly she recalled the day in Meryton and the powerful sensations that had rendered her physically ill when she suspected Caroline Bingley's advances toward Mr. Darcy. Since then Lizzy continually fought the urge to squeeze the jezebel's scrawny neck. Worse yet, with honest reflection, traces of fretfulness persisted, the nearly inaudible voice citing Caroline's finer attributes and accomplishments as a rational reason for Mr. Darcy to capitulate. *What if a woman you did not know he disliked acted in such a manner?*

Indeed, she understood Mr. Darcy's jealousy and distrust far better than he suspected.

Before she formulated a reply, he tenderly grasped her hands and bent until level with her eyes. "My dear, while I cannot apologize for my jealousy, I can and do apologize for succumbing to it before seeking an explanation. That was wrong of me. I humbly beg your forgiveness, on behalf of Mr. Beller as well, for presuming precipitously and casting aspersions. Can you forgive me, Elizabeth?"

His gaze remained direct and his expression serious, but warmth softened the hard edges. The combination made her heart flutter.

Inhaling, she whispered, "I will forgive you, William, only if you forgive me first."

"Pardon? Have I missed some—"

"You must forgive me for envisioning wild acts of violence toward Miss Bingley every time she says your name or smiles at you, or finds some excuse to touch you or...basically anytime she is present."

He stared silently, a smile fighting to emerge, as his eyes reverted to their normal glittering blue and rosiness bathed his cheeks. "If I refuse to forgive you, will you act upon your inclination? A fracas between you and Caroline would be entertaining."

"William!" she huffed through the sudden attack of giggles. Then the sweet pressure of his lips covered her mouth. Amusement, irritation, nervousness, apologies, visions of strangling Caroline Bingley—it all vanished instantaneously.

It began as a delicate kiss, lingering and controlled, then, a minuscule release, only to buss her upper lip before a smooth slide to the left corner of her mouth. A nuzzling caress there was followed by nibbling sucks along the lower lip while gently gliding to the right corner. Leisurely he traveled, a sequence of exquisitely dainty kisses mapping her lips as if a vast, unexplored territory. Judging by the fiery tingles ignited with each touch, she dimly wondered if her lips *had* tripled in size. Never had she imagined that lips alone contained the power to light an inferno within her entire body.

Lost to delicious sensation, she was unaware of him untying her bonnet ribbon until the hat slipped down her back when he embedded both hands into the loosely pinned hair by her ears. On and on the fragile, chaste kisses seared. Distinctly she heard herself whimper when he left her lips, but the whimper turned into a moan when his tactile survey extended to the innervated skin on her face—chin, cheeks, nose, and all points in between were unhurriedly investigated by his insanely arousing mouth.

"I missed you, Elizabeth. Sorely. Say you missed me as well."

The words, huskily whispered amid the intoxication of his warm lips lovingly showering her face, augmented her dizziness. She was clutching tightly to his forearms to remain standing, and the thought of inhaling so as to reply was almost more than she could manage! Nodding an affirmative required conscious effort, diverting her attention from the delirium his touch induced.

"Was that meant as a yes?" he murmured into her ear. "That you missed me?"

She repeated the nod with a bit more movement, a muffled yes passing her lips. An attempt to repeat the word audibly was curtailed when he captured her mouth fully, this kiss firmer and insistent. A glancing caress of his tongue along the furrow between her lips was followed by a muted groan deep in his throat. Reflexively Lizzy parted her lips, inviting him to accelerate the kiss as he had before in this very garden. Instead, he abruptly broke away, and it was her turn to groan.

Crushing his mouth against her left temple, she felt his fingers flex into her hair and scalp. Tension rolled off his suddenly immobile body, the arm muscles underneath her hands rigid. Hot air waved down her cheek with each of his grating exhales, and although the thundering in her ears was most likely her pounding heartbeat, she suspected his heart was in a similar state.

As happened on the day of their engagement, when kissed for the first time, Lizzy experienced a chaotic jumble of sensations. All were blissful, begging for more to truly satisfy, while also, somehow, mysteriously comprehending that, where William was concerned, satisfaction would forever be a temporary achievement. The secrets of lovemaking—as gleaned from books or overheard in conversations—were vague, yet enough that Lizzy understood the pleasurable expression was not intended to be a one-time or occasional event. Physical love was designed for enjoyment with the partner of your heart for all the years granted together—and in myriad ways. Precisely how many ways Lizzy could not fathom. All things considered, kissing was obviously one of those ways!

As overwhelming as the yearning to learn a few more ways to express their love, the garden outside Longbourn in broad daylight was not a wise location for a lesson in lovemaking.

"Tell me, Mr. Darcy, which did you miss most, arguing with me or kissing me?"

The blurted question amazingly defused the worst of the tension. Darcy chuckled, the sound hoarse, but followed with a relaxation of the tight grasp on her head. Withdrawing, he met her eyes and his smile was almost normal. "Of those two choices, Elizabeth, an argument will never take precedence over kissing you." Closing his eyes, he inhaled a massive lungful of air and released it slowly. "That clarified, what I missed most was hearing your voice, gazing into your beautiful face, and simply being in your presence."

Lizzy blushed and averted her gaze. Shakily laughing, she stepped back and nervously brushed at the soil and rose fragments clinging to her apron. "A lovely sentiment. Yet here I am with perspiring skin, tattered garments, hair I fear is mangled, and, as Mama warned, dirt under my fingernails. I am mortified! Under the circumstances, if you rescind your last statement, I could not fault you."

Darcy's initial reply was to kiss both her hands, then secure them around his arm. Walking toward an umbrella-protected table, he said, "Later I will tell you of the time when I was eighteen and became stranded in a rain storm. I was left to walk a fair distance back to Pemberley, only to arrive mud splattered and soaked to the skin, entering the foyer to head to my chambers precisely as my father was welcoming the guests I had completely forgotten were joining us for dinner that evening, among which were Lord and Lady Matlock, a duke who is a distant cousin, and an assortment of other eminent personages. *That* was mortifying! To this day Lord Seymour calls me *Squishy* due to the sound my soggy boots made on the marble floor."

"My word! Squishy, indeed! The image in my mind is..." Laughing and shaking her head, Lizzy trailed off as they sat across from each other at the table.

"Mortifying," Darcy finished for her.

"Was it? Hmmm…I sense that secretly you were amused. These nibbles of your past, doled out sparingly, are intriguing. Such an enigma you are, sir!"

"Am I? Fascinating observation, Elizabeth. I doubt you would discover many people who agree with you. As you once accused, I am a tough nut to crack due to my reticence, but fairly transparent and uncomplicated underneath."

"I beg to differ. Transparent you are certainly not, William, nor are you uncomplicated. You present a cool, unflappable demeanor"— she cocked her head and pursed her lips saucily—"urbane and quite the perfectionist. Almost, dare I say, a dandy. Yet you hint of climbing trees and other daring feats as a youth. I have seen how you recklessly ride your horse, and you mentioned working in the stable yard and training the horses at Pemberley. Now I hear of trudging through the rain and mud, a very Lizzy Bennet sort of adventure! Who would have suspected it of Mr. Darcy? Never fear, however, because I appreciate your complicated nature. It is a challenge, you see, and I adore challenges."

"Not sure if I live up to the label of enigma. Nevertheless, if challenges are desired, then I—"

"Lizzy! Lizzy, where are you?" Mrs. Bennet's screech jolted both of them to their feet. Lizzy rushed to the corner, turned, and stopped short at the sight of her mother charging toward her. "Lizzy! Oh, there you are! My word, look at you! Kitty just informed me that Mr. Darcy arrived a bit ago, wishing to visit with you, she said—why she did not bother to tell me of this I cannot imagine—I was only in my bedchamber and would have greeted him as is proper for the lady of the house to do—and certainly would have diverted him away from seeing you like this. Heaven help us! If he saw you, dirty and…and…so unladylike in appearance and action, I…well, I dare not speak the possible outcome! Fortunate for us, unaware of your poor choice for today, Kitty knew not where to direct Mr. Darcy—"

"Fortunately, Mr. Darcy decided to search the garden before riding on to Netherfield."

Mr. Darcy's resonant voice stunned Mrs. Bennet into gasping hiccups. Gaping from disheveled daughter to impeccable gentleman, her jaw dropped and skin paled to ash. For a minute Lizzy feared she actually might faint.

"Rest easy, Mrs. Bennet. Miss Elizabeth's hobby does not distress me in the least. I daresay her proclivity for outdoor activities is a commonality. Gardening is not my forte, I confess, being fonder of fishing, hunting, and riding, with the occasional vigorous ramble through the wood for good measure. Pemberley boasts a variety of choices, many of which I am confident Miss Elizabeth and I will enjoy together."

How reassured Mrs. Bennet truly felt was questionable. Lizzy strongly suspected her mother's fretful warnings of Mr. Darcy's repudiation due to her wild behavior would persist until the moment she walked down the church aisle. For the present, thank heavens, his serene attitude mollified her—at least in part. Mrs. Bennet insisted Lizzy scurry to her room to wash and dress properly, going so far as to grab her arm and tug insistently.

Resisting her mother's sudden, surprising strength, Lizzy clutched one of Mr. Darcy's hands. "You will stay, yes?" Noting his glance toward Mrs. Bennet and reflexive wince, she added, "I promise to be quick. Papa is in his study and will welcome your company."

Relief flooded his face. "Of course I will wait. After all, I have yet to hear what other adventures occupied your days while I was away. How could I deny myself such excellent amusement?"

ತಿ

Every man has a set of specific activities, best suited for their unique personality, to relieve tension, anger, or pent-up energy. Depending on the situation, the choice may be a placid task that calms, such as reading, painting, or fishing, or it may be physical in nature, the internal pressure needing a tangible, forceful outlet. Shooting, fencing, chopping wood, and swimming—among other manly occupations—are common selections. For Fitzwilliam Darcy, racing his horse at breakneck speeds was by far the preferred method, followed by billiards and fencing.

Charles Bingley, although skilled at horseback riding and the prime outdoor sports deemed essential for a gentleman to partake in, had been raised in London. As a city dweller, his favored entertainments veered toward those readily available indoors. While in boarding school, he discovered a proclivity, and talent, for pugilism. As a rising sport amongst the social elite in England, boxing was viewed as an excellent form of exercise. A purely masculine art form, being able to defend oneself was another benefit of learning to box. Bingley trained and participated in matches all through his educational years but was never one of the champions in the field or interested in fighting as a professional endeavor, so he willingly ended competing when he finished at Cambridge. What remained was a passion for the sport as a spectator, an enjoyment in casual sparring at the gymnasiums in Town, and the yearning to pummel a sand-filled punching bag as a ventilator.

Shortly after breakfast the third morning following Mr. Darcy's return from London, both gentlemen found themselves in dire need of anger relief to save harming a specific person in the Netherfield household. Darcy made for the stables and was likely already miles away. Bingley practically ran to the game room, where his punching bag was hanging. A half hour of unrelenting clobbers onto the beaten-smooth leather surface, with sweat soaking his shirt and dripping from his brow, Bingley had just begun to feel the murderous urges slipping away when the door opened.

"Caroline," he croaked, punctuating it with a resounding wallop that wildly spun the bag, "I strongly suggest you turn right around and walk back through that door!"

"Nonsense, Charles. As if your tantrum will be inflicted upon me."

Should I tell her how many times her face floated on the surface of the punching bag?

"Tantrum?" he asked incredulously instead. "I am the one having a tantrum? That is rich, Caroline. You have been in the throes of a tantrum since my engagement to Miss Bennet!"

"I cannot fathom what you mean." She spoke airily but slid her eyes toward a random corner of the room.

"Then let me explain." Bingley gave the bag a last punch and then stomped to the billiard table. Caroline strolled casually around it as if nothing were amiss. Bending slightly with hands gripping the table edge, he summarized, "Rather than congratulate me, as a normal sister would, you snipe and whine and insult. Incessantly. For weeks. Even when we are trying to have a pleasant breakfast, you persist. Be thankful I have that bag to hit, or the alternative would be strangling you!"

The last he accented with a hard slap onto the felt surface of the table. For one of the first times in active memory, his sister appeared genuinely taken aback by his temper. There was even a faint hint of regret glimmering in her eyes.

"Is it possible, Caroline, to at least *pretend* you care for me? Or has your utter selfishness blinded you to how gloriously happy Jane makes me?"

"Brother—"

"I have been patient, Caroline, because you are my sister. My desire is for familial accord, as I presumed you desired too. Evidently I was mistaken. What is most inconceivable is you not adoring Jane when everyone does!"

"I do not dislike Jane Bennet, if you must know," Caroline blurted and then bit her lip, lowering her eyes.

Stunned, Bingley stared at her for half a minute. Pushing up from the billiard table and crossing his arms over his chest, he mocked, in a voice heavy with sarcasm, "How generous of you to tell me now. Is this a sudden epiphany between the breakfast room and here?"

Huffing loudly, Caroline flipped her arms in the air and flounced away from the table. "I have never hated Jane Bennet, Charles. She is…pretty and sweet, if not too bright, and her manners are…acceptable. I suppose you do love her, as you assert, and with time and proper guidance, she may improve in her elegance and—"

"Is this supposed to be an endorsement? Do compliments choke your throat, Caroline? Never mind," he bellowed when she sputtered an interjection. "All I want are your congratulations, even if false, and then your silence on the subject forever. I am under no illusions that Louisa's pompousness is less than yours, but at least she possessed enough civility, respect, and affection to write with her congratulations. Do you think you can manage that much?"

Hands balled on his hips, Bingley fought the urge to berate further. Willing his vexation to abate, he waited for her to reply, and as the time ticked by, curiosity dampened his frustration. Caroline stood near the dartboard some six feet away, staring vaguely toward one of the far windows. As typical, her chin was lifted haughtily and lips puckered as if a sour taste lay on her tongue. Unusual were the rapidly blinking eyes, the twitching leg fluttering her skirt, and the nervous twisting of the ring on her left hand. Bingley was frequently flummoxed by his younger sister's attitude and opinions, but he was eminently familiar with her mannerisms and expressions. Everything Caroline did was practiced, controlled, and purposeful. A restless, distressed Caroline was an anomaly.

"Congratulations!" Her shrill exclamation; abrupt, jerky pivot; and scowl were wholly at odds with the sentiment. Strangely, rather than Bingley's irritation increasing, ridiculousness struck him.

Snickering, he patted his chest. "Ah, Caroline! How you warm my heart with your well wishes. I pray the effort has not caused you harm?"

After a collected pause and cleansing breath, she repeated, "Congratulations," in a honeyed, sincere tone. "I wish you and Miss

Bennet a lifetime of happiness. I mean it," she insisted when Bingley's brows arched, "truly. Jane is…" She sighed and brushed at something on her cheek. "…a lovely woman. Provincial and not what I wished for you, Charles, but…I cannot argue that you two are suited. She makes you happy," she concluded with a shrug.

"Indeed she does. Immensely so. Thank you."

Nodding once, Caroline turned away and resumed her dreamlike stare out the window. Bingley frowned, more confused than relieved. She spoke sincerely—he felt certain of that—and it was nice to hear the admission. Suddenly parched, Bingley walked to the sidebar and poured a glass of water and then another, drinking each in one long gulp. Caroline remained slump shouldered and immobile other than intermittent swipes at her face and a quivering tic along her jaw.

Bingley's eyes flew wide. *Good God! Is she crying?* The idea was preposterous! He searched his memories and honestly could not remember his sister ever crying—not even when lashed by their nanny while in the nursery. If he had ever given the topic any thought, he might have speculated her tear glands were dysfunctional. It was so inconceivable he experienced none of the standard male guilt or discomfiture at a woman crying. Rather, his inclination was to exploit her rare emotional state.

"Accepting my future with Jane is an important step, Caroline, and I sincerely appreciate your congratulations. Now you must accept Mr. Darcy and Miss Elizabeth."

"That I cannot do."

Leaving the glass on the sidebar, Bingley circled the billiard table at a moderate pace and stopped in front of the window she dazedly faced. Indeed, her eyes were red rimmed and moist, and an unattractive blotchiness covered her cheeks.

Damn it all! Now I feel sorry for her.

"I did not realize your feelings for Mr. Darcy were this strong. Having lost Jane for a time, I can empathize with your heartache over losing the man you love, and I am sorry—"

"Love? What are you driveling now? Really, Charles! Just because you are ruled by maudlin emotions does not mean I am."

"Then…what?" Truly baffled, a coherent sentence would not form. Gesturing at his eyes and then toward her face worked to get his message across.

"You become lachrymose at romantic poetry, tragic opera, and fluffy kittens frolicking. I weep when a drab inferior with an impertinent tongue destroys my future. I cry at injustice, Charles."

During her rant, the pooling tears disappeared and she wiped the residual wetness off her cheeks. Her motley complexion and reddened eyes tipped the scale toward anger rather then sadness. Bingley believed her claims were how she honestly felt. That did not make it sensible or right, however.

"I shan't belittle the intensity of your emotions, Sister. I disagree with your perceptions of Miss Elizabeth but doubt my ability to convince you otherwise. Where you are seriously wrong is blaming her for destroying your future because you *never* had a future with Darcy."

Unfazed, she smiled coolly and shook her head. "You are the one who is wrong. Mr. Darcy and I are alike. I am his equal, not Eliza Bennet. They are a drastic mistake."

"This line of thinking is dangerous. You must see reason!" Bingley rapidly strode until directly in front of her. "Darcy and Miss Elizabeth are perfectly suited, and their love is real. Surely you can see that!"

Staring straight into his eyes, face emotionless, she countered, "I see a man who has been enchanted. Mr. Darcy is not the same, and I would think, as his friend, you would fear for him."

A shiver raced up his spine. "I fear for you, Caroline. Give up these delusions of Mr. Darcy before you cause irreparable damage. Fighting the inevitable serves no one, least of all you."

"I refuse to see *that* union as inevitable. Until the vows are recited before God, they are not married."

"Listen to yourself!" Cinching her wrist penetrated her maddeningly aloof demeanor and placid tone—not much though. Caroline merely turned her head to peer at him through hard-set eyes. Fighting against the panic choking his airway, Bingley chastened, "Stubborn you are but not stupid. A betrothal is as binding as marriage, or near to. Honor is everything to a man like Darcy. If you know him an iota, then you know that. A gentleman never disgraces a lady or compromises her reputation." Gripping her chin hard between thumb and fingers, he glared sternly into her eyes, his words clipped and hard. "Breaking his vow to Elizabeth is never going to happen, Caroline. Accept that and accept it now, or God help me, there will be consequences."

Bingley ripped the leather straps off his knuckles, spun on his heels, and stormed out of the room. He burned to pound the sand bag, but Caroline was too close for him to trust his resistance—especially with her frighteningly calculating, smug expression.

ဆ

"Miss Bingley?"

"Yes! Come in quickly! And shut the door, for pity's sake!" Caroline flew toward the maid, yanked her inside, and slammed the door before the words finished passing her lips. The young servant quailed, but Caroline kept a tight grip on her wrist, demanding, "Tell me."

"The gentleman...came down, just now, and went into the library."

"Ah! Very good. And Mr. Bingley?"

"Not seen him, miss. Must still be in his chambers. He was in a right mean state a while back, stomping and grumbling—"

"Never mind that! I must hurry. You know what to do, right?"

The maid nodded and then hastily spoke when Caroline shot her a dagger-like glare. "In fifteen minutes, I'll come to the library, where you will have the door cracked. Waitin' for your signal, then I go in."

"You must be abrupt and make no noise until inside. Good. This is for now"—Caroline pressed several coins into the maid's palm—"and the rest when I am successful."

Remaining calm and walking to the library at a sedate pace was taxing. Fear that Mr. Darcy may exit the library in the handful of minutes necessary to reach the other side of Netherfield, where the library was located, urged her to hasten her steps. But Caroline's plan depended on her arrival appearing casual, so entering in a rush and out of breath would defeat the purpose. With luck, his tendency to pass extended spans of time amongst the dusty books would be the case this time. She had never understood his enjoyment of poring over boring dissertations by writers long dead. A rousing novel with romance and adventure was comprehensible as a worthy entertainment upon occasion, but a bulky tome by one of those Greek or Roman philosophers—their names similar and unpronounceable— was inconceivable. It was a minor annoying flaw in an otherwise agreeable man, and if advantageous today, she might be able to better tolerate his bookish behavior in the future.

My future as Mrs. Fitzwilliam Darcy.

For nearly three weeks, an appalled Caroline had watched Mr. Darcy act the fool over Elizabeth Bennet. He had remained blind to Caroline's subtle displays of her superiority, further mystifying and depressing her. Hopes that their separation while in Town would break the Bennet wench's enchantment went unrealized, severely vexing and distressing Caroline. Her moodiness spilled over while partaking of breakfast that morning—not a wise move—and she truly feared a line had been crossed.

Then her brother had unwittingly reminded her of a fact forgotten: "Honor is everything to a man like Darcy…A gentleman never disgraces a lady or compromises her reputation."

Caroline Bingley rarely needed to resort to devious methods to get what she wanted, and in most circumstances, it was easier to be forthright. Nevertheless, if required for the greater good, scheming and blatant duplicity were ethically sound as far as she was concerned. If Mr. Darcy was unable to think sensibly, Caroline was fine with forcing the situation.

As silently as possible, Caroline widened the crack in the library door and slipped inside. Her prey stood before a bookcase to the right with his back to her and was running one finger lightly over the spines. He paused a time or two until apparently intrigued by one title. This he pulled off the shelf. As he opened the slim book, Caroline left her undetected pose by the door and quietly moved closer.

Mr. Darcy finally sensed her presence and glanced over his shoulder. A frown flashed across his face, Caroline unhappily noted, but in a second it was gone. Snapping the book closed, he turned and greeted with a proper incline of his head. "Miss Bingley."

"Mr. Darcy," she responded, following with a perfected smile she knew to be seductive, as was her sinuous saunter. Avidly he observed her, but his neutral expression and cool gaze gave no hint that he was affected.

Not for the first time, she fleetingly wondered if his imperviousness was an indication of some bizarre abnormality. Indeed, he was more animated with Elizabeth and stared at her constantly. Yet even with her, Mr. Darcy maintained his rigid composure and a deliberate distance, seemingly at odds with how a man was supposed to act when in love. Goodness knows Charles was forever simpering and gushing florid prose at Jane! It was nauseating, to be honest, and while Caroline never claimed to possess deep passion or particularly wanted to be afflicted so, she understood it to be typical. That Mr. Darcy did not embarrass himself with Elizabeth, as Charles did with Jane, proved to Caroline that his emotions were not strong.

"I came to borrow the poems of Christopher Smart for Miss Elizabeth." He thumped the book against his open palm. "She has never read them, so it will be a treat. Now that I have found it, I shall leave the library to you."

He stepped to the left, but she shifted the same direction and blocked his path. "I was hoping for your assistance. I am searching for a copy of Shakespeare's *Taming of the Shrew*. Do you know if there is one housed here at Netherfield?"

"I believe there is a copy in the collection, yes." He pivoted smartly and strode briskly to a case on the opposite side of the room, tossing over his shoulder as she trailed closely behind, "I did not think you a fan of Shakespeare. You were bored by the Covent Garden production of *A Merchant of Venice* and once admitted you disliked *Romeo and Juliet*."

"I have accepted the errors in my judgment and education. I am determined to broaden my comprehension of fine literature, Mr. Darcy. A worthwhile endeavor, do you agree?"

He did not reply and increased his long-legged pace, Caroline skipping to keep up. Revealing his familiarity with the three shelves of Shakespeare titles, Mr. Darcy unerringly retrieved *Taming of the Shrew* and turned to hand it over. Surprised to find her less than a foot away, she saw him flinch as he stepped backward, only to encounter the solid wooden bookcase impeding.

"Pardon me, Miss Bingley."

His muttered apology and rosy cheeks were frankly adorable, and one of the first indications of a normal male response. Caroline smiled, feeling quite triumphant, and closed the already minuscule gap between their bodies. Fingertips sliding caressingly over his fingers to latch onto the book, she simultaneously leaned forward to press her breasts firmly into his hand and arm. Praying the timing was correct and the maid was lurking by the door, Caroline purred, "Thank you, Mr. Darcy. You are the soul of kindness. There must be some way for me to express my gratitude?"

If not for the other hand lifting to wrap around his neck serving as an unexpected cushion, she would have bashed face first into the hard wood of the bookcase when he abruptly stepped to the side. As it was, she tottered and pitched past the space previously inhabited by him, and emitted a sharp yelp when her arm struck the surface.

Shocked and in pain, she swung her eyes about and instantly felt the remaining blood drain from her face. Mr. Darcy had somehow stiffened his spine so that he appeared a foot taller than his normal considerable height and was glowering at her with intense anger and hatred. Chilled to the bone, her veins then turned to ice when he brusquely bowed and snarled, "Excuse me."

Seconds later, he was out the door, his storming march past the maid causing her to blanch and scurry away—not that Caroline blamed her.

ঙ

Darcy was furious. No, he was something far, far beyond furious. His anger at Lady Catherine on that day in Darcy House was a minor irritation in comparison. For the first time in his life, the urge to harm another human being overwhelmed. Only divine intervention saved Caroline from being hurled into the window conveniently located behind her. And considering how vivid the image and just how satisfying imagining it felt, all the angels in heaven needed to lend their aid, or he might turn back around.

He knew exactly what Caroline had tried to do. The maid—one of the upstairs servants with no purpose anywhere near the library—standing stupidly in the half-open door sealed his suspicions. Rage mingled with self-recrimination and terror. How could he not have anticipated the lengths Caroline Bingley would go to? She had spent the past three weeks engaged in one long ploy to wrest him away from Elizabeth, so why was he stunned at her brazen attempt to trap him scandalously?

Later he could waste time condemning his blind gullibility. For now, the objective was to get as far away from Caroline Bingley as humanly possible—for her sake as well as his.

Not caring who saw him stomping through the corridor, Darcy ascended the stairs two at a time and rushed around the corner toward his chambers. Such was his state of mind that he did not see Bingley's

245

door open, and if the younger man had been any less attentive, they would have collided.

"Darcy!" Bingley gasped, grabbing the jamb to avoid tumbling backward. "What has you in such a state?"

"Your sister," Darcy spat, not even slowing down.

"Caroline?"

At Bingley's amazed tone, Darcy stopped and spun around. "Of course Caroline! Don't be an imbecile!"

"So—sorry…of course Caroline. What…? Oh God, I am afraid to ask."

"She has gone too far, Charles. I cannot stand for it nor subject Elizabeth or myself to her actions any longer. I am leaving for the inn at Meryton." He whirled away and resumed his frenzied pace. The urge to vacate Netherfield was nearly as severe as the roiling hunger to physically assault Caroline.

"Wait! You must tell me what happened Darcy! I have the right to know."

Again, Darcy pulled up short and wheeled about. Not hesitating, he explained what happened in the library, a smattering of curse words and highly unflattering verbiage embellishing the concise recounting. When he was done, Charles looked ill. He also looked very angry and determined.

"It is past time to deal with my sister. Go to your room, Darcy, and stay put. I refuse to allow you to leave."

Darcy's brows rose at his friend's blunt command. He could not readily recall Bingley ever speaking in such a harsh tone—to anyone—and especially not to him. In fact, *no one* ordered Darcy of Pemberley in such a way! The oddity and vague humor of it went a long way toward defusing his violent energy.

Nodding once, Darcy did as commanded. An hour and two calming glasses of wine later, Darcy answered Bingley's knock.

"Caroline is packing her bags and within the hour will be on her way to Bath. Louisa and Hurst can deal with her, not that Hurst will pay her any heed."

Darcy handed Bingley a glass of wine. "I suspect he will thank you for giving Mrs. Hurst a companion. Frees him to pursue preferred activities."

"Caroline will swiftly drown her disappointments in shopping. A lot can be purchased between now and the end of November. Maybe there is a merchant selling character and decency."

"If there is, be sure to tell me and I will find a way to get Lady Catherine to Bath."

CHAPTER TEN
Shivering from the Heat

*T*wo mornings later, the topic of Caroline Bingley's exodus remained a popular one—at least to Mrs. Bennet, who for the third time since sitting down with the Longbourn family for breakfast expressed her opinion on the matter.

"Miss Bingley just suddenly decided to join her sister in Bath? How odd!"

"They are close, Mama. It makes perfect sense Miss Bingley would miss their companionship." Jane swiveled her gaze to Lizzy. "Goodness knows I will suffer the same when Lizzy is in faraway Derbyshire."

"Oh! Do not remind me!" Lizzy accented her dramatic wail with a slap of butter onto the muffin in her hand. "Of course, with so many fine carriages at our disposal, visiting will be effortless. Is that not so, Papa?"

Mr. Bennet's dry retort emanated from behind a newspaper. "I daresay a sturdy, padded coach, as Mr. Darcy owns, drawn by a superlative team of horses will float down the road covering the distance in half the space of time."

"There, you see, Jane? Neither of us shall have a chance to suffer. In a blink, the winter will pass and one of us will call upon the other."

"Besides, you will have your husbands to allay any suffering." Kitty's innuendo made Jane blush and Lizzy laugh.

"I do hope you said nothing to offend her, Jane."

"Who, Mama?"

"Why Miss Bingley, of course! Is that not what we are talking about?"

"I was under the impression we were talking about sturdy carriages and distracting husbands." Lizzy winked at Jane, who was still rosy cheeked. "Either subject is preferable to Caroline Bingley as far as I am concerned."

"I agree with Lizzy," Kitty piped in. "She was most unpleasant. You will not admit it, Jane, but I am not marrying her brother, so can speak my mind. Good riddance, I say."

Mrs. Bennet set her teacup onto the saucer with a sharp clink. "It would not serve your interests to speak harshly of Miss Bingley to Mr. Bingley, Jane. Remember that!"

"Judging by how besotted the two gentlemen are with our eldest daughters, you can rest easy, my dear." All eyes turned to the newspaper shielding Mr. Bennet's face. "My guess is that commentary on the personality of Miss Bingley would delight Mr. Darcy and not be vigorously denied by Mr. Bingley."

"A man's affections are fickle, Mr. Bennet, and should never be tested." Mr. Bennet lowered the paper an inch and peered at his wife. Mrs. Bennet paid him no mind, her attention equally divided between her eggs and her daughters. "Remember that, girls. Always strive to flatter and be the peacemaker in your marriage. If Miss Bingley's abrupt departure is in any way the result of unpleasantness, then you must immediately make amends!"

Jane was staring at her toast. *Feeling guilty for no reason*, Lizzy wagered, so she kicked Jane under the table while turning a sweet smile toward her mother. "Mama, you have nothing to fret about. Jane especially and me, to the best of my capability, were polite to Miss Bingley at all times. Besides, there is no proof that her departure was abrupt, simply that we did not hear of it until afterward. She was bored to tears at Netherfield, that much is certain, and Bath is, by all accounts, much more exciting than Meryton."

"If I had the means to visit Bath, I would hasten there as well." Mary's bland tone drew everyone's attention, even Mr. Bennet, who folded the newspaper. "I read an interesting book about the natural springs and walking trails. A sight to behold."

"I quite agree with Mary, although I do not think Miss Bingley apt to climb rocks or traverse wooded trails. It is doubtful she will do anything more strenuous than strolling through the Pump Room and local shops." Lizzy's speculation earned an agreeing grunt from Mr. Bennet, a giggle from Kitty, nods from Mary and Mrs. Bennet, and a smile and snicker from Jane, who rapidly hid both behind her napkin. Not giving her mother a chance to prolong the topic, Lizzy rushed on. "At the present, I can find no fault in the desire to forego a nature walk for the rigors of battling crowds on a merchant street. For probably the first time in my life, shopping has a great appeal."

Lizzy grinned at her father. Mr. Bennet answered with a groan and unfolded his newspaper. Jane quickly washed down her toast with a swallow of hot tea, wincing at the discomfort but jumping on Lizzy's hint.

"Oh yes! We did not hear the rest of our Aunt Gardiner's letter, Mama! They have returned to Town, but when are we to join them?"

As expected, wedding planning was a sure distraction. "My sister Gardiner requested several days for them to settle in after being away and to prepare for your visit. She suggested the twenty-fourth. Not that it matters to me, since I will be staying here."

Mrs. Bennet's woeful sigh and drooping shoulders momentarily had the desired affect. Lizzy felt a sharp stab of pity render her breathless, and Jane looked on the edge of bursting into tears! The nagging for their father to escort them to London had finally resulted in his assent. Mrs. Bennet had complained loudly—contrary to her recent motherly advice to be the peacemaker—and was only placated when Lizzy and Jane cleverly heaped upon her a mountain of "important wedding arrangements" to handle while they were gone.

Happily feeling essential, Mrs. Bennet reverted to the intermittent doleful expressions and pathetic sighs. It was fast becoming the main reason the two brides-to-be were eager to get to London.

Luckily, before either capitulated and begged her to come instead, Mr. Bennet spoke from behind the paper. "The twenty-fourth will not do. Mr. Darcy and Mr. Bingley are joining the fox hunt, remember? We will leave on the twenty-fifth. I'll write Gardiner." And with that, the matter was decided.

ಬಿ

Mr. Darcy and Mr. Bingley were perfectly agreeable to leave for London on the twenty-fifth. Of course, they were perfectly agreeable to just about anything, as long as it occupied the time stretching until their wedding day—or to be more accurate, their wedding night. Not that either of the gentleman were indifferent to the necessary plans for the ceremony and surrounding celebration with friends and family. When asked, they sincerely proclaimed a desire for their nuptials to be special and even expressed the occasional opinion on the food or decorations. If pointedly questioned, however, they would admit that the night they consummated their marriages was far more important. Unlike the wedding day, where the discussions were open and seemed to involve half of Meryton, Darcy and Bingley separately arranged their wedding nights with only the basic information related to anyone. The following conversation while riding to Longbourn two days before the fox hunt was one of the few.

"Bingley, I talked to Mr. Bennet last evening about my wish to depart with Elizabeth as soon as possible after the wedding breakfast."

"Oh, are you planning to make directly for Pemberley then? Or London?"

"Pemberley, although not in one shot. That would be impossible. Nor do I wish to spend my wedding night in a carriage."

"Understandable."

"I am making alternative arrangements but wanted you to know that we shall not infringe upon your hospitality at Netherfield."

"Much appreciated."

"Furthermore, I will ensure my wedding guests return to London. Your guests are up to you to manage."

Bingley nodded, his eyes forward on the trail as they had been all through the short exchange, as were Darcy's eyes. And that was the end of the discussion touching on sleeping arrangements with their new brides.

Darcy was unsure how comfortable Bingley might normally be in openly talking about matters of sexuality. The reason for his lacking knowledge on Bingley's attitude toward the topic was Darcy's reticence when it came to divulging private thoughts. Intimacy was not the only personal topic Darcy hesitated to speak of, but was the last area he would ever willingly blather about. Thus, if Bingley were the type to engage in ribald humor or bragging about conquests—and Darcy doubted Bingley was—he would have to do it with another man.

Some said that airing one's thoughts or feelings with another person, even a stranger, could alleviate one's angst. To Darcy, the concept of talking to a stranger about a personal topic was unfathomable, but on a handful of instances, he had gained relief or perspective by sharing with his father, cousin Richard, or other close friends. Daily his assurance grew that Elizabeth would be a truly complete confidante in time. He longed for this more than he had previously imagined he would with a wife. Furthermore, he was surprised to recognize how fervently he prayed for their communion to include candor in the bedroom.

Anticipating such a future was glorious. In the present, he needed to maintain a tight rein on his passions. Chatting with Bingley, or anyone, about male-female intimacy would surely be counterproductive. It was also best to approach the honeymoon with a focus on the logistical aspects, rather than solely the privacy of the inn or size of the bed.

Keeping the finer details secret from Elizabeth helped maintain his self-restraint and sanity. Plus, it was fun, as he discovered that afternoon when the couples enjoyed their habitual afternoon stroll.

"Papa tells me you plan to abscond with your new wife seconds after I recite my vows."

"Not quite." Darcy contested, frowning. Briefly he wondered why he bothered to speak privately with Mr. Bennet at all when the older gentleman apparently enlightened Elizabeth anyway.

"Then I shall be allowed to eat first? That is a relief! I would hate to be famished to the point of fainting from lacking energy minutes after we arrive at our destination."

Elizabeth's arch tone and smirk tied his tongue for a couple seconds. God knows he could imagine nothing worse than her weak or sleepy on their wedding night! Did she seriously fear the same? And if she was referring specifically to intimacy, could he resist the sudden urge to lower her to the grassy ground beside the trail, crush his body over hers, and kiss until they were forced apart to breathe?

Speaking despite the tightness in his chest and throat, Darcy charged, "If Mr. Bennet said I wished to depart seconds after the wedding, he was exaggerating my words for humorous effect."

"Shocking! I cannot envision Papa ever doing such a thing!"

"Indeed, quite a surprise." He matched her feigned amazement, and then they both laughed. Less tense after a joke, Darcy assured, "What I did say is that we would leave after the wedding breakfast and a reasonable time for congratulations and farewells."

"So by this vague statement I can deduce we are not spending our wedding night at Netherfield?"

"You are remarkably astute, Miss Elizabeth." He squeezed her arm and grinned.

"Thank you. I try to keep my brilliance in check so as not to astonish too greatly. So, are we heading in a northerly or southerly direction?"

"One of those two, yes. With perhaps a bit of east or west added in."

"That narrows it down considerably!"

"If I give too much away, your astounding brilliance will be left unchallenged. I would hate to be the bringer of such disappointment."

At that, she playfully punched him in the arm. "I am getting the distinct impression you mean to keep our honeymoon a surprise."

"I shall repeat: you are remarkably astute."

Further cajoling was answered with similar evasiveness. Darcy enjoyed the game that would continue to be played up to the minute they entered the carriage on their wedding afternoon. Elizabeth's liveliness and love of laughter frequently provided the diversion necessary when his love, or frank lust, threatened to get the better of him—when, that is, her utter adorableness was not enhancing his passion. Truthfully, as marvelous as it was to be with her, Darcy struggled daily against the tightening coil of wanting her. Not much he could do to rectify the matter other than pray for time to speed by and God to grant him superhuman control.

౭ఎ

The night before the fox hunt passed in much the same way as every night had during the week since Mr. Darcy's return from London. With Caroline Bingley gone and most of the citizens of Meryton and the nearby communities already acquainted with Mr. Darcy and Mr. Bingley—the news of the Bennet daughter's joint engagement not the prime topic of gossip anymore—dinner was enjoyed at Longbourn with only the Bennet family.

Mr. Darcy assured Lizzy that dining in a semiformal manner with cuisine flavorful if simple in preparation was satisfying, and no longer quite as strange and discomfiting as initially. She felt she knew him adequately to believe his claim. He certainly ate heartily. Lizzy was amazed that a man who dined delicately with regulated pacing could ingest so much food. The relaxed manner of conversation the Bennet family enjoyed while eating would likely never be his preference. Lizzy accepted this as one example of how different their upbringings. Since she would soon be leaving her home for Pemberley, learning to dwell in his world meant dining in a higher style, among many other things. Until then, it was a relief to witness her betrothed loosen enough to intermittently engage in light banter and not appear continually startled by the rambling flow of conversation.

After dinner, the couples strolled outside as they typically did. Kitty joined them with her puppy, the small animal impervious to the chilly air as he dashed from person to person. His tail wagged in a blur of motion and yips were ongoing unless he paused for a welcome pet or was stifled by a stick in his mouth. The latter was tossed by whomever he ran to, including Mr. Darcy. Lizzy marveled at his overt pleasure in interacting with the dog he had paid scant attention to thus far.

"I did not suspect you were one to cavort with dogs, William. Do you have pets at Pemberley?"

"Not pets precisely." He threw the slimy stick into the darkness, smiling as the puppy launched bravely into the shadows. "My mother had a corgi when I was young. She was a gift from Lady Catherine, who has several of them. She lived to a ripe age. The corgi, that is, although one can presume the same will be true for my aunt. As Wordsworth wrote, building on Defoe, 'The good die first, and they whose hearts are dry as summer dust burn to the socket.'"

Lizzy snickered, partly from the humor of his comment and partly because it still shocked her when he jested even remotely crudely.

Darcy continued, "Who can resist playing with a young animal? As with children, they have such lightness and innocence. I suppose adults see it as an opportunity, however brief, to revisit a time when life was endless play and joy." He bent to retrieve the stick, bestowed a quick scratch behind the dog's ears, and tossed the stick further away. "Animals are not kept inside the manor on a regular basis. My mother's corgi was the only one. Georgiana has had two or three cats over the years. They never wished to stay indoors for long though and soon joined the mousers roaming the property."

"So you were not a fortunate youth, with young animals to share your innocence and lightness."

"I did not say that. Remember, I tended to spend large portions of my days, then and now, in the stable complex. I never managed to entice a foal to fetch a tossed stick, but they are quite playful. The gamekeeper compound was my second favored place. Mr. Burr is Pemberley's head gamekeeper. He is a remarkable man with an affinity for any animal species, as is Mrs. Burr, for that matter. They raise the mastiffs, who guard the estate, and the hunting hounds. Dogs are vital assets. While not exactly pets, with breeding comes multiple litters of puppies for an active boy to cavort with."

They chatted about animals for a while longer, the others joining the conversation with amusing reminiscences from their childhoods, but sooner than desired, the cooling night air drove them inside. Mr. and Mrs. Bennet were already in sedate repose in the parlor. Mary "entertained" on the pianoforte, thankfully located in the room across the corridor.

Mrs. Bennet jumped up to fuss over the gentlemen, as she inevitably did no matter how often they assured her they were in need of nothing. Before either man could sit, tumblers of brandy were thrust into their hands. Darcy accepted the glass with a kind thanks and incline of his head. Mrs. Bennet flushed and spluttered, but Darcy turned away to acknowledge Mr. Bennet, where he hunched in a corner chair.

While her fiancé and father conversed, Lizzy retrieved her embroidery basket from the closet and the book Mr. Darcy had left sitting on the foyer table: *A Tale of the Four Dervishes*, translated into English some three years ago and sent to Darcy by his uncle, Dr. George Darcy, who knew the author, Mir Amman, from his time dwelling in Calcutta—another tidbit of fascinating information about her future husband and his family.

What remained a mystery was whether translated novels from foreign countries were his typical reading fare. Lizzy had paid scant attention to what Mr. Darcy read during their times together before they were engaged, but she was fairly sure the books she recalled in his hands had varied. Oddly, he had been carrying this book around for weeks. Noting the strip of ribbon marking his place, the page was near the beginning of the book, as it had been when she first saw the book sitting on a table at Netherfield shortly after his proposal.

Before she could puzzle through the possible explanations, it abruptly dawned on her that the ribbon doubling as a bookmark belonged to her. Stopping midstride, a sweet pressure tightened her chest and warm moisture welled in her eyes. She remembered the day vividly for several reasons, not merely because it was the day after his return from London.

That morning had dawned with blue skies and fair temperature, so the couples had decided on a picnic at Oakham Mount. Kitty and Mary were invited, as had been Matty Beller at Darcy's behest. The afternoon had proceeded as one expected with a group of cheerful people enjoying the out-of-doors. At one point, well after eating, Mr. Bingley and Jane had set out for a stroll along the edge of the creek, while Mary and Matty had wandered in the opposite direction down the gentle slope to pick from the clusters of blooming wildflowers fighting the looming winter. Fifteen minutes passed before Kitty had abruptly sprang from the spread blanket to chase after the adventurous puppy. Other than glancing up and laughing at the scene of her sister being bested in the race, Lizzy had resumed reading aloud from a dreadfully written mystery novel serving to entertain.

Another ten or more minutes had ticked away before her awareness that they were utterly alone crept in and her reading trailed to a stuttering halt. A swift look had noted Mary and Matty so far down the hill as to be big dots. Jane and Bingley were almost as far away, sitting on a large rock facing the water. Kitty and the dog were nowhere to be seen. She had not needed to lift her gaze to know Mr. Darcy was acutely aware of their solitude. She had *felt* the intensity surrounding the space he occupied on the blanket. A slight shift of position and peek from the corner of her eye confirmed his familiar penetrating stare.

Heat had flooded her face, and she had been seized by a magnetic pull toward him, no amount of nervousness powerful enough to stop her. Never would she remember how they closed the space. She only remembered meeting his eyes, and then the caressing pressure of his mouth followed by an intense surge of delight pounding head to toe. She might have gasped, or maybe he did, but as rapidly as the kiss began, it had ended. That much she knew for sure.

"William," she had whispered, eyes closed and mouth seeking.

"I love you, Elizabeth." His raspy declaration had passed through lips so close they brushed delectably against hers. Yet rather than close that tragic gap, he had withdrawn further, the fingertips feathering across her jaw the only contact.

When she had finally gained the strength to open her eyes— minutes or hours later—he had been watching her with a soft smile and twinkling blue eyes, but no other sign of wild desire. For a moment, she had wanted to slap him! She knew he possessed phenomenal self-control and suspected he called upon this command in a multitude of situations, but did he have to employ his talent for restraint at the *one time* they were gifted a measure of privacy? Or worse yet, was kissing her so mundane that after a ten-second exchange, he was done?

He had given her no chance to ruminate upon those disturbing questions or blurt them—which may have been a benefit or detriment depending on the answer. Instead, she had been distracted by his playful tug on a green ribbon loosened from the intricate knots and bows on the right side of her bonnet.

"One tiny kiss and you literally unravel, Miss Elizabeth." The shakiness of his voice had restored her sinking spirits somewhat. Then he had twined the narrow ribbon around his fingers, the strip detaching completely from the hat, and her swipes to grab it promptly became a game she was doomed to lose due to his considerably longer arms. Before either had tired of the diverting foolishness, Kitty returned and then shortly thereafter the others, ending any opportunity for privacy, with or without fiery kisses.

Only upon spying the green satin ribbon lying perfectly flat in between the pages of his book did Lizzy realize she had forgotten all about his sneaky possession of her token. Pressing the book to her chest, she inhaled deeply to calm the emotional flutters. That day was the last time he had kissed her, other than on the hand, and had been only the second kiss granted since his return from London. In every way, Mr. Darcy was a gentleman, expressing his devotion to her in dozens of ways, yet physically, he had grown more rigid and undemonstrative. It bothered her more than she had recognized until finding this ribbon.

Shaking her head, Lizzy headed back to the parlor. Her betrothed was a complicated man and, she firmly believed, one with powerful passions. In time, she would unravel him just as he had unraveled the ribbon from her bonnet—in time.

Mr. Darcy was sitting on the sofa corner as he typically did, the space beside him waiting for her. Jane and Mr. Bingley had retreated to the sofa closer to the fire and spoke in low tones. Kitty and the pup had disappeared who knew where. Aside from Mary's continued efforts on the pianoforte, the rustle of her father turning pages in his book, and her mother chattering to everyone and no one at the same time, the cozy room was serene.

"Your book, sir. And a pillow." She handed each to him and then settled onto the sofa, ensuring a good eight-inch gap between their bodies as her parents insisted upon.

"My thanks, Miss Elizabeth. I appreciate your remembrance of my quirk."

Lizzy bent to retrieve her embroidery hoop from the basket by her feet, replying through her laughter, "If wanting a pillow on your lap to prop your book upon while reading is what you consider a quirk, Mr. Darcy, I shall have little trouble performing my wifely duties."

"I—I beg your pardon?"

Sitting back, she turned toward him. Unsure why he had choked on his words or was looking at her with an oddly twisted expression, she flashed a bright smile. "Mama has been educating Jane and I on the scope of our domestic responsibilities as proper wives, you see."

"Oh. I see. Dare I ask what wisdom Mrs. Bennet has passed along?"

"Let me think." Lizzy tapped one finger on her lip, feigning serious thought. "A wife never takes a bite of food until her husband does first. A wife stays at the table until her husband rises. A wife listens attentively to every word her husband says and never interrupts or argues. I may well fail at that one, I should warn you."

"Duly noted. What else?"

Now he was relaxing, the warm smile and tender gaze she adored growing pronounced as she ticked off more nonsensical advice from Mrs. Bennet. "And of prime importance is the fact that a wife should never pester her husband with asking after his needs, or quirks as you dubbed them. She should observe keenly to learn how best to service him and then act in anticipation."

"That is quite an extensive list. You have taken all of this to heart?"

"I am trying," she moaned, sighing dramatically. "Some of these requirements may well take me years, if not decades, to master. Thankfully, I am marrying a man with extraordinary patience who, as he has assured me, demands nothing more challenging than a pillow to prop his book upon. There may be hope for me at this rate after all!"

In the subsequent hour, they spoke occasionally but mostly remained silent as they attended to their tasks. Or at least Lizzy attempted to embroider. In truth, she muddled through the stitches, her consciousness focused almost exclusively on William. The space separating them crackled as if alive, Lizzy swearing she could feel his breath on her neck when he exhaled. He radiated heat, the warmth of his body flowing into her skin and carrying the fragrance of his cologne to her nose. Cardamom and a woodsy spice, vaguely pine but sweeter, mixed with a musky aroma she could not identify. Perhaps it was his natural scent, she thought, a masculine essence unique to him. Whatever the blend, Lizzy longed to bury her face against his flesh and inhale until her lungs filled to capacity.

The vivid image was startling, and for the third time in the past ten minutes, she pricked her finger with the needle. Pain was instantly forgotten, however, when William rubbed one long-fingered, elegant hand along his thigh. Riveted, she watch the muscle tightly sheathed by a layer of fabric harden as he shifted his sitting position and stretched his legs out a bit further. Lifting her eyes slightly, she watched his other hand as he raised the glass of brandy to his parted lips. The tip of his tongue touched the rim, he swallowed a sip, and then the glass was lowered, leaving a glistening sheen of liquor on his lip.

For a crazed heartbeat or two, Lizzy truly thought she would die if unable to lick the residual brandy off his lips. That insanity was followed by a deluge of shivers and a stab of what felt bizarrely like jealousy at the glass itself. Madness!

"Mr. Darcy, the book you are reading, is it an interesting one?"

Where that came from, she had no idea. Clearly he was as surprised, judging by how he jerked, stared at her for ten seconds, and then cleared his throat. "I beg your pardon, Miss Elizabeth. What did you say?"

"I asked if the book you are reading is interesting."

"Oh! Yes. Quite interesting."

His vague tone and confused frown brought a smile to her lips. "Do you think it would be of interest to me? You know how I enjoy reading. Improves the mind, you understand."

"Yes, it does," he agreed, chuckling.

"So, then you believe I may glean value from reading the book your uncle sent? When you are finished, naturally."

"If you wish, Miss Elizabeth. I would be delighted to lend it to you."

"I assume it must be a particularly fascinating story. Or possibly it may be too deep for my young mind to comprehend?" Smoothing her face to as vacuous an expression as she could fabricate, Lizzy noted the confused furrow returned to his brow. The fun of teasing him helped dispel the strange, libidinous musings from moments ago.

"I am positive your mind is adept enough to comprehend any topic."

"I was concerned, you see, as it has taken you more than an hour to study this one page. In point of fact, you have been reading this book for the past two weeks and are only on page fifteen. I can only speculate, but considering how intelligent you are, the only feasible conclusion is that the story is so extraordinary you are rereading each paragraph several times for sheer pleasure. Or it is necessary to do so in order to decipher the author's intent?"

"You have caught me, my dear." Closing the book, he leaned toward her and spoke in a low voice. "The truth is, if you must know, I find myself terribly unfocused whenever I am near you. I am on page fifteen, yet am unable to render an accounting of the content thus far. Does this shock you, Elizabeth?"

Fixed on his dancing eyes, a tingle of delight spiraled about her heart. Smiling, she held up the embroidery hoop. "You see this sampler?"

"Yes, of course."

"I have been working on this for a month and should have completed it in a week. These stitches here are all wrong, and I have had to rip this section out three times! I have lost count how often I have stabbed my fingers. I judge you and I are suffering from the same disease."

Never averting his penetrating gaze, he enveloped her free hand, squeezed gently, and then raised her fingers to his lips. His eyes were captivating, Lizzy breathless as the crystalline blue orbs darkened slightly in what she now recognized was ardor. Pressing her folded knuckles onto the same lush lips she so recently wanted to suck brandy off of, he said, "I am *very* pleased to hear you say that, Elizabeth. You have no idea how pleased."

His muted, husky timbre imbued with emotion sent a fresh cascade of tingles and shivers throughout her body. *Look away from his eyes, Lizzy!* Not that she was listening to rational advice at the present.

"Are you pleased, Mr. Darcy, that I have pricked my fingers?"

"I am William to you, and my mother used to kiss my wounds to make them better. Should I kiss your aching fingers? Will that relieve your pain?"

Without waiting for her permission—as if she would have refused a kiss from him—he separated each finger and unhurriedly engulfed each tip between his soft, warm lips. Mesmerized, she glanced back and forth from his eyes and lips. Time seemed to halt and simultaneously crawl on toward the inevitable kiss to her pinkie. Then what would happen? Would he begin again? Or treat her right hand to the same therapy? Perhaps she should fib and say she pricked her lips a time or two.

Mr. Bennet's not-so-subtle cough effectively interrupted the enchanted interlude. Fortunately, her pinkie was not left out of William's pain-relieving tactic, Lizzy then managing to draw her hand from his grasp and release a quivering exhale. Surprisingly, Mr. Darcy appeared unperturbed by her father catching him in the act of an intimate liberty. In fact, his grin was downright smug!

Picking up her embroidery, more for the desperate need to have something else to focus on beside his handsome face and full mouth she still ached to taste, Lizzy jabbed the needle through a random hole. Searching her numbed mind for a safe topic, she abruptly recalled a piece of information she had forgotten to mention.

"I received a letter from Georgiana today."

"Did you? That would be the third, yes? My sister seems to have forgone writing to me these past weeks in favor of writing to you."

"Oh! I am sorry, William! I have no wish to keep her from writing to you."

Darcy laughed and squeezed the hand she had unconsciously laid on his forearm. "I am joking, Elizabeth. You know how pleased I am that you and Georgiana are friends. What did my sister have to say this time?"

"Nothing of consequence. Female chatter."

As anticipated, he merely nodded at that. Who knew what men encompassed under the female chatter generality, but inevitably it rendered them mute. Probably out of fear that if questioned, even politely, the female would babble on about cosmetics or bonnet sewing or some other equally dull subject. Worse yet, they might launch into a maudlin tale, real or fictional, with syrupy sentiments tossed about and, God forbid, actual tears!

In this case, Darcy's wise silence served Lizzy's purpose because among her enthusiasm for their scheduled meeting in London, Georgiana had revealed a fact Lizzy had embarrassingly not thought to ask about earlier. That is that Fitzwilliam Darcy's twenty-ninth birthday was on November the tenth, just two weeks away.

ॐ

"Can I ask you a personal question, Jane?"

Jane's hands paused mid-twist with Lizzy's hair half-plaited. Glancing upward, Jane met Lizzy's serious reflection in the mirror. "Of course you can. Does this have to do with why you are quiet tonight?"

Hesitating a second more, Lizzy tried to place her thoughts into words that would not embarrass her shy sister unduly. "You needn't reveal too much, but when Mr. Bingley is showing his affection for you"—Jane flushed and focused on completing Lizzy's braid as if an onerous task—"how do you feel? I mean, not so much how you feel in response to his affectionate gestures. Rather, do you feel he...enjoys the moment? Perhaps even wants more? Or...oh bother!"

Jane finished the braid, neither saying more for several minutes. Lizzy detected the unusual awkwardness heavy on the air, yet also sensed that Jane wanted to pursue the topic but needed to prepare herself. Sure enough, once her long plait was tied at the end, Jane sat on the edge of the bed and inhaled deeply.

"I am not precisely sure what is troubling you, Lizzy, but I know I have my own moments of confusion with…that…part of our relationship."

"Do you?" Lizzy jumped from the vanity stool and joined Jane on the bed. "How so?"

"It is the newness of such feelings I suppose. And the mystery yet involved."

"Indeed, I agree it is the mystery." Lizzy bobbed her head firmly. "I will never quite understand why it is believed that girls should be kept uninformed about such things. Why, if not for Mrs. Hill, I would have thought I was dying when I began my courses. Mama told us nothing, and even Mrs. Hill refused to explain why it was happening, only saying it was normal."

"Thankfully for all us girls, you never accept the simple answer." Jane smiled in remembrance.

Where Lizzy had unearthed the book with the short chapter on female reproduction she never revealed. Not trusting Lydia or Kitty, Lizzy kept the shelf of questionable books hidden in Sir William Lucas's library a secret. She had stumbled across it years ago, insatiable curiosity overcoming caution or proper manners, but even after picking the lock, Lizzy rarely risked accessing the books. Nevertheless, she had learned more from Sir William's bawdy books than anywhere else and borrowed the medical text for educational purposes. For one night only, the five of them pored over every word and illustration with a mixture of grimaces and giggles. One night of memorizing that one section was the closest they came to serious education on the subject—that and growing up on a farm, as Lizzy referred to next.

"I have a radical idea that women should be educated as men are. Should I scandalize William and tell him?" Laughing, Lizzy pulled her legs up and rested her chin atop her knees. "If not for seeing animals mate, none of us would have the vaguest idea what married people do. Frankly, I presumed the act was similar, in the sense of being a deed to be done not greatly different than breathing or eating."

"That may be a slight exaggeration, Lizzy."

"Yes, of course it is. But not by too much, you have to admit, Jane. If not for the random whisper or offhand comment or rare affectionate couple, like our uncle and aunt Gardiner, there would be no evidence to point to human intimacy being particularly enjoyable."

"Unless one is male," Jane whispered.

Lizzy nodded, knowing what she meant. Females boldly discussing matters of sensuality and intimacy were expressly forbidden. This mandate was ignored, of course, but circumspectly, with hesitant whispers and the barest knowledge gleaned from questionable sources. At the same time, it was an accepted fact, loudly proclaimed, that men were highly sexual beings. Females were constantly warned against the male species with their "uncontainable lusts" and similar cautionary phrases. So much so that even if clueless what an "uncontainable lust" entailed, you were on the lookout for it.

"In retrospect," Lizzy said slowly, the idea newly forming in her mind, "it is not that the knowledge is unspoken, rather that it is mixed with innuendo and false facts."

"And guilt or shame for daring to let your thoughts drift in that direction."

Lizzy nodded in agreement with her sister's assertion. "Quite so. Are you...afraid, Jane?"

The sharp rap at Jane's bedroom door, followed by it swinging open abruptly, jolted a squeak from each of them.

"Oh! Girls! I heard your voices and decided it was time. Indeed, past time!"

Mrs. Bennet rushed inside, ruffled nightdress and robe fluttering, her tone on the edge of berserk and movements jittery. Even for her it was extreme. Jane and Lizzy exchanged a worried glance and half expected a calamity to hit the house any second.

"Past time for what, Mama?"

"Why, to discuss your wedding nights, of course! So much to say. Yes. Well, we cannot voice such matters where your sisters may overhear. They will need to know in due course, but I am sure my nerves are unable to withstand all four of you staring at me and asking questions! Lydia found out on her own, I daresay, and appeared none the worse for it, so I thought to do the same until Mr. Bennet told me to—"

"Papa told you to talk to us?" Lizzy wanted to drop into a hole and shot a horrified look toward Jane. Surprisingly, aside from high color to her cheeks, Jane calmly watched Mrs. Bennet pace and wore an expression of curiosity, not the embarrassment Lizzy expected and was feeling. Wondering why she was mortified, instead of relieved at the prospect of finally getting answers from someone experienced on the topic, occupied her mind long enough that Lizzy missed part of her mother's speech.

"...be prepared for your husband's demands and expectations. It is safe to presume that all men are not the same in...their urges or how they...pursue relations, but be assured that for most, as I understand it, the need to be with a woman is strong. Animalistic in that respect. Now, what you two can expect on your wedding nights, and as often as your husbands can manage it thereafter, is..."

Mrs. Bennet plopped down between Jane and Lizzy where they sat on the bed, clasped on to each of their hands, and launched into the topic with barely a breath taken. Amazingly, Mrs. Bennet's nerves calmed the more she delved in. Clearly it was an unprepared discourse, with more advice on how to avoid intimate encounters than what those encounters precisely entailed. Yet, amid the rambling, gems of information were interspersed. Grabbing hold of those nuggets was the challenge.

Neither Lizzy nor Jane said much, only breaking in a handful of times with pointed questions or clarification. By the time Mrs. Bennet exhausted herself—an hour later—Lizzy's head was spinning. Then, as quickly as she had arrived, she was out the door with her good-nights tossed over a shoulder.

For easily fifteen minutes, Jane and Lizzy sat in silence staring at their hands, the carpet, the wall—anything but each other. Finally Lizzy murmured, "I cannot decide between 'amorous congress' or 'convivial society' as my favored euphemism. Either is better than hearing Mama use a clinical word like 'coitus' or 'copulation.'"

Jane stared at Lizzy for all of two seconds. Then they fell back on the bed, giggling hysterically. Breathless and wiping tears, Jane gasped, "This is all your fault, you know."

"My fault?"

"You brought up the subject, remember?"

"Oh my! I suppose I did! I had actually quite forgotten."

"You asked if I was afraid and I was about to answer that I was, a little anyway. Now, thanks to Mama, it all seems too amusing to be fearful of."

"Yes, I suppose it is to a degree." Lizzy turned her head to look at her sister, but Jane was staring up at the ceiling. "What were you afraid of?"

Still staring upward and smiling with the recent attack of laughter visible on her countenance, Jane explained, "Nothing for myself. Mainly my fears arose from the desire to please Mr. Bingley as a wife aught while unsure how I could do that when knowing so little. Yet even before Mama's information, I was realizing I had no need to fret over that either. It is God's design, Lizzy, and every woman since Eve has been exactly where we are now. Every man too, for that matter. Whether the first time or the hundredth, sensual intercourse—another intriguing euphemism—is a part of the marriage relationship as God intended."

"So, logically it cannot be a frightening, unwanted activity," Lizzy added when Jane said no more.

"Exactly."

"Even though Mama gravely declared otherwise?" Jane turned her head and looked at Lizzy—just looked at her, no words passing her lips and her expression bland, yet Lizzy knew the message being conveyed. "Right. How silly of me."

"I trust Mr. Bingley and how I feel when with him. I cannot share specifically, Lizzy. It would be too uncomfortable. I can say that I feel wonderful with him, enough so that I am convinced the...rest will be equally as wonderful."

"Of course you are right. Like you, I want to ensure William's happiness and...*satisfaction*, I suppose is the most apt term." Suddenly hit with embarrassment from she knew not where, Lizzy sensed the heat washing across her cheeks and giggles tickling her throat. "Speaking of William's happiness, you must help me, Jane. I learned from Miss Darcy that his birthday is in November. I would like to plan something special."

Jane was thrilled with the idea, and soon the two were plotting various ways to surprise Mr. Darcy, the diversion perfect to relinquish apprehensions surrounding *amorous congress*.

CHAPTER ELEVEN
Emotional Downpour at Darcy House

*D*arcy strolled through his London townhouse's parlor, crossed the entrance foyer, and entered the dining room. Standing behind his chair located at the head of the crisp, bleached-white linen-draped table, he swept his scrutinizing gaze over the room. Of particular study were the gold-edged china place settings and sparkling wineglasses, gleaming silver candelabras and serving utensils, fragrant flowers, and polished chairs with spotless cushions. As in the previous chambers of the townhouse, nothing was deemed inconsequential for his examination.

Hosting formal dinner parties was high on his list of least favorite duties. Nevertheless, when an occasion arose requiring guests at his table, Darcy ensured perfection and protocol down to the tiniest detail. The exacting demands given to the staff and his rigorous character had been put to the test repeatedly since inheriting the title of Master of Pemberley and Darcy House. Over time, he had hosted dozens of gatherings with aristocracy and persons of eminence, managing capably despite his discomfort. Invariably, his guests concluded their evenings satisfied.

History was in his favor, so Darcy knew it was illogical to fret over menus and ambience for the small group of intimate friends and family expected tonight. Yet never had a dinner at Darcy House held greater significance for him personally than the one planned for this evening.

Mr. Travers entered through the servants' doorway and approached his employer. As he traversed the large room, the butler's keen eyes surveyed the scene, undoubtedly detecting a multitude of minor flaws that Darcy would never notice.

"Is anything amiss, Mr. Darcy? Have all your specifications been fulfilled to your satisfaction?"

"Excellent, Mr. Travers, as always." He read the label on the wine bottle the butler held for his inspection. "Two bottles should suffice, but have two more within easy access."

Per standard procedure, Mr. Travers delineated the list of spirits for the evening. Darcy offered one or two suggestions but trusted the butler's superior expertise. As they were finishing, Georgiana glided into the room. She waited until Mr. Travers left before greeting her brother with a kiss upon his cheek.

Referring to the bottle Darcy had been inspecting, Georgiana smiled winsomely and inquired, "How many glasses of that chardonnay am I allowed to have?"

Darcy pursed his lips and frowned sternly. "Perhaps I will allow half a glass."

"A half! I drank a whole glass while dining with Uncle and Aunt last week! I *am* seventeen, William—"

"I am aware, Georgiana. I was present at your birthday celebration if you recall. Why the fervency to imbibe? Could it be nervousness, my dear?" He tweaked the tip of her nose.

Georgiana blushed but tilted her head and arched a brow. "I might ask who has been pacing through the rooms since seconds after arriving at noon? Is compulsively rearranging flowers and straightening pillows a frequent habit, Brother dear? And"—she lifted his hand and twisted until the candlelight shimmered off each shiny fingernail—"am I correct that you buffed your nails?"

Darcy jerked his hand from her grasp, growling, "You may have one glass of wine, perhaps two, little imp!"

"Thank you, William!" she trilled, clapping her hands and bouncing on her toes. "You are the best brother!" Laughing at his sardonic grunt, she then confessed, "It is true that I am nervous about tonight, although wanting the wine is merely because I am curious."

"'Curiosity is one of the permanent and certain characteristics of a vigorous mind.'"

"Samuel Johnson," Georgiana promptly replied, earning a proud smile from her brother. "A 'vigorous mind' is a compliment I accept. And as William Wirt said, 'Seize the moment of excited curiosity on any subject to solve your doubts; for if you let it pass, the desire may never return, and you may remain in ignorance.'"

"A *tragedy*, indeed, to remain in ignorance on the delights of wine," he agreed with false incredulity. Georgiana playfully slapped his arm. "Rather than pointlessly lecture, I will caution with another quote, 'Be not curious in unnecessary matters: for more things are shown unto thee than men understand.'"

"Oh bother! Must you always counter with scripture? I cannot very well argue with God, now can I?"

"You can argue all you wish, Georgie, but I doubt the endeavor will meet with success." Darcy chuckled at her indignant huff, then tucked her to his side for an affectionate squeeze. Shifting into a serious tone, Darcy observed, "Rationally, neither of us have the slightest reason to be nervous. Elizabeth adores you—"

"And she loves you." Georgiana peered up at his happy face.

"So she has assured me." Darcy hid the blush warming his cheeks by bending to kiss her forehead. "Furthermore, Mr. Bingley you are well acquainted with, and our other guests are honest, pleasant people. You will like them, I am sure of it. Now," he said in a brisk tone, clutching her upper arms and stepping away, "let me look at you."

Darcy's intention to flatter with vague comments about her dress or something of that nature, mixed with a tease about her youth, was revised upon honest examination. "My word, Georgiana! When did you mature into this young woman before me? You are a vision, especially in this gown and with your hair arranged elaborately. You"—he swallowed, finishing in a whisper, "you resemble our mother more with each passing day."

"Thank you, Fitzwilliam."

"It is the truth."

The doorbell interrupted further sibling conversation and forestalled either of them giving in to emotional reminiscences. Swiftly they positioned themselves in the foyer to welcome their guests. Darcy's tug on his jacket and Georgiana's pat to her hair were their last fidgety gestures.

Mr. Travers opened the door, two footmen at the ready to take coats and hats, while Darcy greeted with typical pomp and introduced everyone to his sister. Georgiana maintained her calm, a hint of rosiness to her pale cheeks and intermittent glances at her toes the only signs of her bashfulness.

As soon as he could manage, Darcy cornered Elizabeth to clasp her fingers and bestow an earnest kiss to her knuckles. "Elizabeth. My dearest Elizabeth." He crooned her name caressingly. "It is my supreme joy to welcome you to Darcy House. Tonight you are my honored guest, and my happiness is immense. Greater still shall be my euphoria when you are here as Mrs. Darcy."

Darcy straightened before she responded, not trusting his restraint if she extended a similar sentiment. Slipping her arm under his and pressing her dainty hand firmly, Darcy broadcast to his guests, "Dinner will be served at precisely seven o'clock. Miss Darcy and I thought a stroll on the terrace and garden in the fresh, autumn air would be beneficial prior to a bountiful meal."

"Dare I hope you have a trout pond here, as you do at Pemberley, Mr. Darcy?"

"Alas, I fear your hopes must be dashed, Mr. Gardiner. There is a fountain, a large one, in fact, but it never occurred to me to utilize it as a home for fish. Somehow I doubt more than four or five trout would deem it a sufficiently ample habitat."

The fountain he referred to was heard before seen. The mullion-paned glass French-style dual doors opening to the walled rear yard gaped wide, and the musical cadence of bubbling water drifted inside. Leading through the doors with Elizabeth on his arm, Darcy stepped to the right, so as not to obstruct the view for his trailing guests. Elizabeth sucked in a breath and reflexively squeezed his arm.

"Oh! William, it is beautiful!"

Located in the precise center of the enormous rear yard, the fountain's water-filled base was eight feet square with raised sides and a flat ledge for sitting. Constructed of mosaic tiles painted in vivid hues, the tall, central column was designed as twined stems of a flower bouquet. The petals of each colorful flower gracefully curved downward in a cascade, rivulets of water dropping melodiously. A path of smoothly cut stones extended from the terrace and encircled the fountain.

Surrounding and stretching beyond into the dusky shadows, past the reach of the glass-domed torches, was a flat expanse of freshly cut lawn. Bushes and trees of various species were planted amid the gardens and dotted the periphery—some evergreen and others transformed with the colors of autumn—the diverse shapes indicating a rear enclosure enormous and generously vegetated.

Two gaslight lamps illuminated the stone patio where the party clustered in awed admiration. The light revealed cushioned chairs; small, round tables; and potted shrubs and vines, spaced evenly along the wall and railing.

"Mr. Darcy, this is impressive! I never suspected some of the houses in Town boasted yards so generous."

"Some do, Mrs. Gardiner, although not all. My great-great grandfather was friends with Sir Grosvenor. Married his cousin, in fact. This townhouse was one of the first Sir Grosvenor built, purchased before it was completed and designed specifically for my great-great grandfather. One of the requests was a substantial garden area." Elizabeth left his side to join Jane and Georgiana at the fountain, Darcy observing her nimble steps and pleasing figure even as he expounded on the yard's features. "The light of day offers the optimum effect; however, additional torches can be lit if further investigation is wanted. I do assure the lawn is level and free of hazards, so strolling in the moonlight is safe."

Mr. Bennet asked a number of botanical questions—Darcy answering with superb knowledge of the subject—while Mr. Gardiner was most curious as to which tradesman supplied the plants and furnishings. Darcy's conversation with the gentlemen was effortless and interspersed with casual humor. The two older men may not yet technically be Darcy's relatives, but their kinship and easygoing personalities created a family atmosphere often missing when Darcy entertained his own blood relations. Elizabeth interacted with his sister as if she'd know her for years, and Jane and Mrs. Gardiner joined in with their amiable natures, Georgiana soon laughing and talking with barely a trace of shyness. That alone was remarkable enough to melt Darcy's heart and erase any lingering nervousness.

But it was when Elizabeth glanced his direction, as she frequently did outside and when dining, that his soul soared. Laughter, jesting, and flowing conversation trumped the exquisite cuisine and expensive wines as the best part of dinner. Darcy amazed himself with how gregarious and vibrant he acted. He might have attributed it to intoxication, except that he never finished his second glass of wine. The gay company contributed to his unusual ebullience to be sure. The main reason was that, for the first time since inheriting the seat of command, over five years ago the woman he had long searched for to share in his life with was occupying the seat to his right. The awareness that Elizabeth would forever be with him in this room, even if at the far end of the table as proper for Mrs. Darcy, made him giddy. Indeed, astonishingly and refreshingly giddy!

As they rose from the table, the others merrily trailing behind Georgiana into the formal salon, Elizabeth stayed him by gripping his arm.

"Mr. Darcy—"

"William," he corrected, playfully pinching the tip of her nose. "You have successfully separated me from the group, leaving us somewhat alone, and thus you, my love, are obliged to address me by my Christian name."

"William," she repeated, her voice softly caressing his name, which only made him yearn to kiss her. "I want to thank you for a fabulous evening, in case I do not have another opportunity. I also wanted to comment on how pleasurable it is to see you relaxed and enjoying yourself. I admit it is...startling. I hope I have not offended."

"Not in the least, dearest Elizabeth. We have more to learn of each other, I suppose, but it is as I confessed in the Longbourn garden on the eve of our engagement. I have never experienced this degree of giddiness. I am light of spirit and as content as I have no recollection of ever being before, even in my youth." He traced his fingertips down her cheek, pausing under her chin. "The reason is you, Elizabeth. Only you."

He bent closer, fighting the desire to kiss her. It was damned difficult, almost painful, but the presence of Mr. Travers and immobile footmen lining the wall, eyes averted as they silently waited to clear the table, penetrated his haze. Forcing a genial smile, he straightened and escorted her from the room without another word.

Per standard protocol, Georgiana served as hostess for the ladies in the salon while Darcy led the men to the billiard room. The male bonding interval did not last for long, however. Darcy doubted Mr. Bennet or Mr. Gardiner were taken aback when he and Bingley prematurely suggested rejoining the ladies, or that they fully believed his expressed concern over Miss Darcy shouldering the burden. Neither of them argued though, and judging by their rapid steps to the low table laden with sweet cakes and fruit, they were perfectly happy to be there.

Elizabeth sat in the chair Darcy remembered being his mother's favorite. As always, her effervescence filled the room, her light voice lifting above the rest. Whether this was factual mattered naught, because to Darcy it was the truth, and immediately he felt at peace.

Tea, coffee, and additional snacks were served as conversation abounded. A blushing Georgiana, after some coaxing, went to the pianoforte and proceeded to astonish everyone with her talent. Different guests lent their voices, Mr. and Mrs. Gardiner especially skilled with a trio of duets. Jane sang two songs, Mr. Bingley's unrehearsed accompaniment on the second inducing laughter more than awed admiration.

It was when Elizabeth completed her song, the applause swelling, that Darcy stealthily exited the room. The sudden need to breathe cooling air was, he knew, a direct result of the impact upon him as she sang. The sonnet itself was not particularly romantic nor sung specifically to him. In truth, it was not the song at all but rather the accumulated emotions of the whole evening. Seeing Elizabeth in one of his homes, not yet his wife but already fitting comfortably, was overwhelming. Incredible, wonderful, rapturous—yes. And overwhelming.

Standing on the terrace in an area at the edge of the gaslight, he stared into the sky. Inhaling and exhaling at a measured pace, he allowed his love for her to eddy over and through him.

Soon, very soon she will be your wife. The next time you are here with her, she will not depart. Evenings of entertainment or serene family reposes will end with a walk to your bedchamber, and there, restraint will no longer be necessary.

Closing his eyes, Darcy willingly painted the mental picture of Elizabeth in his bedchamber. Effortlessly he summoned the image of her stretched atop the burgundy counterpane wearing nothing but a shift, hair a loose mane spread over his pillows and face alit with desire. Smiling, the Elizabeth in his dreamy mind lifted her hand, palm up and fingers wiggling. *Come to me, William…*

"William?"

Opening his eyes, Darcy turned toward the melodious voice echoing the entreaty whispered inside his head. "Elizabeth." Not feeling slightly surprised to see her standing in the doorway, he smiled and held out his hand. "I was dreaming about you, and here you are, as if conjured."

She laughed softly, left the doorway, and slowly crossed the stones toward him. "Not quite that magical, I am afraid. I saw you leave the parlor and wanted to make sure you were well. And...I wished to share a moment alone with you."

Reaching across the narrow gap remaining, he clasped her hands and drew her into the semi-shadows. Drifting tender fingertips along her flushed cheeks, he huskily confided, "No, it is magic, for I wished to be alone with you and here you are." Bending, he secured her face within his palms and tenderly brushed his lips over hers.

Perhaps the moonlight was weaving a magical spell. Perhaps the magic of their mutual love and desire intermingled with heavenly bewitchment to create an enchantment a hundredfold more potent. All Darcy knew for sure was that moderation was futile. The moment, however it happened, was too perfect for chaste kisses and regulated touches. Nothing rational or deliberate, he merely let pure sensation rule and his desire flare at will. Judging by Elizabeth's arms snaking inside his jacket, hands kneading the muscles of his back, and breasts flattened against his chest, she was of like-minded opinion.

Groaning, he parted her lips, insistent tongue delving hungrily into the farthest reaches of her mouth. Nothing about this kiss was tender. It was consuming and heated, delirious and passionate. Fire scorched from so many points on his body that none could be distinguished. His groin tightened, then hardened into a steely rod in a matter of seconds. The blissful agony of his arousal was desperate for relief—relief that was only dimly gained by cinching one spread hand onto Elizabeth's buttocks and crushing her pelvis harshly into the solid ridge. When she showed no sign of resistance, and in fact moaned and dug her fingertips into his back, he responded with an increase in the wildness of their kiss.

God! Blinding ecstasy! Sheer rapture!

Then, "Elizabeth? Are you out here?"

Mr. Bennet's baritone drifted through the open terrace door, as effective as being doused by a bucket of icy water or struck by a mallet. Darcy released Elizabeth so abruptly that she staggered. Not in much better shape, he recoiled and melted into the shadows. Hating himself for…well, everything to be frank—guilt and shame burned as hot as the remaining passion. *I am sorry*, he mouthed but could not be sure she saw him.

Surprisingly, she turned and walked calmly toward the door. "I am here, Papa. You know me and seeking air in the evening."

"Indeed I do. I saw that Mr. Darcy was missing as well and thought he might be showing you the stars of London."

"No. Not looking at the stars tonight, and I am not exactly sure where Mr. Darcy is. Come, let us go in. I am superbly refreshed now."

For fifteen minutes, Darcy leaned against the cool stone wall while waiting for his blood to stop boiling and body to relax. How she had managed to speak coherently, telling the truth without giving anything away, was absolutely incredible. God knows he could not have spoken with such aplomb. Nor would he have had the chance. Mr. Bennet would have taken one look at his glazed expression and massive bulge in his trousers and either slugged him square on the jaw or hustled Elizabeth out the front door without a backward glance. Either probability was less than he deserved.

Covering his eyes with one hand, Darcy muttered a string of curses. He was so far beyond mortified, even his command of vocabulary was unable to locate a proper word to define how low he felt. Recognizing it was sensible to abandon her to face Mr. Bennet alone failed to expunge his cowardice in doing so.

Coward. Fool. Undisciplined. Dishonorable. Untrustworthy.

If not for the shreds of his dignity reminding him that there were guests waiting for him, Darcy might have been ill. He pulled himself together and returned to the parlor. No one seemed to have noticed his absence, or at least they had carried on in the same vein of lighthearted congeniality.

Elizabeth was in his mother's chair again and immediately swung her glowing, chocolate eyes to him, smiling brightly. There was no hint of negative emotion about her. In fact, if he had to label the arch lift of her lips and tilt of her head, he would say she was smug.

More confused than ever, he made it through the rest of the evening. Once in the foyer, amid servants distributing outerwear, Darcy retrieved Elizabeth's cloak from the footman. Drawing her slightly to the side, he draped the heavy fabric over her shoulders and proceeded to fasten each button with focused intent. The weight of her stare added to the weight of the disagreeable awkwardness between them.

"William—"

"Miss Elizabeth, I am sor—" Pressing his lips into a hard line, he shook his head. Finally lifting his gaze to meet her concerned eyes, he rushed on. "I love you. Please remember this. I shall pray you sleep well and for your shopping expedition on the morrow to be fruitful. As it pleases you and accommodates your schedule, I will be awaiting your return for the thorough tour of Darcy House I promised."

"That will be the high point of my day, *William*," she stressed, staring directly into his eyes. Then she lifted his fingers to her lips, kissing gently. "I love you as much. *You* remember *that*. Until tomorrow, then."

ജ

The Bennet daughters woke in the morning of their first full day in London with wide smiles, and briskly launched out of their beds. Today would commence the serious shopping for their wedding gowns and bridal trousseaux! In no time at all, hasty breakfasts and speedy toilettes were completed, and they were out the door with Mrs. Gardiner gaily leading the way and Mr. Bennet grumpily trailing behind. The driver made for the finer shopping areas in London where, Mrs. Gardiner insisted, the essentials her nieces required for the elevated stations they were marrying into must be obtained. As they rode down the streets lined with glass-fronted shops crammed with merchandise and edged with sidewalks crowded with elegantly dressed people, all their previous chatter, teasing, and list making felt pointless. Imagining had not prepared them for the reality. Mr. Bennet was already pale, undoubtedly from the anticipation of how much of his money would be spent!

Fortunately, as a way to ease into the expedition, their aunt had set an appointment for that morning with her modiste. "After all," she declared firmly, "the selection of your wedding gowns is of prime importance."

In her late thirties, the modiste, Mrs. Carter, possessed higher than average talent at designing, and her crew of seamstresses were skilled, yet her shop was ordinary and prices reasonable. The latter especially pleased Mr. Bennet, who then waved farewell in relief, leaving them with their aunt for several hours. The vast selection of styles, fabrics, laces, ribbons, and the like was delightful, if a bit overwhelming. Eventually, she and Jane settled on wedding gowns fancier than any dress they had ever owned, yet suited to their individual tastes of simplicity and modesty.

All in all, the session was enjoyable. The one surprise came at the reaction from the dressmaker to the name Mr. Darcy. Her eyes had bulged, mouth dropped, and for a minute or two, she was speechless. Then she had sent her assistants scurrying for the costliest fabrics and trimmings in the place, and been stricken with renewed muteness when Lizzy insisted that was not her desire. The whole episode was bizarre, and Lizzy's expression must have revealed her bewilderment because her aunt laughed and squeezed her hand.

"My innocent Lizzy! Even after touring Pemberley and visiting Darcy House, do you remain unaware of Mr. Darcy's importance?"

"I know he is…rich," she whispered the word, "of course, and with money comes power and distinction, I grant, but this?" She jerked her chin toward the still-twittering Mrs. Carter.

"There is wealth, my dear, and there are those who wield power. Mr. Darcy falls into the latter category to be sure. As valuable as that stature is, of greater worth are those who add dignity, character, ancestry, solidity, and similar vaunted English qualities to the wealth and power inherited. Then, one has a name instantly recognized as you have now witnessed."

Nothing more was said, and soon the fun of measuring and being draped with yards of cloth took precedence. Lizzy remembered her aunt's words, however, and frequently dwelt upon them in the month to come.

With most of the morning consumed at the modiste, they only had time to visit a handful of shops before Jane and Lizzy separated for their afternoon invitations. Mr. Gardiner had volunteered to escort Jane to meet Mr. Bingley at his townhouse on Hill Street, in the Mayfair District. Mr. Bennet served as Lizzy's chaperone. Secretly, she suspected the arrangement had more to do with her father's curiosity with the Darcy House library than any favoritism for her or Mr. Darcy. Nevertheless, she was pleased to have him with her.

The Bennet carriage rattled over the cobblestones of Oxford Street, passing one stunning townhouse after another. Lizzy's eyes darted up, down, and side to side, as they had all day while driving through the high-end shopping areas. She had been to London a handful of times in her life but dwelt with the Gardiners in Cheapside and had only skirted the wealthier districts. Bypassing Kensington and approaching Grosvenor Square awarded her an entirely new perspective of the life she was marrying into.

Last night, she had sat in a cramped carriage while darkness rapidly fell, the artificial illumination from gaslight and smoldering lamps ineffective in dispelling all the shadows bathing the grand townhouses. Yet even with limited vision, the splendor of Grosvenor Square and Darcy House had taken her breath away. The impact on a sunny day was unimaginable, and her excitement boosted her sagging energy from the busy morning. Further invigorating was the prospect of wandering through rooms that, in about a month, she would call home. Lizzy attempted to wrap her mind around that fact, as she constantly did with Pemberley, and met with minimal success. The reality of precisely how radically her life would change as Mrs. Darcy, with the expectations and duties thrust upon her narrow shoulders, was easy to shove aside when in his adoring company in provincial Meryton. In London, especially after seeing Darcy House and the modiste's reaction, she felt twinges of nervousness creeping in.

Knowing William would be at her side today, and forever, was comforting. That vision was vitalizing while adding to her nervousness.

"Lizzy, you have nothing to worry about. You are my clever, capable daughter. The girl who once chastised an angry bull and memorized Act Five, Scene Two of *Love's Labour's Lost* just because Lydia dared you can handle any challenge set before her. Including being Mrs. Darcy."

"I do pray you are correct, Papa. It is a different life than I have lived for twenty years." She accented her statement with a nod toward the window she stared out of, the houses increasing in size and ornamentation.

"In some ways, maybe that is true. Nevertheless, my opinion is you are selling yourself short, Lizzy." She turned her eyes to her father, attentive as he went on. "Mr. Darcy sees your capability, even if it took him a while to do so. Moreover, he cares deeply for you so will help you along the way. That said, the main reason you will succeed admirably is because you have watched your mother for twenty years. Just do the opposite of that."

"Oh, Papa!" She shook her head, laughing. Mr. Bennet's grin and humorous advice lifted her spirits to a great degree. Of course, she could not tell him that a portion of her nervousness at the present had to do with what had occurred the night before.

Reliving her encounter with William on the terrace—as she had endlessly all night and morning—was the real reason her insides were coiled in a knot. The kiss and the sensations of embracing his body were, quite simply, the most deliriously joyful five minutes of her life! Instantly, she recalled the taste of him on her tongue, the pressure of his mouth and insistent hands, the sound of his ragged respirations, the heated smell of his cologne, and the glaze of desire flooding his eyes. There was no shame or fear in how William made her feel or in how she obviously made him feel. Her only regret from their interlude was that she stupidly walked away with her father rather than following William into the shadows. Over and over, she envisioned the expanse of darkness, sure that they could have carried on their blissful intimacy for a while longer before forced to return to the parlor.

Then she remembered his reaction. The guilt and shame that was stark on his face. The wall of awkwardness sensed the rest of the evening. And worst was the apology he started to give before she left.

What, precisely, had he wanted to apologize for? The kiss? For becoming aroused while holding the woman he was soon to marry? For leaving her to face her father? Could he honestly think for a second that Mr. Bennet seeing the state he was in would be better than disappearing? Or was it all of these points and more?

Luckily the carriage turned the corner, off Duke Street and onto Grosvenor Square, halting further conflicting musings. There, before her eyes, was Darcy House, and Lizzy sucked in her breath.

Though tiny compared to the vastness of Pemberley, it was still majestic. Constructed of polished white stone that glowed in the sunlight, each of the five bays on the lower level contained tall, multipaned windows allowing beams of light into the house. Dozens of wide windows cut into the flat surface of the upper floors. Flowers bloomed from boxes underneath each window. Ornate iron fencing barricaded the passageway to the basement service areas and curved elegantly up the steps before the gleaming, blue entryway doors.

"It is so beautiful," Lizzy whispered.

"Yes," Mr. Bennet agreed, "but it is just a house. One with a reputedly fine library, I hasten to add."

"I have a suspicion you will enter that room and need to be physically evicted. We best make sure to go there *after* luncheon." Lizzy squeezed his hand and kissed his cheek.

Mr. Darcy and Miss Darcy waited in the foyer exactly as they had the night before. Lizzy's eyes immediately swung to her fiancé, noting as she always did how handsome he was and striking his figure. As detected last evening, there was a distinct difference to his bearing. He seemed to dominate the space more than his stature and presence typically did, which was significant no matter where he was. She surmised it was because, here, he was the master. Here, he was at home and fully cognizant of his place in Society. He wore the aura of power quite well, and Lizzy's insides thrilled in response.

He was also stiffly proper. This, she could not decide how to decipher. Was it normal? Or was it the result of nervousness?

Smiling politely, he kissed her hand and greeted with the common phrases of welcome and pleasure to see her. Searching his eyes, Lizzy felt the warmth and adoration, yet he too quickly looked away. All through lunch, he maintained an attitude that skated the edges of formality and congeniality without dipping one way or the other with consistency. She honestly questioned her perspective, wondering if she was fretting where there was nothing to fret about, but the sporadic odd reactions from her father and Miss Darcy confirmed something was amiss.

Despite this, lunch passed with no mishaps and conversation was light. Miss Darcy was especially gay, so the two young women kept the discourse lively. Immediately upon vacating the table, the tour of Darcy House began, heading up the curving staircase to the upper floors.

The first and second stories primarily consisted of uniquely decorated bedchambers with attached dressing areas. Each were comfortable, luxurious, and modern. At the present, the only occupied suite was Georgiana's. It was the largest and included a cozy sitting room with an old harpsichord she informed had belonged to her mother. The next biggest bedchamber did not have the empty sensation most of the others did, and there was a decidedly masculine quality to the decor.

"This suite is reserved for Colonel Fitzwilliam." Darcy stood close enough to Lizzy that she felt his breath on her neck and could smell his cologne, but he did not meet her eyes when she turned her head. "When in Town, he usually dwells at his apartment near the barracks. If he has no choice due to his work, that is," Darcy explained, laughing shortly. "The colonel much prefers the luxury found here or at the Matlock townhouse. It depends on who is in London at the given time, but he seems to stay here mostly—probably due to the superior-grade liquor and the dart board."

"He shows up on our doorstep like a lost puppy." Georgiana sighed dramatically. "Tragic soul. How can we resist?"

At the top of the stairs leading back to the ground level, they completed their circuit by entering a set of double doors recessed into the wall directly across from the landing. As Lizzy predicted, it was the billiard room. A necessity in a Darcy household, the room included a host of gaming entertainments, including a spectacular billiard table and the aforementioned dartboard. Clearly designed with the male sex in mind, the room was rich with dark woods, brown leather chairs and sofas, and a dark gray carpet. It was a narrow room, extending to the rear of the upper floor, where tall windows spanning the width allowed blazing sunlight in.

"I see the benefit of the location." Lizzy indicated the staircase and polished wood balustrade outside the open doors. "Easy to access for entertaining."

"Indeed, that was the design, as is the location of the ballroom. Shall we?"

Descending the stairs once again, Darcy led the way to a room encompassing one corner of the ground floor, the doors exactly like the ones to the game room and diagonal from the lower landing. Although a fourth the size of Pemberley's, the ballroom was stunning. Dark oak boards, thickly varnished, contrasted beautifully with the gold and cream walls. The sunlight streaming through a bank of windows along the back wall shimmered on the glossy surfaces, dazzling the eye. How the shine from the three crystal chandeliers and dozen wall sconces would warm the ambience at night was a vision Lizzy longed to behold.

As if reading her thoughts, Darcy said, "Sadly, this room has not been used in years—not to its full purpose that is. Family members and friends have amused themselves with casual dancing upon occasion, but we have not hosted a true ball since before our mother died."

"Fitzwilliam and Cousin Richard taught me how to dance in this room." Georgiana's voice lacked the hint of sadness in her brother's. "And my brother has promised that after my debut, we can host a ball!"

"It was a promise extracted under duress," he sniffed. Then he winked at Mr. Bennet—Lizzy's father nodding his head, presumably agreeing with how pretty young girls connived to get their way. "However, with a new mistress of Darcy House, I suppose parties and balls will become a frequent event. God help me."

Lizzy matched his warm smile, and for the first time since arriving, he was her William—the man who gazed at her with love, contentment, mild humor, and longing perpetually hovering underneath. The man who made her heart race and butterflies dance inside her belly. Then, just as she felt the knots of her worries loosening, he glanced away and resumed his businesslike commentary. She was unsure whether to scream or cry but did neither.

Next on the tour were the main parlor, or salon, and the dining room. Since they were familiar with these rooms from the previous night, the examination was quick. Crossing to a far door in the dining room, Darcy entered a corridor that bisected the foyer but veered to the left toward a single door. Here he paused, looked at Mr. Bennet, and announced, "And now the one room I deem is the only one you honestly cared to visit, sir. The library."

Not nearly as large as Pemberley's library—as Lizzy teasingly dangled as bait to a fish—the townhouse's library was substantial. And it was lined ceiling to floor with shelves of books. As predicted, Mr. Bennet immediately lost himself amongst the titles. She chuckled and shared an amused glance with Mr. Darcy. Again, it was brief, a faint flush touching his cheeks as he diverted his gaze and waved a hand toward the end of the library nearest the door.

"As you can see, a part of this room serves as my office. Between work and reading, I tend to pass large quantities of time here."

"Large quantities," Georgiana emphasized teasingly. "He has been known to fall asleep on the sofa rather than walk the astronomical distance to his bedchamber. Your presence will save him from a sore back and twisted neck, Miss Elizabeth."

It was Lizzy's turn to flush at the image Miss Darcy's innocent, jesting statement conjured. She did have a point, though, considering the sofa indicated was not anywhere near adequate for a man well over six feet in height.

Not far from the sofa was an enormous, solidly constructed desk with drawers on both sides, situated before a window facing the rear garden. The surface was cluttered with an array of papers and objects, but oddly organized and neatly arranged. The chair was carved of Coromandel ebony, the leather seat and arm cushions molded in places from his body and worn from long use. Additional wooden cases against the wall behind the chair held some books but primarily objects of an obvious personal nature to Darcy. Lizzy wanted to examine each one, ask questions so as to learn more about the man she loved and was soon to marry. Unfortunately, the tension between them was increasing by the minute.

Leaving the library and Mr. Bennet behind, the trio aimed for the only wing of the mansion yet to explore. That was, of course, the private chambers for the master and mistress of the house. While not exactly an astronomical distance, they were located across the foyer on the opposite wing from the library. Access was via an archway cleverly hidden behind the staircase and an immense statue of white marble.

"Archibald Darcy, who purchased this townhouse and contributed to the design, wanted his quarters on the ground floor, so as to make use of the garden. Tremendous forethought was given to accomplish this while remaining private during social engagements. In my opinion, his solution was remarkably effective."

Lizzy had to agree. The portal was completely invisible unless one knew it to be there. Darcy pointed to several intriguing features as they traversed the short corridor, but his strained attempts to interject gaiety and normalcy were obvious to Lizzy. She suspected they were to Georgiana as well, or maybe she did have a valid reason to excuse herself from the tour. Whatever the case, in a second, Lizzy was alone with Mr. Darcy, and the situation only grew worse.

Entering the chamber once occupied by his mother, Darcy walked away from Lizzy to stand ramrod stiff by a porcelain washbasin sitting atop a gorgeous French commode. Lizzy wandered to the window and then to the small table by the bed. She pretended to intently examine the paintings hung on the wall and embroidered pillows on the bed while he fidgeted and droned on to fill the silence. Lizzy could not concentrate on a single word, not that he was saying anything of importance. Sadness, frustration, irritation, and an unrelenting desire to kiss him combined and roiled inside her chest. Being in a bedroom contributed to her agitation, especially when abrupt visions of them lying on that bed sprung into her head— visions that were shockingly lucid considering how mysterious the act of lovemaking still was to her.

Breathing efficiently was becoming a serious problem, and her mind refused to focus. Surely this cloudiness worsened her inattentiveness and was why she stumbled when a curled edge of rug wrapped around her foot. There was no time to correct her balance, arms flying forward to break the fall she knew was coming and a squeak of shock passing her lips. Miraculously, instead of the hard floor, her hands and face made contact with Darcy's solid chest, the squeak muffled against pliable brushed wool.

How he had crossed the room so fast defied logic, not that she gave the matter much consideration. Every thought spiraled out of her brain except for the awareness of his radiant heat, harsh breathing, wildly beating heart, and firmly muscled arms steadying her. Instinctively, she curled her fingers into his waistcoat and breathed in the musky aroma of his cologne. At the same time, he buried his face into her hair and inhaled deeply.

"Elizabeth. My Elizabeth."

The rough murmur was followed by a series of rapid, frantic kisses to her head, the curved edge of her ear, jawline to cheek, and finally, blissfully, the mouth she lifted in anticipation. In a near repeat of last evening's encounter, they went from nothing to crazed, unrestrained kissing and caressing in seconds. It was glorious! Fire surged through her veins, Lizzy feeling desired, loved, and cherished all at the same time. In those moments, she sensed her heart melding with his and, in a sudden flash of insight, understood why intimacy with the man you loved was a uniquely bonding experience. If loving with touch and shared breath had this impact, the intensity of nakedness and consummation would surely be life altering.

Then, as abruptly as it had begun, the rapturous accord was shattered. Darcy released her with a minor shove and pivoted away, a strangled cry piercing the air as he lunged to the window. Tottering once again, Lizzy watched him lean into the sill with hands balled into fists of steel and shoulders heaving with each rough inhale.

"Elizabeth," he rasped, "you need to leave this room now! Please!"

Automatically she nodded and stepped to the door. Hand on the latch, she stopped. She was trembling and out of breath, as if having run a mile straight. Yet unexpectedly, in the midst of the chaotic emotion, everything clicked into place. Like a bolt from Heaven, clarity was restored, and with it came understanding and sympathy. There was also anger, and it was this she grabbed on to.

Securing the door, she then stormed to where he stood hunched at the window until inches behind him and snapped, "No, William, I will *not* leave! Turn around this instant and face me!"

He did immediately, mouth agape and eyes wide. Lizzy clenched her hands at her waist and let the full fury inside show on her face and in her voice. "Tell me truthfully, Fitzwilliam Darcy. Am I to conclude that our mutual love and desire are emotions to be disdained and ashamed of? Is this contempt and repugnance to continue after we are wed? Or is it that you honestly reckon you are such an uncontainable beast that you would hurt the woman you love? Or do you have so little faith in *my* self-control that you assume I would willingly allow you to ravage me like a bought woman?"

All the blood had drained from his face. *Good. He needs to be shocked!* Leaning closer and lifting onto her toes until almost level with his face, she growled, "Answer me!"

"No, Elizabeth"—he swallowed—"I would never hurt you or—I love you! Please...I have never wanted anything in all my life as I want you. You...are my life...you must know that? Surely you know how much—"

Elizabeth interrupted him, forcing her voice into a controlled level but maintaining her hard glare into his eyes. "William, listen to me carefully. I do not believe any of the questions I asked are true of you. What I do believe is that you are afraid to freely express your emotions. You are wrapped in an inflexible cocoon of discipline and righteousness, and are terrified that if you loosen one single cord, you will unravel completely. You love me and desire me, yet resist showing me how much because you fear I will be disgusted or disappointed if I discover you are not this towering paragon of virtue and excellence you deem yourself."

He never once glanced away from her eyes, clearly hearkening to every word she said and stricken to the core. Suddenly her anger drained away, leaving her with the clarity, understanding, and sympathy. A fresh rush of irrepressible love netted all of it together.

Placing both hands about his face and drawing so close their noses touched, she whispered, "My God, William. Do you not yet comprehend how deeply I love you? You can be free with me and I will *always* love you. I trust you with my life, my virtue, my body, and my heart. You have nothing to fear from me and I fear nothing from you except for this distance between us. I beg you, do not push me away."

"Elizabeth," he moaned, pulling her into his arms for a crushing embrace. "I am sorry. Unbelievably sorry! You are absolutely correct. I have feared...all that you said and more. Opening my inner being is not easy for me. Surrendering to my passionate nature after so long subduing it is difficult. The lack of control is at odds with the disciplined man I proclaim to be."

"There are multiple levels of control, my love. You can remain a highly disciplined man and still, upon occasion, surrender to your passionate nature."

He lifted her chin from where she rested against his heart. "Can you repeat that?"

"I meant that one can be regulated and—"

"No. The endearment."

"My love." She punctuated it with a soft kiss on his fingertips.

"That is now the second time you have spoken an endearment for me. I like hearing it."

"I shall make a point of it, then."

This statement she emphasized by pressing her mouth to his. Darcy unhesitatingly responded but kept the intensity at a simmering degree. Slowly he released her lips, nibbling several tiny kisses along her chin before resting his forehead against hers.

"My Elizabeth," he sighed. "If we are to enjoy these moments as they are granted us in the weeks ahead, you must promise to help me remain a gentleman. I have never, in all my years, wanted a woman...physically...as I want you."

Lizzy knew she was blushing scarlet and thus was glad their eyes were closed. "I promise. As for your...confession...if it is meant to alarm, you have failed. I can only feel joy, and relief, that this is the case."

Darcy chuckled, his breath caressing her cheek and somehow triggering a series of shivers at random spots on her body. "Thank you for understanding my struggles and my heart. Now"—he kissed the tip of her nose—"in light of the former, despite your promise, I am in a bedchamber with you in my arms. Far too tempting for this fallible human male, no matter how highly disciplined. Nor would it be good for your reputation to be questioned about our isolation. Come."

Lacing their fingers together, he bent and softly brushed a final kiss to her forehead. He then briskly started for the door. Returning to the library, they found Mr. Bennet steadily weaving his way deeper into the room, apparently unaware they had ever left. Darcy and Lizzy shared a private smile, neither pointing out to Mr. Bennet his dismal failure as a chaperone.

Instead, Lizzy walked directly to the case behind Darcy's desk and pointed to a miniature Austrian chateau.

"What is the story behind this?"

Smiling, Darcy casually sat on the edge of his desk. Beginning with his first trip to visit his Aunt Mary in Austria, when the tiny chateau was purchased as a souvenir, the afternoon passed in pleasurable storytelling. Only a few were embellished for greater effect and all of them were true. Well, nearly all. Lizzy figured out each time he tried to fabricate an exciting tale.

What was his penance for telling fibs?

A kiss, of course!

~ * ~ * ~

This ends Book One of the Darcy Saga Prequel Duo. The tale of the Darcy and Bennet betrothal period continues in Darcy & Elizabeth: Hope for the Future. Turn to the next page for more information.....

Darcy & Elizabeth

✳ ✳ ✳

Hope for the Future

The final weeks of wedding preparation continue in Book Two of the Darcy Saga Prequel Duo.

Join Mr. Darcy and Elizabeth Bennet, Mr. Bingley and Jane Bennet, and all their family and friends as the double marriage ceremony scheduled for November the 28th of 1816 in Meryton, Hertfordshire fast approaches.

Shopping and adventures in London! More "advice" from wise elders! Mr. Darcy's birthday! Romance! Lizzy and Jane prepare for their new lives and separation! Wedding guests arrive!

Tentative release in eBook and print by Summer of 2014

Keep an eye on Sharon Lathan's blog and Facebook page for updates!

SHARON LATHAN

About the Author

SHARON LATHAN is the best-selling author of The Darcy Saga nine-volume sequel series to Jane Austen's *Pride & Prejudice*. Sharon began writing in 2006 and her first novel, *Mr. and Mrs. Fitzwilliam Darcy: Two Shall Become One* was published in 2009. Sharon's ninth novel was released in March 2014, *Darcy & Elizabeth: A Season of Courtship*, the "prequel to the sequel" recounting the betrothal months before the Darcy Saga began. *Miss Darcy Falls in Love*, Sharon's seventh novel, was selected as one of the thirty-two titles chosen for World Book Night US 2014.

Sharon is a native Californian relocated in September 2013 to the green hills of Kentucky. She resides with her husband of thirty-years, and grown son. Currently retired from a thirty-year profession as a registered nurse in Neonatal Intensive Care, Sharon is pursuing her dream as a full-time writer.

Sharon is a member of the Jane Austen Society of North America, JASNA Louisville, the Romance Writers of America, the Beau Monde and Hearts Through History chapters of the RWA, and serves on the board of her California RWA chapter, the Yosemite Romance Writers.

For more information about Sharon, the Regency Era, and her novels, visit her website/blog at: www.sharonlathan.net -
on Facebook at www.facebook.com/SharonLathanNovelist and
Twitter @SharonLathan https://twitter.com/SharonLathan

THE DARCY SAGA SEQUEL SERIES
SHARON LATHAN
ଔ

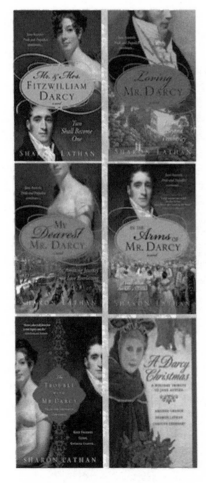

Happily Ever After Comes True...

Beginning on their wedding day, Darcy and Elizabeth are two people who are deeply in love with one another and are excited to begin their marriage.

The Darcy Saga sequel series to Jane Austen's *Pride and Prejudice* is a sweetly romantic, historically accurate tale recounting the daily life of newlyweds Mr. and Mrs. Fitzwilliam Darcy. Through five novels and one novella, Sharon Lathan presents a vision of happiness in marriage.

Meet new friends and family members. Delve deeper into familiar characters and their futures. Dwell in the Regency world at Pemberley and London. Through it all, delight in an unparalleled love story with Darcy and Elizabeth.

Mr. and Mrs. Fitzwilliam Darcy: Two Shall Become One

Loving Mr. Darcy: Journeys Beyond Pemberley

My Dearest Mr. Darcy

In The Arms of Mr. Darcy

The Trouble With Mr. Darcy

A Darcy Christmas

"If you enjoy enthusiastic romance passionately written featuring the redoubtable Mr. Darcy and his wife, then "I would by no means suspend any pleasure of yours"!" *AustenProse*

MISS DARCY FALLS IN LOVE
SHARON LATHAN
ഇൻ

An intimate journey of love, life, and the passionate pursuit of happiness.

Noble young ladies were expected to play an instrument, but societal restrictions would have chafed for Georgiana Darcy, an accomplished musician.

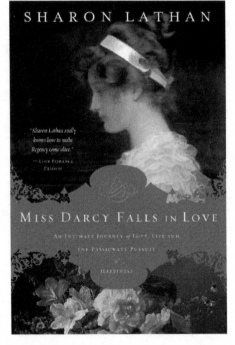

Her tour of Europe draws the reader into the musical life of the day, and a riveting love story of a young woman learning to direct her destiny and understand her own heart.

ഇൻ

"Sharon Lathan has another home run hit on her hands here. Her name is certainly solidified with what good Austen fan fiction should be. Fast-paced and always full of the romance we dream about, Miss Darcy Falls in Love is not one you'll want to miss." *Austenprose*

"If you are a Jane Austen fan, if you love historical novels, then Lathan's wonderfully written, vividly detailed, sweet romance novel will be one you don't want to miss out on!" *Romancing the Book*

"The love, passion, and excellence of style, as well as the writer's superior talent with words is sure to win her new fans or satisfy old fans with this one." *Long and Short Reviews*

"This is a story that fully immerses its readers in the world of the characters, from the rainy streets of Lyon and Paris and the quiet hush of the churches and museums Georgiana visits, to the dazzle and splendor of the society balls that light up the evenings." *The Romance Reviews*

"In the characteristically romantic style of author Sharon Lathan, Georgiana Darcy's story feels nothing like a departure from our most famous Darcy couple, but feels more like a beautiful continuation within the family." *One Literature Nut*

THE PASSIONS OF DR. DARCY
SHARON LATHAN
ॐ

You never know where a life of purpose may lead...

While Fitzwilliam Darcy is enjoying an idyllic childhood at Pemberley, his vibrant and beloved uncle, Dr. George Darcy, becomes one of the most renowned young physicians of the day. Determined to do something more with his life than cater to a spoiled aristocracy, George accepts a post with the British East India Company and travels in search of a life of meaning and purpose.

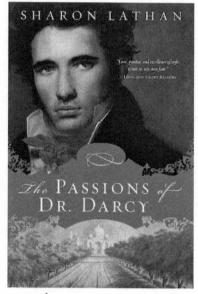

When George Darcy returns to Pemberley after thirty years abroad, the drama and heartbreak of his travels offer a fascinating glimpse into a gentleman's journey of self-discovery and romance.

Explore a fascinating and unique aspect of the Regency period, when the British Empire offered the young noblemen of the day promising adventures all over the world.

ॐ

"A splendid tale of one man's determination to be the best in his chosen profession, and to find love." *New York Journal of Books*

"Lathan obviously spent a lot of time and research to tell of the things happening at this time in history. It is fun, engaging, and full of history. I strongly recommend this to anyone who enjoys historical fiction. It is an amazing book!" *Night Owl Reviews*

"The story is entertaining, especially for those who take pleasure, as I did, in details of 18th-century medicine and learning about the exotic India of this era." *Historical Novel Society*

"Lathan is an expert in character development. We travel across every reach of the Indian subcontinent for over 30 years with George, exploring its vibrant and rich history and the intriguing characters that he meets along the way. It was a journey which I was happy to take." *Austenprose*

A SEASON OF COURTSHIP

Made in the USA
Middletown, DE
26 December 2016